THE THINGS WE DO

Kay Pfaltz

This is a work of fiction. Names, characters, places, and incidents are products of the author's imagination and any resemblance to actual events, places, or persons is coincidental.

ISBN: 0692853545
ISBN 13: 9780692853542
Library of Congress Control Number: 2017903086
Arcadia Roseland, Roseland, VA

For my parents

And to numbers 11, 12, 22 and to all the nameless, homeless animals who pass through shelter or laboratory doors and never leave.

For me, I touched a thought, I know,
Has tantalized me many times,
(Like turns of thread the spiders throw
Mocking across our path) for rhymes
To catch at and let go. [. . .]

How say you? Let us, O my dove,
Let us be unashamed of soul,
As earth lies bare to haven above!
How is it under our control
To love or not to love? [. . .]

Just when I seemed about to learn!
Where's the thread now? Off again!
The old trick! Only I discern—
Infinite passion, and the pain
Of finite hearts that yearn.

—Robert Browning

PROLOGUE

Early Fall 2014

The Things That Are

It's morning when she leads him down the hall to the room. Outside, something timeless, untouched by sorrow, speaks in softer tones. Birds call back and forth and a breeze lifts leaves that no one sees, like the cavities within her heart, shrouded and unshared. But neither song nor touch enters these walls. Her task is to offer some measure of peace and kindness into corners forsaken, ignorant of human love.

She speaks softly: "Come along. You're doing great."

Hours later, she leads him back, two passing revenants to all that shudders. She shuts the gate and there's the click of the latch. From behind the metal links, the brown eyes stare at her and she looks back into them. Eyes that beseech her. She drops her gaze to where the boney haunch hunches and quivers. It's easier to look there than into the dark eyes that keep her up at night. She swallows and glances back to his face but he has turned his head away. And she too hears the voices down the hall and straightens her spine. The girls who clean the runs are dragging the heavy hose and spraying the dogs in each cage with a jet of cold water as they hose the cement floors. As she stands before his run she sees him hang his head and crouch at the sound of the water.

Then the cursing.

"Dumb dog, think I give a damn? Get up!"

They are spraying the dog in the next run, and giving her disapproving looks.

Her heart is beating fast when they approach his cage. She knows each dog and she knows the look that comes into their eyes, some dogs enthusiastic and valiant to the end, but many broken and cowering. Somehow, he seems the most frightened, the most likely to die, and at night he will not leave her mind.

Finally one girl speaks to her:

"Aren't you finished yet? Can you just get out of the way?"

She turns her back on him and hears the water jet into his run. She listens for his cry but she knows there will be none.

"Hey, can you, like, make yourself useful around here? We'd like to go home on time for once."

She glances at him one more time when they move on. His run is a puddle of water still smelling of urine. Water drips from his back and he trembles.

"*I'm sorry. I'm so sorry,*" she whispers to him. But he doesn't look back at her.

And it is then that she knows what she must do.

Late-Summer 2015

The Things We Do

Outside the sun lowered and another day began its descent into past while continuing into the rebirth of the morrow. Inside behind prison walls the call for standing count assured that every girl would rise and assume a uniformity that apart from private inner thoughts never varied. Concurrent to the call for count yet unheard by inmates beside the continued din of the loudspeaker (*Clear the unit! Back to your rooms! Stand up for count!*) was another noise. It signaled the arrival of a new prisoner.

The steel door shut and the sound sent its discord down the hall. A prison guard stood silhouetted with a new inmate in the late-afternoon sun and began advancing forward. The pale girl in handcuffs heard the sound yet did not wince the way the guard had seen others do. She seemed equally accepting of the stale interior smell, but she stopped for just a moment and raised her head. On one side of the hallway were windows, where a beam of outside light cast itself like a bridge. It was to this bridge of light that the inmate let her eyes rest briefly in what was perhaps a metaphorical backward glance, for the long hall leading to the interior of the penitentiary along which she now walked marked the start of each woman's term. The women would not walk this way again until their sentences were over when they would walk in the opposite direction. But rarely were they aware of this and it was enough to keep feet moving forward and not drop to the floor in remorse or despair.

"Keep moving, Miss," the guard warned.

Guard and inmate walked the length of hall and stepped out through the far door and entered the penitentiary. At first the corridors seemed empty. Then the sounds began.

"*Fresh fish! Fresh fish! Fresh fish!*" One voice was joined by another, then several and finally many. The chant rose up pulsating within the closed walls. Someone was banging out a rhythm with her fists.

"Hey white bitch, come here, I got to talk to you. Waz yo name? You got an attitude? Yeah, I don't *think* so. You gonna lose that *real* quick." Laughter.

"*Weta, Weta! Flaca Weta.*" More voices called and yelled as eyes stared down the new inmate, and the noise level rose until two guards ran in to see what was going on. Beating sticks on the walls they shouted, "Shut the fuck up you sorry losers! Get back to work!"

The shackled girl appeared oblivious to the banging and taunting. The guard watched her, perhaps surprised by her neutral reaction, perhaps wondering only briefly what crime she had committed to land her in the god-forsaken place.

But the girl was not thinking any of this, for as the guard nudged her forward, she was thinking she would stay a lifetime and, given the circumstances, it would be for the best.

PART I

PRESENT
Virginia, Early October 2015

The task of the seeker of eternity is to die while living.

—Richard Rose

CHAPTER ONE

Eleanor Hartley walked briskly down the penitentiary hallway. She was often called to the head warden's office, but this time the message conveyed a note of urgency. Out of the corner of her eye she thought she saw a flash of maroon ducking around the far wall. She turned but there was nothing. When she reached the closed door, she knocked lightly and, except for a darting glance over her shoulder, which in its unconscious elegance suggested habit not deliberate thought, she remained still, standing erect and poised.

"Yes?" The call came from within.

"It's Eleanor."

After a moment, the door opened to reveal a large, spacious office with a dark carpeted floor and windows on the far wall. A woman of medium height and build with short, hennaed-red hair and thick black glasses stood holding the door open for Eleanor. She motioned for Eleanor to come in. Then shut the door and smiled, but the smile looked strained.

"Thanks for coming, Eleanor. Sit down."

Eleanor sat in a comfortable leather swivel chair before the desk, while the woman slipped around behind.

"I need your help more than ever."

"Go ahead," Eleanor said.

"Thank you." For a moment Helen studied the woman across from her. Eleanor sat up straight, not leaning back into the chair. She was tall, with a body from which clothes hung naturally and well. Her refined features and precise manners called to mind equally Greek goddesses and school mistresses. Eleanor spoke little of her personal life or of anything apart from her work with the girls, and Helen listened to her more than she did the other therapists who, too often confiding personal details of relationships, children, even fad diets, she had deemed less professional and therefore less of authorities.

"A new inmate was brought in three days ago . . . an unusual case, involving a police officer. There's already been no small amount of press about this, as you could guess. Anytime a police officer is involved." She took a breath and let it out. "We don't know who she is. We just found out her I.D. was faked. Which in itself is odd as we're almost certain she's not a minor, so it's not as if she was trying to buy liquor or get into bars. Fingerprints reveal no past record. The police have been searching for contacts. But nothing so far."

Helen paused and pushed her glasses up onto her head but they fell and landed with a clatter on the desk. She made an agitated sound. "Eleanor, look, you're not immune to the gossip that goes on around here. Our facility needs this case. Our reputation needs it. We need it quite badly, and so . . . ." Helen rubbed the bridge of her nose. "I need you." She paused and Eleanor waited. "Of course it's not our job to do the work of the police. But I thought if you are able to find out from the girl's own lips what happened, and before the police did—"

"What does she say?"

Before Helen could respond there was a loud banging on the other side of her door.

"Not now!" Helen called to the closed door.

"*When* then?" A shrill, yet strangely self-assured, voice hollered back. Eleanor recognized the voice as well as the note of challenge.

"All right, come in for one minute," Helen said, and Eleanor glanced at her but Helen didn't see the alarm in her unspoken question.

As the door opened slowly, a tall, pretty girl in maroon prison scrubs and salient chin walked forth. "Oh, *excuse* me. I didn't know you had company."

"Didn't you, Mimi?" Helen said flatly.

"Hey, Dr. Hartley, how's tricks?" the girl asked, smiling at Eleanor.

Eleanor glanced up, gave a pleasant, cocktail party smile of acknowledgement but said nothing.

"*Pffffff,*" Mimi pushed the air from between full lips in a sound of disgust. "See how she treats me? What the fuck?"

"*Mimi,*" Helen said tersely, and Eleanor noted the pinched together brows and barely quivering lips.

"Well you *saw,* she didn't even say hello. I could die and she wouldn't give a flying fuck. Y'all drinking hooch in here, why you got the door locked up?"

"Mimi," Helen said again, her lips hardly opening this time. "Get to the point."

"Can I sit?"

"No. Get to the point."

"I need to change pods. Shina's plucking on my nerves real bad."

"Make an appointment and come back to see me. I'm in the middle of a meeting."

"I'm here now. Kind of a waste, ain't it?" She smiled coyly.

"I'm in the middle of a meeting," Helen repeated.

"With my girlfriend, Dr. Hartley," Mimi's smile widened. "I can see you are."

"Or better yet," Helen continued. "Why don't you talk out your issue with Dr. Hartley in your next session?"

"You think she cares?" Mimi said looking not to Helen but to the back of Eleanor's head. "You should fire her."

"Actually, I think she does care about to you. Now, goodbye, Mimi."

The girl stood her ground a moment longer, but when neither Helen nor Eleanor spoke, she turned and walked out leaving the door wide open, and hollering: "Yeah, I *know* what y'all are saying about me! Fuck all your lies! You'll be sorry!"

Helen took off her glasses, looked at them then put them back on top her head. "Can you—" She motioned to Eleanor who stood and shut the door, shutting out the sound of Mimi's continued insults down the hall and some other inmate yelling that someone else was a "piece of fucked-up cafeteria fried liver that done be bit off and spit out."

"Can't say there's not a touch of creativity flourishing here at times," Eleanor said, almost smiling.

"That's not exactly how I see it most days. What do they think? That the whole world revolves around them?"

"Many do, yes. But others feel the exact opposite and only hope to be seen."

"How have your sessions with Mimi been lately?"

Eleanor considered the question for several seconds, then said, "Difficult."

"She's been acting out even more than usual. I'd say something deep inside was bothering her. I mean apart from Shina plucking on her nerves," Helen said. Eleanor's steady gaze stated the obvious, and Helen laughed feebly. "I'm sorry. That must have sounded terribly obtuse. Of course something's bothering her. But," Helen waved a hand in the air. "We'll have to discuss Mimi Kramer later. This other matter is somewhat urgent. It really cannot wait. Where were we?"

"You were telling me about the new inmate. I believe I was asking you what she says."

"Ah, well yes. You see, that's just it . . ." Helen paused. "And that's why I need you." She waited a few moments and Eleanor watched her face. "She doesn't speak."

Eleanor nodded. Her eyes flickered over the desk with neatly stacked papers, a single pen in a sleek onyx holder, the phone.

"If you're willing, I'd like you to work with her."

"I'm willing."

"Great," Helen took another deep breath and let it out as though biding her time. "That's a relief. But . . ."

"Yes?"

"There's a catch."

"Yes?"

"She's in for murder."

"Yes. I guessed as much."

"I know that you have an agreement with Lewis."

"Lewis will be all right. It's been a long time."

"Eleanor, I only asked you because you're the best I have. We need this."

"A mute murderer," Eleanor said evenly. "I'd like to try. What do you know about her?"

Helen ruffled through the papers before her, but too quickly to read anything. "There were two murders that night. A police officer—"

"She shot an officer?" Eleanor said quickly before Helen could finish.

"Yes."

Eleanor nodded once, then said evenly, "I see."

Helen sighed. "I suppose we'll get to know her well. She won't be leaving for a long time, if ever. She also shot a Mr. Grady Smith. Notorious drug dealer."

"I see," Eleanor said again, in the exact same tone.

"There was a trial. Quick and easy. She had no lawyer of her own. A court-appointed attorney defended her on the grounds of insanity. Apparently she sat there very calmly. When they told her she might get the death penalty, she showed little or no remorse."

"As if she didn't understand?"

"I don't really know. But yes, I think that was the defense's strategy."

"And it failed to work."

"She admitted to the murders."

"Verbally?"

"Yes. Apparently she barely spoke, but answered questions when asked, and admitted her guilt."

"She spoke then, but not now."

"That's right. That's what I understand. Perhaps she only nodded her head."

"You don't know why she killed?"

"She was most likely buying drugs from Mr. Smith when the police came on the scene. She probably panicked. But it doesn't really matter. The job of the court is not to uncover motives unless it proves guilt. She'd already admitted to killing him. Eleanor, I'd like for you to get to her as soon as you can. If I've seen it once, I've seen it fifty times. The police give up if the victim is not in the public eye. Or if he's African American. Other more pressing crimes come up, and things like this become forgotten. I think sometimes they want it brushed under the rug."

Eleanor nodded in agreement.

"But we could capitalize on this. If she could publicly apologize, or maybe do community service in Grady Smith's neighborhood, I don't know, something. If our facility could help the Black Lives Matter movement, it wouldn't hurt us. And the fact that here we have both a police officer, who happens to be white, and an African American . . . with all that's in the news right now, it's just . . ." Helen laughed half-heartedly but didn't finish.

"What else can you tell me?"

"The police had been after the victim for some time. I can't help but to think they're relieved, and not particularly interested in the details. Aside from the outcry over losing one of their own."

"I see. Any witnesses who might know more of the details?"

"There were two witnesses who confirmed..." Helen stopped without finishing and looked up at Eleanor. Too quickly she looked down at the papers on her desk again, but this time didn't ruffle through them. "Her name and age are unknown. Apparently she indicated that she didn't know her name. The report said she may be slow, you know, mentally challenged. She could have escaped from an institution and ended up on the streets. We estimate her age in the mid-twenties. She's in P.C. right now."

Helen continued telling Eleanor everything she knew about the new inmate, which wasn't much. When she stopped, Eleanor spoke:

"You said you have two witnesses who confirmed, and then you changed the subject. What were you going to say? Confirmed what? Please tell me everything that happened."

Helen hesitated, then in a rush, almost as if she wanted to be rid of the knowledge, she blurted, "It's not pretty. She must have snapped. She shot the first victim three times. Twice straight through the heart and once . . . in the face. She shot the second victim three times."

"In the heart and in the face?" Eleanor asked.

"Yes. Almost as if she didn't want people to recognize them."

Eleanor dropped her gaze to the desk for a moment in a thoughtful silence. When she looked back up Helen was staring at her, her eyes questioning, perhaps pleading. Then, as much to herself, as to Helen, Eleanor asked, "What would make her shoot both the dealer and the police officer?"

CHAPTER TWO

Clutching her briefcase, Eleanor shoved the door to the Volvo shut and walked up the pathway to the old clapboard house as the first of the rain began to splatter down.

Inside she slipped off two tan pumps and walked into the kitchen, dumping the briefcase on the table. Her house was elegant without being fussy; there were the antiques from her family home, a few graceful plants draping down from pedestals. She cast her eyes around the room as the sky outside let in one last shard of light that streaked across the hall and pine floorboards before succumbing to a wall of cloud. There was a moment of stillness when her mind was free from thought.

As the bank of clouds overtook the last of the sun, the interior dimmed, like lights going down in a theatre. Darkness collected within, and silence reigned.

"Lewis?" she called out breaking the spell.

From down the hallway a man emerged in white tennis shorts. He was of equal height to her, and had ruffled salt and pepper hair, matching beard, sinewy and permanently suntanned body that, but for a few sags, looked in excellent shape. He stood in an open space that served as both dining room and kitchen in the quiet before the storm.

"What happened? You're late," he said in a clipped staccato voice.

Eleanor looked out the window to the sodden fields dotted with brown and yellow copses of trees. She saw the lily pond, only minutes before a calm mirror of life above, wince as small beaded pebbles of rain bore into it. As she watched, a strange premonition that she was on a precipice persisted.

"A new case. I had to talk with Helen after hours." She reached up behind her head, and let down her hair, shaking the damp strands like a dog.

Lewis stared at his wife, to the streaks of gray in her hair that once had been blonde. He turned from her, washing and scrubbing his hands in the kitchen sink. As he opened the oven door releasing a savory smell of roasted lamb and rosemary, Eleanor sank into a chair at the table.

"Tired?" he asked stooping over, attention on the roast.

"I'm all right. But Helen has asked me to take the new case."

"Damn, overcooked." He straightened, turned towards her and began setting plates and bowls on the table.

"Looks beautiful." Eleanor filled her plate with green beans, scalloped potatoes with garlic, and the lamb, as Lewis, making noises about what should have been done differently—"any respectable lamb is pink inside not corpse gray"—uncorked a hearty Gigondas and poured the red wine into their glasses.

"You need a break, not a new case."

Eleanor finished chewing a mouthful of beans and looked across the table at her husband.

"Maybe," she answered. "There's more to it than that." She inhaled before she spoke. "Lewis, it's murder. The girl's in for murder." And as she pronounced the word she was unable to hide the fine vibration of excitement rising in her voice.

He put his fork down and stared at her. "Don't kid me."

"I'm not," she said softly.

He snatched the fork back up, leaned over his plate, taking a hasty bite and, with his mouth half full of food, began speaking rapidly. "And what if I say no? No, Eleanor. No.'

"Lewis—"

"You made me a promise. And you made it for a good reason. Have you forgotten?"

"Helen asked me."

"That's not why you're taking it," he said, his mouth full.

"It is."

"If that's so then just tell her no." He lifted his wine glass by its stem and swirled the wine around inside.

"What's past is past," she said to her husband softly but firmly, while thoughts within her mind took on another direction, someone else's words, long ago: *Your past catches up to you at some point. You can't run from it and you can't ignore it. And you're better off facing it early on rather than waiting for it to overcome you in some weakened state.*

"Lewis, the girl doesn't talk. She doesn't speak a word. Helen needs me." She paused. "She asked me to check with you."

Lewis's expression needed no interpretation. "And this is what you call checking with me?"

"The girl's been placed in Protective Custody, in the isolation/segregation unit because they assumed being mute she'd be picked on by inmates. Apparently she hasn't always been mute. Something traumatized her badly. Perhaps the crime itself. Perhaps something else. Helen thought I might be able to get somewhere with her. With time," she added.

"You are making one huge mistake. But of course you know that, and don't seem to care."

"Lewis, don't you wonder why one human being would take another's life? Don't you want to understand why or how the human brain can wander so far from rational behavior?"

"No. I know why. They're all nuts and need to stay locked up."

"Don't you wonder what happened to them to make them take such extreme measures and don't you wonder if maybe, you could help them?"

"What'd this one do? Knife her boyfriend in the back when he looked slant-eyed at another woman?" Lewis asked, chewing the tender muscle of baby sheep.

"No. She shot a notorious drug dealer, a Mr. Grady Smith, twice in the heart and once in the face, and she—"

"*Jesus.*" Lewis took a sharp intake of air through his nose, interrupting her. "Christ, Eleanor." He leaned back in his chair, arms folded across his chest. "You'd think they'd be giving her a medal, not locking her up."

"Well, yes, but murder is murder. And she also shot a police officer."

"*She shot a cop, too?*"

Eleanor nodded. "In the face and through the heart."

"She won't be getting out anytime soon, will she?" He sighed, and there was resignation behind the sigh. "Where do kids learn to shoot like that? *Girls,* at that. Christ almighty."

"I know." She cleared her throat. "Lewis, I'd like to at least try, since I've been asked." Eleanor paused for a moment as if considering something then said, "I'll be okay."

Lewis stared across the table and into his wife's deep-set green eyes.

"Elle," he began, and in the way he pronounced her name, Eleanor heard a voice striving for compassion. But it was as if he couldn't maintain it, and he finished harshly: "I guess I can't really stop you, but I think we both know you're making a mistake." He drank the remaining wine in his glass and reached for the bottle. Eleanor watched him, saying nothing.

After a moment, in which neither one spoke, Lewis looked at his wife. "Why would she do it? Why would anyone?"

She shook her head. "I know," she said. "I know," meaning she agreed with her husband in wondering why. Not that she knew the answer to his question. She didn't.

CHAPTER THREE

A teen slouched into Jo's, coffee shop. Low, below his waist, hung pre-faded, ripped jeans, the crotch riding just above his knees, chains looping from one pocket to his belt. Small silver studs protruded from a brow and around his neck hung an ankh. He wore a backwards ball cap and the grim set of his face looked as though he had never smiled. Before him, as if propelled by immanent force, moved a girl, probably no more than thirteen, her jeans hugging her curves in stark contrast to the boy's shapeless pants.

David Sampson nodded and smiled gently as the young couple walked past to sit in the booth behind him. The girl flipped her hair as she passed but ignored him, and the young man's scowl darkened.

David was used to being hated and called a "pig" or "scum" and all number of other colorful expressions. At thirty-six, he was probably twice the boy's age. But at the boy's age he had decided he wanted to make a difference in the world. To say that what he'd experienced since joining the police force was different from what he'd expected would be no small understatement. He had no friends in the academy. His closest friend was left over from high school, and as usual Steve was late and David sat alone, listening to the quiet tones of the young man behind him. Then the girl's intermittent giggles, punctuated by, "*Stop it.*" More hushed laughter. Then silence. Then the sucking sound of lips meeting lips, an ostentatious noise at odds with etiquette.

He sat, leaning forward, looking past several empty booths to the front window watching the parked cars turn gold, then red, then green from the neon lights of the drugstore next door. A waiter was bringing the chairs from the outside in, and stacking them in a corner.

He saw Steve push through the door, black leather jacket, hair standing up, uncombed. David waved and Steve smiled when he saw him.

"Hey. Thought you were off duty. What's with the uniform?" Steve asked, sliding into the booth opposite.

David looked around the room. "Oh, you know, gives a good impression."

"I get it. Still selling dogs. I never did see why—"

"No."

". . . you thought that was a good idea."

"Because they got a new lease on life instead of being put to sleep in a shelter. But I stopped. I would never do it again."

"I don't know if being experimented on in a laboratory is a new lease on life, but that's not my problem."

"I said I wasn't doing it anymore. I—"

"Oh, I get it. Trying to impress girls with the uniform," Steve said cutting him off. "You seeing anyone?"

"No," David said softly, the way he always answered when Steve asked the question, which was better than what he used to ask: *Are you still a virgin?*

"What?" Steve asked in response.

"I said *no.* You always ask that first off as if—"

"Not seeing *anyone*?" Steve said, shaking his head; Steve who'd been married for four years and was expecting baby number two.

"No."

"Don't you want someone?"

"Yes."

"So?"

When David didn't answer, Steve said more gently, "Hey, you're a good guy. Just because you couldn't save your sister doesn't mean you don't deserve some happiness."

"This isn't about her."

"Just relax, dude. And don't think so much. Sherri says you could have any woman you wanted. Says you got the looks, and you listen to her when she talks."

"Yeah?"

"Sometimes I worry she'll leave me for you."

"Really?"

"So I say to her, no way, he's too idealistic. Head always in the stars."

"I don't know. Just seems that sometimes I lose my stars. You know what I mean?"

"That's just what I'm talking about, dude." Steve laughed. "That's exactly it. No, I don't know what you mean. My head's down here. You think too much with that big head of yours. Look, I'll see if I can hook you up with one of Sherri's friends."

"No, Steve, I don't think so."

"Why? Come *on*."

"I'm not ready."

He thought for the hundredth time how he would have liked to talk to Steve, but he didn't feel Steve would ever understand. Steve thought everything wrong in David's life was because of what happened with his sister, but that was a long time ago. He should never have told Steve about his sister. This was different, and although he'd like to confide in someone, he knew he could never tell Steve. He also knew he would begin thinking of her tonight. He was the reason she was in prison. He had put her there. His mind started reeling and he felt the sickness begin.

". . . got to be kidding, always more than *one* girl . . ." Steve was saying.

"I don't want to talk about it."

"You are the only living, breathing male who thinks you have to wait till the third date or something, who thinks that sex has to be—"

"I said I don't want to talk about it!"

"All right, all right, dude. Calm down." Steve said looking surprised. "But I can tell you, just forget it. Get your mind down from the stars and your body in the sack with the next girl you meet and you'll feel better. Promise."

But David knew that wasn't true. And he knew why.

CHAPTER FOUR

From the front parking lot, Eleanor studied the familiar building with its green roof, high fencing and rolls of razor wire, from which no girl would ever escape. For a moment she watched the brown leaves lift then fall back down around her feet on the pavement. Alight, then lie still.

She could not have known from the day's humble start the significance of its remainder. If she had, she might have discarded her notion that memory didn't serve her, and taken notice of the day around her as it bid her old self goodbye: The brisk air of autumn. The short days and long shadows. Steam, like secrets released, puffing out when she breathed. Trees clinging to their last leaves, the sense of everything on a precipice, the holidays racing towards her, and her world still unchanged.

East of the prison the sun was well up in the sky, spreading morning light over the beige building before her. A little light for the women within whose lives had known such darkness. What their intentions had been in committing the crimes that placed them in prison Eleanor little cared, or rather cared only in so much as she could gain insight, trying not to allow curiosity to spill over into judgment. Today if there was an added lightness to her step it was due to the excitement a new patient always gave to her.

"Why do you do it?" Cory had asked a million times. "You could work in an office, be a nurse, volunteer—"

"Join the Junior League," Eleanor said in unison with her best friend. The words that caused the smile on her face were, at the same time, the very words that had lately begun to give her a simultaneous feeling of exasperation.

Cory tried to help Elle by suggesting jobs that "you'd be so positively wonderful at, honey." And once Eleanor said back, "It fulfills me. Maybe I am sublimating a natural instinct for children, but I don't see that it matters if the result is a good one for both me and many an inmate."

"But *Elle*, they are so *messed-up*. So *danger*-rous."

Psychology had come naturally to her. It was a desire to understand her constant feelings of unease, especially compared to the rest of the normal acting world. And it had worked, for as she came to understand the motivations and actions of human beings, she began to realize she might not be so alone. Other people had lost their parents at a young age. And later in life, she realized that of course there were women who had chosen not to bear children, women whose lives had passed so quickly that by the time they felt ready to care for a new life, the time to do so had vanished.

She inhaled as if to bring the crisp air inside then entered the building. She handed her ID to Officer Harris and he nodded. His eyes lingered on her face for too long a moment.

"Good morning, Officer Harris," Eleanor said smiling.

"Morning, Dr. Hartley."

She always addressed him with "officer," perhaps sensing that he liked it, speaking in the unhurried, low, melodious tone that gave his name and title substance and respect.

Eleanor breathed in the familiar institutional smell, a mixture of stale, close quarters combined with too-sweet disinfectant. She passed through the metal detector and walked down the hall, her heels clicking on the linoleum tiles, her mind picturing Connie, an inmate who had counted every step she took, going to great lengths to avoid the lines between floor tiles.

She remembered one of Connie's last questions before she was released a week ago.

"Come on, Dr. Hartley. Won't you miss me just a little bit once I'm gone?"

Naturally she thought about the inmates once they were gone, but she had never missed one. There were always so many others ready to fill the void left by one. And she was too pleased for them.

She went through the Sally Port to the outside, walking beside the towering fences. The prison was rectangular in shape, with a courtyard, the equivalent of a boulevard in a men's penitentiary.

Entering through another door, Eleanor palmed into the Kronos systems key control box, retrieved the key to her office then stopped before an open door with a gold plate on the outside that read Executive Secretary. She waited until the woman behind the desk looked up.

"Oh hi, hon. Come on in." The woman at the computer was short and round with a cap of dark hair. "Be just a sec."

Eleanor composed herself in a chair before the desk, and laid her briefcase across her lap as a faint, sweetish odor of perfumed baby powder reached her. She looked around the cluttered office, her eyes finding unlikely refuge on a sausage biscuit lying half-eaten in its wrapper. She smiled to herself. When the woman finished typing, she slid her chair back across the floor, and looked up. "What're ya smiling at today, hon? Wish more people would." She shook her head back and forth as she said it, as if in disapproval of something.

Eleanor smiled even more into the candid brown eyes before her. "Oh, I don't know," she said. "I guess I have a lot to smile about. How are things today, Asa?"

"Fine. Just fine. But you may be in for a handful." She was rummaging through something on her desk. Then she set a thin blue file down for Eleanor.

"S'all right here. Rebecca has the dossier, but don't go running for it, I copied everything. Thing is, we don't have very much. That's why Helen thinks it's going to be hard."

Eleanor reached for the folder and opened it. Usually files were anywhere from five to ten pages long depending on past histories. She would scan the personal history, the pre-sentence investigation, the institutional criminal records, then look for additional notes that would help her. She began to read:

Name: *Jane Doe.*

"You've got to be kidding."

"What?" Asa looked up.

"Jane Doe?"

Asa shrugged. "There was an I.D. but it was fake."

Eleanor continued reading flipping through each of the three pages.

Identification pending. Prisoner doesn't speak. No personal contacts. Identification assumed false.

"Helen told me the inmate couldn't remember her name, that she was most likely mentally challenged."

"S'right. Not operating with all her faculties. Mental issues."

"Helen said she couldn't remember her age. That's particularly typical with patients of subnormal intelligence who have endured trauma."

"Hmm, wish I could forget my age."

Eleanor continued to read. "So they're charging her with second degree murder. That's better than first," she said as much to herself as to Asa.

Asa let out a puffing noise that sounded like she might be trying out for a dragon in the school play. "It was no aiding and abetting and being in the wrong place at the wrong time. It was murdering in cold blood with full intention to kill. You ask me, it ought to be first," Asa said while typing.

"Well, we don't know everything, do we?" Eleanor turned a page and there was the mug shot.

A face stared back at her, startling her. It was not the face her imagination had composed yesterday evening, addressing it, coaxing the face to smile, then to speak, the mouth and lips obeying each time. She looked at the real face, and for a second she mourned the imagined other as she concentrated on the pale face and tried to read the eyes the way she did every photo.

Two years into counseling women in the work release program, Eleanor had enrolled in a "face reading" seminar after reading an article in a scientific journal. Out of the four hundred and twenty-one face reading students who'd enrolled in the two-month course, she had scored third behind an ex-policeman and a psychiatrist. Afterwards, she'd been chosen by a well-known psychologist in San Francisco to work for three months on a project that tested the validity of high-scoring face readers' hunches. She quickly improved with practice, realizing however, as she mastered the art to finer and finer degrees, that it was becoming a compulsion, and she found herself not only listening, but obsessively noting what each speaker was also unwittingly revealing via contorted brows or tense cheek muscles.

"The face is the most effective instrument of communication," her professor in Tucson had informed the class then proceeded to arrange his face into several arresting expressions. She'd had no trouble, even in that introductory session, receiving a feeling from each, even if she still had no verbal description to accompany each feeling.

Now she stared at the face in the photograph. In each photo, in every file, Eleanor could read *fear* when the face appeared angry, *violence* when the face looked passive, *smugness* when the face stared back in innocence. She had always been able to read something in the faces bound to the files.

Until this moment.

For, stare as she did at the face upon her lap, she could read nothing. She saw nothing. When usually a detail in the face disturbed her, this time it was the lack of something to grasp onto that caused her to utter a sound, somewhere between frustration, disappointment and alarm.

"Y'all right, hon?"

"I'm fine. Maybe she is mentally disturbed. It's true ...she doesn't look particularly bright." Eleanor mumbled the words to herself.

"I mean if we had a contact," Asa continued. "Parent, spouse, cousin, *something*. But we don't. And, to boot, she doesn't talk."

"Any theory on why that is?"

"Talk to Helen, but . . ." Asa looked up at her, "I think she'll say that's your department. We're working on it. Just other things come up. You know, always something."

"Have you seen her?" Eleanor asked, her voice lilting upwards, her mind hoping against hope to gain some insight from Asa.

"Yes. When we did preliminaries."

Eleanor waited, searching Asa's face.

"I don't know." Asa looked down and away. She looked uneasy.

"Okay. I'll talk to Helen." But Eleanor didn't stand up to leave. Instead she looked at the photograph one more time. One more time the blank face stared back at her. Eleanor stared harder. And it was then that she felt it. There was something in the eyes and brow that became, for an instant, recognizable to her. She closed her eyes the way she'd been taught to do in the class, to let what she'd seen form in her brain. But whatever she'd seen and felt had vanished. When she opened her eyes and looked away from the file her brow was furrowed. She stood up.

"Thanks, Asa."

"Sure, hon."

Eleanor knocked. When Helen opened the door for her, Eleanor saw her face had lost the tense agitation it'd worn in their last meeting.

"I can't tell you how happy, how *relieved* I am, that you agreed. And how did Lewis take it?"

"He was fine."

Helen stood for a moment beside Eleanor. "Thank you, Eleanor. Thank you for doing this. Okay, let's go."

Eleanor walked beside Helen, her skirt forcing her long legs to take short steps. Together they moved through the courtyard, past the last of fall flowers and shrubs that bore evidence of a succession of girls who'd planted them over the years, tended in wistful remembrance of the small acts they'd once taken for granted. The courtyard shrubs were now a testament to beauty's necessity and tenacity within the world of confinement.

Helen and Eleanor passed the pharmacy where inmates lined up on the other side of the windows awaiting their medication. The walls against which they leaned were stained crimson from their uniforms' strong dye, as though a massacre had occurred and no one had bothered to wash the walls of the blood. They walked past women in maroon scrubs, indicating that they were not working, or orange scrubs, which designated working within the prison, or green scrubs for the lucky few tending the grass and gardens.

One day several years back after a long and difficult day, two assistant wardens had become punchy and started calling the inmates the "oranges," the "apples" and the "limes." The names had stuck and even spread, for unbeknownst to them, they'd been overheard making up the new names, and on an odd Thursday, leaving her office, Eleanor heard a guard yell, "Yo! You bunch a oranges, SHUT UP! Or I squeeze the joy juice outta you!" The ladies in the more severe-looking white scrubs were dubbed the "icicles." These were the isolation/segregation inmates, often the most hardcore offenders who had committed the most heinous crimes.

"Hello, Warden Huffington. Hello, Dr. Hartley."

"Hello, Melinda," Helen replied to the woman hurrying across the courtyard in observance of the KEEP MOVING policy.

Eleanor smiled and said hello to inmates, but by name she knew only a handful of women. These were generally the toughest cases, many of them requiring mental health experts: Eleanor or the psychiatrist.

In the far corner of the courtyard, Helen pulled open the door to building four, which housed the offices of the Department of Corrected Education and the Treatment Programs.

"Go on in and I'll bring her to you." Helen motioned Eleanor into a room she knew better than her own bedroom. Dubbed the "psych room" or sometimes the "sick room" pejoratively, it was empty of furniture except for two mismatched chairs on opposite sides of a green metal desk. On the side of the desk were three drawers and an electric buzzer midway down. The buzzer connected to the guard's station and, when touched, would ring four rooms away. The walls were the dirty beige of safari khaki, the tedium broken only by a round clock, three hanging prints and a small window on the back wall. The desk was angled so that Eleanor could turn her head slightly and see out the window.

Eleanor wanted one last look at the photo of the girl she was about to meet, but at that moment Helen walked in, followed by a guard escorting an icicle in handcuffs. Helen leaned over and said softly to her, "I'm sorry. I should have warned you about the cuffs. It's for your safety."

"But I've worked—"

"With certain felons. At least initially," Helen said under her breath. "You'll hold this key yourself every session until the guard returns. Procedure." She dropped a small key into Eleanor's hand.

Helen turned to the girl and said in a loud voice as though she were not only mute but hard of hearing too, "This is Dr. Hartley.

She'll be working with you, as I've explained, three times a week for fifty minutes. Eleanor, this is . . . we don't know her real name. We call her Jane, although we have reason to believe that is not her real name. Perhaps she'll tell you her real name."

As Helen motioned for Jane to sit in the empty chair, Eleanor registered her first split second impressions: *medium height, slim, fair; did not glance around room, suggesting little curiosity, either that or depression, stress, mental breakdown, sense of resignation.*

Eleanor let her eyes run all over the girl from head to toe. She watched as the girl crouched into the chair like a feral cat or dog unused to open spaces. She's somebody's child, Eleanor reminded herself to quell any unease, but the girl did not look particularly dangerous. She glanced away from her only to thank Helen, bidding her goodbye, and Helen's grateful look said back to her, "Good luck."

After Helen had left, closing the door, Eleanor looked again at the girl across from her, taking advantage of her disregard to study her face and catch some initial reading that she could enter into her file. Words will often lie, but seldom the face. Perhaps her muteness would be a blessing not a hindrance. She scanned the features before her now for the hard, embittered lines of many of her past patients, women whose faces read like road maps of their pasts. But Jane carried no map. Eleanor puzzled. The few creases around her eyes indicated that laughter had been present at some point in the girl's life, although Eleanor saw no vestige of it now.

"Hello," Eleanor began.

The girl did not regard her. She sat sideways in the chair, her eyes cast down. But Eleanor knew from her photo her eyes were blue or gray, a shade that could be light sensitive. Here in the interior of a prison, she would have little worry.

Had Jane once sat outside giggling with girlfriends, sipping cappuccinos? As Eleanor looked across at her she thought of the hundreds of girls Jane's age living freely as the earth continued its axial spin. Girls laughing and crying, not waiting for those behind bars to regain lost time. This girl had murdered. She had taken two lives. Snuffed them right out. Probably gotten mixed up with drugs at some time in her life, become an addict, and in the height of desperation, she had pulled the trigger of a gun in some sordid street to obtain her fix.

Eleanor glanced to Jane's arms for the telltale signs of using, but her arms were turned inward. Her eyes traveled up over hunched shoulders covered in the white scrubs. When her eyes moved up further, she saw the face. If, in her past, she'd thought she'd seen a closed face, she realized this face made a mockery of those.

The face before her was shuttered. It let in no light. It was framed by shoulder-length hair, blonde, uncombed. In the eyes gazing to the floor nothing registered. It was as if Eleanor were looking at a doll that a child had discarded. Looking directly at the downcast empty eyes Eleanor smiled.

Then in a relaxed voice she said, "Is it all right if I keep calling you Jane?" Using a name to precede each question would have the reverse effect if it wasn't the inmate's correct name. "Or is there another name you'd prefer?"

Jane blinked her eyes once, but kept her attention on the floor.

"It's all right with me if you don't want to talk. I don't know why you don't want to. I hope I'll find out. But for now let's just say, it's okay. You could do something to help me, though." She said brightly, then paused. "Will you do one thing for me? Will you nod your head yes or shake it no when I ask you a question?" She smiled, but across from her Jane did not move.

Eleanor stared at Jane and wondered what had occurred to cause her to murder.

And become silent.

Perhaps there had been some recent horrific prison abuse of which Helen was unaware. In G.P., General Population, prison abuses were frequent occurrences. It was inevitable that women locked up together in close quarters would get restless and often turn on their pod mates for sexual release or in violence.

"I'm here to help you. I would like to."

The ticking of the clock. But otherwise, silence.

"You can make it easy for both of us, or you can make it uncomfortable."

Again the small sounds, and more silence.

"Should you make it easy, that is to say, talk with me, you may talk about whatever you wish. You choose. Is it a deal?"

Jane shifted in her chair, and Eleanor heard the clinking of the handcuffs' chain.

"Perhaps you feel you've been put into prison unjustly. This is something we might talk about."

Nothing registered. The pale face across from her looked as though it lacked strength or, perhaps more accurately, will. In the girl's posture, too, there was defeat.

As Eleanor studied Jane's face she remembered the words of a poet who spoke of the soul living in perpetual yearning. What had caused Jane to kill? What had caused her to give up? Would she be able to help Jane find peace?

She found herself saying again: "I would like to help you."

Jane moved slightly and Eleanor saw her eyes flicker to one of the hanging prints. Eleanor turned her head and allowed her eyes to rest on the familiar landscape for a moment instead of the quiet girl's face. *Hills and Mesa to the West,* 1945. She had become enamored with Georgia O'Keeffe in a college Art History class and coaxed Cory into taking a trip to Abiquiu, New Mexico. She remembered sitting in a tiny restaurant with Cory, eating *huevos rancheros* outside on a picnic table, the warm, dry air so different from back east.

"I think I could live here," she had said.

"Hmmrf, really?" Cory garbled an answer, her mouth full of eggs. Then her eyes shifted in conspiracy. "Yes, *dahlin.* I could too. *Right here.* Did you see the waiter? *Gawdess* he gorgeous."

"I don't know if I'll ever get married."

That got Cory's attention and she nearly choked on her Coke, spurting half of it out her nose.

"Elle! What*eva are* you talking about? But of *course* you'll get married," she drawled out the words. "And I'll be your maid of *honnah.*"

Eleanor looked now at the hanging landscape, thinking of course Cory had been right on both accounts. She had indeed gotten married, and Cory had been her maid of "honnah." But she still remembered the feeling she'd had then, how her sensibility had matched the barren, scorched, but pure terrain.

"Do you like looking at that? Do the colors please you?" She asked Jane.

Jane removed her eyes from the mesas. Then, for the first time, but for only an instant her eyes met Eleanor's, gazing at her directly as if she had a message to deliver but very little time in which to do so. It was up to Eleanor to decipher the message. Eleanor caught her breath. There again was the quick feeling of recognition—but just as quickly as it had surfaced, it was gone. She knew she had never before seen Jane.

But what she'd seen filter across Jane's face for a brief moment was the most complete look of despair she had ever witnessed on a patient.

A tightness rose in her throat and she made herself breathe deeply. She didn't at first speak, but sat in silence, looking around the room as Jane had. There was the golfing print of St. Andrews in Scotland. Beautiful, peaceful fairways and greens, a sand trap and the North Sea beyond. Light puffy clouds floating in blue. Eleanor sometimes directed a patient towards this print if the patient was feeling anxious.

On the far wall hung Monet's *Impression Sunrise.* Did Jane know this painting? Had she ever taken an Art History class in school? Eleanor doubted it. This vision of a sunrise greeted Eleanor every day she entered the room. She looked at Jane.

A piece of blonde hair fell across Jane's face and Eleanor wished Jane would push it away. It looked greasy and dirty and it obscured part of her face from Eleanor's view. Jane had light brown lashes above her eyes, fixed by a sullen expression. No, not sullen. Defeated. Unlike the rehab patients Eleanor had worked with after graduate school, the offender in the penitentiary often did not see her way of acting as extraneous to or distant from herself, but rather as an expression of her way of being. Her motivation to change was often spurious, if not nonexistent, in that it stemmed merely from a desire to leave prison, not necessarily to change destructive behavior.

"The first session is always difficult. I don't want to make it hard for you." She paused and watched Jane, but saw nothing change in her features. "I think, with time, it will become easier for you."

"You know, it's okay to tell me anything at all. If you're afraid I'll judge you, I won't. That's not my job." Speaking softly, trying to coax Jane to look at her once more Eleanor said, "Perhaps you could indicate to me what you would like to talk about?" She searched for some emotion in the watercolor of Jane's features but, across from her, there waited the same hollow emptiness as if the soul of the girl had long ago fled.

"I know you must be wrestling with," Eleanor looked down to the desk, "probably more than I can imagine. I know you killed a police officer." She looked up. "I don't know why."

She glanced away for a moment and when she looked back Jane was staring back at her—looking steadily into her eyes, not merely staring blankly.

Eleanor continued slowly, not wishing to take her own eyes from Jane's. "I'm not here to judge you. I hope I never will.

None of us is perfect. No matter how hard we try. I guess we all make mistakes. You here in prison aren't the only ones who've made mistakes, you've just been caught at them. But—"

She thought she saw Jane's expression change. What was it?

"Do you have something you want to say to me?"

She waited but there was only the faint ticking of the clock.

"If *you* want to, I'd very much like to hear what you have to say. What you think."

Silence.

"I suspect you'll become tired of hearing me talk. I suspect I'll become tired of hearing me talk." She laughed a small laugh. Jane was looking at the desk between them. She shifted, and Eleanor again heard the handcuffs, this time their metal scraping the metal of the desk. She thought the cuffs steep insurance for the slim possibility of misbehavior here in the psych room with a guard not three minutes away with the buzz of her finger tip. They must be a heavy nuisance to bear in one's lap and Eleanor leaned forward in her chair to observe more of Jane's body. Then she saw a word written on the white cotton scrub bottoms covering Jane's left thigh. Black ink. It looked as if the word began with either an "M" or a "W" but she could not read it and at that moment Jane crossed her right leg over her left leg. Eleanor sat back against her chair. Nosiness wouldn't win her Jane's trust.

"Do you talk to yourself when you're alone? Do you want to talk to me now, but just can't?" She searched Jane's face for a clue, any suggestion, but there was nothing. She'd been with her for forty-five minutes. Time to stop. She pushed her chair back slightly and sat the remaining five minutes in stillness listening to the muffled movements beyond the closed door, to the small sounds of the room, which amplified their breathing and made a cleared throat sound like an old engine starting up. The room was no longer an empty room, not even silent. Just quiet. Eleanor wondered if the minutes felt long to Jane or if, since beginning her confinement, time had ceased to matter.

A sudden knock and noise felt like both intrusion and relief. Helen entered followed by a guard.

"*Well! All done? How'd it go?*" The loud greeting seemed an assault to the quietude. Helen addressed Jane and she too received silence in answer. She looked at Eleanor who smiled up at her and said, "The first day is always hard. Jane did great." She turned to Jane. "I'll see you day after tomorrow."

Eleanor stared after the retreating figures, but when the door closed, she slumped back against her chair. Only then did she begin to understand that the next session with Jane, and the next and the next could well be the most difficult in all her years as a trained psychologist. Only then did she have a the strange flash of premonition that they would become hours out of her life that she would not only remember, but that would grow and morph, stretching shape and intensifying in significance until all the other hours, in subsequent comparison, had paled. Or perhaps, she only hoped they'd become important to her, for how else could she bear the hours with Jane?

CHAPTER FIVE

That evening, more tired than she could remember being in a long time, Eleanor drove well above the speed limit toward the sanctuary of her home. Five miles away she turned up the exit ramp and only then was she stunned to see the flashing lights and the police car nearly in her back seat.

She pulled over and closed her eyes for a moment. Then she waited.

"Ma'am."

She rolled down her window.

"Ma'am, may I see your license and registration?"

She had already retrieved her license from her brown leather bag and she handed it to him. He studied it and she felt him studying her. His eyes were on her in a way that made her uncomfortable. He had short-cropped blonde hair and would have been attractive if his demeanor hadn't been so combative and … menacing. She hadn't spoken a word.

"Mind telling me your name?"

"No. My name is Eleanor Christina Hartley. As it says on the license."

"Mind telling me why you were doing 65 in a 45 mile stretch of road?"

"It was an absent-minded thing to do. I wasn't paying attention to my speed."

"I see. And do you frequently not pay attention to your speed?"

She felt the anger arise then. She wanted him to write her up so she could go home.

"Actually officer—"

"Officer Drakas."

"Actually Officer Drakas, this is the very first time." She knew she answered more curtly than was wise.

He leaned into the driver's side window, glaring in at her. "I'm going to have to write you up a ticket for reckless driving."

She was about to open her mouth and snap, 'Be my guest' or 'Go right ahead,' when her mind gently pointed out the folly of doing such.

More than twenty minutes and one ticket later, she pulled away from the side of the road and drove the speed limit the rest of the way home. As she walked up to her house, she was looking forward to seeing her husband, speaking about her day and eating the excellent food he loved to prepare.

"Late again," Lewis called when she entered. "But don't worry, the ginger glaze burned when I had to answer the phone, so I'm on round two. And pretty damn delicious, if I do say so."

"You seem happy," Eleanor said smiling, shedding shoes and jacket and walking into the kitchen. On her way she glanced at the cover of last week's *Economist.* A young boy of maybe eleven or twelve, an AK47 automatic rifle slung in nonchalance over his shoulder, gazed into the camera with a lingering, confident stare. Unlike the girl she had just met in person, she easily read this boy's face.

"What's wrong with being happy?" Lewis's voice, at once defensive, broke her thoughts.

"Not a thing."

"If not a thing's wrong, then why'd—"

"I didn't say anything was wrong."

"Your tone did."

She stared at him. "It did? I'm sorry. I want you to be happy. I always have."

He shook his head and laughed under his breath. But when she made no comment he said, "Now what is it?"

She looked up.

"*What*?" Lewis questioned.

"I don't know." She opened a cupboard filled with tall, sky blue, blown-glass glasses, retrieved one and filled it with water from the tap.

"Why don't you use the fridge water?" He asked her for the umpteenth time since they'd been married. "Can't understand how anyone can drink lukewarm tap water."

"It's too cold." Her answer never varied.

"Did you make it up the walk okay?"

"What?" She turned to face him, more baffled than before.

"That damn dog relieved itself on our front walk again. Ought to be shot."

"Lewis, it's dog poop," she said, her good mood evaporating and bewilderment growing.

"Exactly! And it's disgusting! No different than if I walked over to our neighbor's lawn and . . ." He didn't finish but Eleanor's mind formed a picture of where his fanciful analogy was going.

"Talk to him, then."

"I did. I told him to keep his damn shitting dog on a leash when he walks by."

There was a moment's pause before Eleanor said, "I met with . . . Jane today."

"Who?"

"The young woman in for murder, remember?"

He grunted.

"Lewis, I want to try to help her. In that way, perhaps I can help myself."

Lewis regarded her. In a softer voice he asked, "Okay, so how'd it go?"

"It didn't go." Eleanor answered. "She didn't talk to me. But, then, I hadn't expected her to."

"Hadn't you?"

"Right you are. Perhaps I had, but I don't know if I'm upset because here's this young girl whose life is ruined and who'll spend the better part of her days locked up in a penitentiary or because of all the injustices of life—some people lucky, some unlucky, you slip up once and you pay for it the rest of your life—"

"Wouldn't exactly call murdering a cop a slip up," Lewis interjected and Eleanor was about to speak when he asked, "Why do you think she did it?"

"Buying drugs from the dealer, I assume. Probably panicked when the police came."

"What's the accepted jurisdiction?"

"The testimony of the arresting officer, what little there is, is that she was, or is, mentally unstable and that she fired in a fit of panic, or rage, or something."

Lewis let out a half snort, half laugh. "In the face and heart."

"Two witnesses."

"Maybe it was self defense."

"I thought of that too. The problem is she sat in the courtroom and admitted her guilt with no mention of self defense."

He snorted again. "She could talk then."

"Evidently."

Lewis peeked into the oven, and a hungry Eleanor breathed in the heavenly smell. "Two more minutes for the salmon." He straightened and cut off the flame under the glaze then reached for the blue and yellow ceramic saltshaker that he and Eleanor had bought on their honeymoon in Provence. He tossed it from one hand into the next with absent-minded dexterity, nodding his head up and down in motion as the saltshaker flew back and forth.

"I can't keep calling her Jane if it's not her name. It's absurd." Eleanor sat down at the old plantation table and ran her hand over its grain, caressing it, as Lewis watched her. "I have to find out about her. At present, she's a blank wall." She remembered the word inked upon Jane's thigh and felt an unpleasant urge to know exactly what it said. "She looks completely blank. I don't know if that's because she doesn't talk, or *won't* talk to me. Or because she really is blank inside there, deeply disturbed. And that's what scares me. I've seen blank looking women before. But this one is different."

"Different how?" Lewis slid a chair over and sat down at a right angle to her.

And Eleanor wasn't sure she could tell him. She frequently glimpsed the emotional inside of a woman by way of her physical exterior and expression. How to explain Jane's detachment? Devoid of emotion? Too simple. Hiding something? Perhaps. Some atrocity must have befallen her.

"So what's wrong? I thought you liked the tough cases. The more looney the better."

"I don't know enough about her to know how disturbed she is. I'm excited, but—" She stopped. Quite suddenly Eleanor longed for sleep. Sometimes into her sleep would drift insights into these women that eluded her by day. Jane's record indicated she was Level 3, the security level of highest risk, both to herself and to others—prisoners whose escape would be dangerous to the public, police or security of the state.

"But you're doubting yourself for the first time."

"Perhaps." She reached out a hand to touch his. His were wiry, competent hands. A few dark hairs covered the backs. She stared at the veins and hair and skin, but as she tightened her grip he shifted casually, removing his hand and stretching his arms up over his head.

"And to top it all off, I got a speeding ticket on the way home."

"Oh Elle, for crying out loud."

"How was your day?"

Lewis gave her a brief commentary of the nurses' incompetence, with the exception of Stacy Sweeney on whom she suspected he had once had a significant crush. He rarely mentioned his patients, whom he saw fewer and fewer of each week, allowing new patients to sign up with younger doctors just beginning their practices and allowing Lewis more time to focus on his childhood and lifelong passion, tennis.

"Did you go to the club?"

"I did."

"Did you play well?"

"I did."

She waited.

"We won. Duncan missed a couple of drop shots, but I made up for it at the baseline." As Lewis continued to describe a shot by shot replay of his match with the enthusiasm that had first attracted her to him, Eleanor found that the details of tennis now bored her. She let her mind float, and she found herself back inside the psych room with Jane. Do your parents know you're in prison? Do you have brothers and sisters? Where did you live? What did you do? Who are you? Why don't you speak? Why did you kill? And *what* is your name?

Then something occurred to Eleanor that hadn't before. She's aphasic! Why of course! Why hadn't she thought of it at once? She would tell Helen tomorrow. Aphasia, the total or partial loss of the power to use or understand words, was usually caused by brain disease or injury. She thought of all the possible causes for the muteness, and possible cures that she'd ever read about or studied. Extreme trauma was the number one cause. She must find the arresting police officer.

"Elle?"

She realized Lewis had asked her a question, and she came back to her immediate surroundings with difficulty, her eyes focusing on the wide windows beyond, surprised to find no bars. "I'm sorry, my mind drifted."

"No kidding."

"I'm sorry, Lewis."

"No problem. By the way, you're on your own Friday night."

"What?"

"I'm having dinner with Cory," he said standing up, not meeting her eyes.

For a moment Eleanor said nothing. "You're. . . "

"She asked us both over, remember? You told me to go. You said you were too tired or too busy, I forget."

Eleanor looked up at her husband then again traced the rim of the table back and forth with her hand. "That's great, Lewis. Yes, I remember. That's great. That'll be fun. Just the three of you?"

"Two. Jim's out of town."

When Eleanor didn't answer, Lewis touched her lightly on the shoulders. "Let's eat. Stay put and I'll serve you."

"Thank you." And as Eleanor looked out the large glass window, the sun retreated like a low tide into the already crest-fallen evening.

CHAPTER SIX

Three nights had passed since David sat across from Steve in the same booth where he sat now. He could hear a group of teenagers behind him talking in low voices, but he couldn't make out their actual words. He heard the voices stop and the kids get up and move to a booth across from him. He could see one young man leaning back in the booth. Beside him two thin black-haired, black-nailed, red-lipsticked girls hunched forward hanging onto his words. The waitress, one David didn't know, took their order then walked over to David. She looked nervous or haggard, maybe fragile, David thought.

"More?" She didn't smile.

"Sure." He held out his cup, smiling up at her. It was after the waitress had poured his coffee and walked away that the call came over the portable perched on his epaulet and he wished that she had heard it, but she was moving through the swinging doors. He glanced to the teenagers, and found only one face turned toward him, and that face was surly.

"*211, I need a back up.*" His department still used a mixed system of plain language and the ten code. The ten code kept air time down, but after a major screw-up when an officer misheard the 10-32 code over a crackling radio, arriving on the scene unprepared to find an armed man intent on using his gun, the use of plain language became necessary.

He slipped from the booth. Then the portable squawked again, this time more urgently.

"*10-32! 10-32! I need a back up!*"

He dropped some bills on the table, nodded across the room toward the haggard waitress and left. Once behind the wheel, he looked to his rearview mirror, and over his shoulder briefly, then switched on the siren as he pulled out. There was the usual beating of his heart and surge of adrenaline in his chest as he bid the squad car to move faster. He thought of Nick. Well, he'd let Nick call the shots tonight, keep his mouth shut.

A mist had settled in the streets, and as he slowed up around Belview Park he could make out two more squad cars.

"One-eleven," he radioed, trying to get the picture.

"*10-33! 10-33! Man down!*"

He parked the car under the branches of the old trees lining the park's perimeter, and slipped out, stepping over discarded forty-ounce bottles and used condoms, hand on his gun, heart pounding in his chest.

Then, as if he'd just stepped into a color world from his own black and white, he began to hear the sounds: Voices. Cops voices, to his left. Shouts beyond. He began to listen for the sounds he'd been taught to listen for. The shouts, but also the silences. He continued advancing. Then he heard a shot. He had his gun in both hands before him now, advancing slowly. Two more shots in rapid succession from the parking lot behind the apartments. Lights on in one apartment building but not the other. He ran to the scene.

Two men were down. David saw Andy, and his pulse quickened. Andy was pulling himself off to the side of the street.

Nick stood in the lot by the apartments.

"Beside me! Back me up, David!"

Gun out before him, heart pumping, David scuttled over to Nick.

"What happened to Andy?"

"He'll be fine. Charlie's opposite." Nick answered in tense phrases like Morse code.

David glanced at Andy and saw he was in pain. He grimaced.

Just then something whizzed close by them. David felt the air beside him change. A bullet hit the wall behind.

Nick whirled around and fired back. A man dropped down, his torso covered by a black sweatshirt, his right arm outstretched and reaching for a gun eight inches away in the dirt. He inched forward on his stomach, and just as his fingers clasped the gun, David saw Nick aim his gun and fire one shot. Nick remained standing with his arm outstretched pointing at the man's still body. Finally he looked up and scanned the apartment buildings. Only then did he let his arm drop to his side and turn to David.

"Fuckin' time we blew them away." He kicked a small piece of gravel with the end of his black boot. "Mother fucking scum of the earth."

David was about to speak when he saw movement in his peripheral vision. He spun around as a young man holding a small sack jumped from the lit tenement window, landing with a thud.

"Freeze! Don't move!" David yelled, gun pointed toward the crouching man. "Drop your weapon!"

"Don't have no weapon!"

"Drop it now, or I'll shoot!"

"Don't have no weapon. For real, man!" The young man moved to open his coat.

Nick was beside David, and two loud cracks sounded one after the other.

The crouching man crumpled on the gravel. It happened so fast, David turned around to look at Nick and saw in the light from the streetlight an eerie, eager glint in Nick's eyes. Then there were no more sounds. They waited standing in the queer stillness, casting their eyes around, not moving or speaking.

Small outside noises—cars in the distance and the flutter of debris came to them out of silence and Nick turned to David and said quietly, "Go check on Andy."

David started toward Andy but stopped midway. He turned for just a moment to watch as Nick walked up to the dead figure and rolled him over. He watched him kneel down. When Nick glanced back over his shoulder, David spun around and walked the rest of the way to Andy.

"Hey."

"Hey, David," Andy answered, looking nervous and scared.

"Where'd you get hit?" David squatted.

Andy pointed to his thigh. "Just grazed I think. Least I hope," he tried to laugh.

It looked bad. It was bleeding a lot, and David thought, *We got to get him out of here.*

"Looks okay," David reassured. "I'm calling the medics then I'll tie it up good. You're going to be just fine."

"Thanks, man."

"What about him?" David nodded to an inert man with his leg buckled under him.

"What's it look like?"

Behind the man, on the side of a derelict building, some gang member had tagged, "*Zong*" in various places, and somebody else had answered back, "*FYOM.*"

"Yeah, I figured, but . . ." David pretended to lean over Andy but he raised his eyes to watch as Nick reached his hand into the corpse's coat. Then he reached into the sack the man had been carrying, bringing out one paper bag in the shape of a brick, and slipped it into his inside pocket. David saw him reach in again and pull out another then open the second bag, and dip a finger into it.

"Tell me what happened," he said to Andy in a low tone, trying to focus, but glancing once more to Nick. When Nick stood up, David dropped his eyes.

Andy was talking and David brought his attention back to him. "What?"

"Nick got him," Andy said under his breath. "Got him good." But when David said nothing, Andy continued, talking fast. "Shit man, they're fuckin' murdering drug pimps."

Still David was silent, trying to decide what he could say and what was best left unsaid.

"David, you got dumb shit for brains!"

"You don't shoot them." David paused, waiting for Andy to argue. Then feeling like a rat, he stated what they had all learned in officer training and what he took to heart. "If you can restrain them without force, then—"

"Aw, fuck that. Look at me lying here. Fuck that! He fuckin' *shot* me. If they fuckin' *shoot* you, you blow their fuckin' *balls* off! If you're gonna quote that bullshit to me, which is what I think your head is made of, then did you ever hear of the *possibility of deadly force*?

"Who shot first? Him or Nick?"

Andy stared back at David. "Nick is the man! I'd rather have Nick on a job than anyone. He doesn't take shit from anyone."

"You think you know, Nick. But you don't."

"What are you talking about? Don't trash talk Nick."

"Andy, that guy there," he nodded to the young man lying by Nick. "He didn't have a gun. He was about to show me he was clean when Nick blew him away."

"And you better thank Nick that he did too, because if not, we'd both be dead right now. Believe some crack-assed drug pimp that he don't have no weapon. That's real bright."

"If you can restrain them without—" David began repeating again, but Andy burst in.

"Either they kill us or we kill them! Take your pick. Besides, they're *they serve no purpose on this earth.*"

"I'm going to call the medics again see what's taking them so long."

"Fucking medics."

"Look, Andy," David said up close to Andy's ear: "I don't like them anymore than you do, but they still have rights. You don't kill them if you can restrain them in other ways. You don't kill them because you're prejudiced yourself and you're taking your aggression and anger out on them. Makes you no better than them. Even convicted prisoners have rights as human beings."

"David, look, you know I always liked you. You're a good guy. But I'm sorry, I'm not sticking my nose where it don't belong and I'm not losing my job to save you." He paused, but he wasn't looking at David. "If it comes down to it, I'll say Nick shot in self defense. Sorry."

David heard sirens in the distance, and turned his head from where he knelt beside Andy as a flood of headlights poured over them creating a ghostly stage-like appearance.

CHAPTER SEVEN

In the locker room of the club Lewis zipped his fly and tucked his racket carefully into its canvas bag.

"Clydesdale Room?" Duncan asked sitting heavily on the bench, his veined legs crossed one over the other like a woman's.

"Can't today. Meeting someone for lunch."

Duncan glanced at his friend who was younger than he was by about fifteen years. He smiled, nodding his head, but said nothing.

Lewis turned his black Z4 into the familiar driveway. When he'd bought the new car, Eleanor had taken one look and stated, "Mid-life crisis car?" He'd laughed with her, but had been silently pissed off. Now as he strode up the walkway he knew so well from years of dinners, he wondered if she'd say, "Mid-life crisis," and leave it at that, or if for once he'd see emotion.

How he used to hang onto her words, finding her the most fascinating woman on earth and marveling that he, an ordinary Jewish boy from Summit, New Jersey, could have snagged the beautiful, blonde-haired, green-eyed New England girl.

On their first date, sitting beside her in his father's Buick sedan, he'd told her about his passion for tennis, and how he'd been proud to be on the team in college, then asked her to tell him one thing about herself that would surprise him, so that they might begin getting to know each other.

She'd laughed, and what a beautiful, carefree sound it was. "I like learning other people's secret thoughts."

At the time it had intrigued him, but now he often thought back to that comment with a small emotion that if he were to analyze, he knew he wouldn't like.

On their second date he stole up his courage to kiss her goodnight in his father's car. And on the third date knew he loved her more than he'd ever loved any girl before and the kiss had turned into more because she kissed him back with surprising passion, a hunger he felt at odds with her more than aloof exterior. And on that soft spring evening in his father's car, with the air gently touching them as if in silent benediction of what they were performing, he heard her cry out and at first he thought he had done something terribly wrong.

It was only later after they'd been married that she'd stopped crying out beneath him, and he knew, in fact, it was this that was wrong, fearing it like he had her first demonstration of letting go, and all the while yearning for it back. But it was too late, for he felt clumsy and awkward with her from then on.

He had tried to eschew feelings of inadequacy, believing instead in his good luck. After making love to Eleanor, he'd feel elation, followed quickly by the sense that he wasn't really the man she wanted. It was the same elation that had followed their marriage—marred only by his disapproving parents, their disappointment reaching its apex when she wouldn't take his name—and just as quickly shadowed by the predictable feeling of not being worthy of her. As time mellowed their differences and left stability in its wake, she became familiar to him, all her human quirks and ticks no different from anyone else's, and these visible flaws comforted him to the point that he no longer felt anxious about her.

But then one day almost exactly two months ago, he'd awoken feeling so unlike himself that he feared rising from bed. The feeling of hope and anticipation that would touch him upon waking—whose promise he'd savor in bed beside Elle as the dawn slowly gave way to morning—was on this day alarmingly absent, and he felt already eaten up by the harsh light and imagined stresses lying in wait for him. And on that day he had played harder and better than usual upon seeing Coralee at the club, and afterward asked her to lunch. As he watched Cory throw her head back and laugh at his jokes the way Elle never did, Lewis knew he and Cory would satisfy what each was imagining. He fell in love not only with her southern accent and sultry bedroom appearance but also with her small, careful gestures, the way she lit a cigarette, the way she straightened the silver at their luncheon table. For those beautiful weeks he had felt light, filled with anticipation, hoping to see her at the club. He had to be careful not to act too happy at home. One evening he'd been at the sink humming *La Donna e Mobile,* in his best Duke of Mantua imitation, and hadn't heard Elle come through the door. But even his turned back had perceived somebody standing in the hallway silent. Then Elle had simply said:

"Lewis?" Making him feel guilty for singing. Making him feel guilty for his long-sought out happiness. So he rationalized.

Eleanor was like an incredible dessert in bed, the kind of sculpted creations he'd seen in *pâtisserie* windows in France, magnificent, mouth-watering, yet so perfect as to be un-servable to assembled groups of friends. Would you slice into it only to find the blueberries and raspberries rolling off of the top, the knife cracking through the thin, hard layer of caramelized sugar, squishing and destroying the perfect layer of cake? When he made love to Eleanor, he felt that she was holding back, as if she was observing the two of them making love, as if—and it took him years to admit it to himself—her heart was not in the act. It was like she was made of stone.

Now walking up to Eleanor's best friend's house, he wondered how his life would have turned out if Cory hadn't moved to Virginia seven years ago. He knocked lightly on the door. In the other hand he held a bouquet of Mums and deep inside his overcoat pocket he carried a mango. When Cory opened the door and stood before him in a red silk blouse and nothing else, he knew his luck had not run out. He handed her the bouquet of flowers.

"Why, *thank* you. They'll sure brighten up this gray day." The word "gray" was spoken lazily in two syllables, gra-ya. "But then again, so does seeing you again."

"I brought you something else," he said and reached into the pocket.

"A *mang*-go." She glanced from it to him. "What*ever* for?"

"Remember," he began and he felt his cheeks flush, but embarrassment faded when he looked into her eyes and saw nascent understanding and a sly smile spread across her face. She grabbed his arm and pulled him inside.

Still clutching the mango he reached his arms under her blouse and felt her flesh, smooth and new like the fruit's silken skin. He let his hands drop down to her buttocks and she arched into him letting out a small sound as she did.

"What's that?" He asked her, standing back and sniffing the air.

"What's what, dahlin?"

"Something smells wonderful."

"Dahlin, I put a shoulder of lamb on the stove and it's cooking with white wine and potatoes, onions and a bay leaf." When he said nothing, she answered the unspoken question with: "I thought we'd need something for afterwards. You *can* stay, can't you?"

"I, uh, I'll have to call Elle."

She placed a deft hand on the lump in his pants and said, "Then call her. Tell her you'll be late."

"Now?"

"Of course. I can do two things at once, can't you?"

On Coralee's bed, he bit into the mango and tore off the skin. He pushed Cory down and smeared the sticky orange fruit over her belly. Then he moved it down.

"Now I need to lick it off of you." He put his face down onto her.

"Dahlin," she said. "*Dahlin*!"

He loved her raw eagerness, her clutching legs, the way she had of clamping herself so tight that he didn't want it to be any tighter and then rocking up in that intoxicating way, the two of them locked together, the shoulder of lamb cooking away in the oven. When he felt Coralee shudder, he stopped abruptly, swapping positions, bringing her down on top of him, grasping breasts—copious breasts, the same body part yet so unlike the medium-sized, restrained bosom of his wife. Lewis groaned a few moments before Cory released the theatric howls he loved.

Weak and limp, she sat back down astride him, breathing hard for a moment, then pushed herself up with exaggerated effort, turned to face him and collapsed by his side.

He watched, then slipped his arm around her as she lay against his chest. He closed his eyes and drifted off into unsettled sleep. He felt her nudging him in the ribs and heard her voice.

"Dahlin, I think I lost my earbob in your den. Would you have a wee peek?"

He opened his eyes. "What did they look like?"

"Dahlin!"

"I'm sorry. I was focused on body parts not ear…bobs."

"They were Tiffany. And they were my *fav*-orites."

"I'll look."

"You were spectacularly impressive that afternoon, if I do remember correctly. I do *so* enjoy sitting on you."

Lewis grunted but remembered how he felt making love at home. The rushed and forbidden aspect intensifying the sex to such a height that he now became aroused just thinking about it.

"Has Elle said anything?" Coralee asked studying the thick dark underbrush of hair on his chest, forearms and armpits.

"No she's too busy living in the minds of looneys to notice."

"Well, that's Elle." Both *well* and *Elle* were two syllable words. She shifted away from Lewis and put her hand up momentarily to shield her eyes from the persistent rays of afternoon sunlight beneath the partially lowered Venetian blinds. "She can pick up on things that the rest of us would never see. If you lie, if you twitch your face muscles, she'll know, you know."

"Don't worry, she doesn't look at me anymore," he said with more passion than he liked.

He watched the sunlight catch the diamond ring on Cory's left ring finger. He reached to touch her belly and felt the sticky mango and smelled its lingering trace together with her musky scent, and he thought of the big cat cage in the zoo when he was a boy. The stench was ferocious, but he felt drawn by its powerful horror as he looked upon the dangerous cats trapped behind bars. Now a smell similar and powerful in its own fecundity aroused him like none other.

"Oh, I'm sure that's not true," she answered.

"Loves those girls in the prison more than me. I tell you, I—" he didn't finish.

"I'm sure she loved you once, but now *I* love you more," she said to him, pulling him into her, nuzzling against him.

There was laughter coming from a neighbor's yard. Diminishing light touched the end of the bed, giving the entwined couple sunlit stockinged feet for a moment before fading as a cloud overtook and the walls of the room lost their momentary brightness.

"Do you ever talk to her about it? She being a shrink an all."

"That's exactly why I never would. Hell will freeze over before . . ." He reached for Coralee, and offered the straight, white teeth in a smile his wife rarely saw. "This is my way of talking about it."

When Lewis left, Coralee did not have the good, if temporary, feeling of being fulfilled that she'd had a month ago when the affair had turned from flirting and emotional tension to the physical. Or even two weeks ago. His words stalked around in her mind like crabs to nighttime carcasses.

Loves those girls in the prison more than me. I tell you, I—

She had nuzzled into him, smiling and pretending, but her thoughts had taken a different turn. He still loves her, *dammit.*

I don't think she's ever cared whether I lived or died.

Coralee knew it pained him to say it, and she also knew that his assertion was false, but she'd said nothing. She loved Eleanor, but her desire for Lewis was something she felt powerless to fight. She separated the two, love and desire, and over the past two days found herself staring into the mirror in the mornings, or sometimes blankly out the window, speaking to herself, rationalizing, long conversations directed to whom? To Elle or to God? She knew what Eleanor would say in the situation, for she remembered a moment, long ago, walking beside Eleanor after their English Lit class in which they'd been studying passion and the Romantic poets. They were so erudite back then, gathering together in dorm rooms to drink Dubonnet, light cigarettes and eat smoked oysters on Ritz crackers while discussing Kierkegaard and Wittgenstein, love and sex. Coralee had never forgotten the remark as Eleanor turned to her, the breeze catching her hair and blowing it up from her shoulders, creating an image of nonchalant beauty that Cory was able at that moment to admire free from envy because Eleanor was, as her best friend, something of her own possession. Yet even then, in their early carefree college days, she had known Eleanor would always remain an inscrutable presence to those who sought and tried hardest to be closest to her.

"In my opinion there's only one reason to resist desire." Eleanor had spoken with the assurance of youth.

"What?" Coralee asked.

"Love," Eleanor answered.

But Coralee had not understood. It was only now that she could.

CHAPTER EIGHT

"*No. Stop it. I don't want to,"* Cilla whispered back to the voices, but today they were relentless, urging her towards the thing she did not want to do.

At 5:30, she was supposed to rise, but often she was just too tired because the voices had kept her awake all night. Other nights she was woken by flashlights in her eyes during the three early morning shift counts. After the 5 a.m. count sometimes she stumbled out of bed into the cold dankness of her cell. She would try to move on the bed without it creaking in order not to wake her cellmates who would then yell at her. The older woman was a little kinder to her than the teenager, but each morning Cilla felt anxiety knowing that she was disrupting their sleep and that either one might at any minute jump up exasperated and frustrated. The constant anxiety and attention to consideration created a tension, an artificial politeness that she'd not known at her old institution. And then there were the voices. If she messed up, they got so mad at her. But for good reason.

At 6:00 a.m. the officers who hated her would begin screeching over the loudspeaker. Names and commands blared out. Her ears strained to hear whether her name was being called. All the screeching and loud blaring only intensified the voices that no one but she could hear, as if her voices, in vying for her attention needed to treble their volumes. But she thought to herself, as if there was any *choice*? Of course she would always choose *them.*

She had never told nice Dr. Hartley about the voices she heard in her head because she expected Dr. Hartley already knew. In a way she suspected Dr. Hartley heard voices too.

They had a bond that way. But Dr. Hartley didn't know about Lelia yet. She would tell her soon and nice Dr. Hartley would say back in her beautiful, soothing voice, with her beautiful movie-star looks, "I know, Cilla. I understand. I had my own—"

"*WHO THE FUCK STOLE MY FUCKING RESEES CUP?!*"

Cilla jumped as if someone had smacked her from behind.

"Pipe down, J-cat," someone called. "Your fat ass ain't gonna starve, that for sure." Laughter.

Cilla was on constant alert, tense, near tears. Her sessions with her therapist provided the only down time, save for sleep and then even her dreams were alternately filled with horrid visions of floating jellyfish-esque dead babies on top of brackish brown water, strange futuristic cars driving across the still water's surface and then Lelia's demise. The voices scolded her for letting it happen out there on the road, and they were becoming relentless: *"Why'd you kill your baby girl? Your very own baby girl? Killer, killer, baby killer.*

Lelia lay still before her eyes at the edge of the road. It was then the voices had begun again. The voices had first started softly in her twelfth year, when her parents let the people come and take her from the only person she had ever loved as a child. Her older brother by nine and a half months. Her brother fought and screamed but he couldn't stop the people who came, and the people put her in the bad place. That's when she'd started hearing the voices.

Now, she wondered if the voices were really in her head. Maybe they were in her gut. Because two days ago she'd heard the lady in the TV say that in our guts there lived millions of little things, and these millions of things could change our behavior and make us do things we didn't want to do. She could understand this. So maybe we weren't really one person walking around—we were all these tiny, little, crawly things.

After years in the bad place and no contact from her brother, the "event" happened—the event with another patient in the bad place. A male patient. And the event, which was against her liking, had produced Lelia.

Lelia's birth freed Cilla from the bad place and Cilla went to live in the "house" with the other women and the other babies. The voices subsided. But then she killed Lelia. She didn't try to but she guessed that it was her fault. If her older brother had been there with her, none of it ever would have happened. The voices started getting louder and louder until she could take them no more. The people intervened again, but they didn't take her back to the first place where the event had happened. They brought her here, to prison.

When Lelia came back to her with long green hair and sparkling lights at Christmas time, the voices spoke in softer tones...but only for a while.

At midday Cilla felt the best she had in seventy-three hours and twenty-two minutes and she sat down at the communal table in her pod. The table with chairs around it stood outside her room, always inviting *her* to sit at it like the other inmates did. But rarely did she listen to it and sit. She felt too exposed. But on this day, she felt good. Well, she felt okay. She ventured forth, leaving her room, sat down and started writing a note to Lelia. And the voices began again, but with such force that she called out answering them.

"No, I can't do *that.*"

The girls in her housing unit looked up at her then ignored her. Except for Mimi Kramer.

"Who you yelling at Cilla? I don't see no one sitting with you."

Cilla took her lower lip between her teeth, horrified she'd spoken to the voices out loud. She wondered if Mimi had voices. She knew Dr. Hartley liked Mimi better than her because Mimi was pretty. She often wondered what Dr. Hartley thought about her once she had left. She wondered if she talked to other people about her. She kind of hoped that she did.

"Don't be dry snitching on Cilla," someone said to Mimi in a lazy, I-don't-give-a-damn tone. "She chatted out, and you know it. Probably always been OMH, ain't that right, Cilla?" Cilla said nothing because she didn't understand the language the girls used. Even when someone told her OMH meant Office of Mental Health, and it was used in place of "crazy" she still didn't understand.

"Hey! I'm talking to you," Mimi yelled towering over her. Cilla hunched her shoulders as if trying to make herself smaller. Mimi turned to the pod. "Y'all see anyone but fat back Cilla sitting there?"

Still biting her lip, Cilla risked a glance at Mimi, straining her neck because Mimi was one of the tallest girls in the pod. Mimi's weight was shifted and her head cocked. She had a small head and small feet of which everyone knew she was particularly proud. She had strawberry blonde hair and big, voluptuous lips like Angelina Jolie.

"All you ever do is buy oatmeal cakes and Oreos from the Com and stuff your face. How many pounds you gained since coming here?"

"Leave her alone, *Creo*," said Shina Jones, a tall, elegant black woman. She stood, stretching like a cat, slowly, with power contained before the single bound onto prey. Something in her movement was like a low warning, or perhaps a forewarning.

"Roll up your window, bitch," Mimi said and gave her the finger behind her back. She returned her attention back to Cilla. "Too fat you can't even stand for counts. Spend your time in the Ding Wing, right? With Dr. Hartley, right?"

"Hey you monkey mouth, I said *leave* her, or I gonna bust your pretty prison pocket good," Shina warned again, but she walked into her cell, and flopped onto her cot with a book.

Cilla bent her head down, her pen still in hand, and focused her eyes on the sheet of paper before her.

"Kiss my sweet ass," Mimi said to Shina's closed door.

Cilla had never before heard the likes of so many colorful words and far from horrifying her, they fascinated her. She'd try them out for herself, lying in bed, whispering softly, "Kiss my sweet ass." Or "cunt-licker, cock-sucker, mother-fucker, meat wagon, lock-in-a-sock," liking the way the new words sounded with only a nebulous understanding of their meaning.

Mimi laughed then snatched the pen and sheet of paper from Cilla's hand.

"*Dear Lelia, I am sorry,*" Mimi read aloud from the paper. "*I am sorry I let you get squished and I am sorry not to be with you right now. They say I will be coming home soon. I hope so. I will decorate you and comb your long hair. I bet you have grown tall.*" A diabolical grin spread across Mimi's face. "Who you writing to, Cilla?" Cilla blushed from ear to ear but could not bring herself to look again at Mimi. The whole pod was staring at her now. She knew now the voices would punish her for exposing Lelia's choice of return. But she knew why Lelia came back to her as a tree. Trees live long lives rooted to the earth and no one can carry them out to the road to get run over. Lelia wanted to be with her always. But, after the psychiatric institution, neither Lelia nor Cilla had bargained on Cilla's incarceration in the women's state penitentiary.

Glancing once at the unit manager, Mimi waved her trip pass in the air, slipped outside the doors and let Cilla's pen and papers fall from her fingers. She exited the building as Cilla followed her, bending over in great effort to retrieve her pen and missive to Lelia, knowing the voices had seen it all. If she lost that pen she'd have no way to write to Lelia and the voices would sure be mad. And with good reason. Oh, poor Lelia.

"*You!* Trip pass?" The guard shouted at her.

Cilla stared in terror at the guard.

"Where's your trip pass?" The guard yelled again.

Cilla staggered backwards. "I was getting my pen back."

"Getting your pen? How's your pen get out here? You're in an unauthorized area. Get back in your pod this minute!"

Tears streamed down Cilla's cheeks. The voices were telling her to lie down, sleep, eat a banana, a moon pie. But they urged her to do other things too. The thing she didn't want to do.

She stumbled back into her unit greeted by the stares from lounging inmates in the smoked-filled pod.

"Yo, Cilla, you dumb mother-fuck. Why you run out the pod like that with no trip pass? Why you let Mimi mess with you? Just forget it, girlfriend. Let it be.

She grabbed her blank papers from the table, crumpling sheets as she did and headed for her cell, but she tripped, falling down and banging her knees before she reached it. She heard the laughter behind her.

"Law child. That be one fucked-up little white bitch."

"Little, my ass."

More laughter. Maybe the solution the voices offered was for the best after all.

The only other inmate Mimi picked on more than her was the girl everyone called "Mute." But Cilla envied Mute, because she was around Mimi only one hour a day, during Association, when girls were allowed free time to mingle in the courtyard. The rest of the time they said Mute stayed locked up on her own because, "she done splattered someone's brains all over the street from here to fucking Kansas City, and you be careful, you turn your back, she just as soon knife you too." The girls also said the C.O.s "had their way" with Mute. Cilla wasn't sure what way they had, but she wished she could stay locked up on her own like Mute. She'd gladly give them their "way" with her too. She might even splatter brains to Kansas City if she could stay locked up away from Mimi.

It was on a dark, overcast day the first time Cilla had seen the mute girl being led around the courtyard in handcuffs by a guard. The guard was a little short man, with chocolate bar colored skin, who Cilla liked because he was gentle and kind so unlike most of the other guards. Cilla eyed Mute with curiosity the way all the girls did, though always giving her a wide berth. Because she was "dan-ger-rous." She was always dressed in the white scrubs, like "a fucking Al-*bi*-no." Mute scared them all. She could feel it. Scared them all, except for Mimi. Mimi seemed to have it out for her.

She remembered watching as Mimi sauntered over to Mute one time when the guard let Mute walk a few yards away from him. Mimi standing as she always did, with one hip pushed forward and her toe pointed out. Cilla studied Mute's reaction. She walked over so she could hear what Mimi said. The voices had told her to, "*Take studied note of external occurrences around you.*"

"Hey, how come you don't talk? You can tell me. I won't tell," Cilla heard Mimi say.

The girl, whose gaze was on the prison wall, or perhaps just beyond, seemed completely oblivious to Mimi, and Cilla watched as her eyes appeared to rest on the thick bank clouds beyond the wall.

"Hey Mute, you deaf too? What's wrong with you? You stupid? *Hey, listen.*" Quieter now and Cilla couldn't be sure what she heard. She strained to hear. Mimi leaned in and said something to the mute girl. Cilla couldn't hear her words, but she saw Mimi was getting angry. "I'll be your friend. Like you got any choice. You got zero friends." Then she laughed.

The girl continued looking to the clouds. Mimi stepped around in front of her so Mute would have no choice but to regard her.

"I know you go to see my prison bitch, Hartley." Cilla strained to hear but could only make out a few words: *Dr. Hartley, skittles* and *talk to me.* Then she heard: "Am I right?"

And "What, do you just sit and say nothing?" And "What does she say to you?" Cilla guessed they were talking—well, Mimi was talking, rather—about Dr. Hartley and for some reason that pleased her. She wanted to hear more of this particular, one-sided conversation. She heard Mimi say clearly: "Don't make me ask twice." Mimi must have gotten tired of talking because she stopped when Mute still said nothing back to her. Mimi leaned in closer and whispered something to Mute.

The mute girl's eyes glanced sideways at Mimi, but otherwise ignored her. Cilla believed that this was a mistake. She wanted to tell the voices that she was taking "studied note" and she believed this was a mistake not to obey Mimi when she was talking directly to you, but just then Mimi raised her arm to push Mute, leaping toward her in the same moment that the mute girl took a step forward, and the result was *not good,* Cilla decided. The result was that, handcuffed, Mute was unable to steady herself and she bumped into Mimi. Mimi shrieked, grabbing at the cuffs and jerking Mute down on top of her. Cilla watched, taking studied note, as she listened to Mimi's screams echoing around the courtyard.

"*Help!* She tried to get me! Get her off of me!"

The guard was there in an instance pulling Mute off of Mimi. "Get off of her right now! What's gotten into you?"

"She tried to kill me," Mimi panted, letting herself be pulled from the ground by the guard. "She tried to kill me. She murdered a man, you know."

"You mind your own business," the guard said to Mimi.

By now a small circle had formed, and the guard shoed inmates away. Cilla couldn't see the mute girl's face, and a strange desire rose in her to tell the guard what she had seen, that it was not Mute's fault. But she did not, and as he escorted Mute away from where Cilla stood, she heard him saying, "What you go and do a thing like that for? Can't leave you for a minute. Now I gotta tell what you did. Don't like to think what'll happen to you, now. Hmm, hmm. Don't like to think." Cilla could no longer hear and she let her eyes fall on Mimi. She saw that Mimi was smiling.

CHAPTER NINE

As Eleanor walked into the D.C.E. building, she thought about the strange attentiveness with which Lewis had served her breakfast for two days straight. But as her mind switched to thinking about her next patient, the unease this caused remained, yet changed shape.

Priscilla Hankins reminded her of one of those china cows used for pouring milk, except where cows had full-lashed, large eyes, Cilla's were small and startled eyes like an animal who'd been crept up upon, constantly darting about as if for preservation. Overweight, she walked with difficult, side to side motions like a pendulum, her inner thighs hindering normal movement. With each new human encounter, she winced like a dog used to beatings, used to people dismissing her from the outside. Yet no matter how discouraging she found Cilla's case, Eleanor would not give up until Cilla was released.

Over the past two weeks Cilla had become increasingly remote and Eleanor was at a loss as to why.

She glanced up as Cilla, hair flat on one side, lumbered into the room, her metronome movement steady, her demeanor self-conscious. Cilla was eight minutes late. She remained standing, gave the chair a dubious glance as if to say, "You want me to sit there?" She persevered two more steps, and let her body drop into the chair like an anchor.

Eleanor observed the unresponsive eyes, and she knew that she loved this girl for the suffering she'd endured, and that this love, begot of pity, might well outlast those first loves born of passion and desire.

She began the session the same way she did every time:

"Hello Cilla. How are you today?"

"Okay."

For several months Eleanor had greeted Cilla each session with a genuine smile, hoping to coax her patient into copying the expression. She realized to an outsider that the smile might seem to mock. But research proved that on seeing a smile, one instantly smiled back, even before the conscious brain was aware of the emotion being expressed. Facial expressions constituted a system of unconscious communication that was built into human biology long before language, and most researchers accepted that facial expressions were innate, not merely something babies learned by watching and copying those around them. It explains why athletes, blind from birth, smiled at the moment of victory no different from their comrades who could see.

Conversely, Eleanor learned that by simply forming the expression of anguish or anger on her own face, she would internalize those feelings—emotions delving into her from the outside in, in what seemed at first a paradox from the standard notion that they occurred from the inside out. After standing before the medicine cabinet mirror in her bathroom, contorting her face in fear while observing the adrenaline flood her chest, or into a vicious scowl and noticing as her heartbeat increased, she knew that Cilla's permanent frown could well be causing the girl to feel even more miserable each day, just like taking a dose of anxiety or fear from a bottle every morning.

"Have you had a good week or a bad week?"

"Ummm, okay."

"Okay, as in between good and bad?"

"Uh-huh," Cilla answered.

"How was your horticulture class?"

Her face reddened. She looked at the floor.

"Are you okay, Cilla?" When Cilla didn't answer, Eleanor asked gently, "Do you need to confide...do you need to talk to me about something? You're safe in here, you remember that, don't you?"

"Uh-huh."

"Did you have a good time in class?"

"I didn't go."

"I see." Eleanor nodded. An entire opera was staging itself across Cilla's face—conflicting emotions, surfacing then disappearing, that Eleanor found hard to read. "Why didn't you go?"

"I . . . didn't . . . feel . . . well."

Eleanor watched the lie spread across the girl's face.

"Cilla?"

"Uh-huh?"

"It's okay that you didn't go. I'm not upset with you. Quite the opposite. I'm here to help you share what's inside of you. You're safe here, okay? No matter what you say." She paused, questioning the veracity of her words and the safety within the prison walls, but it was too late. "Is there something you want to talk to me about?"

Cilla stared at the floor, holding back tears.

"Cilla, would you like to tell me what you're feeling right now?" Eleanor asked softly.

"Nothing."

Eleanor paused, then said equally gently, "You feel *something* don't you?"

There was a long pause, in which Eleanor was about to speak, but Cilla answered, "I feel very confident today."

Eleanor opened her mouth, and shut it. To doubt Cilla's words, even though she read their opposite on her face, could undermine the girl's attempt at positive self-esteem. She hesitated another moment, then said: "That's good, Cilla. But, you know, if there's something you would like to talk to me about, you may. Anything at all, Cilla." She waited, observing the girl before her. "Is there anything or anyone . . . bothering you?"

Looking down to her lap, Cilla did not at first speak, then finally shook her head, "No."

When the fifty minutes were up, Eleanor ended the session in also the same way as she always had:

"Take care, Cilla. I'll see you next week."

"Okay."

As Cilla left, Eleanor felt relief, but relief was quickly shadowed by a feeling that would sit with her the rest of the day—a murky depressing feeling, like walking into a cloud and shivering. She trusted her intuition, but she wouldn't have the time to analyze it until later, for today was her busiest day. Her next patient made Cilla seem like a piece of sponge cake. Her next patient was Jane. She shuddered inwardly, but quickly thought back to one moment, the first time she'd sat in this room with Jane, two days ago. It was that initial look on Jane's face, and she knew that, without that look, she probably never would have stuck with the difficult case. She pictured Jane's face when she felt her nerves the most frayed: Jane's eyes, filled with silent sorrow, gazed back at her urging her not to give up. Or so she thought.

She would begin by attempting, under no circumstances, to call the girl Jane. This simple omission of name was far harder than it seemed, however, for Eleanor had been trained to use a patient's name frequently. Eleanor glanced at the clock just as the guard knocked.

"Please come in."

And as Jane walked in for her second session, Eleanor let her eyes study her. All day yesterday, she had tried to remember certain features in her face, but could not. Unable then to bring forth her particulars, she now let her eyes devour the face then transmit the image to the storage of memory. Yet the confidence with which she'd spoken to the Jane in her mind—easy, even jovial, insightful conversation—was nowhere present in this small room.

"Hello," she said.

Jane sat down on the other side of the desk, the handcuffs falling on her lap.

"Thank you," Eleanor said to the guard as he retreated pulling the door shut. She looked back at Jane and said, "Have you thought about our first session together?"

She watched Jane's eyes shift from the floor behind her to the floor beside her; watched as she shifted slightly, turning in the chair so that her body again sat sideways to Eleanor, not facing her.

Eleanor continued asking Jane general questions about day-to-day life in prison, and Jane sat quietly in her chair, sometimes shifting her gaze.

"I wonder if you could tell me about a typical day for you. I know for most of my patients in G.P., the days are structured, with classes and work, work study, library time, trips to the commissary and mess hall, meals, walk, counts. I think there are four formal counts where you're required to stand and several intermediate counts. Am I right?" She paused, waiting. "I always wondered what that was like. Tedious? Or just plain strange. But you're not in G.P. You're in segregation, for your own protection they tell me. Is this true? Is it for your own protection?" Eleanor waited again. Jane did not move. "Do you feel you could harm yourself?" Another pause, which elicited nothing from Jane. "Or that the other inmates could harm you?"

Jane made no attempt to respond or even act as if she'd heard Eleanor. The normal maximum sentence for an inmate confined to isolation/segregation was thirty days. Thirty days in which she spent twenty-three out of twenty-four hours in her cell, meals brought to her. A shower once every three days. The remaining single hour she spent outdoors for recreation, handcuffed. But Helen had indicated that Jane, being mute, might stay in isolation indefinitely.

"Do you not want to look at me today?"

Again she noted the girl's rounded shoulders and slumped posture and found her own shoulders straightening in response.

"You know, one of the hardest things in life is living with your regrets."

No response.

"But what's past is past. There is," she hesitated before saying the next words to a convicted murderer serving out her time in a women's prison, "There is a future for you. You can serve time then get parole for good behavior. You're life isn't over. Sometimes awful things happen to us in life, or maybe we do awful things, but we go on."

Slowly Jane raised her eyes, aiming her gaze at Eleanor, as though challenging her to continue, to tell her more about the great things she would from now on do, like reading for the one hundredth time *About Herpes* and *Stay Free From Hepatitis B* and all the other fascinating handouts that inmates received in the Inmate Orientation Packages.

Eleanor stared back, pleased that she'd at least gotten Jane to look at her. She searched her face for the micro expressions for which she'd been taught to look. Many of the women she worked with wore faces on which past experiences, imperfectly erased, were palimpsests of their lives before, painfully visible for Eleanor to read. But whoever had erased Jane's past had done one hell of a good job.

Looking back at Jane, Eleanor said in a low voice. "I'll talk about whatever you want me to, but you're going to have to help me."

She waited, sitting silently, giving Jane the chance to speak. Or making her uncomfortable enough in the silence to break it. But Jane did not.

So much can happen in a second. So many actions or expressions can occur simultaneously. Jane could raise her eyebrow conveying to Eleanor the inner working of her tangled mind, in a moment so slight that it would, outside of prison amidst ordinary conversation, flow into the next expression undetected. Or, in some unconscious movement, she might tilt her head a quarter inch, offering in the expression uncertainty or vulnerability or a question perhaps.

Eleanor remained still and determined. She focused on Jane's face, ignoring her body as body movement distracted. Jane turned away first, but it was not an angry movement. It was most nearly a shrug, a gesture made with the carelessness of the self-assured, and Eleanor was surprised.

"Do you find yourself bored in these sessions with me?"

Nothing.

Eleanor began a procession of questions, seriatim, interrupted with pauses like caesuras that gave a rhythmical cadence, her tone gentle, yet steady. If she was not expecting Jane to answer, she was very much hoping that one question would at least educe a change in expression.

"Did something happen to you to make you stop talking? Or lose the desire to talk?"

As Jane stared to the floor, Eleanor kept her eyes on Jane's face and the top of her head, where the blonde hairs crisscrossed over each other.

"Did something happen that wasn't your fault? That was perhaps, unjust?" She waited quietly for five minutes or more, but Jane offered nothing.

"Look, I don't really care if you killed someone. That's not my concern. My concern is to help you." She paused. "Shouldn't your parents or relatives know where you are? Don't you think they should know what has happened to you? Or do you believe they wouldn't care?"

As Eleanor continued, she leaned forward on the desk, aware of the soft flow of words that floated over to the girl two feet from her. She watched Jane carefully. Rarely did she move, and Eleanor could not place what emotion was keeping Jane so determined not to cooperate.

"You know, there are many women who have been sexually abused. It is, unfortunately, quite common. It is also nothing about which to be ashamed. And holding it in can actually harm you. I wouldn't want that for you. Would you want that for you?"

Jane shifted and Eleanor watched her eyes.

"Have you . . . ever in your life been sexually abused by anybody?"

No blush in the cheek or face to indicated shame or guilt. No contracting muscles to indicate revulsion or fear.

"If you have, you are not alone."

No change of expression. No movement. Just nothing. *Nada. Niente.*

"Did you lose someone very close to you?"

Eleanor stopped. There it was!

People betray themselves not with their words, often carefully chosen and released, but with their expressions. And there in Jane's eyes, flickering for a moment, Eleanor had seen life.

She waited and watched. But, if she'd really seen a flash of something, now darkness had returned again to Jane's face.

"If you want to talk to me about something you feel is very difficult to talk about—"

Eleanor jumped at the sound of a knock on the door. She gathered her thoughts quickly and turned towards the clock. Amazed, she saw time was up.

"Yes, come in," she called out. She looked quickly back at Jane. "Our time is up. That went by quickly this time, don't you think so?" Eleanor's own face begged Jane to nod and acknowledge what she'd said. But Jane was rising to follow the guard out the door, leaving in her wake a seated and depleted Eleanor.

After Jane left but before the door had clicked shut, Eleanor heard the voices outside the room.

"Look, there she goes."

"She the one?"

"Yeah, back door parole, baby."

"Mute mother-fucker."

"Look-it, the guard has to stay with her." Whispers mixed in with the other voices from the inmates.

The air inside the room felt dense and Eleanor blinked once as if trying to see through it clearly. The clock on the wall ticked like someone was tapping nails into the desk. Had she really prompted Jane to recall something from her past? Now she wasn't so sure. It was possible she'd only imagined that the face had changed. The clock ticked out its seconds and Eleanor jumped up, pushing through the door.

She walked down the hall to her office and began scribbling notes into a notebook. Forty minutes later she sat behind the same desk listening to Mimi Kramer.

CHAPTER TEN

Eleanor had become accustomed to what had first both alarmed and intrigued her about Mimi Kramer: her unusually small head. Mimi's small skull was covered with long golden hair, beneath which two greenish hazel eyes observed the world from what some might consider an advantaged bias. They were eyes that gazed directly at Eleanor. The exception, Eleanor had learned, was when Mimi was lying—in which case she refused to look at her therapist, often squinting at the desk instead. Mimi was attractive. Yet where Eleanor had found Cilla downright homely at first glance, compassion for the girl had come quickly and easily. There had never been any such feeling for the good-looking girl across from her now, whose face would one day be shaped by the thoughts which lodged within her mind.

"How have you been, Mimi?" She noted two large Band-Aids on the right side of Mimi's neck.

Across the desk, Mimi tossed her hair and smiled. Mimi knew she was attractive. "Dandy, Dr. Hartley, just dandy," she said.

"Yes? How's your work study going?"

"Why'd you say that? You doubt me?"

Great, Eleanor thought to herself. She knew Mimi well enough by now to know that she took great pleasure in recounting the week's injustices, telling her therapist in vivid detail all about the awful things the awful girls with whom she was forced to "cohabitate" (her word of choice lately) did to her.

"I'm not doubting you. What happened to your neck, Mimi?"

"Shina stabbed me. She got it in for me." Eleanor searched Mimi's eyes, but now Mimi was not looking at her.

"Are you feeling okay now, Mimi?"

Mimi shrugged, the wounded neck disappearing for a moment into her shoulders. Eleanor waited, expecting the usual diatribe against Mimi's archenemy, Shina Jones, but none was forthcoming. Just as Eleanor was making a mental note of it, the eruption came:

"Shina tried to kill me! Don't you care?"

Eleanor waited.

"Me and you should stick together. Those people are trying to take over."

"What people? Take over what?"

"Our country!"

"Who do you mean when you say 'those people', Mimi?"

"You know who I mean. They weren't born here. They want to get rid of all of us and take over."

"Mimi, do you mean black people? African Americans?"

"They don't belong here. Muddy up our race. Just like Shina. I know about her momma and daddy. Gross."

Eleanor inhaled and looked down. "I don't think your people were born here either, if you mean indigenous to North America. Have you considered that?"

"Shina's got you all fooled. She ain't who you think she is. I oughta kill her. I'd do it for you, Sugar Lips. I would. Then we could cohabitate together."

Eleanor made a larger mental note then proceeded carefully.

"Taking another life is not something about which we joke." She spoke clearly.

"If I killed her she could go to hell where she belongs."

Did Mimi know what she was saying? She studied Mimi's face to see if veracity was present next to guile.

"I think it's the people who kill who are, historically, more designated to hell than the victims," Eleanor replied calmly.

"Shina's not a Christian."

"Does that matter to you?"

"I bet she wasn't even baptized."

Eleanor waited.

"I hate her. I hate them all."

"Are you talking about black? Muslims? Who do you hate, Mimi?" Eleanor asked, feeling the emotion creeping in, and trying her best not to show it.

Mimi leaned back in the chair fixing her eyes on Eleanor. "If you don't do something, you're gonna be sorry. Someone needs to take her out before she kills me."

Warning bells rang in Eleanor's head, but she silenced them, focusing on Mimi's inner eyebrows, watching for any facial muscle movement that clearly contradicted the asserted words. She thought to herself how easy it was for her to simply close her eyes, yet shutting her ears was harder. Now she would have to speak to Helen. The emphasis had shifted from Mimi's fantasy of killing Shina (jealousy perhaps? with the obvious racial hatred) to Mimi's fear of Shina (more racism, misplaced anger?)

"Mimi, Shina can't bother you if you don't let her. What other people do to you is their problem. How you react is yours. Conflict can't survive without your participation in it. What I am asking you to do, as part of your work in therapy," Eleanor spoke deliberately, but emphatically, stating the girl's name if she broke eye contact with her. "What I would like for you to do, for one week, is to *not* think about the other girls. I want you to focus instead on yourself and your life. Even if you're in here now, you can be planning for the time when you will be out. You can be thinking about what you would like to do with your life. And when you're out, I sincerely doubt that you will see any of these girls again. They will cease to matter to you. But I can promise you that there will be other people who will fill their places. Brown people, white people, lots of different new people with whom you'll have to contend, and the very same problems will arise if you do not address them now. We share our planet with all number of races and that's part of the beauty of it. Did you ever think instead to get to know someone first and find out if you like their insides, so to speak?"

When Mimi sat silently, sulking, Eleanor continued: "Therefore, what will matter is the preparation you did while in here to help you interact with all these different people, black people included," she said deliberately. "And I'm here to help you with that. How you conduct your life and what you do with it is up to you. So from now on, every time you start thinking about Shina, when you start dwelling on her the way you do," Eleanor knew that would irritate Mimi, but she didn't care. She was not here to placate her destructive thought patterns. "Then you *stop.* And you tell yourself, not now, and you shift your thoughts to your cosmetology studies, or anything that makes you happy rather than angry."

"Why do you think I'm angry? I'm not angry. You should see Shina."

"And you think about you. Not Shina. Not anyone else. Because you're the one who's important, remember? Not them." She saw Mimi suppress a little smile. "Okay? Will you do that?"

"Why don't you stop having sessions with Shina. She's a whore."

Eleanor sat quietly.

"And Cilla. Dumb as fuck. And *Jane.* Her tongue is cut out. She probably did it herself. Why do you keep seeing them? They're all liars."

"I can't talk about them, Mimi, you know that," Eleanor answered, suddenly startled. Was Jane's tongue really cut out? Was that why she couldn't speak? And if it was, did she do it herself, in a psychotic episode?

"Y'all better watch out for Jane," Mimi continued. When Eleanor said nothing, Mimi spoke louder, "Jane's buying cleaning detergent in the com. Wanna know why?

"No, Mimi, I don't."

"She's going to make a bomb with it and blow up this place."

Eleanor was relieved of responding back to Mimi when the guard came.

When Eleanor reached her office, she closed the door and took a deep breath. Exhausted and famished, she opened the small refrigerator that perched beside a file cabinet, and stared at the only food left, one medium-sized mango. She began methodically slicing off the skin and cutting up the flesh into bite-sized pieces. Two hours later she was back in the psych room.

CHAPTER ELEVEN

"How you doing today?"

"Hello, Shina. How are you?"

"Linda thinks you're a repressed lesbian."

"Linda's entitled to her opinions."

"And you know what that crazy cracker bitch ask me?"

"Shina, how about if we talk about you and what you think instead of about what Linda thinks?"

"What *I* think? I could give two tits what you are, less what you do with it."

"I didn't mean what you think of me, unless of course it affects—"

"Yeah, yeah, I know. You mean how I gets along with my fellow inmates." She raised her nose to the air and sniffed carefully, as though she might be able, here in the psych room, to smell its previous occupant. "Well sister, I tell you. I get along just fine with everyone except one."

Eleanor waited.

"Don't sit there like no blind possum."

Eleanor shifted. "Go on, Shina."

"Shoot, you think just 'cause I'm locked up in the pen, that I'm bad. Well I can tell you about bad."

"I'm not judging you, Shina."

"You talk of right and wrong, good and bad. I'll tell you about good and bad. You do *good*," she raised her fingers in quotation marks. "And you get walked all over. Now, to me that's *bad*. There's only money and power in this world and if you don't believe me, look around at who's running the world. Money and power, and I aim to have me some. This here being in prison is only a lesson."

"Yes, that's right, Shina. It *is* a lesson."

Shina nodded. "That's good. You and me's on the same page again."

"Yes, that's right. We are."

"Now, you probably sitting there, all perched and pretty, waiting to hear who I have trouble getting along with."

Eleanor said nothing.

"I was talking about that mis-di-*rect*-ed, shrunken-headed, weaselly creodont." Shina winked across the table, like she and Eleanor were in on something together.

Eleanor opened her mouth, searching for the right response.

"I told you before, Hartley, don't play dumb. It don't suit you."

"Weaselly *cree*-o-dont?" Eleanor repeated.

Shina let out a riotous belly laugh. "Yeah, don't you think? Fits her like a condom fits a pecker!"

Eleanor sat back a few inches in her chair. She knew full well Shina was referring to Mimi, who ever since arriving at the prison found it her role to record Shina's every movement, as if it were some unofficial position she'd been assigned by penitentiary staff: "Special agent Kramer on Operation Shina Duty."

Shina Jones, the product of a black father and white mother was, by all accounts, the old-time miscegenation proponents' glorious high card, until she landed herself in prison. Shina (pronounced with a long "i" as in Shy-na) was not only beautiful: tall, dark, elegant and exotic, but she was bold, confident, fun and, as Eleanor had quietly learned, she had an I.Q. hovering around one hundred and forty.

Bearing twenty-four years of emotional problems, Shina had coped remarkably well in life until one day last year, high on crack, she and her confederates decided to hot wire and steal a Mercedes SUV and tour the city of Washington D.C. She rammed into a prominent politician's Audi, and when the police came after her, she gave them a run in four wheels that made the prix de Monte Carlo look tame, almost succeeded in giving them the slip, but when she didn't and was finally stopped by a police blockade in central Virginia, she offered the arresting officer, "the best fucking blow job you ever had in your life" if he let her off.

Another officer might have eagerly bartered, but she'd been caught by Officer David Sampson who, although impressed by Shina's good looks, driving ability and spunk, believed he had become a policeman to make the world a better place, and not to receive gratis blowjobs. He also believed in "going by the book," and thus gave Shina the book, where another officer might have been more lenient, not to mention accommodating. Shina was arrested and found guilty of grand theft larceny, assault and evading an officer. But she had earned so many points on her E.S.C. (Earned Sentence Credits) she would be eligible for parole in the spring, and ready to terrorize yuppies, police officers or whoever else offended her own code of ethics.

Now as Eleanor sat opposite Shina, she longed to get her talking about her plans once out of prison. In past sessions, she and Shina had engaged in some stimulating and insightful talks, and Eleanor often felt in high spirits afterwards, feeling she'd performed the work she was meant to with competence. But today Shina was not going to offer her anything.

"Weasels and such aside, do you want to tell me about your week, Shina?"

"Now do a rooster lay an egg?"

"Not that I'm aware of. How was softball?"

"Ball of fun."

"Would you like to elaborate?"

"I'd like to confabulate." Shina winked.

Eleanor smiled. "Very well. Anything exciting in the cafeteria this week?"

"Hartley, baby! You scraping the bottom of the conversation barrel today."

"Then help me out, Shina."

"Cafeteria, hmmf. The grubbish they serve . . . stuff ain't fit to eat."

"I gather it's not the tastiest."

"What you eat at home, Hartley? You a good cook and all?"

Eleanor waited.

"Go on, Hartley. Ask me stuff."

"What are you reading this week, Shina?"

Shina's expression changed, and Eleanor saw interest.

"I'm reading about udder enhancement."

"Utter en-*hance*-ment? Like a complete makeover?"

"No, not like a complete makeover."

Eleanor waited.

"*Udder* enhancement. Just like it sound."

Eleanor nodded.

"I can see you don't have no *i*-dea what I'm talking about, but you the one asking me what I reading. So now I'm gonna tell you and you gonna sit there and listen." She straightened her shoulders and puffed out her chest. "You heard of getting bigger boobs? Boob job?"

"Hmm-hmm," Eleanor nodded warily.

"Well, same thing." Shina brought her voice down to a whisper. "'Except this time we enhancing the *udder*."

"The udder," Eleanor repeated. "Like the udder of a cow."

"Maybe you seen a frog with an udder, but I ain't never have."

"You're reading about cow udders?" Eleanor sensed she was being taken for a fool, but she persisted.

"There you go, Hartley. Takes you seven tries for everyone else's one, but you got it. Now you cookin' Hartley sister." Shina leaned back, evidently pleased with herself.

"Well, Shina, no one ever said you didn't read some interesting things," Eleanor said, wondering why Shina was toying with her.

"They ain't nothin else to do round here. Where you get that fine jacket, Hartley? You styling today!"

"Did anything special or exceptional happen this week?"

"Shoot Hartley, think you get bored and tired a looking into other people lives, asking us all these *so-tell-me-about-your-week* questions? What's wrong, don't got nothing good cookin' at home?"

Eleanor shook her head and sighed. "No, Shina, I don't get bored. It's my profession. I love it, and I'm lucky to have a profession I love. I think you too would thrive performing a job you loved doing when released from here. If it feels boring to you, then help me out. We're in here for nearly an hour, as you well know by now. You can talk to me about any problems you may be having."

"Hartley, I ain't got no problems. It's other peoples got the problems. I ain't done nothing wrong." Eleanor knew that if she listened to the inmates and took their word, everyone in the entire place was innocent.

Shina's prison experience judgment saw the world not so much out of frosted glasses, but rather from the mentality of, "I can imagine what it's like to be in your fancy-ass Lexus, but you ain't never experienced, and therefore can't imagine, life on this side of the prison." It was the same attitude that made her feel superior to the upper-middle classes.

"Well, you'd be surprised to know that that's what everyone else says," Eleanor replied.

"I ain't everyone."

"That it's always somebody else's fault. Never one's own."

Shina glared at Eleanor. She pushed her chair back, brought her feet up onto the desk, crossed her legs, and crossed her arms behind her head.

"Hartley, if I was to tell you even half of what goes down around here, I'd shock your pretty blonde hairdo. Who you have do up your hairdo anyway?"

"All right, Shina. Shock me."

This surprised Shina, and Eleanor watched the muscles on her smooth forehead contract ever so slightly. Those minuscule movements that most people were unaware of making conveyed to Eleanor a world of valuable information. An eyebrow raised a fraction higher. A twitching mouth. Shifting eyes that refused to look into your own. Eleanor liked Shina Jones. She liked her a lot and didn't want to see her talents go to waste. But she also felt little amused when Shina slipped into one of her moods as she had done today. Eleanor wondered what was plaguing her enough to produce the antagonistic attitude.

Across from her, Shina took her feet off the desk, scooted the chair forward, pushed up her green sleeves and placed her chin in her hands, the long brown arms forming a V at her elbows.

Her face was of a shade of rich sienna that made Eleanor think of delicious desserts. She thought of the faces of models between the pages of *Vogue*. Shina's high cheekbones were topped by almond shaped greenish-brown eyes. She had once had a profusion of long healthy black tinged with blue plaits that Eleanor had seen only in the file photo.

"Sure you know what you saying, Hartley?" Shina answered back slowly. Then in one magnificent movement, she laced her slender fingers together in a fist, raised it quickly into the air and brought it crashing down upon the desk.

Eleanor jumped.

Shina smiled. "Just checking, Hartley. Don't want you go thinking you got me all figured out or nothin'. Shock me, you say, ummm-hmmm. Did I do good?"

Startled, Eleanor did not speak for a moment but sat regarding Shina, observing that she was not smugly smiling, but sat almost as if she regretted what she'd done. "I'd like to help you figure yourself out," she said. "Go on, tell me what goes on around here."

"Maybe I don't want to."

The words, spoken too slowly, had the flavor of thick impending snow and Eleanor regarded Shina trying to see past the voice like seeing past the mist to the trees—branches moving, telling her something. The story of the wind, perhaps.

"You try and convert me to some mealy-mouthed limpet."

Again Eleanor waited, watching, but when Shina did not respond Eleanor said, "I'm not interested in converting you to anything, unless it's converting you from misery to happiness. From the prison of your mind to freedom, and . . ." She stopped and, thinking not of Shina for one moment but of Mimi, she finished the sentence in the quiet of her own mind: and from cruelty to compassion. How the girls in prison could be so cruel . . . . Then again, could one really blame them?

"And what, Hartley?"

"Go ahead, Shina, tell me what happens that I don't see. Maybe it will help me to better understand."

"Hartley, Hartley, Hartley," Shina said drawing out Eleanor's surname like she was a teacher yet again disappointed in her pupil's performance. "I think you come to regret what you ask." She stared deep into Eleanor's puzzled eyes across the desk, then began in a voice different from the one Eleanor knew, a flat monotone, raspy like dry dust blowing.

"Creo-Mimi always picking on poor fat Cilla. You talk about udder enhancement. That girl's got some udders on her, but she sweet as can be. Never hurt no one. Child of grief. Messed up in the head real bad, hears voices and talks right back to them, but of course you know all that, don't you? Low man, low woman on the pole, if you know what I mean, and I always feeling sorry for her. But, damn, she tires me out, you know what I mean?"

"That's kind of you, Shina," Eleanor responded, a picture of Cilla forming in her mind, and with it an accompanying feeling of disquiet.

"But I be sliding from our subject, ain't I?" Shina smiled, but when Eleanor said nothing, the smile faded and Shina resumed. "Creo-Mimi, you know she get all Princess-and-the-Pea like if you mess up her routine." She didn't wait for Eleanor to reply but continued: "Rodent-head Mimi stole Cilla's pen because she said Cilla stole hers, but Cilla didn't. So Mimi throw Cilla's pen out by the guard so Cilla'd have to go get it. Out she go, and back she comes in big fat trouble."

Eleanor opened her mouth to speak, but Shina waved a hand silencing her. "No, you wait. You asks for it, Hartley, so you gonna sit there and listen. I told you one day you gonna learn that when you asks for something you gotta take the consequences of getting it. The Lord works in not so mysterious ways. And don't you know I'm right?" She smiled again at Eleanor looking like the Lord's temptress. Then she crossed her arms and continued. "Next day, Creo-Mimi bought her own pen from the Com. Might be something about Creo and pens. Might want to make a note of that. You listening to me, Hartley?"

"Yes, I'm listening, Shina."

"Anyhow, she lost this pen or hid it more likely under her mattress an accuse me of stealing it. And me and you both knows, you couldn't no way pay me to touch anything she touch. So she see me writing letters in the pod, grabs my pen out my hand, just like she done to poor fat Cilla, and runs around screaming I stole her pen. I coulda strangled her right then and there on the spot. Don't no one fuck with me like that. So when I get up to get my pen back, she start pretending it's a knife the way she's holding it and going for my face and eyes. Before she could stab my eyes out, I grab her but the slippery eel gets loose and damn if she don't take that new pen to her neck and shove it in." Shina paused staring across at her therapist perhaps waiting for the appropriate reaction. But when Eleanor offered no immediate response, Shina narrowed her eyes, and continued with an air of impatience. "Then she yelled that I done it. Blood coming out of her good, and you know damn straight, girlfriend, you gotta push a pen in hard to make you bleed like that. Could you stab yourself, Hartley baby? I couldn't no more stab my pretty neck." Shina caressed her neck, rubbing both hands up its sides slowly.

Eleanor felt the hair on her arms prickle as if a cold void had settled around her body. She felt icy as if standing in a freezing pond. She watched Shina's face. "She stabbed her own neck, Shina?"

"Didn't think she had it in her, did you? Yeah, that crazy bitch got it in her, and a lot more. She's traumatizing Mute. Much as you can traumatize a person in one hour."

Eleanor sat quietly for a moment looking at Shina. Then she said softly, "Mute?"

"Hartley, I told you, don't play dumb. You know Mute. You have sessions with her."

"You mean Jane."

"Uh-huh," Shina said. "If you so sure you know her name, why don't she know her name?"

"You mean Jane's being picked on during Association? What does Mimi—" Eleanor stopped herself, feeling contrary emotions: the one, guilt, reaching towards disgust in the moment Eleanor recognized it, knowing who, in this session, she was here to help. And the other relief, if a wispy relief that she'd observed then caught her near misstep. Later, when she allowed herself time to reflect, she would feel shock, for never once in her years at the penitentiary had she needed to question her own probity or fear a breach in professionalism. She was about to speak when Shina interrupted.

"Hartley, you either blind or you don't get out in the pen much." She laughed as though she'd told an especially funny joke, then stopped and looked directly across at Eleanor, no trace of amusement in her eyes. "Cause there's some bad stuff going down, Hartley. And I ain't talking bad as in good. I talking bad as in real bad. Mimi ain't the only one messing with Mute."

Eleanor's thoughts were racing and before she could plan an appropriate reply she found the words forming. "What do you mean, Shina?"

"I mean the guards are messing with Mute. You know, *messing*."

Uncertain what to say, Eleanor sat still, without speaking, waiting, hoping and dreading for Shina to say more.

"Cat got your tongue, Hartley? Maybe I should take your job, you know, try it out for a spell. You might come to thank me." The twinkle was back in Shina's eye. Eleanor was grateful, yet disappointment, cold as winter's ice, settled in her gut, joining an emotion bleaker than failure.

"How'd you like living in the same pod with Lizzie fuckin' Borden?"

"Shina—"

"Just quit it, Hartley. You come in here and ask me, *How your week go, Shina? How you getting long with your fel-low in-mates, Shina?* Well, why don't you come stay one night, and you see for yourself how you like living with my fellow inmates? Then you see I'm doing pretty damn fantastic for what I have to put up with here. You also see what I telling you is true. But no, you go home each night to your fancy la dee da house, with your pretty little rich husband, your pretty little children all going to college to learn nothing except how to drink beer, roll around drunk, hump each other and look down on black people. Hmmpf, they checked in with Oprah lately? Or my girl, Bey? You go home to all your rich stuff: bottles of fine wine and paintings on the wall of nothing I ever seen in the real world. Few little red lines here, few little gray lines there, most pitiful paintings I ever seen."

She waved her fingers in the air like a conductor, pointing off to the walls so vividly that Eleanor turned her head to behold the pitiful paintings. "Why rich folks have to buy all that stuff? Not happy, that's why. Yeah, I know what it's like, think I ain't never been in no rich person's house before? *You* the one haven't ever been in *here*. I ask you come on in here and try living with the green-eyed swamp monster from the East lagoon. Try it for just a day, see if me and you don't arrive at some the same conclusions." Shina slouched back shaking her head and brushing her hand in the air in a final, disgusted manner. "I'm trapped."

"Can you describe the feeling?" Eleanor asked quickly. "Of being trapped?"

"You know for a psychiatrist, you one dumb bitch. I ain't trapped. I'm getting out in one hundred and sixty-four days." Shina looked up proud then dropped her eyes uncharacteristically to the floor. "Sorry. Didn't mean to call you a dumb bitch."

"That's all right, Shina."

"That's a fine looking blouse you got on. Color's wrong though."

"Do you want to describe feeling trapped?" Eleanor uncrossed her legs, then re-crossed them.

"No. But that color sure would do right by me."

"Has it ever occurred to you that maybe Mimi is jealous of you?" Eleanor asked, then thought silently to herself: Jealous because you possess beauty of the soul not just of the face, jealous because you're intelligent, jealous because you're fearless, and jealous most of all because you're respected by all of the girls save her. "Has it ever occurred to you to show compassion toward someone who angers you instead of releasing your own anger? Sometimes the people who torment others the most are the ones with the deepest wounds inside. All they're really trying to do is obtain your approval, to receive love and acceptance, but they don't know how so they strike out in anger and garner whatever attention they can."

"You think Mimi wants my approval, mmm, mmm, mmm," Shina stated, shaking her head. "You something else."

"I wasn't speaking of Mimi, specifically," Eleanor said clearing her throat.

"Don't worry, I won't tell the authorities on you." Shina winked at her again.

Exhausted by evening, Eleanor looked to her home as a safe sanctuary at least for the temporal dark hours of night. Her drive home from the prison took her twenty-five minutes, and it afforded her time to reflect on the day and, in theory, switch gears leaving her work behind. She'd slip Dvorak or Prokofiev into the CD player and let the music and the car's lulling movement be the transition she needed after leaving the women in the penitentiary behind.

She pulled into the Exxon with the little old-fashion market attached and slid out of the Volvo, listening to her stomach announce its hunger. She stood in her wool suit, pumping gas next to the good old boys in their pick-up trucks, their own stomachs tucked tight into shirts and hanging over jeans.

"Afternoon, Miz Hartley. How're things over at the prison?" Freddy Phillips asked as she walked across the uneven wooden floor planks to pay for her gas.

"Hello, Freddy. The women are fine." Eleanor hesitated. Freddy saw her look over her right shoulder to the cooler.

"Can I get something for you, Miz Hartley?"

"Thank you, I'll get it. I can't remember if we're out of milk."

"Better safe than sorry's what I always say."

"Yes, I believe you're right." She strode over to the cooler, sliding back the glass door, as Freddy caught Little Eddie's eye.

"Mangoes!" Eleanor exclaimed. "I love them. When did you start carrying mangoes?"

"Since people start asking for them," Freddy answered, but he said it in a way Eleanor knew meant he didn't approve. Mangoes were foreign fruit, not grown around here. "I'll buy a couple." She looked at the exorbitant price and changed her mind. "On second thought I think I still have one at home."

"Righto."

"Is it true we're getting a storm?"

"Yup. S'what it looks like. And in for more weather this weekend."

"Thank you, Freddy."

"Thank you, Miz Hartley. You have yourself a good evening now."

She was walking to her car when Little Eddie made a sound part whistle and part exhale. "That's one good-looking woman. Cool as a cucumber. Wonder if she lets it rip in the sack. Can't really imagine her with that high-strung husband of hers."

"Not bad," Freddy answered. "But nice too, always real polite with me. Now, there's a lady. Never could figure, though, why she'd want to spend her time with a bunch of drug addicts, thieves and murderers, but then there's no accounting for some people's common sense. Most people's actually."

Eleanor walked to her car carrying her milk in its brown paper bag, unaware that both Freddy and Little Eddie were staring after her, not because she wasn't used to people perceiving her as beautiful, a sentiment with which she had rarely agreed, but because at that moment the wind had picked up, blowing dust and someone's empty McDonald's bag against her shins. Eleanor breathed in the air, acknowledged that Freddy was most likely right about the weather, and felt a strange, uncommon foreboding. The same foreboding she'd felt when Cilla left the psych room.

As she drove home the feeling persisted.

Our subjective happiness is not all that matters. Agape - selfless love of other without any objective, personal gain or strings attached. For so many years it had been her creed in working with the girls in prison. For the first time she wondered if for all those years, she'd been merely filling her ego, smoothing it over from the trauma she herself had suffered as a child instead of giving back, genuinely desiring to do good and help.

"Why have you chosen psychology?" Dr. Tucker, her undergraduate advisor had asked her. "I believe you could do far more with your grades and abilities. Medical school, law school."

"It interests me, and I would like to try to help people." She remembered wondering then if it were not a profession of looneys for looneys, to use one of Lewis's favorite descriptive nouns. She remembered thinking that only people with messed up backgrounds and insecurity complexes would choose to go into such a profession, and they would be good at it, that is if they weren't already too far looney. This was why at age twenty she knew she would make a good psychologist.

"Well then, you should pursue it. I think you'll be very good," Dr. Tucker conceded.

But now, for the first time, driving home, Eleanor wasn't so sure.

When she pulled into her driveway she saw the neighbor with the brown dog whose excrement had pushed her husband over the edge. She waved to her neighbor and watched the dog, aware not exactly of aversion or fear, but a feeling that questioned the human canine bond, which seemed of late to enthrall so many people. She had nothing against dogs, but she was suspicious of the love showered on animals, as if it was filling a void that should rightfully—and healthfully—be filled by a human companion. She knew she judged ardent animal lovers in a way that suggested they hadn't succeeded in a human relationship and were only giving their dog or cat such an intense love to fill a gaping void.

"Lewis?" she called, once inside, letting her briefcase collapse on the hall table. "Lewis?" She glanced out a front window and saw what she hadn't noticed walking up the tidy flagstone walkway. His car was absent. She placed the milk inside the refrigerator realizing she'd been wrong about the other mango. It wasn't there.

Slipping off her shoes, she padded down the hallway to the den and flipped on the gas fire. Her feet had high arches and her ankles were thin-boned and delicate, prompting Lewis once to call them the sexiest part on her body, then to laugh and add, no, just the sexiest ankles he'd ever seen. And she'd been pleased with him for according the ankle importance alongside the breast, the leg or the buttocks.

She collapsed into a leather armchair, reached for foot and ankle, massaging gently with her fingers. She'd read once that the ankle was frequently the first thing to go on a body.

Sunk down in the big welcoming chair, she watched the orange and blue flames leap, raising their hands insistently like kids in a classroom vying for attention. Like women in a prison, fighting each other. Fighting themselves. Seeking her help? She wasn't so sure. She reached her hand underneath the worn leather, slid out a fat Webster's dictionary, heaved it onto her lap and began flipping through pages: a's, b's, c's, . . . the sheer pages peeling reluctantly away from each other like the outer skin on a onion. She could have Googled the word, but she preferred the pages of the dictionary. She stopped in the c's, scanned down the page and read:

crenulate

crenulation

creodont - any of an extinct suborder (Creodonta) of small, primitive, flesh-eating mammals with small brains.

"Well. I'll be." She read the entry again then began laughing in a low melodious tone, her head resting on the back of the armchair.

"What's going on?" Lewis stepped down into the den.

"Oh hi, darling. Just Shina Jones proving she knows more than I do, yet again."

"What?"

"Shina Jones." She set the dictionary down, sliding it back under the chair, but as she did her eye caught the glitter of an object behind the chair's leg. She touched it, and glanced up at Lewis but he had turned from her. She saw his back, the light sweat through his white shirt. She prodded the object once more, and something fluttered inside her. The gold curled into itself like a snake and she didn't want to pick it up, but she did and she knew she'd seen it before somewhere in a pair.

"Your good-looking black girl." Lewis answered, walking down the hall and Eleanor rose, feeling her legs heavy as barbells as she followed him, the earring clutched tightly in her hand. She dropped her eyes to the thin-piled Turkish runner and felt its pressure beneath her stocking feet, imagining that each color produced a separate sensation. She willed her feet to keep stepping forward.

"She's black, yes," she said with considerable effort at controlling her voice. "She's beautiful, yes." She stood beside the table while Lewis unloaded Chinese take-out. "She's also very intelligent. Maybe too intelligent." She dropped the earring into her jacket pocket.

"Why?" Now Lewis sounded interested.

"I'm not sure if people will ever take her seriously. Perhaps because of her looks. I suppose she'll be forever trapped by her beauty and people's wrong perception of her. Just as Mimi is trapped by her obsessions, needing for the world to love and want her."

"Hmm," Lewis answered after a moment then said absently, "Which one is that?"

"Why the take-out?"

"Got home late."

"So I see. Is everything okay?"

"Of course it is," he answered and when Eleanor said nothing, he offered, "Stopped over at Duncan's. I called you. Left a message. Don't you ever check your messages?"

To an outsider Eleanor knew her husband's response sounded passively innocent, if a bit defensive, thus she could only blame herself for feeling compelled to note the downward ducking of his face upon answering her question, and his turning away, not to mention the trifling issue of finding a woman's earring, not her own, beneath the chair in the den.

His back was to her now and she was glad. And maybe it was Nicole, Duncan's wife, who wore Chanel No. 5, Eleanor tried to reassure herself. Many women did. Her best friend for instance. The old, unresolved queasiness that she'd felt since she was sixteen began to insinuate itself inside her, and she felt the desperate need to gulp down water. She wanted to go home. That feeling that came to her in dreams sometimes of searching for home. But she was home. What was she searching for?

"How's Duncan?" she asked, filling a glass quickly.

"Same old Duncan." Lewis's back was still toward her.

Finding nothing to say, Eleanor did what she always did when she felt emotional anguish nudge. She worked. In college when Jeremy had dumped her after only two months of dating she decided it was better to throw herself into her work to the exclusion of all social activity. Her work, or self-discipline, phase had lasted six months. Years later, married, her life running smoothly, and yet she still found that work provided her with the most enduring gratification.

Now she forced her mind to review each patient, knowing better than anyone that instead of evading the uncomfortable feeling she should speak to Lewis. But she did not, and her thoughts jumped first to Jane, then Shina, then Mimi, Cilla, Lisa, Tammy, Deborah, Cassandra and back to Jane again, over and over. She decided Jane must have gone through some significant trauma. She mustn't get discouraged or Jane would perceive it, consciously or not. *La speranza e sempre l'ultimo a morire.* Hope is the last thing to die. Ankles the first, hope the last.

Eleanor sat across from Lewis, scooping from the white cartons spoonfuls of chicken, onions, bean sprouts and baby corn onto her plate. When she slid the containers toward him, he shook his head. "I'm not really hungry. Stomachache."

Rehabilitation was a process of slow growth, Eleanor thought to herself, often imperceptible, just like growing into adulthood. There would come breakthroughs in therapy where both patient and therapist would connect and gain simple or stunning insights. But more often recovery from a trauma, even the trauma of daily life itself, would be a gradual progress often only apparent in the backwards glance, a declaration: "Ah, but I no longer feel that now."

Lewis began to hum, and Eleanor glanced over to him quickly. He stopped, but she'd seen the smile on his face.

"Have you seen Cory lately?" she asked him.

"No, not lately. Have you?"

CHAPTER TWELVE

The following week, Eleanor sat in the psych room with her eyes shut, and thought about the girl she called Jane and inmates called Mute. But what was a name? Actually, she thought, it was a lot. Countless studies proved that certain names predicted more success and stability later in life, where others predicted the opposite. What was Jane's name?

Outside, the dry dirt made ticking sounds as it blew in a sudden gust of wind against the small window. She turned as if expecting to see someone outside the window, but there was no one there. She could hear the noise from the corridor and the courtyard beyond, distant and angry, sometimes the release of laughter, but when the guard shut the door, all sounds would ebb away save her voice, the interior pulse of the room and the sound she hoped to hear: Jane's voice.

Eleanor turned and raised her wrist to her nostrils and sniffed. Scent molecules reached her brain from her nose in increments of time less than seconds and she responded, not so much in reaction to the smell, which only made her remember her mother, but in reaction to what she had done.

She remembered walking past the perfume counters under the harsh bright light of the department store. It was fun for her, in the way that doing something you never allow yourself to do, even if harmless, was fun. She wore makeup sparingly, and rarely did she spend money on accessories, among which she counted perfume, or frivolities, such as going out to lunch, primarily because she hadn't the time.

It'd been a long time since she could recall having fun. She could still hear Coralee's remark from well over a year ago after she'd declined a luncheon date with her friend:

"Elle, it's one thing to be good at what you do, but it's a-*nutha* tale all *togetha* to quit engaging en-*tire*-ly with the outside world, and simply stop having *fun*."

Eleanor used perfume when she and Lewis went to the symphony or to friends for dinner, but she didn't find it appropriate with her work at the prison. Now she realized that her patients, sitting across from her, might also be able to smell that timeless, rich and classic scent, no different from Lewis and perhaps wonder why she had, after months, suddenly decided to apply perfume. Mimi would have her own egotistical assumption. None of the others would probably care.

She had studied Lewis's face as he sipped his coffee. She'd felt guilty, suspicious, juvenile, and devious all at the same time. If she once in a while had what she considered petty or immature urges, she had over the years rarely given into them.

Until the point when she actually bought the Chanel No. 5 and not Chanel No. 19 or 22, extending her arm furtively across the counter to retrieve her credit card then the shiny little black and white bag with the string handle as if it were filled with black market goods, she had rationalized her actions, fully aware she was rationalizing, explaining to herself that she was merely shopping for perfume to wear for herself since she seldom did.

When she thought she saw Lewis tense, and when she thought he acted strange eating his two slices of wheat toast with butter, she too became guilty. Once arriving at the penitentiary, she scrubbed and scrubbed at her wrists under a stream of hot water, until only a trace of the scent remained. Ashamed, she decided simply to throw out the bottle, or give it to Coralee, wishing too late she'd never done what she'd done.

But despite her best efforts her mind persisted in offering images of Lewis with a fuzzy, out-of-focus blonde. Lewis removing her clothing slowly then removing his own. Eleanor felt a rock lodged in her stomach and her brows knitted together before she stopped, realizing her fantasy—herself—was the cause, not Lewis. The self-help culture and consciousness of recent decades that espoused the power of positive thinking and the importance of thought often led the public to believe fallaciously that here was a new point of view and way of life, when Marcus Aurelius and Montaigne, among others, had understood the principle hundreds of years earlier using the strength of imagination and a positive attitude not for new cars and larger flat-screen TVs, but for virtue and goodness.

Footsteps outside the room stopped her rampaging mind, and she tried to relax her face muscles and put on an unstrained smile as the girl called Jane entered. But on this day she did not say hello. She merely sat quietly. She nodded to the guard, and watched as Jane sat down across from her.

Jane looked up and their eyes met. Again Eleanor felt a question coming from Jane's eyes.

"Hello," she said quietly across to Jane, not taking her eyes away from her face. "How are you today?" She spoke the words as softly as she could and with what she considered a large dose of compassion, and that wasn't hard, for there were no combative gestures in Jane's movements like she'd seen with Shina or Mimi. Just the look that Eleanor had noticed on the first day—was it a cry for help? Or was it only quiet resignation? Jane did not look disturbed to Eleanor, and yet she'd learned from experience that to believe the guileless poker faces she worked with daily and think otherwise could lead her to destinations visited only in nightmares.

"Another session," Eleanor stated.

Jane regarded her an instant longer then dropped her eyes.

Eleanor smiled. "I wish I knew your real name."

Jane remained in the same position staring at the desk. It was possible she'd lost her memory in the trauma. That would explain a lot.

"This may sound silly, but do *you* know your name?"

Nothing.

"I want to help you. I know, you probably think you don't need help. You probably think I'm the one who needs help." Eleanor tried to keep her own sarcastic thoughts judiciously to herself. "Well, you're right. I do need help. From you. Some acknowledgment."

No response. Jane's eyes on the floor now. Eleanor watched, suddenly tired, as though Jane's resignation had seeped into her.

"Can you help me?" Eleanor asked searching Jane's face. "You do help me sometimes. Your expressions speak to me even if your voice does not."

Jane raised her eyes to Eleanor, apparently listening, at least observing. So Eleanor continued.

"It's automatic. You know, how a dog will wag his tail, no one tells him to do so, but he does anyway. Or bark. Bark from pleasure, bark from pain. Bark from excitement." Eleanor stopped abruptly. Because up to that moment, she had believed the mask across from her impenetrable. But in those few fleeting seconds, Jane's face had altered so much it was as if another girl sat in her chair.

Eleanor backtracked. *Quick, quick*! What had she *said*? She'd been speaking of involuntary actions, a dog wagging its tail. But of course! *Of course.* Jane had murdered *involuntarily*. Involuntary manslaughter. Murder without intent. And yet the expression she glimpsed had not been the familiar one of combined anger and despair that shadowed the faces of women who'd acted rashly and, now disbelieving, wondered what they, ordinary women until bad luck beckoned, were doing living behind bars. No, on the face before her, grief creased the normal features, reaching across to therapist so that Jane's pain was like a flash card, forcing Eleanor to revisit her own buried sorrows.

It was now obvious to Eleanor that Jane felt remorse for what she'd done, but then why had she killed? There wasn't a whole lot that made sense with this case, but her thought at the moment was that this girl across from her was no murderer. She had shot two men, that much was true. But she was no murderer. The deed had distressed her into silence. And Eleanor resolved to find out more about the victims.

As the thoughts bounced off each other in Eleanor's brain, her own eyes never left those of her patient's face. Jane had recovered herself quickly and expertly as if challenging Eleanor to believe that she had ever seen anything mark the impassive face that sat before her.

"You killed those men, I know. Did one of them try to hurt you? Did you feel you had to? Remember, I'm not here to judge you. What you did is in the past, but you and I are sitting here in the present. And I'm here to help you. I very much want to." Silence. "If you talk to me, I may be able to help you."

To Eleanor's surprise Jane turned to face her, and as she did, she brought her eyes from the floor and looked into Eleanor's eyes directly.

Could a woman's past life be encapsulated in one glance? She'd witnessed it before in previous patients, patients she'd been able to help. But the person across from her hid her life and emotions like the thief hid his identity, as though her life now depended on it.

Eleanor found the more a criminal lied, the more she tried to control her facial expressions and suppress emotion. There was, however, one crucial exception to this theory. The criminals, honest or lying, had to possess a conscience. Remorseless psychopaths laid the way for Eleanor's theories to break down. And it was into this category that she'd been compelled to dump Jane, until a few moments ago.

"Okay, let's try an exercise together. You're the teacher, I'm the pupil. If I get a question right, you nod your head. Or you can raise a forefinger, it doesn't matter, you do what is most comfortable. But let me know. So, nod your head if I'm right or getting warm. Shake it, if I'm completely wrong."

"Ready? Here we go."

"Your name is Jane."

Eleanor watched, but Jane sat motionless, back to staring at the floor.

"Your name is not Jane."

Nothing.

"You're here in this room with me."

This time Eleanor observed that Jane took a deep breath, letting it out softly.

"You shot a man." Eleanor had decided in her sessions she would stick to talking about one man or the other. Not both.

Nothing.

"You shot a man and he died."

Did she see Jane's muscles contract, or did she only imagine it?

"You shot a man involuntarily, without intent. You shot a man in self-defense."

Aware that she was holding her own breath, Eleanor let it out, watching and waiting for some illustrative gesture from Jane. But Jane produced nothing.

Eleanor rolled her chair forward, removing her hands from her lap and, placing them on the desk, leaned forward towards Jane. She repeated herself, patiently and softly.

"You shot a man in self-defense."

Jane's eyes widened, and she winced. She wrinkled her nose, and squinted. It was like a face waking from a nightmare.

But the words were the same Eleanor had used seconds ago with no adverse reaction. Jane moved back in her chair away from Eleanor, and on her face was an accusing look, one that Eleanor had no trouble reading. Revulsion.

"What is it?" Eleanor asked gently, while inside her thoughts were racing, *Don't lose the thread. I've upset her. Think. Think. What did I say?*

Jane looked like she was experiencing pain, and again her expression pained Eleanor, yet at the same time Eleanor couldn't help being fascinated by it.

"I'm sorry," she said. How easy it was to read pain in another's face. And how painful. "What is it, Jane?" She asked a second time, realizing too late she'd used the name. "What did I say that hurt you?" Her voice, soft and kind, matched what she was beginning to feel. She did not want to hurt this frightened girl. "Can you tell me what upset you just then?"

Without the wheels of Eleanor's chair, Jane's chair scraped on the floor as she pushed back in retreat. Eleanor stared at her. She shook her head once, wanting to say, *No, stop.*

"You needn't pull away from me." She stopped and began again: "You've done well today. I know it isn't easy. I know it's not easy either being here without your friends or family." She waited. "Is there someone you can contact from here?" Eleanor knew from Jane's chart that she had no family, and made no phone calls to the world outside the prison. She didn't write letters and she hadn't made friends.

Jane must have sensed the session's end nearing, for she'd shifted again. She glanced at Eleanor and Eleanor fired the last question at her without realizing the results she'd achieve.

"Is there someone you love who you would like to see again but . . . cannot?"

Bingo!

The face crumpled. The head tilted down to avoid Eleanor's direct glare. Two knocks on the door and the guard entered.

"Wait!" Eleanor said. "Just one minute."

But Jane was already rising, face averted, and Eleanor knew that fifty minutes was fifty minutes and to try to go over time with one patient would be a mistake that would come back and bite her like a cold, brutal wind.

That night as Eleanor lay her body down in bed beside her husband she fought not to sniff the pillows and sheets that she and Lewis had picked out together at Belk long ago. Yet her nose sniffed, somehow beyond her control. Clean and fresh. She swallowed as relief flooded her.

"Goodnight, Lewis."

"Night, love."

She awoke around midnight. Dark storm clouds were moving with eerie speed across a waxing moon, and the glow from the moon threw ghostly light down upon the bedcovers. Eleanor squinted, looking at the moon, sensing that it contained the wisdom she sought but lacked. She rose and stood by the window, staring down to the lily pond, a piece of dark satin with a moonlit milky gloss covering.

Had she dreamt hearing the voice? She struggled to remember the dream and caught its aura but the dream kept retreating until it had lodged in a recess where she could no longer follow. She turned and looked at Lewis lying alone in the bed in the pale light. When she turned back to look at the moon it was with a silent plea for help, praying that daybreak would become a single syllable upon the tongue, a voice breaking solitude, a requiem of answers.

CHAPTER THIRTEEN

Two days later Eleanor arrived at the psych room earlier than usual after conferring for a few moments with Helen. Under her arm she carried two rolled posters. She shut the door behind her. Still standing, she looked around the room. She knew that if she were to leave any legacy behind, it was here within the walls of this one small room.

She surveyed the posters on the room walls. The O'Keeffe hills and mesas, the swank putting greens of Scotland and the calming Monet. The hills and mesas and the putting greens hung side by side on the left wall of the room as one entered. The Monet rose vertically on the back wall by the window.

Eleanor unrolled the two new posters onto the desk, rolling them backwards several times in an effort to straighten them. The first poster was a well-known, now practically clichéd, Hopper painting of a woman alone in a train compartment reading a book. Outside her compartment window awaited the dark and somehow ominous American landscape.

The second poster was of a fifties family, standing stiffly and smiling wide, forced grins before a brick ranch house. In long since invisible ink Eleanor knew it must have once read, "All American Happy Family." There was mother in pink frock and matching pink and white checked apron to show she'd been fresh at the muffins.

Eleanor let out a strange sound. All of a sudden, it was too much. The apron. She couldn't look at that apron, but she found that she couldn't take her eyes away from it either. "*No,*" she whispered, as her own mother's apron flashed across her mind. "*Stop it,*" she said aloud. "Don't remember," she said to her brain. "Why did I tell Helen I do this?" She let go of the poster and it rolled back up like a snake coiling to strike.

She fell into her chair and let her head rest on folded arms. But her elbow touched the edge of the poster and she jerked her arms away from the paper like it was contaminated. "Get a hold of yourself." She took a deep inhale breath, unrolled the poster and let her eyes rest again on the happy family.

There was the father with his dark navy suit, innocuous striped tie and short, neat haircut above small tidy ears, grinning like Mr. Rogers. Modest brunettes both mother and father. Sis, with her hair in a perky pony tail, beaming, perhaps practicing for the Homecoming Queen and little Tommy, as Eleanor had dubbed him, about six or seven years old in the forefront grinning like he'd just heard for the nineteenth time, "Now smile, Tommy. Smile nice for the camera!" There was even a loyal and faithful family dog, the ubiquitous beagle, sitting beside little Tommy, mouth open, smiling in imitation of his family, if just a bit more tongue.

The third poster was an explosive de Kooning. The colors jarred Eleanor, and she did not find it particularly pleasing. Blacks and grays. Cooked-lobster red in the lower right-hand corner, blue-red in the center. The painting reminded Eleanor of death and destruction. Murder. She stood weighing the various positions, in the number one slot or the number two slot, like an interior designer sizing up spaces to hang a precious Munnings or Stubbs in a Fifth Avenue penthouse.

"Just hang them," she muttered, pulling forth the sticky tack. Hopper first on the left wall. De Kooning on far wall. Happy Family beside Hopper in the center of the left wall, opposite the desk.

The knock interrupted Eleanor's thoughts and she felt caught off guard. Still standing she said briskly, "*Come in.*" She watched as the same guard ushered in the girl wearing the same steely cuffs.

"Come in. Hello. Thank you." She took the tiny key and watched the guard shut the door.

Instead of quickly slumping down into the chair as she habitually did, this time Jane remained standing before Eleanor, her cuffed hands creating a sense of even more vulnerability. Her face, shed of the usual vacantness, looked abashed, as if more than prepared to accept the blame for her crimes. Eleanor was as close as she'd ever been to her and she looked into the blue-gray eyes, eyes that looked back at her with soft bewilderment and seemed to be asking a question, not insistently, but gently with all the time in the world. Eleanor felt her heart jump inside her chest, and as she did, she blushed. What followed next Eleanor could not say, but Jane, inches from Eleanor, took a step backwards, her lips parting as if to speak, then she stood motionless in the center of the room still facing Eleanor. And Eleanor, desperate to understand what was going on inside the girl's head, watched as she swallowed.

"Hello," Eleanor said.

Jane stood.

"You may sit. I was standing because I just changed . . . I just hung new posters." She had not intended to announce the new arrangement to any of her patients. Rather to wait and observe their reactions, if any, but she found the words sprinting from her mouth and once the words had left their starting blocks, Eleanor felt their banality, as if she'd rushed into the room to tell Jane about her plans to redecorate her kitchen. She clamped her lips together to prevent a further breach, but kept her eyes on Jane to record any change across her face. But Jane did not even glance to the new posters, her eyes falling to the floor as if whatever life had been present when she stood in the room speaking silently to Eleanor had vanished.

Eleanor sat too, but turned her body so that Jane couldn't help but see the de Kooning and in the next instant Eleanor stared stunned as she beheld Jane's reaction.

Jane looked beyond therapist to the print and Eleanor watched as the ends of her mouth moved in a grimace and her eyes creased at the edges.

"You don't like it?"

At the sound of Eleanor's words, Jane met her eyes, and Eleanor felt walloped as if she'd been slugged with a baseball bat in a dark alley.

"Does it make you angry?" Eleanor urged turning her body to look around at the poster, even though she could see the turbulent brush strokes with her eyes closed. The volcanic force and harsh, jarring colors certainly could be a trigger in precipitating a reaction such as anger or fear. She turned back to face Jane.

"Or did I make you angry in asking?"

Jane remained looking at her, which was unusual.

"Does changing something that you'd become used to bother you?" Perhaps she loved Monet's sunrise as much as Eleanor did, but in going mute had no way to communicate her feelings. "Change is difficult for all of us throughout our lives. But it's also inevitable." She watched Jane's face.

"If it's the artist, Willem de Kooning, I understand. He certainly could be somewhat unconventional, I suppose you could say. He was interested in both figurative and nonfigurative approaches to painting, and he had a strong influence on American Abstract Expressionism. Dutch-born American, I guess he painted mostly in New York." She spoke, giving Jane a brief history of the artist, hoping to settle her into a protective place, a gentle lullaby, where Jane would trust her therapist. Speaking not too academically, she hoped, but also not patronizing her either, wishing for Jane to see that she thought of her as someone she could talk to about interesting ideas. Maybe

Jane could trust a person who interested her, who taught her. Maybe Jane would at some point desire to speak back, offering her own opinion on de Kooning.

"Anyhow if you find that painting—it's called *The Time of the Fire*—if you find it unpleasant, I understand. Actually, I agree with you. What about these two?"

Eleanor rose from her chair, moving away from the desk to the wall, aware of her own movement, aware that Jane's eyes now skittered over her body. She'd worn a beige herring bone suit, the skirt just above her knee, the jacket short and fitted. A pale egg-shell blue shirt open at the throat, and a simple pearl necklace with matching pearl earrings that had been her grandmother's. When she first started working at the prison she debated for days on the appropriate manner of dress, finally deciding she wouldn't dress down because she worked in a prison. She would dress in the same way she would were she the managing director at Saatchi & Saatchi or the C.E.O. of Goldman Sachs, showing the inmates due respect.

Standing, Eleanor pointed her finger first to the Happy Family thinking that the woman's isolation in the Hopper perhaps too difficult initially.

"Maybe this poster is more soothing," she said aloud to Jane, but no sooner were her hand and finger poised, than she stopped still as if struck, watching Jane's perfunctory glance at the Happy Family morph in ghastly recognition.

The expression in the eyes and brow that had first beckoned to Eleanor from Jane's mug shot, however faintly, had deepened into one of desperate pain. She saw Jane's chin lift and her eyes grow wide. She watched her eyes focus and zoom in, her head moving forward, pulling her shoulders and torso with her as if someone had pushed her from behind.

Too close to the poster, Eleanor stepped back swiftly to be by the desk to see the trajectory of Jane's eyes—riveted on which family member? *Little Tommy*! But Jane had snapped her head away from the poster, closing a door. Eleanor saw the emotion flood Jane's face, and a shiver ran through her like a conduit of energy that had originated in Jane and now sparked some flame within her.

She sat down quietly. For several moments she did not move. She felt uncharacteristically overwhelmed with desire to touch Jane and offer her comfort but she knew she could not.

"Are you okay?" she asked gently.

Jane's posture was closed, huddled like a person who was cold. Eleanor saw she was trembling. What had happened? What was she afraid of?

"Jane?"

No response. Eleanor found herself speaking in her head to Jane, bargaining with her. Here, I'll give you, what? What could she give to Jane in exchange for her revealing her private thoughts? Her anguish? Her real name?

"Does . . . did that poster make you think of your own family?"

Very slowly Jane raised her head. Very slowly she raised her hands, palms down, parallel to the table, and Eleanor stared. Looking into Eleanor's eyes and not once blinking, Jane took her palms and moved them slowly but emphatically from left to right, the chain linking the two cuffs, giving a small jerk as she did.

Eleanor caught her breath.

Keeping eye contact with Jane, she nodded and said in a voice one level above a whisper, "Okay. Enough."

And together they sat across from each other, for the rest of the session, not speaking a word, Eleanor glancing only occasionally at Jane, but Jane never once looking again to Eleanor.

Eleanor found herself looking to the Happy Family. She'd seen it, hadn't she? All right there spread out across Jane's face: the anguish, the love, the loss. Where was her family now? What had happened? She moved her eyes back to Jane and found her as before, closed off from her and the world.

When the guard came, Eleanor said, "Thank you," quietly to Jane, and Jane raised her eyes to meet Eleanor's.

"Come in," Helen called.

"May I sit? Do you have a second?"

"Of course. What is it? You're all out of breath, but you're smiling." Helen smiled back at Eleanor as if receiving smile contagions.

"Yes, I am, and well I should be. She nodded her head to me."

"What?"

"Jane," Eleanor stated. "She nodded to me on her way out just now. I think. I could be wrong. I keep replaying it over and over and doubting myself. Thinking, maybe she just dipped her chin down, trying to scratch it since her hands are shackled. I think she should have the handcuffs taken off, by the way. Will you consider it?"

Helen nodded, a nod directed more to the rush of words and enthusiasm that she saw so seldom in connection to the controlled and elegant woman before her.

"I believe she consciously and intentionally nodded her head to acknowledge my presence."

"What did you say to her?"

"Nothing. That's just it. Nothing. We were sitting in silence. We had been."

"So she appreciated your coming into her world?"

"Yes, she did but I'd upset her. Remember the poster I told you about, the Happy Family?"

"Uh-huh."

"I asked her to look at it and she did and it upset her tremendously. She wanted to cry, but she didn't want to cry in front of me. That's not behavior you see with the mentally disturbed. Even with fairly healthy girls, it takes effort and control to put away tears when there's a torrent just waiting to flow the way hers were. I saw emotion. So now at least I know she's not devoid of feeling."

"That's good."

"That's great. It makes it a whole lot easier. But I have to understand what happened to her family."

"I'll look into it, Eleanor. I wish we knew about her family. I wish we could find someone, anyone. You know, we've never had a case quite like hers before. I'd like to find a contact. We will. They're working on it. Of course she must miss her family."

"Perhaps. Or maybe she had a rotten childhood and that's why a humongous poster of childhood happiness upset her."

"Mm-hmm, I see."

"But she kept staring at Little Tommy. Maybe she lost—"

"Who?"

"Oh. Little Tommy. That's what I named the young boy in the family. See, I wonder if she lost her little brother."

"Yes, but maybe," Helen ventured, "you should be wondering if she lost her child. Her own Little Tommy." Helen said slowly, regarding Eleanor sitting across from her.

CHAPTER FOURTEEN

Two days later, Eleanor walked down the hall, her face lowered, eyes on the floor tiles as her mind thought about one person and one person only. She thought she heard running footsteps but when she stopped and looked around there was nothing.

She opened the door to the psych room and sat down. A moment later Mimi Kramer walked through the door with the sexy swagger of a runway model and a lit cigarette between her lips. Eleanor watched her.

"Mimi, you know smoking is forbidden."

"I got me a hookup. Got me one for Ramen, too."

"Please, put it out or I'll have to report you."

"*I'll have to report you,*" Mimi mimicked. She sat down and took one long drag on her Marlboro Light before stubbing the butt out on the floor with the toe of her shoe. Raising her head back up and pouting at Eleanor, she let the smoke out of her mouth, blowing it across the desk into Eleanor's face, a purple-gray genii set loose like a curse.

"Thank you for putting it out, Mimi." Eleanor said without emotion, trying not to let the smoke cause her to cough. "How are you today?"

"Look, I stole these from Lateisha. She snitched on me." Mimi held out a box of Gummy Bears.

Eleanor did not answer but held eye contact. Mimi popped a Gummy Bear into her mouth and flicked her tongue over her lips. Eleanor's mind flickered to her request to Helen last week:

"I don't think I'm helping Mimi. I wish to be removed as her therapist."

And Helen's response: "Eleanor, if your father tied your hands with duct tape and threw you off a bridge, you might be sour on life and act out too. I need you to stay with her. You're the best we have. No one else has gotten anywhere with her."

And when Eleanor had not, out of her own slight despair, responded, Helen had added, "Eleanor, think about what I just said. Have compassion for her. She's crying out for help. We both know that's why she acts out."

Eleanor knew that Mimi's life before prison was a case of abuse that would cause even the most jaded rehab specialists to take pause. She knew Helen was right and that Mimi's father had repeatedly molested her, using her for an assortment of sexual experiments, and then in a fit of delusional rage tried to throw her from a bridge, her hands bound. Now, as she regarded Mimi she wondered what choice a young girl had in such a situation but to flee from home. Yet what awaited her on the street? Trapped either way, she finds nothing but the inertia of any trapped situation, which often leads to crime.

When Eleanor didn't respond, Mimi said, "I suppose you know Mute got a detention." She waited across from Eleanor, her eyes glistening like she might be trying out for Ilsa Lund in *Casablanca*. "But of course you know everything."

"Mimi, I'll remind you again, we're here to talk about you."

"It involved me," she stated and stared back at Eleanor, and Eleanor felt a sudden dread for the upcoming time she was to sit in the room alone with Mimi. Compassion, she said to herself. Just why was it so hard with this particular woman?

"How did it involve you?"

"Because," Mimi said slowly, dragging out the word, "She jumped on top of me and tried to do the deed with me. Then she tried to kill me. She's going to the hole for sure this time." She watched Eleanor. When Eleanor did not speak, Mimi continued. "You don't believe me? You go ask the guard. Go on, ask him."

"How does that make you feel?"

"Wouldn't you like to know?"

"Yes, I would." Eleanor watched Mimi. "Does it make you think about your father? Are you angry at him for what he did to you?"

"No. I'm angry at *Jane.* That's what you call her isn't it? She may be deaf and dumb, but she sure can write." Mimi said, waiting. "Do you know what she wrote?"

Eleanor didn't answer.

"She wrote that she hated you and she hated her sessions with you worse than when the girls were sticking the broom up her ass." Eleanor tried not to wince. "She wrote that she wished she didn't have to have three sessions a week with you." As Eleanor listened, Mimi kept talking, but then her voice changed. "I heard her." It was a whisper. A challenge. A sneer.

"You heard what, Mimi?"

Mimi looked at Eleanor with eyes that radiated triumph and said, as if it had been the moment she'd been waiting for, "I heard Mute crying in her cell. She was moaning and whining. And *talking.*"

Eleanor watched Mimi's face. Direct, if angry, eye contact; no evasive glances. She doubted Mimi was lying. Had Mimi heard Jane actually speak intelligible words? Yet Jane was in segregation. How would Mimi hear her? Probably one of the girls placed in isolation had spoken to Mimi during Association. Eleanor knew not to question her, yet she felt herself yielding to an internecine urge. Then, as if from someone not herself, she heard:

"It might not have been Jane, Mimi. You can't be sure."

Mimi erupted. "You think I'm deaf? *Sorry.*" She sang the word in a screechy, sing-song voice, *saw-ree.* "I know where that sissy noise was coming from!"

"Mimi, it seems like Jane is a source of agitation for you. Any thoughts on why that is?"

"Fuck you."

"I can't imagine she interacts with you since she's locked away. Right?"

"Why are you taking up for her?" Eleanor couldn't decide if Mimi's tone bordered on frantic or indignant, although she had no trouble registering the fury. "I told you she jumped on top of me!"

"Mimi," Eleanor cut her off. "Why does Jane bother you so much?"

"I don't know, ask her!" Mimi said, misunderstanding.

"Are you frightened of her?"

"Are you kidding me?"

"Do you find her attractive? A rival of sorts?"

"*Fuck you!* You'll be sorry and don't say I didn't warn you."

"You brought up Jane. You can change the subject if you choose, or you can tell me why you brought her up." She watched Mimi's expression flip-flop between resentment and fury. But if Jane were an issue, Eleanor rationalized, Mimi should be talking about her. So what if she gained insight into Jane from another patient. She was here to help them all, and human nature allowed that she could not possibly feel the same about each of them. "Do you feel about Jane the same way you feel about Shina? Do you feel antagonistic thoughts?" She spoke evenly but felt she was walking across black ice.

"I don't care about Shina. She's a slave, and I'm her master."

Eleanor shifted and observed herself in the moment, observing present become past, a detached spectator, not part of life. She saw herself as a psychologist sitting before a mixed-up and unhappy girl, objectively studying the frozen action of a postcard. Then, feeling herself enter the postcard, she spoke.

"You don't care about her, and yet—"

"I don't care about Shina. Because I can kill her if I want to."

Again the warning bells. They were, however, becoming fainter with frequent and overuse and Eleanor silently cautioned herself to heed them. By right, Mimi could be put into isolation with a comment like that, and if Mimi's face gave Eleanor no real reason to fear her words, the emotion behind the words did. Eleanor put her chin down almost touching the top of her throat for a moment. She remembered something she'd read: *One doesn't necessarily kill because one hates. One may also kill because one loves.* The bell went off in her brain like an egg timer on a stove, and she knew it was telling her to do something.

"Has Shina offended you?" She asked softly.

"*Fuck you.*"

Eleanor waited.

"She calls me made-up names because she's so stupid she thinks someone'll believe her. She stands there calling me names from the other side of the bathroom door. I mean," she laughed but the laugh lacked conviction. "How weak is that? She called me a, a . . . All-girl-act." Mimi glanced up quickly at Eleanor.

"An *all girl* what?"

"See what I mean?" Mimi lounged back in her chair.

"What's an all-girl-act?"

"I'm sure you can guess."

"Is it prison talk?"

"Prison talk," Mimi repeated, mocking.

"Well?"

"I ain't telling you. Unless . . ." Mimi smiled. "Unless you have the mute idiot transferred to another prison."

"Why would you want that, Mimi?"

"Because she's got a knife under her mattress, and she's waiting her time to use it on me."

When Mimi's hour was up, Eleanor felt enormous relief, but also a growing unease that her session with Mimi had taken a sharp turn down a potholed road. Twenty-five minutes later when Shina Jones sat before her in one of her more elevated moods, Eleanor knew talking would be easy.

"Hey, Hartley, how's life?"

"Hello, Shina."

"Sharonda's twins 'bout ready to pop out of her."

"How does that make you feel?"

"No, no, Hartley, put a lid on it. Let's lay down some ground rules so you and me be real clear." Her smile stretched from cheek to cheek. "Sharonda ask me to help her name her babies, and let me tell you, I got it all figured out. Hmm, hmm, all figured out.

"Did that feel like an honor, to help her name her twins?"

"Hartley, when you in these sessions with me, you got to abide by the rules. Now, don't you want to know what names I got picked out?"

"Yes, I would like to hear," Eleanor said smiling across at Shina.

"Two prettiest names your ears ever did hear." She waited.

"I'm listening."

"Emesis and Diarrhea." She grinned again.

For a moment, Eleanor's smile lingered. Then slowly the corners of her mouth uncurled, her face arranging its question mark. "A joke?" She said to Shina. "You know the meaning of those two words, of course."

"Hartley baby, I may be in the pen, but I ain't stupid. My body's locked up but my mind, see, my mind it wanders free as a bird. It soars over everyone else's, most especially those pig-faced, fat-ass, honky Bosses." Shina had on several occasions explained to Eleanor some of the prison lingo used so Eleanor could better understand her patients. 'Boss' was a term used to refer to the guards, derived from, "Sorry son of a bitch" backwards. Shina finished by hitting the desk once and stating, "Can't no one tell me that those two names aren't the prettiest sounding names."

"Have you presented your chosen names to Sharonda yet?"

"Oh yeah, girlfriend. She loves them. She all kinda puffed up like a peacock thinking her babies gonna be princesses. Princesses with the prettiest names in town."

Eleanor was about to speak but decided there were worse things than naming your children vomit and excrement. And Shina had a point, when taken away from their meanings, the two words were indeed quite melodious. She decided to use Shina's buoyant spirits to her advantage. "Speaking of vocabulary, Shina, Mimi says you called her a— I think the phrase was all-girlie-act."

"Now Hartley, don't go bringing up Creo when I feel so fine today. Don't go trapeezing all into my mind, ruining my mood for no reason at all that I can see."

"Very well, then."

Perceiving Eleanor's words as reproach, Shina let out a string of four-lettered words, followed by, "Fuckin' A right I call her an oliguriac! She sit on the can for forty-fuckin'-five minutes trying to piss! 'An I got to hold it for her! There now, Hartley. Happy?"

Shina wiggled her hands in the air like a spider. "Happy now? You go ruin my mood. Why you have to go bring up Creo? Just stirring up trouble. Hmm-hmm. Stirring up trouble, nothing better to do." She shifted her body away from Eleanor in an obvious sulk position, the opposite picture from the woman who had strode through the door ten minutes ago.

"Shina, I'm sorry," Eleanor replied surprised, but grasping what had happened—the usual brew of human emotion saddled with miscommunication—she added, "I'm sorry I brought it up. The reason I asked you is, actually, because I hadn't any notion what that word meant and I was simply curious. I wasn't upset with you."

Shina's mood improved. "Keep talking, Hartley. You doing better. Little bit better. Don't let it go to your head or nothing." She turned her body back, smiled and patted the desk as though it'd taken an active role in her exoneration.

"I'll try not to let it go to my head, Shina. Now, perhaps you'd like to tell me the meaning of that word."

Shina leaned over the desk low towards Eleanor, and whispered, "It mean she got a problem with her piss. Oliguria."

"*Oh,*" Eleanor whispered back. "Shina," she continued in a low voice as if others were outside the closed doors listening to them talk about the inner workings of Mimi's bladder. "You have an amazing vocabulary. Did you ever consider doing something with words or language or speech or something like that?"

"Yeah, I considered it."

"And?"

"Hartley Honey, I'm in the pen-i-*ten*-ery. I'm still considering it. Just calm down."

Eleanor nodded.

Shina grinned, white teeth against brown skin. "Now, you want to tell me about your week, Hartley?"

"I would much rather hear about yours," Eleanor answered for she had never once in her fourteen years at the penitentiary spoken of herself or her personal life. But she let herself smile back at Shina.

After Shina's comic view of life, Jane's detachment was hard for Eleanor to take. Determination and pride, mingled with another emotion that Eleanor pushed from her mind, not because it was unidentifiable, but because by identifying, she would have to analyze herself and the logic of her sessions with Jane.

Jane walked in eight minutes late. Eleanor watched her eyes flicker once to meet her own as if wishing to offer an explanation, but in the next moment, Jane shut her eyes briefly and she sat down. The guard closed the door behind, leaving Eleanor and Jane to the muted hush of the room.

It came over her then, suddenly, the lightened, uplifted feeling as though she were beholding a gentle moonlight scene. There was a rush like coursing water in her abdomen. Then she noticed for the first time that Jane was not handcuffed, and she blurted out: "Oh! Your handcuffs are gone." Regaining her composure she added softly, "I think I was behind that particular decision."

She smiled at Jane, but Jane was not looking at her. Eleanor again felt the flutter in her stomach but differently from before.

"Last week, we sat in silence for a while. I think maybe you liked that?" She was trying to get Jane to look at her.

Jane moved her shoulders, but did not look back at Eleanor. She sat hunched over, her left arm resting on the armrest, her right arm hanging loosely in her lap, her legs uncrossed. Nothing written on her thigh today.

"I can do that again with you. If that's what you would like." She spoke in a soft and low voice, a voice she knew she used for Jane alone. She expected to see Jane nod her head wearing a grateful expression. She waited, watching, and when the expression didn't come she felt all the progress of their past work, which had culminated in that real or imagined nod of the head, vanish.

Without thinking what she was doing, Eleanor stood, took two steps to stand directly beside Jane then knelt down as best as she could in the tight wool skirt.

"Jane?" She questioned, looking up into her face. "You've been crying."

Jane's eyes had little choice but to meet Eleanor's, and they did, bloodshot and red, with alarm.

Uncertain what to do next Eleanor rose, but against her will. "I'm sorry. I'm sure there are circumstances of which I'm unaware that make you cry. I'd like to help you."

Nothing from Jane. And Eleanor waited, watching Jane's face, feeling hope drain from her body. She sat silently for some length of time.

"Have you thought anymore about the poster?" She cleared her throat. "Look." She heard the exasperation and began again in an intentionally softer voice. "Would you face me, please?" To her astonishment, Jane straightened, turning her body so that she faced Eleanor squarely. Eleanor read her face. Even more astonishing. No trace of anger. Just the red eyes, giving away Jane's secret.

"Thank you," Eleanor said in a soft whisper. *A child might intuitively seek guidance and discipline without knowing she was seeking them.*

"As I've said before and as you know, it's my job to try to help you. It sometimes won't be fun for either of us." Eleanor wished she could say aloud to Jane, "Do you have any idea how much you, one person, have made me doubt my own capabilities as a psychologist? A psychologist who was until quite recently fairly confident and, I suppose you might also say, effective in what she did."

"I think during our last session the poster of the family upset you." Eleanor glanced at the poster and suddenly found the smiling faces inexplicably sickening. All those upturned mouths and white teeth now seemed to taunt her, and she found herself wondering about their whereabouts at present. What had become of them? She began to imagine that the smiling faces of sister and Tommy had turned to a life of drugs, crime and dereliction. Maybe one or the other was even now in the state penitentiary. Perhaps the father had been caught in a corporate scandal, greed winning the battle of conscience, and his wife had yielded to an extramarital affair. Appearances could, after all, be deceiving.

She snapped her head back, debated about asking Jane to regard the poster and decided one bullying session during the fifty minutes was enough.

"Mother, father, daughter, son, even a dog." The dog was just somehow too much, and since Lewis's outbursts, darkly comical.

As asked to do, Jane remained facing Eleanor and Eleanor scrutinized her face without shame. There was a strange mixture of emotions that for an instant she couldn't name, nothing familiar, yet neither anything she feared. She thought how often words had spoiled an emotional moment for her, and now they were the very thing she needed for that same sense of fulfillment she'd always found in their absence. How often had she watched people, anguished or fidgety, embarrassed or guilty, smother their emotions under the cover of words.

But not Jane. For Jane there was silence. Silence was her cover. Silence was her nature—a silence that Eleanor had come to regard not as stubborn or challenging but as a language unto its own. The space of what is not said, a lacuna. In her silence Jane spoke more than all her other patients who, filling their sessions often with angry words directed at anyone except their righteous selves, strengthened her belief in the predictability of human nature while crushing any hope that one's soul or better self would evolve and triumph. In Jane's silence there was the purity of restraint and the ability to hear without reacting. It was a thoughtful silence, and it encompassed not only respect, but kindness.

Without taking her eyes from Jane, Eleanor said: "I wonder if you lost someone very close to you." She paused before asking: "Did you lose a child?"

There it was, so fast Eleanor's left lobe could not begin to verbalize what she saw. Something had flickered in Jane's face, a light being flipped on, freeing it of the placid mask as if someone had momentarily stopped the film projector midway, allowing Eleanor to view what normally couldn't be seen. She believed no one else would have seen it, not because it had registered too fast, but because no one else knew the face before her as well as she did. Eleanor was seconds from identifying the emotion that had shadowed Jane's face and thinking these thoughts when she heard footsteps running outside in the hall. There was no logical reason to feel alarm, but still she tensed. Her skin prickled and she glanced beyond Jane to the door.

Jane turned in her chair to see what Eleanor was staring at just as the door crashed open and Mimi Kramer stood in the doorway.

"*She tried to kill me*!"

"Mimi, you know you can't be in here," Eleanor said as calmly as she could, wondering how it was possible that Mimi was standing there.

"*Anything she says is a lie! You must listen to me before it's too late.*" Mimi reached for Jane pulling her up from her seat by her waistband, then wrapping her arms around her in an awkward embrace. "*Why'd you do it? You're sick.*"

Eleanor rose from behind her desk, as Mimi let go of Jane and she faltered back into her chair. Eleanor reached out to Mimi, hoping to instill calm, but it was a mistake. Mimi lunged at her, pushing her against the wall. And as Mimi grabbed for Eleanor's wrists, pinning her against the Happy Family, Eleanor was conscious of leaning back against the mother, wondering if Jane was now looking at the poster and what she must be thinking. She was aware of feeling not fear, but self-consciousness. Then Mimi was pressing her body against Eleanor. She began to move her torso up and down, rubbing into Eleanor while squeezing her wrists hard.

"*It's what you want,*" Mimi crooned into Eleanor's ear, while her face morphed to half grin, half grimace. "You've been asking for it ever since I sat down across from you. Tell me you love the way I feel." She removed a hand from around Eleanor's wrist and cupped her breast for a moment. Eleanor could smell

Mimi's breath, full of cigarette smoke, inches from her face. She saw her eyes up close and blurred. She smelled her skin, a sour aroma of sweat and smoke.

"You've been asking for this ever since I walked in that very first day. Telling me I fill your needs like no one else. But that I can't tell a soul."

"Mimi, *stop*," Eleanor gasped.

"You don't even tell yourself the truth."

Mimi pressed harder against Eleanor's body. Over her shoulder she called, "Watch us, mute girl. Watch us do it together against the wall. It's not the first time we've done it." And into Eleanor's ear Mimi said loud enough for Jane to hear, "We ought to make her pay." She flung her head back, laughing. Eleanor heard Mimi's laughter in her ears and tried to shift to see what horror might have cast itself across Jane's face, but Mimi's head was blocking her.

"*Mimi. Stop it right now*," she said in a low voice as she flapped her arms, struggling against Mimi's hold. Mimi was hurting her. "I will speak to you in private, but please *stop this right now*."

Mimi's laugh filled the small room. "Is that all you can say? What about, 'Mimi, I want you?' Did you tell her about that? 'Mimi, you're beautiful, but you can't tell any of the girls I'm telling you this. It's against regulations.' And what about the letters? '*Meet me in the psych room after Association. No one will suspect. No one has to know. Mimi, meet me in my office at 5:00. I'll write you an appointment—*'"

"*Mimi hush!*" Eleanor said again, gasping for air."

"Come on, make me come. Don't worry about her, she can't talk!"

"*Mimi, stop!*" But Eleanor could not finish her sentence because Mimi's right hand was now around her neck, choking her. She flailed her right arm as Mimi held her left wrist against the wall with one hand, and continued holding her neck with the other hand. Eleanor began to gasp then choke and she found her mind confused, remembering Shina had told her something about Mimi, or Mimi about Shina, and she hadn't spoken to Helen. What a fool she had been assuming she knew best.

If Mimi was worried she'd strangle her therapist, she gave little indication as she continued her low, menacing laugh, twisting her body against Eleanor's in exultant triumph as though she were a dancer on the stage and not an inmate in the psych room of a prison.

Eleanor's legs gave way and she began falling toward the floor. Her thoughts were becoming blurred, but she saw the flash of white at the same time she heard the jarring sound of the buzzer, blaring into her ears. Who had pushed that buzzer? But Eleanor knew.

Time became the amorphous putty of slow motion, stretching the seconds so that in some phantasmagoric dream, Eleanor watched clearly as Mimi sailed backwards across the room, crashing into the desk. Too late Eleanor yelled out as she saw Mimi's spine hit the edge and watched Mimi slither to the floor and scream. But Eleanor found no relief in Mimi's release for the sound that trilled from Mimi's lips was a shrill scream, a scream that raised hair on her arms. Then there fell a hush.

Jane broke the stillness first, moving quickly. As Eleanor sat up against the wall, realizing that at any minute a guard would enter, Jane reached out to her, looking at her with more emotion than Eleanor had seen. She saw Jane hesitate and she heard footsteps racing down the hall. *No Jane,* she cried. *No.* But no words came out, and she realized she only cried out in her mind. Jane wavered for only a moment as the loud thumping came nearer, then she crouched and put her arms around Eleanor, lifting her, Eleanor's soft shirt hot and damp with sweat. And when the guard exploded through the door, Jane was holding Eleanor in her arms.

"*What are you doing? Get your filthy hands off her!*"

Like waking to familiar if harsh surroundings from a dream, Eleanor saw a massive woman with a stern face advancing toward Jane. Jane's back was to the guard but Eleanor saw the guard's arm raise a wooden slapstick high in the air. Eleanor began to yell, but already she knew she was too late.

"*No!*"

She heard the raw *thunk* of the stick as it hit Jane's skull so close to her own, and Jane crumpled to the floor, releasing Eleanor from her arms.

The guard stood in the center of the room, her face set with anger, yet creeping into the ugly look was the hint of a self-important smile.

"What in the name of Sam Hill is going on here?" The guard demanded of the room.

Jane lay on her side and Eleanor saw blood beginning to stain her blonde hair. She knelt then felt dizzy and sick.

"*Owww,*" Mimi groaned from the floor. *"Help me. She tried to kill me,*" she said rolling over and pointing to Jane.

"Well, she won't kill you no more," the guard said comforting Mimi. "She won't touch another living individual for as long as she lives. And that might not be long. Are you all right?" The guard addressed Eleanor.

"Yes," Eleanor gasped, pushing Jane's hair from her face with a trembling hand. "But Jane did not assault me. Mimi did."

The guard looked harshly at Eleanor who knelt beside Jane, then at Mimi. The poster of the Happy Family had fallen to the floor, a tear through its center.

"*She's lying.*" Mimi rasped. "Because she likes that murdering piece of shit lying there. Look in her pants." Mimi pointed to Jane. "Go on, see what you find." Mimi was pulling herself up against the desk, whimpering as she did. Eleanor stumbled to a standing position, rubbing her neck. She watched, turning her head from Mimi to the guard. Her neck and back ached and her thoughts were too mixed up to comprehend.

The guard bent over Jane reaching and groping around under her elastic waistband, as Eleanor stared in outrage. But in the next instant the guard's face puckered and she jerked her head, her eyes glaring at Mimi then at Eleanor. She raised her hand for them to see what it held—a glinting pocket knife.

"It's a good thing I was here to rescue you both. Your fate might have ended up at the end of this." She waved the little knife in the air as if it alone were capable of killing two women.

There was a stunned silence. Then movement. The movement was Mimi's as she shifted her weight and groaned. She spoke, slowly:

"Now who's lying?"

Eleanor looked at Mimi then to Jane lying motionless on the floor then to the guard. When she looked back at Jane there was fear, hard and cold in her gut like she'd swallowed a damp stone.

PART II

PAST
Virginia, Late August 2014

I was a-trembling, because I'd got to decide, forever,
betwixt two things, and I knowed it. I studied
a minute, sort of holding my breath, and then
says to myself: "All right then, I'll go to hell"—

—Adventures of Huckleberry Finn

CHAPTER FIFTEEN

W*ww.craigslist.* Left click.

Pets. Left click.

He waited, staring at the screen, his right leg jigged up and down. Then there was the rush as the listings popped up.

Golden Retriever puppies. Purebred Australian Shepherds. Chihuahua pups $200 each. He knew which were reputable breeders and which were backyard breeders. His eyes caught what he was looking for.

Older dog. Free to a good home. A phone number after the ad.

Puppies. Free to a good home.

He replied back using the 'Doglover' moniker.

Six dogs, moving must sell, $15 each, OBO.

He bounded with the light step of a confident man out his front door. There, parked on the curb was his shiny silver Dodge Ram 3500. He hopped in, backed up and drove toward town. Turning into the Wal-Mart parking lot, he saw the object of his desire: one of the last remaining payphones. He lifted the receiver and began punching in the number. As he waited, ear up against the old fashioned receiver, two young women passed, eyes riveted to phones. He watched them, following them with his eyes into the parking lot until they disappeared behind a parked SUV.

Twenty minutes later he was in the truck driving east of town. He pulled up to the low ranch house and looked over his right shoulder toward the front door. He got out and walked up the front walk noticing the unkempt appearance of the yard. Purple morning glories climbed up shrubbery, clinging to whatever they could, summer abundance, or maybe neglect. On the front step he knocked and waited. An older woman with red eyes opened the door to him. When she didn't speak, he wondered if she'd forgotten their conversation of a short while ago.

"Tom Johnson," he held out his hand and smiled at her.

"Mr. Johnson, come in. Forgive me, this is so . . ." Her voice caught and he hoped to hell she wouldn't break down. "So hard for me. I love Tippy more than . . . ." She stopped and reached into her dress pocket for a crumpled Kleenex that had obviously been used more than once. As she blew her nose, he stood waiting, attempting a look of concern. "I don't have words to say how much he means to me." She spoke softly, as if to someone other than him.

She stepped back, letting him enter and pad forward on the carpet. He smelled an unpleasant smell and only realized its source when she led him through to a corner where a little dog lay on a worn and faded plaid dog bed. The smell of unbathed dog. The dog looked to be mostly beagle, with a black back and brown face and sides.

"You see, my husband and I got him together two years ago. We've only had him that short time, but I love him so much. He's so sweet. He was a stray, not in great shape then. We named him Tippy because of the white tip on his tail. I always say it matches the white stripe right down his face. You see it there, don't you? Do you see the white tip and the white stripe?"

"Yes ma'am. I see the white tip and the white stripe." There was indeed a white tip, but the tail itself looked unrelated to a dog tail. It looked like it might be better used to tie up a garbage bag, ropelike and mangy, with hair missing in places. A rattail.

"When my husband died last year, little Tippy was all I had. But I can't stay in this house. My children are moving me to a home." He could see her tearing up again. He stood awkwardly. "I've fallen twice now and my children are afraid I'll break a hip. I did three years ago. My children all live in the city and none of them can take Tippy." Again her voice caught. Again the used Kleenex came forth.

"Rest assured Mrs. Cuddin, old Tip boy will have the very best of care. I live alone too. And I'll look after him like my own child."

"I don't know how to thank you. I just kept thinking how awful it was for him to have been out on the streets, all starving and scared, and then he finally got love and warmth and a good home. Only to have to have the rug pulled out from under him just when he'd gotten used to us and being loved and cared for. So, I really can't thank you enough."

"Well, if you think he'd want company other than just myself, maybe you know of some other dogs around here who need good homes."

"Oh, I don't think . . . ."

He waited but she only blew her nose. "Well, in that case, let's just take little Tip to his new place." He produced a slip lead and walked over to the small dog. He heard the woman sniffling after him.

"Tippy, this is Mr. Johnson who is going to love you like I told you, just like you're his child. He has a warm, soft bed for you and he'll feed you and love you. Don't you worry, you'll have a wonderful life." She bent down, as best she could, next to the dog who looked back at her with quiet eyes. "I love you so much, Tippy. Always know that." Then she stood waving a hand in the air. "Go on. Please, just do it quickly. I've said goodbye to him one hundred times. I can't . . ." She was openly crying now, blowing her nose and honking like a lone goose.

He slipped the lead over the dog's head and tugged. The little dog didn't move.

"Oh, Mr. Johnson, can I please have your number? I'd just like to be able to call and know he's okay."

He handed her a business card he'd had made for this very purpose. "You can call anytime." He tugged again and pulled the dog to a sitting position. Tippy looked once to his mistress who was crying and did not see the look. He pulled again at the leash and the dog turned his glance to him, then slowly gathered his hindquarters under him and seemed to push himself reluctantly to a standing position.

"He's not that old, don't worry," she said quickly. "He was a stray, so who knows what happened to him out on his own all alone. The vets think he's only a few years. He's just a little stiff and maybe arthritic from his time on the street," the woman said. "You will give him the Dasuquin twice a day, won't you? Here, there's a good half bottle left. They're expensive. But you'll get more from the vets, won't you?"

"Of course." He pulled and found the dog following him quietly. The woman continued crying softly and he said goodbye. Once outside, it seemed to take forever to walk the dog down the front walk, a walk that should have taken seconds. Come on, dog, he thought. He didn't have all day. He bent to lift the dog and pushed it into the crate. He glanced to the house but didn't see the woman at any of the windows. He bungeed the crate in place and slipped around and got in.

He called on two more ads, and when he'd loaded all the dogs successfully, he pulled into the local shelter, parking out of the way where his truck was not visible.

"Hey girls, how's it going?" he called walking in and smiling his liquid smile, which was easy to do if he felt the girls' glances traveling over him. The one named Donna was always out front. And today she was the only one there. She sat at the desk and behind her was a messy array of files with papers sticking halfway out, books, ointments, a cat arching its back then lying down just above Donna's head. Donna was a big, buxom woman with dirty blonde hair, competent looking hands and arms, and a no-nonsense manner. Sometimes she chewed on her pen like she was smoking a cigarette. Today she was running the leaded end of a pencil through her hair against her scalp. He smiled. He liked her, but it was Carol he always hoped to see.

Carol had long dark hair and a beauty mark mole between her upper lip and cheek. She had a round, yet slim little figure that he liked to imagine in his quiet moments. Once he had seen her walking out the dogs, three dogs at a time. She knelt and spoke to them like she could understand their thoughts. He liked the way she moved, and he often thought of her kneeling and whispering like that in dog tongues.

"Hi, Officer Drakas," Donna said. "We're fine. How're you today?"

"Can't complain." He paused then asked the question he always did. "Any unadoptables?"

Donna rolled her eyes. "It's getting worse and worse all the time. People unable or unwilling to care for their dogs and cats ever since the economy went south. Dropping them off here like we had unlimited resources and space. I know some people really can't afford, but—"

"And that's why I'm here to take the hard cases off your hands."

"And you're a godsend and I bless you every day I wake. I don't know what we'd do without your help. How many you taken in now?"

"I don't know. It doesn't matter. We all just try to do what we can, right?"

"You've done your share," Donna said. "Well, we've two that could really stand to get out of here, if you're sure you—"

The doors to the runs burst open, letting in the sound of barking. Carol walked around the desk and stood by Donna. He let his eyes rest on her. She looked up from the desk and their eyes met.

"How's Petey doing?" she asked him, flipping her dark ponytail with a casual movement.

He stared at her. There was something in her body language that challenged him, something full of feisty spunk, and for a moment he felt he'd like to take up her challenge.

"*Petey*," she said before he had a change to answer.

"Just fine. Loving the life of a house dog. He licks me in the face every morning." There was a beat in time when his breathing quickened, and she just stared at him. Then she spoke.

"Petey's a girl."

Another pause and he felt the tension in his jaw begin. He remembered to consciously relax his mouth the way the massage therapist had instructed. He smiled. "We know that, Carol. But Petey would *like* to be a man, top dog, Alpha, if you know what I mean, so we call him Petey Boy. Her. Makes her happy." He wrote notes and statistics on every dog he liberated from the shelter but away from the notes it was hard to remember. There'd been so many.

"We've two in the back who are older. They'll never get adopted," Donna said.

"They deserve a good home," he offered. "Better than cement runs enclosed in four walls. It's a prison. Sorry, I know you girls do your best here, but they deserve better than cold, dark runs at night."

"I couldn't agree with you more," Donna sighed.

"Hold on a minute." It was Carol again. "I think someone asked after them."

"Who are you talking about?"

"Who are *you* talking about?" Carol said softly under her breath to Donna.

"Waggles and Max."

"Exactly. Somebody wants them."

"What? When was that? I didn't hear." Donna looked up at her with a frown.

"Mr. Drakas, we'll call you," Carol said. "But, don't hold your breath, this lady was pretty insistent about those two."

"Any others need good homes?" He asked doing his best to smile.

"Nope," Carol quickly. She didn't smile back at him.

"Okay, girls. See you later." He winked and walked out through the heavy glass doors. Once in his truck he glanced back toward the shelter. "Feisty bitch," he said. But he smiled.

CHAPTER SIXTEEN

When he had driven off, Donna threw her hands up in the air. "What was that about? No one has asked after Waggles or Max!"

"Donna, look at me. No, really look at me and answer me with an honest heart."

"I'm looking at you and I don't have the time for this."

"Do you really believe that man is giving a home to all those dogs?"

"Yes! The man is a godsend."

"I don't believe a word he says. Have you ever been to his house?"

"Of course. We checked him out in the beginning when he offered to take those six hound mixes."

"How long ago?" Carol asked.

"I don't know, but he hasn't moved, has he?"

"I've asked him three or four times if I could come see Petey and Sallie. And every time he has some excuse why I can't come see them. He asked to take me out to dinner though, the creep. I don't trust him and I'm beginning to fear the worst. You heard him, when I asked after Petey, he didn't know who I was talking about! I'm beginning to think those dogs aren't there. Petey, and sweet Sallie, what a beautiful old hound. She should never have gone to him. I loved those two. Donna, are you listening?"

"Trying not to."

"Where did they go? Don't you want to find out?"

"They got a good home. And we have so many more to worry about." Donna got up from the desk and pushed through the door to the runs. Carol followed her closely.

"Did they? Did they get a good home?"

There were the dogs, large and small, some barking wildly, leaping up against the closed doors of their runs, others quailing in corners. But almost all bore eyes into the girls, and the backdrop of barking continued. "Nick's right," Donna said. "Look at them. This is no kind of existence. I mean we don't gas them like some places, but they hate it here. They're terrified."

"But what if Nick's is worse?"

Donna spread her arms wide, half turning toward Carol as if to say, "What do you want me to do?"

"We're here to help them find good homes and Nick Drakas is not one. He's taking them somewhere, I can feel it."

"Your mind is out of control. He's a good man, Carol."

"He's a creep. I get the creeps every time he walks in here."

Donna stared at her.

"People sell dogs all the time. Slaughter houses pay. Dog food—"

"They don't use dog meat in dog food!"

"Think again. Dogs used as bait, bear-baiting. Pitbull fights. . . ."

"He's a *cop*," Donna said over the barking dogs.

"Exactly. Who in his right mind would want to become a cop in today's world? I just need to see Petey. I need to know she's all right. And sweet Sallie. The sweetest hound I ever met. I can't think—"

"Carol, I can't think either with you going off the deep end all of a sudden." She began to say something then stopped abruptly. "I can't deal with it right now. Not now."

"All right, but please don't adopt any more dogs to that man. If those poor dogs met their end because of Nick Drakas, I'm going to—"

"Call the cops?"

Carol pressed the base of her palm into her eyes. "Just promise me, okay?"

"Okay, but my promise is only short-term until you come back to your senses."

CHAPTER SEVENTEEN

"Sure you're all right to close up?" Donna called out to Carol as the sun started its descent late in the day through summer's rich green leaves.

"Happy to," Carol said back. She was cradling a small yellowish dog and it wiggled as she kissed the rose-colored nose.

"And thanks again for staying past midnight last night."

"Someone had to whelp the pups."

"I'll do it next time. Thanks for closing up. I gotta go by the grocery store, fix two meals, got laundry to do. . . ." Her words trailed off as she pushed through the door. "You're the best," she called back to Carol. "Even when you're going off the deep end."

Carol watched as the car pulled away then she set the small dog down and picked up the phone. The phone rang and rang, and she was about to hang up, when she heard the voice at the other end answer. The voice sounded far away.

"I need your help," she said into the receiver. A pause. "That's right," she said and smiled. "Can you come over here now?"

Thirty minutes later a young woman walked through the heavy glass door of the shelter. She had shoulder-length blonde hair and a gentle face. When Carol saw her, she couldn't decide if she felt like jumping up and down or crying. She gave her a quick, heartfelt hug and a peck on the cheek.

"What's up?"

"I need a favor," Carol answered.

"Go on."

"First I need for you to tell me if you think we're doing any good in caring for the dogs here." She motioned with her elbow toward the runs.

"Of course."

"Donna said they're terrified and hate it."

"I'd agree with that."

"Sylvie!"

"But what's the alternative? Point, counterpoint. Homeless dog, home with dog. Think of some of the new beginnings we've given human and animal."

"You're right. Come sit." Sylvie sat on the edge of the desk and Carol fell back into the chair.

"They get to know love, the bright, pure notes of love."

Carol smiled, and repeated Sylvie's words. "'The bright, pure notes of love.'"

"Life without the love of something is meaningless. Love turns the world, fills the cracks, ship to shore, lonely no more. Whether it's love of human, love of music, love of tree with hopping bird, love of verse and penciled pearl, or love of cold, wet, wonderful noses. It gives a grail of meaning."

"You're a little crazy, but I guess that's part of why I love you."

"Love tempers life. And you find them love, don't forget."

"You're right," Carol said again, blowing out. "The one-eyed, toothless little monster got a home. His lady worships the ground he walks on, stinky little thing. That was a miracle if ever there was one."

"Exactly," Sylvie answered. "And miracles happen in threes. One, two, three. Be prepared for more."

"You always say that," Carol said, tilting her head to the side and smiling up at Sylvie in a dreamlike fashion. She closed her eyes, as if pausing from life, or at least slowing it down. "And that in itself is reassuring. You are. You just being there, always. You and your three miracles. I hope you're right," Carol said, opening her eyes.

"Maybe the real miracle is that we've been able to help so many abandoned animals find happy forever-ever-after homes. Without this as their interim they wouldn't have gotten there. "

"Yes, you're right. I just needed to hear it from you. You're always so calm and levelheaded. I worry too easily."

"I only ever see you working hard to do your best. So, what's up?" Sylvie asked again.

"My worry got activated. I've got a hunch about one of those happy forever-ever-after homes. And it's not so happy."

"The hunch or the home?"

"Both."

"Go on."

"I think some of our dogs are ending in a research facility. Maybe a lot. I don't suppose you'd go undercover again. It could get you out of the house," Carol said, her voice lilting up as her brows rose to match.

"I don't need to get out of the house."

"You said you hated your new apartment."

"I never said that. I just said. . ." But Sylvie didn't finish.

"What's wrong?"

"Nothing. I think of life as a gift. It's just that it gets a little shadowy in that little apartment, that's all."

"Shadowy? Inside?"

"Like someone cast a long, slivered shadow."

"I've never known you to be afraid. What's wrong?"

"I'm not afraid. I—" Sylvie began to speak, and again stopped. "Anyhow, I can't just leave work."

"Then what's the point of working for animal welfare groups if you can't go help when help is needed?"

"Not sure they'd see it that way. I.D.A. is a legitimate organization. They don't break laws."

"Who's asking you to break any laws? Observation, that's all. We need information."

Sylvie ran a hand through her hair, pushing it from her face.

"I'm thinking about the lab near your new place." Carol said beaming at Sylvie like she'd won a free trip to Bermuda. "You're the best at not falling to pieces."

"DVX?"

"That's right, you could walk if you wanted," Carol said, her beaming light fading just a bit. "You said it's been calling to you since you moved in."

"I said it's been calling to me? It's ominous. It speaks in low rumbles."

"You always say you want to make a difference in this screwed-up world."

"Sometimes it's a beautiful world."

"Have you felt that lately?"

"I love this world." Long pause in which Carol studied her best friend. "Sometimes I feel it. Outside. I don't know, maybe not so much lately. But how can going undercover at that place do anything? I mean of course except to torment me throughout my waking hours for the rest of all eternity."

"And your non-waking hours too. Nightmares, hallucinations."

"Good to know you're on my side."

"Sylvie. No one can keep cool like you can."

Sylvie shook her head. "I don't know."

"Do you remember you made a promise once?"

Sylvie was quiet for a few seconds. She turned to look at Carol. "I remember."

"Does that mean anything?"

"Yes. Okay."

"Really?"

"What, tell me you weren't expecting I'd say "yes". Sitting there counting the seconds, tick, tock, tick, until I did."

"I knew you would because you're a saint and one of the most compassionate people to walk this earth. A saint and an angel. And." Carol squinted like Sylvie might hit her. "You're Jane Dunlap."

"What?"

"I have an I.D. for you."

Sylvie shook her head.

"I just know you better than anyone else does. You thrive on adventure. And, Sylvie, I'd trust you with my life."

"No pressure or anything. What do I do, have Jane Dunlap sign her paychecks over to me?"

"Yes, exactly. Just like you did before. Look, here's what I think. I think it's bigger than we can imagine. And I think that cop, Nick, is supplying dogs to DVX. It's the only logical place around here without major transport. Is anyone on to you?"

"I don't think so."

"You have grace points in heaven. Sainte Sylvie, they'll call you." Carol opened her mouth like she wanted to say more but instead she looked to the closed door behind which dogs barked.

As if reading her thoughts Sylvie said, "I know."

"Don't we all want the same thing, to be happy, not to suffer?" Carol asked.

"Even a housefly wants that."

Sylvie had spoken with a straight face, but Carol laughed a slightly hysterical laugh. "Even a housefly. That's why I love you so much. I don't feel like a freak around you. I can speak my thoughts freely." She looked up. "Sylvie . . . I know you'll end up with a beautiful family. If it's what you want. But until that day, I want you to know that you have a family with me. With Matt and me. Whenever you need us."

Sylvie nodded briefly."Sure, thanks. Now. . ."

"Yes, work to do. Okay, do you remember Petey and Sallie?"

"Of course."

"I want you to check DVX and see . . . ." But Carol couldn't finish and Sylvie touched her arm lightly until Carol cleared her throat and began again. "See if they're there." She fluttered a hand into the air like DVX lab was behind her.

Sylvie saw the tears coating her eyes and waited for her to go on. When she didn't, Sylvie said gently, "I have to get the job first. It's a long shot, Carol."

"No, it's not. You always succeed when you set out to do something. You'll get it."

"Okay, and if I get it, and, if they're in there, what am I going to do?"

"You'll think of something. You always do."

"No, really. What will we do?"

Carol shook her head back and forth, her eyes damp. "We're going to do something that will make Nick Drakas never, ever touch another dog again."

CHAPTER EIGHTEEN

"One, two, three." Sylvie walked down the three cement steps of her home, which consisted of four rooms that were part of a larger old brick house in a neighborhood that had once been occupied by stately homes, but was now considered one of the bad sections of town, many of the large homes abandoned or filled with college students at best, and squatters and drug addicts at worst. Her separate entrance was on a side street and since her landlady, who used the main house as her painting studio, only came a few times a year, Sylvie was completely alone in her small space, the rest of the house left vacant except for an easel and cans of paint stacked everywhere.

Old established trees grew out of the sidewalk, and Sylvie wondered how they could survive like that, even while knowing their roots must seek and reach nourishment below the hardened surface. She touched the huge oak closest to her entrance, speaking silently to it. The great branches spread out offering silent wisdom, while the roots vanished deep beneath the concrete. Morning sun was like the touch of warmed stone on her arms and she breathed in the day's particular smell, a mix of late-summer vegetation combined with gasoline fumes.

She parked on the road wherever she could find space, and yesterday she'd left her old Peugeot with two wheels upon the sidewalk, and two in the road, as if it'd fallen asleep in drunken slumber. She thought of Carol's question. "Have you felt it's a beautiful world lately?" It was a beautiful world, the natural world most of all. There she could always find beauty and steady herself. But lately, she sensed the howls and growls of life closing in. Perhaps something missing. Maybe she had told Carol she didn't like her new apartment, but it was more that she just didn't care. It was four walls, a place to eat and sleep. Then she considered Carol's words about a family and shook her head.

She walked for two blocks, nearly to the convenience store that sold hotdogs and fish sandwiches. She glanced in to the old man with chocolate skin and albescent hair who was always behind the deli case. She waved, and walked past. There was the Peugeot as she remembered, leaning and lopsided, looking none too sober. No windows banged out. A small comfort, that. Getting into her car she felt a thought pressing her. She wanted to make a difference, even a small one. Maybe this, if she got the job, would be it. She started the car and drove to DVX.

DVX Laboratories was one of hundreds of labs tucked away incongruously around the country, often in the shadowed corners of poverty-stricken America. Although some of the largest labs were university labs such as U.C. Davis, Columbia and Santa Clara, or huge operations like N.I.H., other labs operated on the sidelines, hoping to remain hidden, conducting their experiments that furthered science and health away from critical eyes. DVX took money from huge pharmaceutical companies to test insecticides and other chemicals used in companion-animal products. Bayer, Eli Lily, Novartis, Merck, Sergeant's, Welmark and Merial, the maker of Frontline flea and tick products were only some of the many corporations that paid DVX to feed experimental compounds to dogs and cats and test chemicals on their skin.

Sylvie pulled into the parking lot and ran a hand through her hair, glancing in the rearview mirror. She needed to look respectable but a little shabby, as if she'd take any job. She got out of the car, shut the door gently and looked again at the massive windowless building that hid itself in the undesirable pocket of town, the low income housing projects in its backyard. Along one side of the building, just beyond the parking lot, barbwire stretched between locust posts. At the building's rear, a cement wall, tattooed with graffiti and sprouting weeds in front, separated DVX's back entrances from a crenellation of shotgun houses and abandoned buildings with busted-out windows and caved-in roofs.

She inhaled, breathing in the smell of cooking somewhere. The air felt good on her face. She walked toward the beige monster, understanding from her previous lab work what she could expect within. In her hand was a fictitious resume. It paid to be nice to people. When, about a month ago, a woman in the parking lot dropped and spilled her grocery bags, Sylvie had helped her, running after vagrant cans of Orange Aid as they rolled under parked cars.

"Girlfriend, you need you a free burger and fries you come see Bodacious Wanda at *Wendy's*! That's me. I'm the manager there and I'll set you up right! I'll see you eat some goodness!" Sylvie had not taken her up on the free burger and fries, but, after telling Carol she'd try for DVX, she had walked into Bodacious Wanda's *Wendy's* and asked for a particular favor.

Sylvie had done her homework and knew where the entrance door was, but she doubted if very many people would find it without prior knowledge.

As she got closer she imagined she could hear the frightened cries that ricocheted throughout the building at night, animals who wailed not so much from the physical pain they endured as from loneliness. But she heard not a sound and she knew that many labs installed soundproof walls so that any unlikely passerby would never hear the sounds of terror which emanated from within. She stopped before the door for just a moment considering if she should proceed with Carol's idea, wondering if she could ever really help, and how her life might change if she got the job.

Then she pushed open the door.

The silence that greeted her seemed at once more ominous than any amount of barking. She tipped her head unconsciously as if trying to hear what she'd expected to hear. But there was only silence.

She stepped forward and let the door shut behind her, observing a front reception desk with a computer, stacks of papers and medical journals. Two chairs against a wall and a small table between them, as if the receptionist might receive visitors and serve tea. Behind the front desk there were swinging doors that Sylvie guessed led back to the bowels of the lab. The strange silence of the front room gathered and she tried to hear evidence of life beyond. But it was deathly quiet. Just as she was straining to hear something, a man burst through the swinging doors carrying in his hand something Sylvie couldn't see. She stood very still, and watched as he foraged through the papers on the desk. She stepped forward and, when she did, he saw her.

"Who are you? What do you want?" He said backing up.

She glanced to his hand and saw syringes. She paused then said, "A job."

"Oh, *ah-hah,*" he coughed not looking directly at her. "I don't think we're hiring. What kind of job? Are you a . . . ?" He stopped, shook his head, looked around the room like he'd forgotten what he was looking for then looked up at her sharply. "We're not hiring. I'm sorry."

She stood where she was. "I really need work," she said, using the slight southern accent she'd used undercover before. "Please. I'll do whatever you need done. Who can I talk to?"

"I'm sorry." He hesitated then turned and, without speaking to her again, headed back through the swinging doors. Sylvie stood there for a moment, more surprised than affronted. The feeling seeping into her was relief. She'd tell Carol she'd tried her best. She was about to leave when she heard a strange noise. She turned at the sound of it, a smacking, flapping noise. A woman was walking from the doors through which the man had just exited. She was looking at Sylvie with brows not so much furrowed as they were pinched and questioning.

"Dr. Donaldson told me to come out. He said someone had come in looking for employment."

"That's right," Sylvie said surprised. "I'm looking for work. I have a resume. Here."

The woman regarded her, and took the resume. Sylvie saw her nails were bitten. She glanced at the resume but Sylvie could tell she didn't read it. "How do you know about us?" She asked, addressing the resume not Sylvie.

"Everybody does, don't they?"

The woman looked up sharply from the resume. She wore a pair of tennis shoes that had seen better days, and had on a white lab coat, unbuttoned over a T-shirt that read: *Lord, give me coffee to do the things I must, and wine to accept the things I cannot.* "No. I would very much doubt if *everyone* does," she said. "What do you know about what we do? And, more to the fact, what can you do?"

Sylvie was staring at her and reading her shirt at the same time. Before she could answer, the woman walked closer to her. "Are you one of those PETA people? Because if you are you can scram right now."

"PETA?" Sylvie repeated while keeping the woman's gaze and attempting a perplexed expression.

"Look, if you think you're going to come in here and free the animals, you're in big trouble. We call the police on people like that. It's a felony." She accentuated the word.

Sylvie looked at her for a beat in time then said evenly, "I'm not fixin' to free them. I can clean their cages out though."

The woman eyed her. "Let me ask you some questions. Of course you know you'll have to go through a formal application process, background check and all that entails." She stared at Sylvie as if trying to stare her down.

"That's all right," Sylvie answered back evenly. "I don't have a record."

"Are you in good shape?"

"Yes."

"Do you have kids?"

"No."

"Do you have scheduling restrictions?" When Sylvie looked blank, the woman said, "Like working weekends or nights."

"I need a job," Sylvie answered, her tone striving for a blend of humility and strength. "I'll do what you need."

"Why don't you begin by telling me what your last job was and why you left it?"

"I worked at *Wendy's.* I'm a good worker and they liked me but I got allergic to the grease smoke. And before that I worked at a packaging store. I packaged parcels, taped up boxes, sent them out."

"What'd they pay you?"

"They paid me good enough."

"Rule number one. Don't get smart or you're out of here. I asked *what* they paid you."

"Eight dollars an hour. Before that I worked stacking carpets. I'm strong."

"Maybe, but it sounds like you've had a lot of jobs. You don't stick them for long, do you? Why'd you leave the packing store?"

"I guess I didn't like it."

"Yes, and if we train you here and you *guess* you don't like it, you going to up and leave and run your big mouth? That just doesn't fly for us here." Her thin zipper lips were like a crooked twig turned down across her face. One wispy brow twitched and her chin jutted out. "We don't need that kind of attitude."

"I won't quit. My situation is different now. I need the work. I'd be grateful to you and stay put."

"Tell me something." Sylvie felt the woman's eyes and tried to relax. "Do you like animals?"

Sylvie considered the question only for a moment. Then she answered, "Yeah, I do."

The woman stared into her eyes. Sylvie looked away.

"I'm sorry, we just don't have any positions right now."

She nodded her head. "Okay. Thank you for coming out to talk with me." She was turning toward the door, when her eyes fell to the computer again. She stopped, turned around and said, "I can type."

"We aren't looking for a typist." But the woman remained standing looking at Sylvie and Sylvie saw the hesitation.

"Look," Sylvie said stepping closer to her. "I need a job. I'm quiet and gentle, I'll be good with the animals. You won't be disappointed."

Silence.

In which Sylvie didn't move.

"All right. I'll tell you what we do need." She looked at Sylvie in a new way. "But first you'll need to fill out some forms. I can't promise you a thing until you do that. Then you'll have to be passed by a committee. Then, maybe. Look, I wouldn't be standing here wasting my time if we weren't incredibly understaffed with a whole lot of mental morons working, and a whole lot of menial stuff falling on *my* shoulders."

"Thank you."

"Don't go thanking me yet. Just come along."

Sylvie followed the woman through the swinging doors, taking quick sideways glances. She realized what the strange sound she'd heard had been. As the woman before her walked, the sole of her tennis shoe, unglued, smacked upon the floor with each step. Sylvie breathed in and out slowly. She smelled the interior air spiced with disinfectant but it was not enough to cover up an acid odor. She heard muffled sounds, but they were human sounds and metal sounds, not animal sounds. No barking dogs or shrieking monkeys. The ominous feeling grew stronger and she imagined demons morphing out of darkened energy, gaining shape and substance until they became poison to the world.

They turned down a hallway and the woman stopped abruptly before a door on the left and opened it.

"Go in and sit."

Sylvie walked forward and was about to sit when she saw a row of cages attached to the walls and eyes staring back at her.

"Don't mind them. We're short on space," the woman answered her startled reaction. Sylvie turned away from the eyes looking back at her and walked to an empty chair on the other side of the desk. The woman rummaged in a filing cabinet then dropped a packet of information and a pen onto Sylvie's lap. "Begin with this. I'll come back in ten minutes." She turned to leave, but stopped. "Remember, this doesn't mean you got the job."

Sylvie nodded. When the door had shut, she watched it for a moment, feeling the room become quiet in a way that disturbed her, for the room was not void of life. When she heard the woman's footsteps retreating down the hall, she rose and walked over to the cages. Nine cages, three rows of three stacked on top of each other. Inside the cages were cats, but only four were looking back at her. There were cats curled in balls or lying in awkward positions facing away from her. One cat appeared to be tranquilized, and it wore a helmet with metal coming from it. She squinted to better understand what was going on with that cat. She heard footsteps outside the door and stepped away quickly, falling into the chair. The footsteps passed. She picked up her packet of information and began to read.

Is a career in laboratory animal science for you? To find out answer these questions:

- *Do you have respect for animals?*
- *Would you enjoy the potential to work with a variety of animal species every day?*
- *Would you like to help save lives by finding cures and treatments for medical diseases?*
- *Would you enjoy discovering new methods to help make your pets healthier?*
- *Do you want to make sure household products are safe?*
- *Do you want the satisfaction of knowing you have a crucial role in the advancement of science?*
- *Are you are reliable and committed to the health and well-being of animals?*

She checked "yes" and flipped the page filling out her fictitious name and education. And when she glanced up toward the cages, one more pair of eyes was watching her. She gazed back into them and this time did not startle. If this was to become her new job, she would have to get a grip. But my God, she'd forgotten what it was like. And maybe that forgetting was nothing more than survival—how people went about daily life, finding joy, even goodness when they knew the homeless lay shivering on cold nights; when they knew across continents thousands were starving, suffering, crying and dying, while the kings and queens played war. She heard the slapping shoes outside the room. The door burst open.

"How are you doing?"

"I'm fine."

"I need to ask you some questions." The woman sat down behind the desk. "Bring your chair chair."

Sylvie scooted her chair over.

"Okay. I'm going to read some things to you and you tell me if you have questions."

"Okay."

"Laboratory animals are used for the regulatory testing to assess the safety, efficacy and/or potential adverse health effects of new chemicals and products such as vaccines, medicines, food additives, pesticides and industrial chemicals." The woman read in a monotone voice then looked up. Sylvie knew she was being studied. Maybe she was in an experiment, herself. Sylvie smiled, the uncontrollable smile of the person told terrible news. Pure reaction.

"Testing results are used for risk assessment, decisions intended to safeguard human and animal health. However, chemical toxicity and vaccine testing can cause injury, disease, and mortality involving significant pain and distress. Alleviation of pain and distress in animals during testing is problematic because regulations allow treatment only if the treatment does not interfere with the study." The woman looked up, again, scrutinizing her just as Sylvie was swallowing and attempting to take a deep breath.

"Are you okay?"

"Yes," she said quickly, nodding her head.

"Are you following what it says? Do you understand what it's saying?"

"Yes."

"Okay, then tell it back to me."

"What you just read?"

"Yes, explain what I just read in layman's terms. I need to know if you really understand."

"Animals are used in testing chemicals, vaccines, and such. And . . ."

"And?"

"And the tests can cause pain, but we're not allowed to alleviate—"

"Actually, *you* are never allowed to alleviate their pain. You just do as you're told. But *correct,* the doctors are not allowed to. Go on."

"The doctors are not allowed to alleviate the animals' pain if this interferes with the experiments and with the test results."

"Good. That's right. We don't want you, or anyone else, to get here and then freak out when you realize the nature of what we do."

"I won't. I'll just do what I'm told."

"Good. Now, some questions. Do you like animals?"

"Yes."

"Have you ever had pets?"

"Yes."

"Have you ever had a pet rabbit?"

"No."

"Do you like rodents?"

"Yes."

The woman looked up. "You do?"

"Yes."

The woman shook her head, but continued. "Have you ever had a pet rat or a pet mouse?"

"No."

There was a knock on the door simultaneous to it opening.

"Sharon? Can we see you a minute?"

"I'll be right there." The door closed. "I sometimes wonder if I'm the only one who works around here," the woman muttered to herself. "You'll learn the doctors are, well they're kind of entitled. They think they're God's gift. Excuse me, but it's true." She stood. "Read this. You tell me honestly if you understand it and if you think you're up for the job. It's not a job that you yak about to your girlfriends either. You know what I'm saying?" She dropped a thick, thirty or forty-page packet onto Sylvie's lap.

"Yes." And with that, Sylvie sat alone with the cats for the second time.

Three packets, one committee—which she assumed meant the helmet-wearing cats because the only human other than herself was the woman—and one interview later, Sylvie left hours later with a job as the person who led each 'specimen' from the kennel to the treatment room. Sounded easy enough.

When she exited the lab, she stretched up her arms to the sky, as if she were the one who'd been cramped in a cage. The day had turned overcast, a hazy gauze unrolled itself covering the sun, leaching light. She drove home, walking up the steps, one, two, three, and opening the door she never locked, even in the bad neighborhood.

"I got the job," she said without emotion into the phone, after calling Carol.

"Sylvie, that's wonderful!" When Sylvie didn't answer, Carol said, "Not so wonderful?"

"I'm exhausted. I feel their distress. And I wonder if I'm making a really big mistake. There were these cages of cats and, never mind, you don't need to know."

"You're exhausted. You feel everybody's pain and distress, you always have. You're afraid you're making a mistake. But, you're a saint."

"No, I'm not. I'm crazy. Listen to this. Can I read you something?"

"Of course you can."

"They gave me this huge packet of cloak and dagger horror to read. Listen. Adverse effects on animals can be caused during such testing from acute and chronic chemical toxicity and by induced infections that occur during vaccine potency testing. Various clinical signs are indicative of a moribund condition in—"

"Stop. We know all that."

"It goes on to say that the total number of animals experiencing severe pain and distress exceeds one million, which I'm sure is a low estimate given that there are hundreds of millions of animals in labs in the U.S. alone, let alone around the world." She stopped. "Carol, the woman was reading it to me and I wanted to laugh. You know sometimes when someone tells you something awful and you can't help smiling? And I had this thought that maybe we're the ones being experimented on."

"Sylvie."

"Maybe all the piercing pain and all the secret sorrow in the world is because some greater beings made of air or something are performing their own experiments on us, and—"

"Sylvie," Carol said drawing out the name slowly. "Have you taken your medication? You sound strange."

"Seriously, how do we know we're not? By some beings from another planet. You know how proponents of animal testing say that the animals don't know any different, well maybe these beings on other planets are saying that about us and we really don't know.

"Sil, take your medication."

"I'm not taking it much anymore."

"What? Do you think that's a good idea?"

"I think I don't need it all the time. I'm okay."

"Well," Carol seemed to consider then said, "You probably need to sleep. You can write your Sci-Fi novel, but right now I think you need to sleep."

"I'd forgotten what it was like. Before when I did it, I was idealistic. I thought I could save the world. But I don't think I can save the world now. I doubt I could save even one dog."

"Do you remember what you said to me once? You said, 'They can feel just like we do.'"

"Carol," Sylvie said in a whisper. "How can I help them? They're stuck there, behind bars, until they die."

There was silence in which neither girl spoke.

"You'll figure something out, Sylvie. You always do."

CHAPTER NINETEEN

David was walking out the police department doors when he saw a sleek red convertible pull up to the curb. A Corvette. He craned his neck to better see through the windshield. The car door opened and Nick hopped out. Startled, David took a few steps back, holding open the door.

"David!" Nick was leaping up the stairs two at a time. "David, my man. Just the person I want to see."

"Really?" David followed Nick, stepping back inside.

"You bet. Got a proposition for you. A good one. You can help your buddy and make some cash too."

"What's that, Nick?"

Just then Nick scowled, and David turned to follow his gaze. Officer Branston Bread, who they all called Slice, was walking toward them.

"Hi, David," Slice said. "Nick," he nodded.

"How's it going, Slice?" David said, turning and smiling. Slice had a shy, but genuine manner, and David appreciated that about him.

"I don't know," Slice said. "Some days better than others, I guess." He hesitated for a few seconds then walked past them.

Once he was gone, Nick leaned toward David and spoke. "I'd stay clear of him, if I were you."

"Slice? He's one of the nicest guys I know," David said, surprised. "And brave, too."

"He's a fuckin' ass-wipe. My grandmother's a better shot than he is."

David stood dumb.

"Look, you want to make some easy dough?"

David hesitated, still considering Nick's odd assessment of Slice.

"David? You awake?"

"Easy dough? Sure, who doesn't?"

"I've got this little Good Samaritan thing going. You'd be great at it because you've got that face everyone trusts. Help me out, make some money," he said again.

"Sure, Nick. I'll help you out."

"Great. Remember my aunt who died?"

"No, not really."

Nick sighed and looked away. "Well, she did. Terrible tragedy. David, you have no idea what I went through and what I'd give to have her back. Truly a tragedy. But the thing is I can't. I can't get her back. I can't ever see her again. I can't ever talk to her again. It's like the irrevocability of death, you know? And none of it should have happened."

David nodded.

"The hardest thing for me to take is the fact that her death could have been prevented if there had been more research available. Cancer, you know. Today there are drugs available to help, but the research is expensive."

"Yeah," David answered, nodding again, wondering where Nick was going with his dead aunt.

"In order to save lives, human lives, laboratories need to test on animals to gain knowledge and find out if drugs are safe, you know what I mean?"

"Sure."

"I wish there'd have been more information for my poor aunt." Nick looked away and David thought he heard a sniff. He didn't remember a thing about Nick's sick aunt, but it had obviously shaken Nick up. He wished he'd been there for Nick at the time of her death. Just then somebody went whistling down the hall and Nick said to David, "Come on, let's go outside."

They stepped outside and David saw small birds pecking at crumbs. The birds scattered, flapping gray wings as the two police moved closer. When David looked back, Nick was looking at him intensely.

"What I do is I go to the animal shelters and take the dogs and cats that nobody wants, see, and I take them to the labs where they're used to test drugs for people. The labs care for the animals. They feed the dogs, give them a place to sleep. These dogs get a chance at life where they would have been killed within days at the shelters, see? It's like they end up martyr dogs, sacrificing their own lives, doing something good for human lives. Maybe they don't know it but they become the unsung heroes."

David nodded.

"It's win-win all the way around." Nick paused. "So if you help me out I can pay you anywhere from $20 to $100 a dog. You bring me ten dogs in one week and you've made yourself a grand. Not a bad deal, huh? Oh, and by the way, I've even bought you a van. Not much of a van," he laughed. "But I bought it for you."

"Are you kidding me?" David found himself saying.

Nick smiled. "No, I am most definitely not kidding you. Are you in then?"

"What about you? How will you get paid?"

"Don't worry about me. I'm trying to help you a little. You know, a buddy thing." He slapped David on the back. "I'm doing it in my aunt's memory."

David smiled. Life was good, and he was part of a special brotherhood. "Thanks Nick. I'd like to be a Good Samaritan. What do I do, go to the shelters?"

"Yes, you go to the shelters. Ask for unadoptable cats and dogs, the ones they're going to kill. And you can also answer ads, you know like, 'free to a good home,' that sort of thing."

"Do I tell them the home is a lab?"

"No. No, David, you just tell them you're taking the dog for yourself. You tell them what a good home you'll give it."

"But—"

"It's a white lie. That's all it is. Just a little white lie for the good of all, see. You're helping give peace of mind to someone who can't care for their dog. They don't really need to know the details, do they? They just need to have the peace of mind that their dog is going somewhere good or maybe doing a good deed for someone. Dogs sacrificing themselves for the greater good."

"Like those dogs that went up into space?" David said remembering how oddly guilty he'd felt as a child when he'd learned about those dogs, thinking how they would die up there alone and confused. "Laika, wasn't it?"

"Yeah, yeah. Like I said, it's win-win from whatever angle you look at it."

"But what if they want to check up on their dog or something?"

"Well, you can't let them now, can you? Just give them a fictitious phone number. Remember David, you're helping a lot of people who would otherwise die. Think of my poor aunt. And you're helping a lot of dogs who would otherwise die. We're the law, David, remember that. And sometimes you must know when and how to, ever so slightly, bend the law for the greatest good for the greatest number of people. John Miller, right?"

David shifted his weight. "I don't know. Let me think on it."

"A thousand bucks or more a week. Wouldn't think there was much to think about." Nick's tone had changed. "Besides, this is not something that's broadcast on national TV, if you know what I mean. Let's see, now that I've confided in you, I'm kind of in a bind. What do you want me to do, go to Andy and ask him and say that you wouldn't do it? I kind of need an answer, now that I've placed my confidence in you."

"It means I have to lie to people and I guess I feel I've spent my whole life trying not to lie, not to steal, you know, that's why we became officers in the first place."

"Is it?" Nick narrowed his eyes like he was trying out for the villain on Broadway. He looked at David and David saw a strange face, like there was an electric current that jumped from eye to eye in the form of a twitch, and the vein on his forehead bulged. Nick turned to the side, but this time David didn't hear him sniff. Instead he watched as Nick spat. He heard the not so quietly hidden curse under Nick's breath and it gave him the feeling he'd had as a child when he'd done something wrong.

"Christ, I should've never told you," Nick said turning back around, his face lowered. "You're no different from that pussy Slice."

"Wait a minute," David said.

Nick looked up.

"Isn't there any other way I could help you out?"

Nick stared. When he spoke again his voice stroked David like a gentle hand coaxing, persistently pushing a young boy toward home plate to bat for his very first time.

"Well, let me see." He rubbed his chin. "Maybe there is, my friend. Well, yes. Yes, there is. Transport. You could cargo the dogs to the labs. That would help me out a lot, and you got the van. And I'd pay you. Of course it wouldn't be the big bucks."

"That's okay. I'll do it. And Nick, I can follow up on some of the ads. It's okay. I'll do it in your aunt's honor."

"Well now, thanks David. You won't regret it."

CHAPTER TWENTY

On her first day Sylvie was given a cursory tour of the lab that made her feel like she was not welcome and that staff didn't want her to know much of what went on except what she was paid to do.

"This is where you'll come to find out who you're leading out," the stout woman who had interviewed her said. Sylvie found out her name was Sharon not because the woman had introduced herself but because she'd overheard the name on the day of her interview.

"Through that door are the mice and rats, but you're not in charge of them. You'll be leading out the canine specimens only."

"And what's that door over there?"

"Don't ask questions. Rule number one."

"Yes, ma'am."

"Here. You'll wear this. And it's up to you to keep it clean. We'll take it out of your first paycheck." She handed Sylvie a white lab coat.

"This is Mike." Sharon introduced her to a guy holding a hose.

"Hi," Sylvie said to the man who nodded at her and looked, with his short-cropped hair, huge frame, and the position in which he pointed the hose it at her, like he'd enjoy blasting her with a jet of cold water. He didn't say hi.

"And this is the door out. You do not use it to enter and leave your workplace. You come in the front, where the secretary's desk is. And the time clock. And don't forget to punch in and out or you won't get paid."

"Is there a secretary? I haven't seen one."

"Did you forget rule number one already? Don't ask questions!"

Right, Sylvie thought to herself. Something up with the secretary.

"This door is for transport. You understand that don't you?"

"Uh. . ."

"Transport means new specimens coming in. We use humane endpoints because we're a contentious facility. We care about the specimens. But that would also mean that we need more specimens more frequently. Get it?"

"Yes." A feeling of unease crawled up the back of her neck.

Sharon unlocked and swung open a large metal door. "The vans will back up here and you'll be expected to lead the specimens into the facility."

"Okay."

"Come with me."

Sylvie followed Sharon down a corridor that seemed narrower than the others, but maybe it was simply the gray walls.

"New specimens all go in the holding cages first." She pointed to more cages and runs. Sylvie saw three dogs, the closest one was shaved underneath its throat.

"Okay."

"Put on the coat. Cleanliness is vitally important around here." She emphasized the word "vitally" but the way she said it made it sound more like an infectious disease. "Now, go to the board, you'll find the slip leads hanging next to it. Look at the list and lead the specimens to the research room where the techs and doctors are waiting for you. They'll do it themselves, sometimes." Sylvie detected contempt. "But usually they're too busy. Anyhow, they don't like to. It's up to you to get the right specimens to them and on time. This is important work that they do. They want accurate results. Things depend on their work and their accurate results."

"Yes, ma'am," Sylvie said.

"Oh, and don't touch them. It's against the rules. Just slip the collars over their heads without any contact. It's for your safety as much as theirs. You don't know what they may have on them."

Sylvie read the list of numbers: 12, 14, 15, 16, 18, 19, 22, 23, 24, 25, 26, and 35.

No names just specimen numbers. The runs were all numbered so this became the easiest way to identify dogs. If dogs were left unnamed workers were less likely to become attached to the animal as a sentient being.

Sharon left and Sylvie was on her own. She walked up to the first run. Behind the wire fencing she saw the dark eyes of a hound staring back at her, watching. Number one. In the next run a cocker spaniel, its coat damp. It shook then walked closer to her sniffing, its nub tail wagging. Number two. Then two beagles. They looked just like somebody's pet Snoopy. Numbers three and four. In the next run was tiny poodle with enormous teats who panted wildly. Number five. Sylvie bent down, looking at her through the metal gate. None of the dogs barked.

"Are you scared?" The tongue curled as she panted and saliva dripped. She heard a noise and turned halfway to see Mike at the end of the hall watching her. She jumped up, and continued walking.

There were three women and one man who cleaned the runs and who were to provide water and food on a regular basis, but Sylvie saw empty water bowls and runs with puddles of urine. Sharon had told her a veterinarian was called if dogs developed severe infections, pain or abscesses.

She continued walking and looking into the runs. Some dogs walked up to her wagging tails. Some scurried to the back corners of their runs. The lab tested, among other things, the effects of acute toxicity poisoning in both human products and animal products. Her job was to fetch and lead each dog from run to research room and back again if the animal was still a viable specimen.

There were some large breed dogs: a Golden Retriever mix, number six. Then two more, a hound mix and a German shepherd, numbers seven and eight. More beagles. She knew that often beagles were bred in the lab. The reason made sense to research. If different breeds and ages of dogs were used in experiments the results could vary greatly. Beagles of the same genealogy were used and highly prized for keeping the research accurate and stable. Beagles were food motivated, which worked well in research facilities where the animals needed to cooperate with staff. Beagles also had easy-going temperaments and were often friendly and social. When such a variety of breeds and sizes were used as they were here, she guessed the experiment needed different gene pools for efficacy.

She stopped before a run and stared at a small, male beagle, who stood trembling. The tail that curled up and under his belly was missing hair in places, like a rattail, and he cowered in the corner and would not look at her. One long impressive stalactite hung from his mouth and on the floor beneath his mouth pooled a puddle of frothy drool. Her mind was churning over a mish-mash of knowledge she thought she'd put behind her. The little hound looked like maybe he had something other than beagle mixed in, though the face was clearly beagle. Large, fear-rimmed eyes cast a surreptitious, darting glance up to her then quickly away. Looking beyond his fear, she saw a brown face with a white stripe down it. He had a black back with brown sides, and three white feet. On the scrawny tail pressed to his belly there was a prominent white tip. Number 11. She felt a dull ache in the area around her heart.

Number twelve was lying down when she approached. She unlatched the gate and stood for an instance the way she'd been taught. Sharon told her that some dogs snapped and lunged at the handlers. She spoke softly and gently.

Number 12 was a large mixed-breed with tufts of cream-colored fur that curled softly reminding her of a large lamb. Number 12 lay on the concrete, and as Sylvie entered, she turned her head. Sylvie stood quietly, beholding the large, female dog and as she did she felt something test her resolve. Perhaps wondering what she was doing, the dog rolled her brown eyes up to meet Sylvie's own. There, deep within the eyes, Sylvie thought she saw a question. Maybe the dog was not timid, just gentle. There in the eyes, coexisting with confusion, was also wisdom. And there, perhaps unfairly, was a knowing. Sylvie had an eerie feeling that this dog knew her fate and that she wanted to die.

"Hi, big girl. You're very beautiful. Okay if I call you blue-curls, like the flower?" She spoke quietly and advanced forward two steps. The dog then shifted her weight and pushed up from the hips, her forepaws bent and it was then that Sylvie saw she was old. As Sylvie approached, the dog rose to a standing position. Sylvie wondered how long the old dog had lived in the concrete run. She slipped on the leash, but not before first breaking the rules and stroking the cream head and neck. Then as her fingers gently massaged around her neck Sylvie suddenly jerked her hand away like she'd been burned.

"What was that?" she asked the big dog.

Her fingers had felt something sharp and wiry. She let them again touch the dog's throat and she saw that it was only stitches.

"Come on, there you go," she said softy, leading the dog and pushing away her thoughts, walling up her heart.

One of the run cleaners, a girl named Swenson, was walking brusquely by. She had a sullen swagger but Sylvie knew it was best if she befriended as many workers as she could, without raising suspicion. Sylvie turned around to her just as she was passing.

"They don't," she began. "Any of them, bark." A statement, really, to which the woman with the cold, angry eyes squinting back at her could have easily ignored.

Damp, lanky bangs covered her forehead. "Yeah? What do you care? It's a damn good thing." She had met two of the cleaners, Kate and Swenson, and the impression that they needed the money and would do anything for a quick dollar took shape in her mind. One conversation, or verbal exchange, was enough for her to realize they cared little for the dogs in the runs, viewing them as obstacles to their own happiness.

After 12, she retrieved 14, 15, 16 and 18. Then 22 and 23. It was late in the day when a tech approached her and asked her to lead 12 back. Sylvie did and the old dog plodded along quietly beside her, not resisting at all. Sylvie opened the door, walking the dog forward.

"Did it go okay?" She asked number 12 conversationally. The old dog dropped to the floor, resting noble head between front paws. Sylvie exited silently and peered in at number 11.

She was under no circumstances to go into the runs unless the specimen was marked on the board, but she looked up and down the hallway and when she saw no one, she entered. Number eleven didn't at first look at her, but when she dropped to his level she saw his eyes dart once her way. She crouch-hopped over to him. He was trembling as hard as when she first observed him, and she knew he could bite out of pain or fear. Perhaps because of his downtrodden manner, she persisted.

"Hey, little guy." She held out her hand for him to sniff, but he did not. She heard a noise and turned her head. The sound was like someone in the distance crying: a harsh, fricative, almost human sound. But the sound was coming from number 11. His head hung and his sides expanded every time he made the noise, a whispered, whining, squeaking noise like someone creaking open a door.

She inched her hand toward his back. He didn't move but kept up a low-pitched version of the sound. She touched him, stroking his back. He didn't flinch. His coat was damp from water or perhaps something else and in his eyes there was the look she'd seen before. She heard a door open and close, and she got to her feet and slipped out of his run. She glanced back at him, but she had to keep moving.

When she had finished, her back ached and her head throbbed. She walked outside into the fresh air. The sun was sinking, less than five minutes above the horizon.

Once home, she fell onto her sofa and called Carol. Carol answered on the fifth ring.

"Sallie and Petey weren't in there," she said to Carol. "Can I quit?" She heard yelling in the background.

"Hold on a minute, Sil."

Sylvie looked at her clock. She'd be getting up to go back to that place in twelve hours.

"Sorry," Carol said. "It's a zoo over here. Matt's sister and kids. Be glad you live alone."

"Yeah, be glad you have people around you. It feels a shade too shadowy. Just a bit. . ." She searched for the word. "Lonely" wasn't it, but she couldn't place the emotion newly snaking its way around her.

"You don't sound like yourself."

"I'm okay."

"Sylvie, thank you. I guess I should feel relieved they're not there. But it only means that now I have to go to Nick Drakas's house."

"Then I'm coming, too."

CHAPTER TWENTY-ONE

On her fifth day working at DVX, Sylvie walked to the board with the list of numbers. Out of the four doctors that she'd seen or met, only one acknowledged her, the rest ignoring her as if she were one of the animals on which they experimented, no more than an ambulatory bit of flesh to assist in various research projects. It was the big money pharmaceutical companies who funded the research, and she was well-versed in the controversy surrounding any accuracy of using animals to test human products. She wondered if the researchers were.

Animals were different enough from humans to render many results inaccurate; humans could die as a result of animal testing. And yet, she thought, animals were enough like humans, sentient beings with equal, or arguably higher, emotional intelligence to make animal experimentation morally wrong. These thoughts, however, she kept to herself. It seemed so obvious to her, and if any of the researchers felt a twinge of conscience, they didn't show it. She assumed they believed in the rightness of what they did, just as she believed in what she was doing—lying, breaking the law. At least she hadn't stolen or murdered.

She read the numbers and walked toward the runs where the specimens lived out their days. As she approached she felt as though she could hear the gathered thoughts of each animal. Maybe it was only her own. She'd read that many of the dogs took on neurotic behaviors such as incessant spinning in circles or rocking back and forth. Some of them pulled out their hair or bit their own flesh from physical discomfort or psychological anguish. She saw none of that here.

Her first dog was number 2. She glanced up and down the hall and when she saw no one around, she walked passed 2, taking her time, stopping before each run to speak softly to the dogs within, her nose wrinkling at the harsh, anthropic chemical smell. Some of the dogs just watched her. Some came up to her perhaps seeking food, those who'd been bred in the lab and knew no other life. She was walking and stopping, walking and whispering words of encouragement, when she came to number 11. She leaned her face against the metal links. He stood pressed against the far wall, his complete inanition reaching her like a greater aura.

"Hey, little bit," she said in an uplifted voice. She wanted him to turn his head toward her and look. She felt somehow if he did, he'd be okay. But he didn't, and she had to keep moving.

"Hey, pretty girl," Sylvie called to number 12 through the gate. Number 12 did not raise her head. Something was wrong. She reached to her back pocket for her phone to snap a picture, but stopped. She couldn't bring herself to do it. Again, she glanced over her shoulder then opened the gate. She heard voices down the hall and froze. The voices faded and she stepped forward kneeling down.

"Hey, sweet girl." She lay a hand gently on the big dog and felt her side moving with each breath. But apart from that she lay still. Sylvie jumped up, ready to run for help. Then stopped. She leaned down and kissed the top of number 12's head, stroking her soft, wavy fur.

"I love you, you big beautiful dog." She knew her words were not helping the dog, only herself, but she wanted the dog to feel someone had loved her, at least once in her lifetime. The feeling again visited her—this dog was asking to die. She exited the run, and walked back to where the numbers hung, feeling her heart was being torn from her. Number 12 was not on the list. "Damn it," she said to herself.

Where was the veterinarian? She was standing debating what to do when Swenson walked up behind her.

"Hey, new girl. Sharon said for you to dump this." She held two buckets filled with excrement.

"Sharon asked me to?"

A snort. "You too good?"

"No. Where do I . . ." Sylvie began.

"Go out that little door there."

Sylvie held out her hands to take the poop buckets from Swenson, the odor wafting its way up to her nostrils. She walked to the little door Swenson pointed to, feeling wary. Above the door the read lettering said, "Emergency Exit Only."

She pushed the handle and a blaring alarm went off in her ear. The noise startled her so that she dropped the buckets, nearly spilling feces over the edge. She turned around and saw Swenson and Kate laughing.

Then there came footsteps running, and voices calling. Calling and running and coming toward her as if out from crevices in the lab. Swenson swooped by and grab the buckets. "Little drama breaks up the boredom," she said as she brushed against Sylvie and retreated. Then Sharon was walking toward her, and Sylvie didn't like the set of her face.

"What do you think you're doing?" Sharon yelled. "Did I tell you to open that door? No! You are never to open that door! Do you hear?"

"Yes," Sylvie answered. Behind Sharon, Sylvie saw Swenson watching her.

"You pull a stunt like that again, and you're outta here. Now go! They're waiting in the treatment room."

"Sharon, I—"

"*What?*"

"I was on my way to get a dog when I saw that number 12 was really sick."

Sharon's frown darkened. "I'm sure 12 is fine. Get the specimen you're supposed to get and don't keep them waiting!"

Sylvie didn't move. She knew she could lose the job but she spoke the words anyway. "She's really sick."

"For God's sake. How would you know?"

"Because. . . I don't know how I know. I just know. She needs a vet now."

"Yeah? You just know? You and God, right? Well, we're going to get something straight, right now. *That* is not your call to make. That is not your job. The specimen will be *fine*."

Sylvie felt her insides quiver, tighten then spill like punctured sausage casing, a thin membrane vainly trying to hold in all that wept and anguished. If she pleaded with Sharon, she'd put her cover in jeopardy, and then what? Could she forsake the life of one for the welfare of many? And just how was she helping any of them? Her heart argued against her mind in a combat of wills that went on silently. Before she knew what she was doing, the word was leaving her mouth. One word, but it was enough. "Please."

"You cannot get attached to the specimens. I had a bad feeling about you when I first laid eyes on you."

Sylvie took a step backwards, thinking quickly. "Sharon, number 12 is on my list," she lied. "And if I can't get her to stand up, what do I do? That's why I wondered if you could just send a vet in there. That's all. I'm going to get number 2 now." She turned and walked backed to number 2, eyes on the ugly floor, not looking in any of the runs, aware that Sharon was watching her. But as she passed number 12 she could see out of the corner of her eye the dog had not moved.

It took her two hours to work her way through the list. She stood dumbly staring in at number 11 as he cowered against the far wall, his pathetic white-tipped tail perpetually flattened against his tummy. She could do nothing to alleviate his misery. She felt only slight relief that he was not on the board today. He needed a break. Out of all of the dogs, he looked the most wretched.

She glanced at number 12 and immediately sensed a difference. She entered but knew before she lay a hand on her curly lamb-like coat that the life inside had gone. She knelt, squeezing her eyes shut.

"Beautiful, blue-curls. Your life was not in vain. I saw you. And I'll work in your honor." She stroked the big dog's head. Then relief hit her like a physical force, for death was preferable.

She wiped at her eyes and went to find Sharon. She had to knock on what she called the "cat room" door, the room where she had first sat to fill out her application. From behind the door she heard, "It's open!"

She cracked the door and stood in the doorway.

"No! You have got to be kidding me. But why am I not surprised? Can we get something real straight here? This is not the standard for someone in your position. I mean, hello, I have work to do."

"I'm sorry. Number 12 is dead. Just want to know what I need to do." She spoke dispassionately and was aware that Sharon was regarding her differently.

"Oh." Sharon flicked imaginary dust from her sleeve. "Well, if you can lift it, take it to the freezer."

"I haven't been to the freezer."

Impressive sigh. "Come on, I'll show you. Is 12 large or small?"

"Large."

Sylvie gathered her strength to walk back to number 12's run. Sharon came behind her, rolling a wheelbarrow, her shoe slapping. Sylvie expected they'd wrap number 12 in some kind of large trash bag, but they did not. They lifted together, and as Sharon rolled the dog down the hall in the wheelbarrow, Sylvie wondered how much the others knew when they watched.

They turned a sharp right corner and Sylvie saw a large silver walk-in freezer that rose from the ground nearly to the ceiling. Sharon pulled open the lever and the smell that hit them at once was not that of rotting carcasses but a simultaneous harsh and sugary disinfectant. It burned up into Sylvie's nostrils causing her eyes to tear, for which she was grateful. Because in the next moment as she and Sharon heaved the body of number 12 up onto the stack of dogs, Sylvie cried out.

"What's the matter with you?" Sharon asked.

"It stings my eyes."

"Get used to it."

"Okay, I will," Sylvie answered because she could not tell Sharon that there in the stack of dead specimens she had seen the bodies of her two friends. Sallie and Petey.

CHAPTER TWENTY-TWO

It was harder than he thought. Telling the old couple his name was something other than it was, and in so doing, making him feel like someone other than he was. He remembered their faces as he led out their dog, the old man thanking him.

"Thank you, Frank. This means more to us than we can say."

"You'll take good care of him forever?" The woman asked. David smiled at her but he couldn't answer. "He'll love you forever," she was saying now somewhat feverishly. "And if anything happens, you call us, Frank. Don't hesitate to call us. And you'll call with updates, won't you?" Her voice desperate.

"Millie, that's enough. Buddy's in good, capable hands." Her husband put an arm around her shoulders and tried to steer her away from watching the Labrador walk from their house for the last time.

"Goodbye, Buddy!" the old woman was calling. "Be a good boy for Frank!"

He wanted to drive away quickly, from the house, the woman and most of all from the name Frank.

He remembered Nick leaning into the van yesterday, and tapping the steering wheel. "Never answer questions. You ask them."

"Right."

"There's a good man. Can't thank you enough."

"Anytime, Nick."

"And, uh, David?"

"Yes?"

"You need to pick an alias. Don't use your name."

"What?"

"Yeah. Just common sense, is all. You don't want to use your own name."

"Why? You didn't tell me—"

"Sorry, I thought I did. But let's just say it's best not to mix up our police line of duty with something extraneous." He'd patted David's arm.

Nick paid him for each dog he collected and he picked up three more dogs. Then he drove to DVX laboratories. He glanced back to the four different dogs in their crates in the back. Maybe he could ask about getting updates on them, like that poor lady said. Come by and see them, give them treats. The people in the lab might be pleased if someone cared about what became of the dogs.

Two blocks over behind DVX sat a derelict neighborhood, home to drug deals, busts and murders. Shoot 'Em Up Alley the cops called it both because of the needles and the murders. He knew the neighborhood well only by hearsay. No cop wanted to take a call in this part of town and they avoided it except when they had to. He drove around looking for the back entrance and when he couldn't find it, he parked and walked around the building. It was three in the afternoon and he glanced over his shoulder through the Ailanthus and shrubs to Shoot 'Em Up Alley, all of a sudden grateful to Nick for this extra bit of work and cash that took him to the laboratory and not to the back alley. He found the door Nick described and headed back to his van, peering in at the dogs and feeling discomfort in his stomach as he did. Several pairs of eyes watched him through the holes in the crates.

He backed his van up to the metal door as he'd been instructed, got out and knocked. When no one answered the door he frowned and banged against it, harder. Still no one. He was getting back into the van to drive around to the front when the door opened and he saw her for the first time.

"Next time ring the bell," was what she said to him. "You've brought dogs." More statement than question.

"Yes, it's my first time transporting. I'm not sure how it works."

"Unload them one at a time and I'll lead them in." She walked out to the van and looked in at the dogs. "Can you open the door?"

When he unlocked the side door, and slid it back, she slipped in and he watched her let each dog sniff her. When they had, she stroked them. He saw her make an expression he couldn't interpret and he wondered if he'd done something wrong. He didn't want Nick on his case with the first shipment.

"Your first time," she said and glanced in his direction.

"Yes." He stopped, uncertain what Nick would want him to say. "I'm doing it for a good friend of mine," he finished.

"Right." Her hand in the crate rubbing the ears of one of the dogs. "I'll be right back. Go ahead and take off their collars," she said and he watched her walk back through the metal door, straight shoulders and back beneath a white lab coat that hung down over brown jeans. She seemed a contradiction for although she moved with a brisk and confident step he had a feeling even then that she would keep to herself.

When she came back she had a leash. "I'll take them one at a time if you don't mind waiting."

"I don't. I'd be happy to wait all day if you want." He smiled. His eyes were on her as she opened the crate doors and continued interacting with each of the dogs. Two small ones. One medium-sized. And Buddy, the Labrador. He watched as she took her time, talking to each one, reaching in for a small dog, carefully lifting and speaking to it, then stroking it in her arms. He felt a confusing emotion then. She didn't look his way or speak to him the whole time. She only concerned herself with the dogs so he didn't ask questions, and tried to think how to make himself useful.

"Where did you get these dogs?" she asked, when she'd led all of the smaller dogs into the building and returned for the last dog.

He stared. "Where?"

"Yes," she answered standing directly before him and looking him up and down. "Where did you get them?"

"Oh, where! Let's see, I got them from the shelter. They were the ones no one wanted and were going to be—"

"I know," she cut him off. "Which shelter?"

"Um . . ." She was looking at him, waiting. "Like I said, I'm new at this. I don't really remember."

There was a pause in which he understood she knew he was lying. She stepped around him and wedged her hip up into the van and slipped the lead though the door of the crate, and over Buddy's head. He watched her lay a hand on the dog and gently stroke its fur. "*Hey there, big guy.*" He heard her say the words to the dog and then say something else, but her head was in the crate and she was speaking softly. Then to him, over her shoulder she said, "You just came from there and you don't remember?" But it didn't sound like an accusation, merely disbelief. And that's when he said it.

"Look, maybe they didn't come from the shelter, okay. But I can't tell you. Not now at least. If I told you, you'd have to promise me—"

She ducked her head out from the crate, and smiled at him for the first time. "You would not believe how good I am at keeping promises." When she smiled her gray eyes lit up like the windows in a house at Christmas. He noticed a dimple indented on each smiling cheek. His body tingled as she looked into his eyes.

She slipped out of the van and was several inches from him, regarding him in a way he could feel in his stomach. Already he trusted her. "I could get in really big trouble."

"I understand." The words were spoken kindly. She steppe closer and gently laid a hand on his arm.

He was swimming in a sea of warm joy. Without waiting for his courage to fade he blurted: "Would you have dinner with me?" As soon as the words were out, his face flushed from the top of his hairline to his throat.

"What?"

"It's just that I can't talk about it here."

"Then give me your number."

He stood staring at her, his heart hammering his chest, waiting for her to pull forth a phone or something. When she didn't move, he grabbed a pen from the glove box, wrote down his number on the only clean corner of a used napkin and handed it to her.

"Name?" She was smiling again, and looking into his eyes.

"David. David Sampson."

"Thanks, David. I'll call you."

"I'm sorry, what's your name?"

"I'm—" She stopped. And he waited, sensing something had just upset her. "Sylvia Jane. I go by both, but call me Sylvie." She hoisted big black Buddy into her arms, like he was a Chihuahua not a Labrador weighing seventy pounds, and set him onto the pavement. Then she was leading him through the doors to the lab, and he wondered how she'd ended up with a job like that.

TER TWENTY-THREE

It was late on a day of many animal surrenders and only one adoption that Carol lifted the ringing phone and heard Sylvie's voice. She listened, feeling the tears pushing to squeeze out her eyes and down her cheeks, their stain upon her face like the billboards shouting outrage against war or any horrific practice, but at the same time she felt something become dead inside of her, whether from anger or despair she didn't take time to figure out. But the deadness was what caused her not to cry. She only said into the phone:

"Are you sure it was them?"

"I'm sure." There was a pause as if Sylvie was waiting for Carol to react to the news. When she didn't Sylvie filled the silence. "I'm sure. I wasn't going to tell you. I've waited three days. But then part of the reason I'm at DVX is to catch Nick Drakas in the act, if he's doing what you think he is. So, you needed to know." She paused again and then the words spilled out: "But what does it matter if it's them or some other dogs? I no longer know why I'm doing this."

"It matters that Nick Drakas is a liar and a crook, and who knows how many other dogs dropped off at shelters are being taken to labs? I'll tell Donna tomorrow." Her voice quivered.

"I know I could blow my cover if I quit, but it feels harder this time."

"I understand if you can't. I won't push you to do something we both know I could never do. What is your gut saying?"

"I don't know. I don't know anything except sometimes it feels like this world is only about suffering, and where is the good or even the lesson in that? I watched this big, beautiful dog die. Gentle and curly as a lamb. I thought I'd blocked that kind of pain away somewhere, so I could get on with life. And then Petey and Sallie . . . ."

"I'm so sorry you had to see, Sil."

"And then this guy came by with four dogs. He said it was his first transport. I don't know if he was telling me the truth or not, but he seemed somehow sweet or innocent, or something. Maybe just stupid and doing it for the money. I asked him where he was getting his dogs and first he said from the shelter. When I asked him which one, he said he didn't know."

"He's lying."

"No kidding. He flustered all up then he said he didn't get them from the shelter but he couldn't tell me where right then. He asked me out to dinner and gave me his phone number."

"Sylvie, that's what we've wanted. Can you find out more? Who's he work for? Is he coming back? Cuddle up to him, Sylvie. Make him trust you. Do—"

"Would you *stop*? I don't have to cuddle up to some creepy crawler who transports dogs."

"Okay, okay, I'm sorry."

"I mean—"

"I know. You're right. I'm sorry," Carol said.

"It's okay. I'm just—"

"I know."

"It's okay," Sylvie said again.

"You want to know what I think?" Carol asked.

"Not particularly."

"I think that you don't give guys half a chance."

Sylvie laughed.

"And you don't allow yourself any fun, like you think you need to be punished or something. You're the best person I know, Sylvie. So you missed out on childhood, so did a lot of people. You're not responsible for the world's problems. And you just said this guy was cute and sweet." Carol squinted her eyes when she said it as if Sylvie might hit her through the phone line.

"I did?"

She stopped squinting. "Something like that, didn't you?"

"He was kind of cute."

"Look, I'd do it in your shoes if I wasn't married to the greatest guy on earth."

"I know you would. And I know Matt is the greatest guy on earth, and you deserve every bit of that."

"You're the best friend a girl could ever have. Matt's at the doctor's today. He's had this pain in his abdomen. I'm sure it's nothing, but I finally got him to go and check it out."

"Let me know. I'll try to get a photo of Petey and Sallie."

"Good. And think about going out with Mr. Cutie Pie."

"I'll think about it. I'll tell you where we go in case he's a serial killer. I guess it can't hurt."

"I love you, Sil. You're a saint. And you know those three miracles you're always going on about? You're the biggest one."

The next day Sylvie felt no more like a miracle or a saint than Stalin, as she entered each dog's damp and stinky run, looping the choke lead around necks and tugging dogs down the hall to be injected with chemicals.

Looking in to number 12's run, she saw a new dog, another beagle, and she wondered how easily it could smell and sense the previous life and death. When she got to number 11, she gasped. Something close to panic twisted in her stomach. There he was like before against the wall, standing up, but shaking so violently she thought he was seizing. He was turned in the other direction and she saw what she hadn't seen before. His side was one massive burn—red, raw skin in a rectangle six inches long. She entered and he cowered at her approach, crouching lower as though he could escape her.

"If I could take away your pain," she began but didn't finish and she squatted next to him, reaching into her jeans pocket.

"Here, try this." She held out a piece of chicken she'd snuck, but he turned his head away from her. "No wonder you're so thin, if you don't eat," she teased, but she wanted to wrap her arms around him and take him away from his pain. "You're just a little weed," she continued. "Scrawny and thin. Not a beautiful flower, a scrawny little weed. But that's okay. You don't have to be beautiful for me to love you. But, you do need to eat." The scrawny weed emitted the smallest whimper. It sounded to her like a last cry for help. And she thought to herself, maybe it was best if he didn't eat. "A hunger strike. I see." This time she reached to touch him. "I can understand why."

He wheezed.

"*Weedy,*" she whispered. "Weedy, I love you. I know you're going to die." She moved to slip the lead over his head. "And I love you all the more."

She was leading number 11 down the hall, when something caught her attention. Behind a door next to the supply room, a door through which she'd never entered, she heard voices. Somebody whispering and somebody speaking normally. She heard distinctly a harsh, "*Hush!*"

She stopped and stood still before the closed door, Weedy beside her. She cocked her head.

"*You're really going to stand there and tell me it's about saving lives?*

Yes.

And nothing to do with fame or financial rewards that might accompany research success?

Oh, come on! No!

And how driven are these very same people by the need to bring funding dollars to their research institution?

No, they may be driven to find a solution but...."

Sylvie heard the door to the research room open down the hall. A doctor stood in the doorway. She walked toward her, leading Weedy.

That night she called Carol, as much to report the events as to keep her sanity.

"Tell me again why I'm doing this?"

"We can help. We need to raise awareness. People have no idea what's going on."

She told Carol about the odd conversation she'd heard behind the door, but Carol didn't seem to care. She seemed distracted, and Sylvie stopped trying to paint the picture for her.

"You're going to get photos, and we can help end suffering to millions of animals," Carol was saying to her. "And save humans too. Remember Vioxx which was tested in both rats and dogs, and caused more than 130,000 heart attacks?"

"Speaking of drugs and hospitals, how's Matt?"

"We're waiting for the results. Thanks for asking. How are you?"

"Okay. Weedy, the little beagle I love, wouldn't eat a nice piece of free-range chicken."

"A beagle that won't eat."

"He's in pain. He has a burn the size of a football on his side. All bloody and raw. And then he lies down on the wet cement. I go to sleep at night thinking how it must sting. I can't get him out of my mind."

"Sylvie, wait a minute."

"Okay, not quite the size of a football."

"Sylvie."

"What?"

"You said 'Weedy'."

"Yeah, the name just came to me. He's scrawny and pathetic like a little weed. Not a beautiful flower. Not that any of them in there have a chance at being flourishing flowers, but—"

"Sylvie," Carol cut her off. "You cannot name them. You'll just make it that much harder for yourself."

They said goodbye and hung up. And to the approaching night Sylvie said, "It's already hard."

CHAPTER TWENTY-FOUR

The phone was ringing, a jangling noise that jarred him. For as long as he could remember he had lived his life waiting for a certain phone call, at first tormented. As he grew to be a man, he worried still, dreading the call. But the call never came. Still, he waited. He'd prepared himself, speaking to his captors in his mind, defending his actions. He dared not believe the call would be put on perpetual hold and even began to think his true punishment lay in eternal wait.

He stood up from the leather couch, and stretched his arms over his head. He advanced toward the ringing, and looked to the caller I.D. without recognition.

"Hi, David. It's Sylvie."

Relief fluttered within him like a louvered blind opening to light.

"Hi!" He said with the excitement of newness, not caring about playing it cool with her.

"Do you want to meet me and talk?"

"Yes. Where and when?"

"I volunteer over at the shelter, walk out the dogs for a friend who works there."

"Okay." His mouth dropped its smile.

"But sometimes I just go to the coffee shop." She laughed, and the laugh was lighter fluid to the embers of his desire. "And sit outside with the dogs to get them acclimated to people. How about you meet me there. Next Thursday, twelve o'clock. Jo's Coffee."

"Jo's? I know it well." Smiling again. "I'll be there."

She was seated when he arrived. He saw she had already ordered and was sipping from a cup of something, holding it between her hands. Soft light filled the terrace of the coffee shop. Around her at other tables, young people stared at computer screens or phones. There was the clink of cups touching saucers, the clicking of fingers across keyboards. When he approached her table from the side she didn't look up, although the dog with her raised its nose to the air and he wished he could recognize the breed, but he couldn't and he didn't know much about dogs and therefore didn't know how to act around them.

"How's the lab work going?"

She looked over slowly, the way people did who weren't certain they were being addressed, and glanced up.

"Oh, hi. Sit down." His self-esteem withered a little, thinking she sounded less than thrilled he'd shown up, but she scooted her chair over to give him room at the table.

He pulled a white plastic chair out from its wedged position under the table and sat next to her. His large body scrunched uneasily sitting in the flimsy chair and he coiled up his legs and heavy black boots sideways to avoid kicking her dog.

"Hello," he addressed what he thought of as a rather ugly dog. "What's his name?"

"Her name is Lilac."

"Lilac?"

"Yup, isn't she the cutest little thing? Pretty like a lilac."

He smiled reaching under the table to pet the cutest little thing who curled her lip when he stuck his hand down. Even though he didn't know dogs, he knew enough to know people loved to talk about their animals. Just then the waitress walked up to their table and he ordered a coffee. Sylvie glanced up at her.

"So tell me about Lilac," he said.

She regarded him for a bit of time, as if sizing him up, perhaps deciding which version to give him, how much energy to expend on him.

"I wonder how often dogs save people in awkward aardvarkian situations."

"What?" he asked, leaning closer as if proximity could help him decipher the message that seemed to come from other planetary realms.

"She's been at the shelter five weeks."

He knew he'd received the short straw, but something made him persist. "Is that long for a dog there?"

"Are you kidding? Some shelters euthanize after three to five days. No one's even looked at her."

He knew why no one had looked at Lilac. She looked like a nocturnal rodent some creature had unearthed, eaten then regurgitated. But he kept that to himself.

"So, what do you do with her?"

"I try to take her, and all the ones like her, out and get them used to people. So many just need a chance. She's not nearly as frightened as she was."

David made an appropriate noise, but she seemed not to want his admiration and continued as though not hearing. "When I first started volunteering she wouldn't look at me. She just huddled against a far wall. Reminds me of—" She stopped.

"Of what?" he asked, but she didn't answer. She was watching the sidewalk and the road before her, not looking at him, and he took the opportunity to study her. Her worn out jeans, old sweatshirt, scuffed clogs. She didn't look rich, but her skin and hair were neat and clean, and she had an aura, a kind of glow that he associated with good health and clean living. Her hair, the color of morning wheat, was pulled back in a short ponytail. She had eyes that reminded him of his mother's pewter, polished, clean and clear. And lips, sweet lips, he kept glancing to when she spoke.

Still looking away, she said, “We have to get them socialized, friendly with people, because if not . . .”

“They kill her.”

She turned to him then.

“I mean . . . euthanize. Sorry.”

“She’s safe. It’s a no kill shelter, fortunately. But . . .”

Again she didn’t finish and he sensed something important. He repeated her word, “But?”

“But if we don’t adopt out, we can’t take in any more. If Lilac doesn’t find a home, then there’s no room for new ones coming in. Then those ones are, as you say, killed.”

He nodded ardently as if this was important. Never having thought about the workings of an animal shelter before, it was a foreign language to him. He noticed she did not invite conversation from him, unless it was to talk about the dogs. Yet he sensed a kindness and he realized, it was this that drew him to her first at the lab. “We take in dogs from Animal Control, but they have no choice but to euthanize when they become full.”

“So either way. . . .”

“Yes.”

David looked at little Lilac who he now found a bit more comely and who now lay her head across Sylvie’s brown clog, and he was filled by a sudden sense of love and devotion. Not for Lilac. But he wanted Sylvie to lay her head against his shoulder. He would tend to her every need.

“So what kind is she?”

“A mutt.” She smiled and the smile zinged right through him, as he relived the feeling from the DVX parking lot.

“Why don’t you take her?” He offered, amazed that any words came out at all.

This time she really looked at him, and he wondered what kind of faux pas he’d made.

"You're absolutely right. I should take her. Let's see, I work, and I guess I've always felt it'd be unfair to leave a dog in a little apartment all alone."

"You live alone then?"

"I really should adopt twenty from the shelter and then at least they'd all have each other. You have no idea how many there are, just in our shelter alone." She nodded her head across the street in a way that made him wonder if the shelter was around the corner. "I could though, couldn't I? Fill the vacant part of the house with twenty dogs. Turn it into a sanctuary." She turned to him. "What a great idea."

He listened intrigued, wanting and needing to know everything about her, everything she ever was or saw—a feeling akin to longing to rifle through her coat pockets. What does this ticket stub mean? With whom did she sit down beside? What does she read? Where does she go? What time does she go to bed? What does she think about and believe in? And what are her greatest fears and joys?

"Uh, would you like more coffee?" he asked.

"I'm fine."

There was a silence that she didn't seem to mind or even notice. He was raking his brain for interesting threads, wondering if he should reach down to Lilac again and talk about her, but he felt he'd somewhat exhausted Lilac.

When he glanced at her, he saw she was looking out toward the street again. He rotated his head but observed nothing of interest, only cars driving back and forth in both directions. He noticed a squirrel begin to dart forward into the traffic then turn around and scurry back up a huge tree with branches outstretched like beckoning arms. He longed to engage her in heartfelt conversation. Share his soul and all his childhood sorrows. Leaves blew, curled and brown, from the tree, settling on the sidewalk. He cleared his throat.

"Where do you live?"

"What?" she said.

Just then a car screeched on its brakes in front of them so loudly David jumped. His hand flew automatically to where his gun would be. A motorist was shaking his fist and cursing out the car window. David heard someone behind their table mutter, "*Chillax.*" David glanced to Sylvie, wanting to comfort her by touching her. She had reached down and was stroking Lilac who, now standing, visibly trembled.

He shook his head. "Stupid people don't know how to drive."

But Sylvie made no attempt to comment and silence again reigned.

"So, do you like work at the lab? Have you been doing it a long time?"

Her hands were still under the table, on either side of the dog, soothing her. She didn't answer him right away, but when Lilac settled and was lying again this time on her other shoe, she turned and looked at him evenly. "I should probably tell you that I'm not a fan of small talk."

He felt the flush to his face. "Oh. Yes, silence is golden, sorry, well. . ." There was a pause in which he waited for her to say something. When she didn't, he continued, unable to keep the golden silence. "It just seems odd, you liking animals and working somewhere like the lab."

She seemed to be examining something on the table when she spoke. "Does it? Why would you think it odd if I liked animals?"

"Just that I've heard they're not that kind to the animals."

"Then why are you transporting them to a place that will be unkind?"

Considerable pause. "I just did it to help a friend."

"Where are you getting them from?"

"Different places."

"Where?"

"I know that—"

"What?"

"My friend. I know he's gotten them from the shelter."

"And you?"

"I can't tell you here, we're in a public place."

"Oh, come *on.* Whisper it then."

"Come to my house. I'll cook you a meal. I'll tell you then." She didn't speak, and she shifted away from him. "I promise I'll tell you."

"I met you here today so you'd tell me." Her tone had gone glacial.

"I'll tell you. I will. I give you my word."

"Why should I believe you?"

"Because you can," David said, struggling with what to say. "Just trust me."

"I don't know you. For all I know you could be a serial killer."

"Well, I'm not."

"How do I know?"

"Because. . . I'm a police officer."

She turned to him. "You're a *cop*?"

He opened his wallet and presented his badge. At the next table, a young man with tattoos and hair pulled up in a man bun looked at the proffered badge then at David.

Sylvie stared at it then glanced quickly away. "I had no idea." After a pause, she said, "I'm sorry, but most cops I know are the last people I'd trust."

"Do you know many police officers?"

"No."

"Then you shouldn't judge all cops. I became a police officer to make the world a better place. Safer."

"You're a cop and you're breaking the law."

"What? No, I'm not."

"What you're doing is illegal. Not to mention despicable." Before he could defend his actions against her accusation, she twisted her body to face him, and looked into his eyes without blinking. "You must know Officer Drakas, then."

He felt her studying his face and he looked away, anywhere but into her searching eyes. "Okay, I know him."

"He's the friend you transport the dogs for, isn't he?" He could feel her eyes on his face when she said it.

"Come over, let me cook you dinner. I like to cook."

"Answer me that one question honestly and I'll consider it."

"Okay, yes. Yes, he is." His silence then was almost petulant. Or perhaps it was born of fear.

"We'll talk and you'll tell me everything?" she said.

"Yes. As much as I can. Where do you live? I'll pick you up."

"Slow down, I'll drive myself, and I'll call you."

"Let's see, in case you don't, can I have your number?" He pulled out his phone, but she leaned back, fished around in her jeans pocket, and pulled forth a receipt. He flagged down the waitress for a pen.

She scribbled something, held it out to him, and reached into her pocket again.

"I got it," he said.

"Don't worry about it." She placed three tens on the table, five times the price of their coffees. No wonder she has old clothes if she pays for coffees like that he thought, but the gesture touched him.

"I have to go."

He watched her get up, push the chair back and speak gently to the little dog, telling it not to be frightened. He watched her walk to the sidewalk, her slim hips in the worn jeans. There was a man in the yard across from Jo's raking leaves, and David watched to see if he would look up and follow Sylvie with lustful eyes, for already David had taken possession of her. But the man did not, and David watched her as she bent over and scooped up the little dog, saying something he couldn't hear. He watched as she walked across the traffic with the dog in her arms.

That afternoon returning home along the avenue bewitched by the lowering sun, he felt a yearning. He had a part of her. He fingered the receipt with her number in his pocket. As he walked he hummed a song filling in its melody with the lyrics of her name, the name and number making her understandable to him, like a scientist might feel in labeling a very beautiful or very poisonous flower.

The thought came to Sylvie a week later during a glorious patch of Indian summer. She stood on her front step. All around her was the warm, transparent air of late September that singled the day retreating soon into evening, the summer into fall, and then the rush toward winter. She'd begun using her woodstove to warm up her rooms at night, but she knew during the day it was not yet cool enough to leave a dog in a car unattended. She would need help and she couldn't implicate Carol. She dialed David Sampson's number and listened to his phone ringing, picturing what his home would be like. Small, probably neat for a male, but still a bachelor pad. When he answered, she could hear the eager surprise in his voice and it wearied her. But she knew then that she would use it to her advantage.

"I need your help."

"I'm all yours."

As she explained her plan and he listened without butting in, she felt a wave of gratitude toward him.

Her plan was simple. Slip number 11 some Ace or other sedative and tell Sharon he'd died. With any luck she wouldn't see Sharon and she could just get him outside. If she saw her, she'd show her the body briefly. David would be on hand to whisk him away. If suspicions were raised, a cop in uniform wouldn't hurt one bit. She couldn't risk leaving number 11 in her car if the temperature rose. But neither could she wait until the permanent cooler weather. He'd be dead. Weedy was coming home with her to live out his final days. And at that moment it seemed like the only good that would ever come from her undercover work at DVX.

She'd gone over the plan again and again in her head and she knew it was flawed. She knew she could lose the job and expose herself. Or worse, she could be arrested for stealing. Stealing what? Public property? But she didn't care, for she had seen the fate that befell number 12. If she could pull this off she'd at least have saved one. She was aware of her own need to care for an animal in need. But she knew that she wanted Weedy more than she'd ever wanted anything in her life.

David had asked her why she didn't adopt, and the question stuck with her for a week. She would talk to her landlady next time she came. Maybe she could offer to buy the old house. But right now, she needed to take the neediest, the most likely to die. She would have Weedy to come home to each night and care for without the knowledge that she led him to his death and, with that small something to hang onto, she vowed to stay working at DVX for as long as she could, offering what paltry bits of love she could to all the others she couldn't take home.

"Wow," was all he said at first, and she froze as fear skulked its way into her gut and stupidity skipped alongside, gloating. She stood still realizing her mistake confiding in him. The law, no less. But she'd been so sure he'd want to help. And then, too, she could always report him if he tried to talk. With that thought, the fear shrank back just a bit. "Okay, I will," he conceded, "But let's meet and talk it over. Get it completely ironed out. No room for error, right?"

"No room for error," she repeated, squeezing out a smile. But within her gut, there registered potent reluctance.

CHAPTER TWENTY-FIVE

The next day when Sylvie arrived at DVX she walked to the board, trying to ward off a growing anxiety for the cockamamie plan she'd conceived. There was now a vague yet building fear blowing down her neck, hissing, "*Turn back, all ye with un-executable cockamamie plans. Turn back, before it's too late.*" She breathed to steady herself, but succeeded only in breathing in the smell that greeted her daily: bleach, disinfectant and despair.

She was standing before the bulletin board, reading the numbers for the day when her hand flew to her throat.

No. Not him, she begged in the echoing chamber of her mind. But number 11 was clearly posted, and the dread that slipped in through some crack and sought her out, began seeping through her like fog settling over a low valley.

There was nothing she could do. For a moment she turned from the board and wandered the hall like a ball kicked in the wrong direction then forgotten. But brain linked to heart and, governed by an emotion stronger than fear, she stopped. She collected herself and walked back, working her way through two-thirds of the numbers on the list, stroking the backs of the frightened dogs. Until it was time for number 11.

She approached his run and saw him lying awkwardly on his good side, the burned side exposed. When she unlatched the door, he didn't raise his head. His neck was extended and he looked to one spot a few inches before him. He'd begun to tremble with her entry into his run. She dropped, wetting her knees on the damp floor.

"*Weedy,*" she whispered. She touched him ever so lightly all around the wound. He lay staring ahead, his only movement his quaking body. "Weedy, little sprout, little snout," she said, speaking quietly. At the sound of her voice, he coughed, and she took advantage of his preoccupation to slip the lead over his head. But she didn't stand. Instead her fingers sought his domed head, massaging the base of his ears, stroking, stroking. Then she began to sing softly.

"*Get up, now*!" The words hissed behind her back. Sylvie leapt to her feet, whirling around as her heart pounded. She stood looking face to face through the link gate with big, burly Mike. "*Sharon is down the hall.*"

Stunned, Sylvie murmured, "Thank you." Her already shredded nerves, unraveling to their last end.

She stared after Mike as he moved past, then looked back to Weedy, the leash lying as limply as he was. She bent, reaching for the end of the leash, but she did not know how she could walk him down the hall to be experimented on any more. Again, she dropped down to be next to him. Perhaps that was when a new idea first began to form in her mind, shaking her branches, rustling her leaves, whispering, whispering.

She heard footsteps in the hallway coming nearer. They stopped and she knew someone was standing behind her outside the run. This time she turned her head slowly. Sharon was staring through the metal mesh at her crouching beside a specimen.

"What do you do if they won't get up?" she asked quietly.

There was a pause in which Sylvie understood the disastrous consequence of her question.

"I'll show you what you do." Sharon opened the door, snatching the leash from Sylvie's hands. In one quick motion she jerked number 11 to his unsteady legs. "This is the job we're paying you to do. Can you understand that? And can you understand that this is *not* my job to do? If it was the job they were paying me to do, I'd be good and well doing it. But I've got my own work to do. I've got a lot of important work to do. So, tell me if you think you can do your job or not."

"I can," Sylvie said, as she glanced at number 11's side. He had stumbled then righted himself and he stood shaking more than ever. Sharon saw her looking.

"If that sort of thing bothers you, you need to let me know now." But she didn't snap out the words, and for the first time, Sylvie thought she heard compassion in Sharon's voice.

"No, it doesn't bother me. I do feel for him though." Perhaps it was a mistake but she persisted. "It must hurt." As Sharon narrowed her eyes, Sylvie continued. "Will they give him a break? For his sake as much as for their sake. I mean, they want healthy dogs, don't they?"

"We do want healthy specimens and we do what we can for that end. But sometimes the experiments are such that we can't help it. I'm sorry. We try. We do use humane endpoints." There was the ominous phrase again. "To terminate the pain or distress of the experimental specimens," Sharon continued. "Rather than waiting for their deaths as endpoints." It sounded like Sharon had memorized the handout. "It may be time for him. You're right." Sylvie felt her body seize. Sharon opened her mouth as if to say more but stopped and turned on her heel. "Go. You need to do your job."

"Yes, ma'am."

When Sharon had left, Sylvie's desire was to reach for Weedy and hold him in her arms. Her desire was to soothe him and tell him she loved him because she knew this might be the last time she saw him. Humane endpoints. She knew there was nothing she could say or do that would soothe him. Weedy would have to walk down the hall beside her on his own wobbly legs.

"Come on, Weedy. Please, come." And as she walked off leading him toward the treatment room, it was one of the lowest moments of her life. She thought of describing everything to Carol and receiving some relief, but something within her knew that just as she could offer Weedy no comfort, neither could Carol offer her comfort. Carol wasn't here to see and feel this.

In the late afternoon, when the run cleaners had finished hosing down the last runs and filled all the water bowls, Sylvie entered the treatment room to begin the task of leading dogs back again. They didn't all return. Some dogs remained in cages in the room, while others she never saw again.

When she'd led back the last, she hovered in the room until a tech jerked his head up and stared, questioning.

"Yes?" was all he said.

She was afraid to speak and bother him, afraid to find out what she needed to know.

"Do you want something?" he asked, watching her. He was a tall, thin, dark-haired young man about her age with thick black glasses, and now he inclined his head, and squinted behind the glasses as if studying her like he might study a specimen. She had seen him before. She stood dumbly, noticing that underneath his white coat he wore a pink shirt that contrasted with his dark hair.

"Is that it?" She managed to squeak out. "No more?"

"That's all today," he said and returned his gaze to the computer before him.

She turned around. But her legs wouldn't walk. She wanted to punch her fist through his monitor. Weedy was not returning to his run. In that one horrible moment, Sylvie knew she had to get out of there. She couldn't stay another minute. Weedy was dead and she hadn't even given him one hug or word of comfort. She had simply led him to his death. All else dropped from her mind, and she didn't realize that she was still standing in the room until she heard someone talking.

"What's your name?" It was the same technician.

"Me?"

He smiled at her in a mocking way as if to say, "Anybody else in the room but you and me?"

"Uh, Jane. It's Jane Dunlap."

"Are you okay, Jane Dunlap?"

"Fine," she snapped. Out of politesse she ought to ask his name, but she also knew that if she had to stand and make pleasant conversation with the person who very likely had ended Weedy's life, she would explode.

"It's a hard job what you do," he said looking into her eyes. "I mean, if you have any ounce of compassion at all." She was surprised and stood waiting for more. But she couldn't wait much longer for the scream brimming low in her chest was like something crawling across her to the point of no tolerance. Still, she stood, wavering in her intention. During her hesitation he didn't speak but seemed to be watching her again.

"I've got to go," she said.

Walking quickly with eyes to the floor, she exited the room and willed that she not see Sharon. She pushed through the door to the front foyer, grabbed her timecard and clocked out early. Then she was running to her car, and it was only once she had backed out of the parking lot and driven a block, away from possible prying eyes, that she pulled over to a dead end street. To her left, the windows of a crumbling red brick building were knocked out. The other houses were made of wood shingles and half the roofs had caved in, creating gaping-holed, hyperbolic set pieces, uninhabitable, except to the pigeons and rats.

Life was sorrow. Life was suffering. All around you, hiding in the rotting houses. She put her head on the steering wheel. Where was the joy? It was like the faintest trace of perfume fading just around the next corner. After a moment, she raised her head and glanced in the rearview mirror. There was movement. A solitary figure in a hoody slinking toward her car. She put the car in gear, gunned it for a show of bravado, turned around at the dead end and drove off. When she reached her side street, she felt calmer. But Weedy was still dead—as were so many, who she could not help. She never could have. She had to quit.

CHAPTER TWENTY-SIX

But Sylvie did not quit. Perhaps she might have if she had not answered the ringing phone that night to a hysterical Carol, sobbing on the other end.

". . . pain in his stomach, and turned out they think it's his pancreas and the doctors give him only a few months. *Months.* What am I going to do?"

Sylvie listened, trying to understand her friend through the tears and all at once it was her, not Matt who was suffering a further blow to the gut. She couldn't think what to say to Carol except, "I'll quit the lab and help you look after him."

"No. The only good I've ever done in the world is through you."

"You do good every day."

"No. You do all the good. I've always known it. I just need to cry. His parents are coming. I can't believe it. I can't take it in. Only months. I may need to spend time over with you."

"Anything you need."

"I need for Matt to get better again."

The news stunned Sylvie but it was because of Carol's words that the next day she was walking back through the front reception of DVX and clocking in—that small something inside of her (the best part of her, the part that believers would call the soul) was urging her to do what she could. To help soothe where she could. Although, had she not returned, her life would have turned out very differently.

Did she imagine it or did the runs smell more strongly of urine and feces on this morning than on other days? She found out why when, turning a corner, she bumped into a sweating and puffing Sharon.

"Oh, thank god you're here. It's just Swenson and me. Two of the cage cleaners quit without a word of notice. Can you believe it? If they think they can skip work every Friday and take a long weekend then come groveling back on Monday, they have another think coming. They'll not be getting sent a paycheck, is all I have to say. Can you hurry up and help? I need you to finish up here, then go to the treatment room. You know what to do, right?"

Sylvie nodded.

"Great. Thanks so much, Jane. I have a boatload of important work to do."

It was the first time Sharon had ever thanked her. Sylvie took the mop and bucket from Sharon and then the long extension hose that workers fired into the runs, after bleaching. When Sharon had gone, Sylvie bent and sniffed the mop bucket water, jerking her head back. The bleach vapors burned her nostrils. She knew where the cleaners dumped the gray water, and she considered dumping the bleach and filling the bucket with plain warm water. But if Sharon found out, she'd probably make her use extra bleach.

She began dragging the mop and bucket to each run, sloshing the mop in the burning bleach water, ringing it out and mopping up the urine. She scooped up each dog's excrement and dumped it into a bucket then into a green trash container. Lifting the lid, the stench assaulted her.

She pointed the hose into the runs, apologizing to every dog, and trying to aim as far from each as she could. Craven animals crouched and slunk to corners. When she had proceeded in this fashion through all of the runs, she carried the empty bucket to the treatment room as Sharon requested.

Three technicians, cloaked in white, stood like statuary when she entered. The dark-haired man who'd addressed her yesterday was among them, but all three heads were bowed. They didn't look at her as they hovered over a steel table, and she easily slipped by them. The techs, intent on their work, didn't at first notice her standing in the room. When they did, they looked annoyed.

The nearest one to her looked up. "Yes?"

"Sharon said to clean the runs in here."

"Cages," he corrected and nodded with his chin to the back of the room. She walked past them to the far wall where there hung cages, stacked one over each other, in the same fashion as in the cat room. Some contained animals and some did not. She scanned the cages. Her eyes fell upon a motionless black back.

She froze. She was afraid to move forward. She would know that black back anywhere, but then again would she really? She crept closer and craned her neck around to the side and there it was: Weedy's white-tipped, scrawny rat tail. "*Oh*!" she cried in joy, quickly swallowing the sound and glancing toward the techs' table. But no one turned toward her.

There, lying on his side was Weedy. His back pressed against the cage door and his face pointed away from her. She rose up on her toes, peered in and saw closed eyes. Her joy vanished. He was dead. And, because the cage cleaners had quit, no one had removed him. She leaned in closer and sniffed. Then she, too, closed her eyes, and she stuck a finger through the metal and poked gingerly. The techs were speaking to each other in low voices. Weedy's side was still an open wound, only the outer edges succeeding in scabbing over. Sylvie spun around to look once more at the techs then opened the cage door and placed a hand on his neck. It was warm, and he twitched ever so slightly. He was alive.

It was at that moment that she lost rational thought. She needed to get him out of there. She would tell the techs he was dead and carry him out to her car. Then regaining some sense, she knew they'd see at once she was lying. She was still standing there when she heard one of the techs cough and clear his throat, and she realized she had no idea how to clean these cages with a mop and bucket. She walked back to the techs at the steel table standing awkwardly behind and cleared her own throat.

"Sorry, but I've never cleaned the cages before."

In the center of the three, a woman turned around, her hands covered in long plastic gloves. "You use the spray bottles on the shelf. Spray and wipe with the roll of paper towels."

"And one of the dogs is dead." No sooner had she spoken the lie than she began to feel her heart pounding, *thu-dump, thu-dump, thu-dumpa, dump.*

"Which one?" A pause in which Sylvie felt she could hear the breath not only of the woman before her, but the breath and beat of every animal in the scaffold of cages behind her.

"The one that looks part beagle."

"Let me see it."

Clock time, bell chime, horror time, ghost crime. Taut drumbeats took up the space of Sylvie's heart beneath her shirt. She stood without moving. "Right there." She pointed across the room. "Back up against the cage. Stiff as a board."

"Okay, take it out and bring it to me."

Sylvie nodded unable to speak. She felt her knees and legs unsteady and didn't trust herself to walk back. But as the woman turned back to the table, Sylvie said to her back. "Sharon said to take all dead specimens to the freezer."

"All right then, to the freezer," the technician answered without turning to look again. Sylvie heard the low muted voices of the techs and made out: "... *the problem?*" And she imagined an underlying irritation or frustration behind the muffled words.

"Dead specimen."

"Umm."

"The one we were going to terminate today anyway."

"Hmmm. Saves on gas."

"Necrotomy?"

"Too damaged."

She stood stunned with the realization of what had just happened, juxtaposed with what had almost happened. Then thrill, swift and consuming, a scarlet sunrise breaking distant hills. But just as suddenly, the rush she felt was replaced by dread darker than nuclear winter. *What if Weedy cried out when she lifted him? What if he wiggled and squirmed as she walked past the table?* She cast her eyes around the room for a towel or anything, and spied a foot-long roll of gauze. She reached and tore, and opened his cage door again, whispering, "*You cannot make a sound. Please, Weedy.*"

"Do you need some help?" She whirled around and found herself looking into the dark eyes of the young man who'd spoken to her the day before.

"*No.* I mean, you're busy, I'm so sorry. No, I'm fine. Please, go back to your work. I didn't mean to disturb you."

"I don't mind. Here, let me help you."

"It's okay, really." She stood, her back blocking Weedy from his view. She looked beyond him to the other two at the table, willing them to call him back. "Thanks, but I'm fine. I was explicitly told not to bother y'all." She attempted a smile. "I don't want to get in trouble."

"You're not going to get in trouble. Shout if you change your mind and need some help."

With her back against the cage, and sweat dripping from her underarms, she watched the young man walk across the room. *Shout?* Then, trembling she turned slowly back around, her breath coming out shallow and quick. She reached into Weedy's cage.

He was limp in her arms when she lifted him to wrap the gauze once lightly around his body. He let out a small gasp of pain.

"*Shhh. Please,*" she begged him. She continued wrapping. It looked like a shroud. But the white was turning a brownish color where it touched his large wound, and she wondered if he were dead would he draw so much color? She let him fall back into the cage. He didn't move. She draped more gauze, hiding the blood spot. The moment had come. She lifted him into her arms and stood holding him, but she couldn't move.

"*Okay. Here we go,*" she whispered. Her legs were shaking as she inched forward.

Silently, she glided past the techs all huddled together at the steel table. No one even looked up as she passed, an apparition herself carrying the even stranger phenomenon swaddled in white. Weedy made no sound. No cry of protest, pain or the unfairness of life. Just nothing.

A second later, she was out and closing the door gently behind her. There was the sunrise in her heart again, beaming golden rays brighter than before. She'd take him to her car and tell Sharon she had to go. Whatever had gotten the two run cleaners, had gotten her too. She'd quit. She was about to push the top of the gauze away from his head, when she looked up. She was face-to-face with Sharon.

"What are you doing?"

"I . . ."

"What do you have there?"

"Taking a dog to the freezer."

"Give it to me. I'll do it."

Sweat beaded on her forehead, announcing her guilt to Sharon. She stood frozen for a moment clutching Weedy to her chest, silently beseeching him not to move under his shroud of gauze. Just then the door opened and the dark-haired tech walked out, glasses fallen onto his nose.

"Sharon, we need the results FedExed to Pfizer. They were supposed to have them by now."

"I'm sorry, Dr. Watson. Jane, here, button-holed me in the hallway. Kept asking all these really stupid questions."

He looked at Sharon, then at Sylvie.

"I just need the results FedExed. *Now.*" He spun around, pushing up his glasses. Sharon snapped her head back to Sylvie and barked, "Dump that specimen and get back to work!"

"Yes." She walked in the direction of the freezer, feeling Sharon's eyes on her back, her mind racing, but grateful to that tech, or young doctor, rather. She'd put Weedy in a run with another dog. But what if, frightened, the other dog attacked him? She'd put him in another beagle's run. She'd call David and tell him she needed his help. She back tracked, then stopped. She ran the other way. Stopped again. Ran back. Stopped. She stood thinking.

"*Screw it,*" she said aloud. And she turned toward the doors leading out.

"It's the other direction!" Sharon's voice called after her. "Please tell me you haven't forgotten where it is."

"I haven't forgotten." Sylvie pivoted in the direction of the freezer still able to hear the not so subtle muttering. "*Imbeciles who work here. What, like, is a low IQ a prerequisite?*" Sylvie hurried on. She could no longer hear Sharon chortling at her own wit. She paused, ready to turn back to the runs, but when she glanced over her shoulder, Sharon was still behind her, a dogged shadow. She had no choice but to take Weedy to the freezer.

She pulled open the glistening steel door. A cold silence. The dull marble eyes of a hound mix stared back at her. It was wedged into the middle of the stack of faded fur bodies. The smell of disinfectant twisted into her nostrils like death's omen. She had to lean against the bodies, pressing against the hard, cold column of legs, tails and snouts, holding Weedy above her head.

No! Yes, you must. But I can't! But I must. What choice do I have? The battle in her mind raged for seconds that seemed like hours, as she lifted Weedy's living body onto the pile of the dead.

But just as she was about to place him in with the other bodies, she brought his face up close to her own, pushing away his shroud for only a second and in an urgent voice, said to the half-closed eyes, "*Weedy*. Forgive me, and live for me! I'll return, *I promise*."

And she lay Weedy's small frame on top of the stack of dogs. No movement, and he made for a strange and ghostly vision, wrapped within his gauze, as if only he had been given a proper burial. She dredged her waning hope, brightening to think that skin of flimsy cloth might keep him warm until she came back for him. She'd only be a minute. Two at most. Sharon would be busy sending the lab results and she could hustle Weedy outside.

She ran back to the bulletin board, knocking into Swenson, who shoved her back, hard. "Watch the fuck who you bump into."

"Sorry!"

Swenson glowered at her, but Sylvie couldn't think even to apologize. She knew Weedy would die in there. The chemical disinfectants alone would probably finish him off. In his condition, he couldn't stay in there more than a few minutes without freezing. She had to know where Sharon was so she could get Weedy outside. She grabbed a leash and ran to get her first dog, but turned around, crazed like a madwoman in her indecision. There wasn't time. *Run, run,* her mind taunted. *Run through cloacal halls, watchful bowels, to distal room of tethered cats. See Sharon waiting in her web.* She ran down the hall to the cat room, knocking lightly and not waiting for a response, she opened the door. Sharon was laughing. There she sat hunched over the desk, her fingers racing over her phone's keyboard, she remained unaware of someone standing in the doorway. When she realized, she leapt as though one of the cats were on fire.

"Can't you knock?"

"I did."

"Well, *what?*"

"I need to know if you've got any new cage cleaners hired. I'd like to go out for lunch."

"Are you kidding me?"

"I'm sorry, Sharon. I'm just tired today."

"Oh, and if I was tired, do you think I could just up and stop? You think I don't know you're up to something? I'm going in to talk to the doctors about that dog."

"No, don't. Wait till later. Till they're done. They're right in the middle of something important. I didn't know how to wash the cages, and I had to interrupt them." And as she said it, she realized she hadn't cleaned one cage. "They won't want to be interrupted yet again. You can talk to them later about it." She paused then added. "That dog was dead. They all saw it."

Sharon sucked in air and let it out dramatically. "Look at me and you listen to me." Sylvie did and as she looked, she was acutely aware of the clock ticking above Sharon's head. "Just get the runs cleaned. I don't know if we've got new cage cleaners hired," she mimicked Sylvie's voice. "Take the dogs to the treatment room like you're paid to. They're waiting on you and you can be sure they won't do it themselves. Then make sure the way is cleared of boxes and garbage outside, they're coming to empty the freezer today."

"The freezer?"

"Yes, the fuckin' freezer! Excuse my French, but we can't keep dead bodies forever."

She fled the cat room, not caring whether Sharon followed her or not, and raced to the freezer, but before she reached it, a doctor caught her, agitated.

"Please, we need number 22 immediately. We've been waiting." She handed Sylvie a leash.

"Okay, I'll be there in ten minutes."

"We can't wait ten minutes. *Now.* Whatever you're doing can wait." She stood staring at Sylvie.

Sylvie nodded her assent, and walked to the runs. Number 22 was a large hound mix, and he stood, watching her enter, his flop ears pricked.

"You're handsome. Well, here we go." But, when she tried to lead him, 22 planted himself, locking his knees.

"I know. And why not save you? What good saving Weedy? What good will it do? None. Because he's dead now anyway. You know that, as well as I do. But then again, I hear that freezing to death is not such a bad way to go." She blithered to 22 and, as she continued her softly-spoken, if one-sided, conversation with him, he un-planted himself, waving his tail back and forth, as he walked beside her. And sewn in hurried step to hasten that strange tapestry of fate for girl and dog, she led him down the hall. Before the swinging doors, she stopped.

She laid a hand on the hound's hunched back and the movement of his still wagging tail passed up through her fingers to lodge in her heart.

"You beautiful boy." He looked up at her and she at him with eyes that spoke what neither one could say. "Tell me you have tasted fresh air, and muddied big dog paws in river banks and groundhog holes. Tell me this isn't all you've ever known of life." She waited for unspoken words to worm within her mincemeat mind. But all around, only the stealth of laboratory sounds. She bent and kissed his head and entered.

She handed his leash over, then she was turning and running, tripping and stumbling. Back to the freezer. And skidding around the corner, when she came face to face with two men she'd never seen before.

"Well, you're in a hurry, Goldilocks!"

She could utter nothing in response, and the men stepped past her, the one who'd spoken opening the freezer door.

"*No*!" She yelled, finding her voice. "Just a moment! We're using the wrapped up one in an experiment."

"Whatever you say, Miss Sunshine."

She pushed past, grabbing Weedy's body and feeling for warmth. But there was none.

"*Weedy,"* she cried and slipped out of sight of the two men. She darted down the hall, holding him against her chest, and burst out through the specimen delivery doors. Once out, she felt for his heart and then in one glorious moment, there was the faint beat beneath her hand. She pushed the gauze away from his face, and looked down at him. His eyes moved watching her.

"*Weedy,*" she uttered the name she'd bestowed. He was alive. She turned so the sun's rays were touching them both.

"Hang on, Weedy. Stay with me." Reaching into her back pocket for her phone, she dialed and got David's voicemail. She squatted partially, balancing Weedy on her knees and typed with clumsy fingers:

Urgent. Come to the lab. I need you immediately!

Her own heart was pulsing out its fear in disjointed beats. She sent another text to David:

Be discreet.

She hugged Weedy, trying to warm him up, and realized just how thin he was. It was like holding a large, scrawny chicken. His bones stuck into her hands and his head hung over her arm.

"Weedy, are you with me? *Come on, we're almost there.*" As she spoke the words meant to soothe, she heard their urgency. As if to confirm her mounting fear, the sky darkened with the sudden swirling and swooping of starlings, moving in one black roiling wave. They ebbed, and above was the eerie evening yellow that falls just before dusk. But it was only three o'clock.

Sylvie startled as she noticed a large truck backing up to the door from which she'd come. The prize model truck of child of yore had come to life—a massive monster dump truck with a tarp-covered roof.

She moved a little away from the truck and squatted again, her back up against the side of the building, Weedy cradled in her arms. She began unwrapping his shroud, lifting him as she took off each layer. She focused on his sweet domed head instead of his side's raw and pocked pomegranate flesh.

"I'm taking you away from that nightmare, forever." His body jerked, contorting in her arms, and he heaved and gasped, eyes shuttered.

"*Weedy, no.* Please, Weedy. Don't die." The convulsions stopped, but she felt tremulous, herself. She rubbed his shoulders gently to warm him. "You're *free.* You're finally free. It's all going to be over. I'm taking you away forever. It's all going to be okay now. For you, for me." In her arms, he moved like a bird, light and wounded, and he had tan lashes on soft beagle eyes that were now partially opened. Eyes that she had seen so often filled with white-rimmed fear, not looking her way. Now they fluttered to look around, and closed again as if the effort was too great.

"*Weedy, please. Don't give up now.*"

He started to emit a rusty sound. And it was then she felt a love so pure and an urge to protect so powerful that she didn't care who walked out and found her holding him. Her lips touch the top of his head, her nostrils breathing in the rancid smell of him. She was stroking the funny fur and speaking softly to him when the door burst open. She jumped, clutching him in her arms, no longer emboldened by love, but instead painfully frightened by what she had done.

But it was just the men unloading the freezer and the antiseptic chemical smell curled out and over her, as the men performed their work. She hadn't thought about how the removal and disposal was accomplished, but this seemed too awful an ending for dogs who had given their lives to humans in the name of science. She looked down at Weedy, and shivered. The men hoisted down the tailgate and Sylvie gasped, looking in only once, before turning her face away.

"Yeah, might want to find a different spot for your lunch break," one of the men called over to her.

Sylvie nodded to the man, and asked casually, "Where do you take them?"

He stared back at her but in his gaze there was no malice.

"The bodies," she said. "Where do you take them?"

"Dump them. There's a landfill we use. They're dead. We dump them."

A chill—a memory from her past—made her shiver again and she hugged Weedy tighter to her breast. Just then her phone buzzed.

R U in the prking lot?

Cradling Weedy between her elbows, replied back:

Yes! Hurry!

When David pulled up in his squad car, Sylvie experienced a moment too good to be true, looking from David to the laboratory door and she was immobilized. But as David pulled to a stop, she ran to his car.

"You really are a cop," she said to him when he got out.

"Yeah, and I could get in big trouble for this." He bent to the ground, and she threw him a glance.

"Stretching," he said, pushing back up. "Get stiff driving around." He stood staring at her holding the bruised and bloody dog with dangling gauze.

"I can't blow my . . . I mean I have to go back in and finish working." When David didn't say anything, Sylvie explained, "They were about to kill him, and I couldn't live with myself if I didn't get him out of there. Can you understand? I need you to keep him in your car till I get off. Whatever you do, don't let anybody see him. And promise me, you won't let anything happen to him. He's already been through so much. I'll be finished in a few hours. Keep him in the sun. Warm him up."

"Why does he need to warm up?"

"Don't ask me questions now. Just please do it. If anyone comes out, leave. Drive around the block." She stood holding Weedy as though unwilling to give him up. David opened the passenger door for her and she set Weedy onto the seat. He raised his head looking up at them, his brown eyes holding the fathomless silence of a lake. Then he seemed to crumple, letting out the strange sound, before lowering his head onto the seat.

"Hey, boy," David said, reaching a hand to pat his back. Weedy flinched.

"That's too rough. Best not to touch him." She leaned over his furled body. "Weedy, we're almost home. *Live*, Weedy. Live for me and our new life." She moved fingers lightly over him, but he made no more sounds. Ducking back out, she turned to David. "I want this more than I've ever wanted anything. Can I count on you?"

"Yes. But then what?"

"I'll take him home and you've saved the day."

"That wasn't really what I—"

"Can you be back to pick me up at five?"

"I'll be here."

"I don't know how to thank you. Truly."

"You could have dinner with me," he said sheepishly.

"Consider it a date then."

She turned and headed back into the lab. Then stopped suddenly and spun around, her intuition screaming. But David was driving out of the lot.

The first person Sylvie saw when she entered was Sharon.

"Where have you been? Do you want to be fired? What's in your hand?"

"Parking lot trash," Sylvie said, balling the bloodied shroud smaller and smaller.

"They have been needing the specimens and I had to lead them out myself!" Sylvie had a vision of Sharon jerking and pulling dogs down the hall.

"I told you I was going out for lunch. I drove to get a latte. What's up?" She asked smiling dumbly.

"We're short-staffed and this is the day you decide it's time to be Miss liberal latte and what, write poetry or something at Starbucks? Are you freaking kidding me?"

"I'm sorry, I'm tired and I needed the caffeine to get through the rest of the day." Sylvie had never heard Sharon speak quite so effusively. She'd learned to take Sharon's outbursts with a bit of salt, for Sharon was mostly fluff and bluff and Sylvie realized she wanted her there. Still if Sharon fired her—and at that moment nothing would have pleased her more—then at least she'd have Weedy. She would have saved one life.

"About that dog, I talked to the doctors."

Sylvie tensed involuntarily then told herself to relax. Weedy was safe.

"They said they didn't see it."

"The one guy was standing right there."

"Well, where's the dog then?"

"Do you want me to duct tape your shoe? I could fix—"

"Mind your own business. Where is that dog?"

"In the freezer. Dead. They took it away. *Now,* what did they need me to do?"

For once Sharon looked beaten at her game. "Go check the board. And just no more freaking lattes, hear? No more."

"Whatever," Sylvie said under her breath turning from Sharon.

Sylvie walked back to the bulletin board. Now her perennial cocktail, a mix of futility and despair for each dog she led to the experimentation room, was topped with the rotten fruit of exhaustion. The adrenaline that had energized her dipped proportionally as the stress rose. She glanced to the clock every time she entered the experimentation room.

But when five o'clock trickled in, oozing inky angst, and Sylvie burst out the doors, David was not there. She scanned the parking lot, deciding she'd give him five minutes for traffic, but when twelve minutes had passed, a feeling crinkled inside her, so suffocating it was like someone walking up to her and slowly wrapping her in Saran Wrap. She texted him but received nothing in response. Prickles of fear coated her body. She ran a hand through her hair, then batted at the air as if ridding the suffocating slime of anxiety. The world tilted and dimmed. A car backfired in the distance. The air blew through the remaining leaves on the trees.

She stood in a moment of immeasurable regret realizing that she had handed off little Weedy to someone who could just as easily dump him as the men emptying the freezer. Or turn her in for theft. Or, the thought stuck her like a needle piercing skin: David could sell him to different lab. She was reaching into her pocket to send another text when she saw the white squad car turning into DVX. She squinted into the lowering sun.

The car swung round and she ran to passenger side, nearly tripping over a discarded plastic container, lunging for the door, but she saw Weedy even before she opened the door.

"He's sitting up! Oh, thank you! Thank you!" David grinned. He was getting out, and she ran around to him and threw her arms around his neck. "I can never thank you enough for what you've done." She watched his grin vanish, and she turned to follow his gaze. Two doctors were walking from the lab.

"Get in and drive," she said in a hushed tone. "*Now.*"

"Hey!" She heard a voice calling and she ignored it. She jumped into the squad car, wedging beside Weedy. "Drive!"

David put on his siren and whirled out of the parking lot.

Sylvie wrapped Weedy in her arms and hugged him close, as he scrambled in her lap. "I didn't say make a scene!" she yelled over the siren.

David turned it off. "Sorry. Now what?"

"Drive around for a moment more then take me back."

He passed the shotgun houses with windows knocked out and the jagged glass daring entrance. Rust flaked from fire escapes, and vine-strangled Ailanthus invaded houses, growing up, around and, in some cases, through them. Graffiti, the neighborhood's personal wallpaper, decorated every surface.

"Savory neighborhood," she said, and didn't tell him she lived nearby.

"You're telling me. Even the cops don't like it," he answered.

When he returned to the staff parking lot of DVX, the doctors had gone and only Sylvie's car remained. Sylvie lifted Weedy ever so gently and placed him in the front seat. Then she saw the note beneath her wiper.

"When would you like to have dinner?" David was asking her.

"Give me a few days. I gave you my word. But I need to get used to my new situation. And you know . . . you can never tell anyone about this. Not now, not ever."

"Your secret is safe."

Sylvie waved her thanks again. The sun was low and slanted, and translucent light settled over tree branches, enfolding each individual leaf in a haloed glow. She picked up the note. *I would like to take you to dinner,* the note read. Nothing else. No name.

CHAPTER TWENTY-SEVEN

Sylvie slowed the car to a stop before the old oak. For a moment she couldn't get out. *Number 11 was in her car.* She turned and stared at Weedy, feeling both disbelief and joy. His eyes were open.

Stepping out and walking around, she opened the passenger door, and cupped her hand under his small beagle face, quietly massaging his dewlaps. She watched his nose twitch from side to side as he smelled the outside air, his whiskers sticking out like a catfish. She marveled at the small snuffling sounds, beautiful sounds. In the lab he'd not wanted to sniff her. She leaned in and gently lifted. She could feel his body tense against her embrace, but she also felt the moment it relaxed, perhaps only in habitual resignation.

She glanced up and down her street and saw no activity save for a squirrel and some sparrows hopping about the base of one of the oaks. Holding Weedy like something sacred from the reliquary shrine, she walked up her front steps, in through the door and, balancing him in her left arm, locked the door behind her.

"This is the living room," she said standing in the front room with the wood stove. She stood transfixed, as if regarding her home for the first time. The sofa, offering cozy comfort, stretched on her left. Behind it book shelves stuffed with books and two potted plants, an aloe and a spider. Next to the bookshelves was an old turntable and stereo. Windows along one wall, framing the outside street. To the right was the blue soapstone wood stove.

She set Weedy on the sofa while she fluffed up two fleece blankets and fixed a little nest. Nudging him toward the nest, she said, "Have you ever known soft comfort or were you born in that lab? Not talking, are you?" He kept his head lowered, but when she walked to the kitchen, she glanced back and saw him stand then turn around a few times, and crouch back down. She opened a drawer and rummaged through the twist ties, cheese knives, candles, scissors, a mortar and pestle, before finding a small can opener. Next she grabbed one of the cans of dog food she used for luring strays off the streets and when she scooped some into the metal bowl, she looked up to see Weedy watching her, his ears pricked, his eyes alert.

"Well, that's the best look I've seen." She was smiling, scooping food, when all at once she stopped, the day catching up with her, her adrenaline spike dipping. She put a forkful of dogfood down into the bowl, and ran over to him. There she knelt on the floor before her sofa.

"Little Weedy," she said. "I remember the first time I saw you. I remember thinking you'd die." She let her fingers run over his wound ever so lightly and he winced. "I won't let you suffer ever again. You're here." She hiccupped, put her hand to her mouth. "Sorry." She paused. "But the rest are all still there." He seemed to be listening to her, but when she reached to pet another part of his body, he shrank against the back of the sofa, and when she spoke to him in an upwardly lilting voice, he didn't move his tail. He just stared up at her with wary eyes, watching. Then he made the sound that would haunt her. It was low, and vaguely human in its pain. And she looked back at him, not knowing how to help.

She rose, opened a bottle of Tramadol whose expiration date read two years earlier, and put it in a food ball. She brought the metal bowl over to where he lay on her sofa.

"Weedy, I'm going to try to help you feel better." She offered him the food ball and watched as he took it softly between his teeth. She tried to look at his teeth to get a possible indication of age but decided that playing around in his mouth was not in either his or her best interest. When he swallowed, he sniffed her fingers for more. "Here you go," she said placing the bowl before him.

He sniffed at the food. She looked at him then picked out some of the food with her fingers and offered it to him. He took some from her fingers, then stopped and glanced back at her.

"It's the same as the other, minus the drugs. Go on. You need to eat."

In a flash he had risen and spun around. He heaved and retched onto her couch.

"*Weedy*. What is it!?"

When he vomited up the small amount of food she'd offered, he stood, hunched and coughing, the vertebrae in his backbone prominent, giving him the appearance of a miniature Stegosaurus. But the worst part was the look of dejected pain he threw her way, the whites of his eyes falsely guilty.

She felt a different kind of fear then, a fear that ran its clammy, seeking fingers up her own hunched spine. And as she watched for what he'd do next, it grew.

After fifteen minutes of stroking him while he coughed, lay down, stood up, looked agitated, coughed and finally lay down again, Sylvie picked up her phone. And put it down again. She sat beside Weedy on the sofa, letting him be, not reaching to touch him this time. She watched as the sunlight moved down the far wall until it was no more. Outside above the tree branches, the sky turned from orange to slate, as the birds and the squirrels and the outside world waited for the day to yield to that familiar, obliterating darkness.

"Don't die, Weedy. Please live." She wanted to stroke him and comfort him, but she was afraid. She sat in the stillness beside him listening to the light tapping sound on the windowpanes as insects fluttered against them seeking the light within. In the distance a car alarm went off. She reached for the phone again, but one more time put it back without dialing. And in the silence of quiet things not spoken, she heard answers she didn't want to hear.

CHAPTER TWENTY-EIGHT

The next morning, Saturday morning, she sprang out of bed before dawn and ran to the sofa where Weedy had slept the night.

He was still there. A part of her thought the doctors would come fine him and take him away.

"You look comfy." He lay curled in the same spot where she'd left him. "How was your first night?"

After carrying him around to the back and watching him stoop, she could hold out no longer, and when she picked up the phone this time, she dialed.

"Carol, I need to talk to you. So you need to tell me if you can. I can't imagine what you're going through. Call me back."

Carol called before Sylvie had even fed Weedy.

"I'm okay. His parents are here. *Driving me crazy,*" she said in a whisper. "But really trying to help. We're all . . . it's a shock, but it's better right now. I'm okay for right now. For this moment."

"You sound good," Sylvie said surprised, sinking relief-filled, into the susurrus of her friend's voice as it stroked frayed threads of nerves.

"Living like the animals do, in the moment. And I can better help Matt if I'm strong and present."

"You're amazing."

"Staying present is keeping me sane."

Sylvie nodded and said again, "You're amazing."

"Okay, something's wrong, Sylvie. What's wrong?"

Sylvie opened her mouth, her thoughts unrolling toward an outcome she hadn't considered completely. If she told Carol, she would implicate her. And she couldn't do that.

"You're waiting to tell me something." Carol's voice rising, sounding less like a Hindu sadhu and more like the friend she knew.

"Nothing to tell."

"Sylvie." Carol now spoke more like a parent to a child. "I'm okay. I'm dealing with Matt's illness one day at a time. But I know you, so tell me what's wrong."

"I'm fine."

"No, you've quit, haven't you? You're afraid to tell me."

"No."

"Then what? Just tell me. Let me help."

"I've stolen a dog from DVX."

For a few beats there was only silence.

"Very funny."

Sylvie didn't know what to say and when she didn't answer, Carol said, "It is funny, isn't it? Because you haven't really stolen a dog. First of all, it's impossible, you couldn't, and apart from that Sainte Sylvie would definitely not do that to her dear, beloved friend Carol when her beloved friend is going through such sucky hell right now."

"But the sad thing is she would and," Sylvie let out her breath. "She has. And that's not the worst part. The worst part is that—"

"Please tell me you're drinking shots of Tequila at 8 a.m. in the morning and that this is some kind of really bad, perhaps typical, but really bad Sylvie joke."

"Hmmm, where'd I put the breakfast Tequila? Nope, don't see it. I can't oblige your fantasy." After a pause when Sylvie waited for Carol to speak and she did not, Sylvie said softly, "Carol . . . I really . . . have . . . stolen a dog." Then quickly she added, "But I don't think anybody knows or ever will. They think he's dead. And he might, die that is. That's why I called you. I'm scared. I think I've done a very stupid thing. But I love this dog more than I thought possible, and I'm scared something in the experiments has made him unable to ingest or digest food, like he's too toxic inside and he vomiting and I'm afraid he's going to die right here, and I feel that if he dies then I don't want to go on and—"

"Stop it." Carol cut her off. "Don't say that, you have to go on. I need you to go on. Back up. How—?"

And as Sylvie explained how she'd hidden Weedy's body in the freezer, and called upon David, she anticipated Carol's stunned reaction.

When silence greeted her after her narrative, she said, "I know at this moment you wish you'd never met me, you're mad at me, and all the harmonic notes that could have been are now minor keys, off kilter. I know that saving one is stupid, and risking my cover is the opposite of what you wanted."

When she heard the sounds down the phone line, she stopped talking. She pressed the phone into her ear and listened to the wet, gray tones of sorrow.

"Oh, Sil, I could never be mad at you," Carol said crying softly. "I'm so proud of you. I wish it'd been me. My god, how *are* you?"

"I feel like a piece of limp linguine."

Carol sniffed. "If I'm upset, it's only because I worry about you. And now I'm going to worry about you every single night. What if they find out? I don't know what I'd do if I lost you. Not now with Matt. Not ever."

"You won't lose me, because they're not going to find out. But—"

"And," Carol said somewhat urgently. "Listen to me. You've saved one life, Sylvie, and that matters. Anyhow, it's done now. Crazy, yes. Not to mention stupid." And Sylvie, who'd been on the verge of losing it herself, laughed a little peck of a laugh. Carol continued. "But it's okay. You've always been a little crazy. And, it does matter, Sylvie. It matters to that dog, doesn't it?" she said. "But don't do it again. Unless of course you think you can get away with it a second time."

CHAPTER TWENTY-NINE

Throughout the rest of that day Sylvie jumped at the slightest sound. If she had thought about having Weedy or any of the laboratory dogs home with her, she thought of the comfort one might bring, knowing she'd saved a life and adding a grateful companion to her small family of one. She was not prepared for stress.

By Sunday afternoon, she knew she could not go into work and leave Weedy. She would have to call Sharon.

"Sharon, I'm sick and I don't want to spread whatever I have to—" She stood in her small front room, before the woodstove, reciting like she was practicing lines in a Broadway play.

"You be dissentious Sharon. I'll be jaded Jane. Ready?" she asked, addressing Weedy. "Sharon," she coughed twice. "I've come down with something and—" She gave Weedy a pathetic look, and began again.

"Sharon, I've stolen one of specimens, relieved him of an imminent endpoint, but because that endpoint might come soon, I need to stay home and care for him." Weedy watched her. "That was a joke. Funny, ha-ha," she cajoled. "Wag your tail or something. Okay, now I'm going to do it. No barking, right?"

She picked up the phone and called Sharon's mobile number. Coughing, she told Sharon that she was sick and wouldn't be in till she'd recovered for fear of spreading her germs.

"Are you freaking kidding me? Sick? You looked fine to me on Friday."

"I—"

"The hangover flu? Is that what you mean?"

"No, I—"

"You know you don't get paid for sick days until you've been here six months"

"I understand. Thank you. I'm sorry, I have to go lie down," she said and hung up as Sharon was saying, ". . . teach you to drink so much you puke your guts and can't do the job I'm paying you to do. Well, no paycheck."

She let out a long exhale breath and turned to Weedy who was on her sofa twisting his neck, trying to lick his wound.

"That's done." She approached him slowly. He didn't cringe when she sat down beside him, and she spoke softly, stroking his back. "This is your new home, little Weedy." She felt her heart expanding if she even looked at him.

She spent the next two days with him in the exact same way: hardly leaving the apartment, stroking him, coaxing him to eat, and driving him to the shelter vet. But when the shelter vet could not help, she drove him to a vet two hours away lest her theft be discovered. Tests revealed an ulcerated stomach.

"He'll heal, but it could be slow. He'll need a special diet," the vet said. You said you found him on the street?"

"Yes."

"Funny, he has the tattoo of a laboratory beagle."

When Sylvie got Weedy back home she was shaking. She called Carol to see if she could come over.

"Beer? Glass of wine?" Sylvie called as Carol walked in and sunk down onto the sofa next to Weedy. She raised a hand to let him sniff, but didn't try to reach for him.

"Just some sparkling water if you have it. So you're Weedy. Hello, funny face. Or should I say, hello, stolen goods?"

"Not funny," Sylvie said from the kitchen.

"How's life in the Witness Protection Program?" Carol asked Weedy.

Sylvie retrieved a bottle of San Pellegrino and two glasses, and sat down on the other side of Weedy. She poured the water and set one before Carol.

"How did life get like this all of a sudden?"

Sylvie shook her head.

"Wasn't it just a month ago that Matt was healthy and well, and you hadn't risked jail time by committing a felony?" Carol asked, reaching for the water and drinking half.

Again Sylvie shook her head. Over the weekend the weather had changed. The days were marching toward full-fledged autumn. The sun's warmth lingered in the shortened afternoons, but by dusk there fell a welcome chill to evening's air. In the fall and winter Sylvie used the woodstove for heat, and placed onto it orange peels, which released the sweet, rich aroma of baking orange, a smell that had not only become her favorite winter scent, but one that enveloped her with quiet contentment.

"Does he pee and poop all over?" Carol asked, alternately wringing slender hands and pulling at a thread on the sleeve of her navy blue sweater.

"No, hardly at all. It's weird but I think he's been housebroken."

Carol looked at him, then at Sylvie. Her expression changed. "Oh, no."

"Yes. He could have belonged to somebody. To somebody who loved him and is looking for him at this very moment. Now, I'm doubly scared. Scared the lab will find out, and scared his people will recognize him. But I guess, if they want him, I should be happy for him. And for them. I haven't even had him a week, and I don't know what I'd do if I lost him. I love him so much already."

Between them Weedy perched not quite sitting but not lying all the way down either. His burned side faced Sylvie, and he gave off an odor that Sylvie assumed would lessen as he healed. "It'd break my heart if his people took him back. I want him with me forever," she said to Carol. Weedy kept his head lowered and forward like he was trying to get underneath something, and he cringed often, even when the hand touching him was stroking gently. "I think I'm going to hell."

"Now is no time for drama, Sylvia Marie."

"Remember when Huck Finn decides to commit to Jim?"

"Not really."

"Well, that's the feeling I had. And this foreboding sense that I really am going to hell."

"Steel one dog and you become a drama queen and a Christian."

"If you had been there, you would have done the exact same thing."

"Yes, exactly. I know."

But Carol was not at the lab, and Sylvie found herself wanting to share details with Carol that she wouldn't understand. The desire to dump all her fears into Carol's lap percolated, and maybe she would have tried had it not been for Matt's illness.

"I don't know if I admire you or think I can never trust you again," Carol said breaking Sylvie's thoughts. She looked to Sylvie then to Weedy. She seemed to study him. "He resembles a mottled, bedraggled seagull." She flapped her arms, giving her best impression of a mottled, bedraggled seagull. "Sainte Sylvie, patron saint of dispossessed dogs."

Sylvie shook her head. "I just had this feeling that going undercover was not producing the kind of results we wanted. You have to reach people in other ways. Through compassion or . . . . You can't lecture people. Even the horrific facts don't change people. They only push people farther away." She stroked Weedy's back. "Why don't more people see it?" She asked turning to Carol.

"It's inconvenient. Most don't want to know. That, and the majority of people don't question something if it's always been done like that. Slavery. Animal exploitation. Chemicals on plants you eat. Look back into history."

"Look around now," Sylvie said.

"So taking Weedy seemed to you like the only good thing you could do. I know you a little bit." Carol put out her arm to stroke Weedy's funny fur, then grabbed Sylvie's hand and squeezed.

Sylvie was about to say, "It's okay," but she stopped. In one week the life she knew had turned upside down, raveled to a point of unrecognition. She thought of Carol, and how her life had just as radically changed. Neither of them spoke. She could hear the bubbles in her glass fizz.

Finally, Carol said to her, "What do we do?"

"I don't know. Be the best we can. And maybe the world changes slowly if enough people do that."

"Be the best we can," Carol repeated.

"Something like that. Cultivate goodness inside. I don't know. But I know I couldn't have lived with myself if hadn't taken Weedy."

"Think, Sil, Weedy might have been one of the dogs Nick brought in. We have to put an end to it. To people like Nick who do it for money. At least if we stop him, we've plugged up one hole."

Sylvie listened. But when Carol stopped, Sylvie said quietly, "You think if you stop Nick you can stop it. You think then your own pain will end. But it won't. It'll go on like it always has."

"I don't know what to do for him. I just want life to go back to how it was," Carol said after a few minutes, speaking aloud Sylvie's thoughts. "He's in pain, Sil."

"Just be with him. Tell him how you love him."

"I am. I'm there for him. Like you are for those dogs. And somehow it just feels right having someone like you in there who loves them and cares."

Sylvie nodded.

"But, the thing is, I don't ever want to put you in harm's way. I never—"

"You weren't the one who told me to steal a dog. But I have. And no one can ever know."

"I know."

"Ever."

"Sylvie?"

"Yeah?"

"You were thinking of the promise, weren't you?"

Outside a car zoomed past, the base pounding out notes. Then it faded and was gone.

"Maybe."

Sylvie remembered her promise. She and Carol had been in college. They'd gone to the landfill because Rita, the girl everyone looked up to, told them they could find all sorts of cheap sofas and shelves: "Very sort of sultry and bohemian, sweeties, you know."

"The landfill?" Sylvie questioned.

"Discarded wares from rich residents. Madame de Pompadour's escritoire, that sort of thing."

They had not found Madame de Pompadour's escritoire, but they'd found something else.

"What is it?" Sylvie called to Carol, but before Sylvie could reach her, Carol screamed.

"It moved!"

Sylvie was by Carol's side looking at a black trash bag. Together they untied the red plastic tabs, Carol turning to Sylvie, "And why did I read that last Stephen King?"

"God, it stinks! But somebody is in there, Sylvie."

"I know. I'm going to look."

"Oh Sil," Carol said turning away, holding her nose. And only then, when Sylvie had gingerly opened the black plastic to see, did her cry leach in whispered, "*No.*"

Inside, the soft brown head limp. Eyes shut, mouth open, gray patches of skin showing through mottled brown fur.

"We have to get it out," Carol cried. "Be careful."

Sylvie pushed the plastic away from the dog, and saw what had befallen the rest of her body. She quickly covered it so Carol wouldn't see swollen puppies still at gibbous mastoid teats.

"Carol," she said as calmly as she could. "Come here. Sit by me. She won't live much longer. But I want us to be here for her." Carol, crying the grief whose provenance belongs to the unexpected and shocking, sat without questioning.

And there Sylvie and Carol had huddled together next to the dying mother, stroking her fur as the stench from the landfill rose up around them, filling their senses in a paradox made macabre next to their love for the helpless animal discarded with garbage. And when the dog took her last breath, the two girls sat surrounded by trash and death, and vowed to help the animals, to end exploitation whether at the hands of cruel owners, medical students, drug companies, industrial farming, or general abuse.

"Your life was not in vain," Sylvie said to the mother dog, the first of many times she would iterate the phrase in reverence and in pain. "We saw you."

"We'll help, no matter what it takes," said Carol.

"I promise."

"And I promise."

They stood up, holding hands, and as they did, a bald eagle swooped slowly over the mounds of trash. When it had flown out of sight, Carol turned to Sylvie: "Did you see—?"

Sylvie nodded. "And look at the sky."

"What about it?"

"The different layers of clouds." Cirrus clouds wisped their way overhead in the silent space that carved out both death and soaring eagle. In the distance, dark violet thunderheads towered as a backdrop cloaking rain.

"Onion-skied," Carol said looking to where Sylvie pointed.

"Onion-skied?" Sylvie questioned.

"It's like peeling back the layers of the world. And if you could just peel back enough, the answers would be revealed."

"There aren't any answers to this."

As if both remembering that day together, they turned and looked at each other. Sylvie spoke first. "It feels so long ago. We were so young."

"It wasn't that long ago, and it's not exactly like we're fossils now."

"I feel like a fossil," Sylvie said.

Carol began laughing hysterically, and Weedy glanced up. She stopped as suddenly as she'd started. "I don't know why we're here. I don't know why Matt is sick." Then she was crying. Sylvie stood and moved closer to her, scrunching in on the other side of Weedy. She put her arms around Carol but didn't say anything. Carol continued through her tears, "I've got to say it. Sylvie, you're strong, stronger than anyone I know. Please let me say it to you."

"You can say it."

"I just have to say it, please."

"You can say it," Sylvie said again, without any idea what Carol needed to say.

"Okay. Matt isn't just sick. He's going to die. And probably soon. We all know that. But I haven't let my mind go there."

"What can I do for you?" Sylvie asked.

"Just be there, like you are. Sylvie?"

"Yes?"

"Do you ever wish you could trade it all in? Just go back to being a child again, and be taken care of?"

Sylvie watched the flames through the glass door of the stove. "I don't know if I have the same memories as everyone else does about childhood. I remember one time, though. I was lying on the sofa, and my mother was in the armchair beside me, and we were both just resting, nothing was wrong. And I had the sense of being taken care of. The peace and comfort of it. The sense of security, even if there isn't any real security. I think that's the feeling I'm always looking for."

"*Someone to watch over me,*" Carol began crooning to the room in general. "Me too. To be taken care of. And now I have to take care of Matt. But who is going to take care of me? Apart from you, because you always do." She lay her head against Sylvie and sniffed, and Sylvie stroked her back like she stroked Weedy. The fire in the woodstove burned and the crispy orange peels released their aroma. After some minutes, Carol's tears slowed, then stopped. She sat up and looked around like she wasn't quite sure where she was.

"We can't marinate in our misery."

"No," Sylvie agreed.

"Your apartment is cozy and warm. Why do you say you hate it so much?"

"I don't hate it. Suddenly everything is different. I have someone to come home to, and this little place is filled with love. I love our home."

Carol smiled. Then she continued talking to Sylvie as if she had never spoken about Matt, asking Sylvie trivial questions as though her life depended on it: how long she thought she could stay at DVX, what she would say and do, who she trusted there and so on.

"Are you going back?"

"Yes, at least to say I quit."

"I feel like it's all my fault. I put you up to it. You did it for me."

"And for the animals," Sylvie cut in.

"What I'm trying to say is that I know it traumatized you. I'm trying to apologize. And I'm trying to tell you, I'm so glad you got Weedy. I'm so happy you rescued one."

Sylvie was quiet. "Thanks. And you know, maybe I will go back. Maybe I'll continue for a while. Like you said, I think loving those dogs may in some weird way help."

Carol looked over to her with round cocker spaniel eyes, on which tears had begun again to form. "Oh Sylvie, you're so brave. And you always say and do the right thing." Sylvie scoffed. "No, I mean it. You're the bravest and most calm person I know in the whole of the northern hemisphere."

"I guess you don't really know that many people, after all."

"Shut up."

"I'll continue for a while, try to get an ally in one of the techs. There's this guy, a doctor, and I think he might just fancy me."

"That's great."

"I knew you'd say that."

"Well," Carol's voice was uncertain and weak from emotion. "I mean for your sake. You should have some fun in your life."

Sylvie didn't answer, and asked instead, "Do you think that while your in-laws are there, you could come over here and check on Weedy, let him out, when I'm gone?"

"Of course. I'll pay you if you let me hang out here. Give you my 401K and throw in dental."

Sylvie looked at her sideways.

"Okay, that was mean. Yes, I'll happily help you look after Weedy. I could even take him with me to the shelter on days I go."

"You're still going to work?"

"Matt insists I do. That he not screw up my life. Talk about saints."

"You can take Weedy, if it doesn't make him think he's going back in one of those runs."

Carol turned to Sylvie. "We'll all get through this. Me, you, Matt, Weedy, in the way we're meant."

"I—"

"Matt has been amazing. You'd think I was the one sick. He wrote this out for me." She stood up and reached into her jeans pocket. Then she read: "*Prison walls cannot confine him who loves, for he belongs to an empire that is not of the world, being made not of material things but of the meaning of things*....Antoine de St-Exupéry, *The Wisdom of the Sands*. Matt said I have to hold onto the meaning of things, which means love."

"I'd agree with Matt. I believe in love," Sylvie said.

"I know. 'The bright pure notes of love.'"

"You can love the flowers and the trees and the earth itself. Life is a gift, as long as you can love. And so you just keep loving Matt, and—"

"I will. And you keep loving little Weedy there." She looked at Weedy as she said it. "Do you realize you are the luckiest dog in the world? Give him time," she said to Sylvie. "He'll know it soon enough."

Sylvie shook her head in an I-don't-know-what-got-into-me sort of way.

"You'll manage somehow. He's not behind bars. He's free as long as he stays with you," Carol said and Sylvie stood and hugged her.

And after Carol walked down the steps, Sylvie returned to Weedy and watched as his tail feathered shyly. "Oh!" She leaned down to kiss his nose and he didn't duck away from her.

She spun around. "Carol!" she called. But Carol was driving away.

As the late-afternoon sky changed from yellow to blue to gray, and then to black, Sylvie ran a bath. She folded a towel and laid it on the bottom of the tub. She wiggled her hand in the water to test its warmth, then ever so gently she lifted Weedy and placed him in. His tail clamped to his belly like it had at the lab, but he didn't struggle, not even when she scooped cups of warm water over his back. She worked up a frothy, white lather, massaging the vertebrae that protruded and the rib bones that were like the fragile vaulting of a broken barrel. His wetted coat showed up the angles of his frail frame, and for a moment Sylvie closed her eyes, letting her suds-covered fingers feel his feeble will, allowing her mind to remember how he looked in the stinking run when she would have to turn away and leave him behind.

She began to sing: "*Someone to watch over you, over you, little Weedy,*" just as Carol had sung earlier. A soapy bubble, with oily hues of pink and blue, rose upward, drifting gently. Then popped.

And she knew then, in that moment, that she would do anything for him, no matter what. It was as if she had felt this all her life. All love and tenderness converged down into her sudsy hands as they held him steady in the tub. Everything else in her world could stop and she would have this one little dog, and this one tiny, yet momentous deed that she had managed to pull off, a pinprick of light casting its beam out across a dark ocean. The darkness ran through her as she thought about what it would be like to lose Weedy, but she pushed it away, focusing on the moment, the small sparkle of light, just as Carol was doing with Matt.

CHAPTER THIRTY

In the morning Sylvie got up and donned the large overcoat, hat and dark glasses she'd taken to wearing when out, in case Sharon should, in a strange kind of Murphy's Law like way, drive by and see her. Weedy himself wore a little T-shirt that Carol had brought, together with cooked chicken and rice, and containers of broth.

"Come on, little guy," Sylvie said stretching the T-shirt out as much as she could so it didn't rub against his side.

The first time she slipped the harness over his head, he sat still, as though resigned to his fate, perhaps forever expecting to be poked and prodded. But on this day, she watched as he raised his face—a sweet face she now found beautiful—toward hers as if to say, "Are we going?" And out they walked together, into the cool morning air, Weedy sniffing the sides of trees just like any other dog.

"There you go!" Sylvie said to him as he raised a leg against a tree. "Good boy!" Over and over she wondered where he had come from, and if he'd ever known a life outside the lab. She stood feeling the air on her skin, watching him sniff the earth. Weedy glanced up to her for direction and she swallowed, as tears blurred her vision. The solid ice of fear was melting and filling her veins with a trickle of love, at first tentatively, even mistrustfully. But as she grew to believe this newly revolving carrousel that was her life, and as one day became the next with Weedy adapting, eating, walking, and stretching like a normal dog, her love, which in the great scheme of things was but a drop, grew to hold within that drop the reflection of the sun and stars anew.

"You'll never go back there again. I will, but you, no. But then what about all the others? Well, I won't think about that now. Thank you, Miss O'Hara. I'll think about that tomorrow." Weedy walked stiffly to the next tree, nose to the ground, breathing in rich, earthy scents, so foreign from the smells of the lab. "I have an idea. Follow me. I know a field."

She walked to the end of her street and turned. Her eyes skirted the road, latching onto every passerby, sizing up, and determining if she and Weedy were safe. Weedy nosed his way along the street. When Sylvie arrived at a barbed wire fence, she lifted the lower wire and coaxed Weedy under. She swung her leg over, looking one way, then the next. Beyond the barbed wire was a football-sized field, covered in dried brown grass. Yellowed hues of goldenrod and Jerusalem artichoke bedecked the perimeter. And thistles put forth the last of purple flowers, seeding offspring before a hard frost.

"What do you think, little Weedy? Do you feel like a real beagle now?" She scanned the field for the white cottontail of a rabbit, but saw only birds flying above. She and Weedy walked on, while underneath her step the dried grass crunched and the crows cawed out in language only they understood. The day held brilliant clarity and in one joyous moment, she dropped to her knees, startling Weedy, and grasping him at the same time. "I love you so much!" All around the low cant of time marching forward. All around the low chant of hearts opening to love. She plucked a little purple clover flower with which to press into her journal and remember that singular moment and her sudden joy.

As stress and worry over him waned, she found she was not prepared for the gratitude that having him brought. Now there was a liquid quality to time and she found herself willing it to slow. Once Weedy began keeping food down, she'd sit, watching him with his head in the metal bowl and his legs sprawled outwards—just your average dog in a household. Not a specimen behind bars in a laboratory, awaiting his humane endpoint.

In the evening she gave him the pieces of chicken that Carol bought at a local farm, and poured in the broth together with rice and sautéed vegetables. Weedy stood on tentative legs, but legs that were growing stronger each day. He stood with legs braced and strangely bowed as if prepared for someone to grab him while he ate and take him away. And Sylvie smiled, sometimes laughing outright, as he slurped and splashed the food.

It was only when the police car passed her house, its siren blaring full force that she understood what she should have understood at once.

Weedy was tucked beside her on the sofa. She stroked him with her left hand, while her right hand held a book. When the sounds of the siren approached, Weedy raised his head and looked around, eyes large, ears pinned to his skull. Then, without warning, he flung his head back, his muzzled pointed skyward, his mouth rounded like an instrument. But no sound came forth. Sylvie watched and stared in horror as she listened to his airy, rasping vocalizations.

Only then did she realize. Only then did she understand that he would never bark his enthusiasm, just as he had never barked his pain. And she wanted someone beside her with whom to share the unspeakable, and she wanted Weedy to know how sorry she was, but all she could say was, "*Oh, Weedy, no.*"

That night, Sylvie opened her front door and stood holding him in her arms as she listened to the outside sounds and breathed in the air as the day ended and night began. Light dripped and fell from the stars. A bright star, or perhaps a planet—Venus or Jupiter—had risen near a lopsided moon. She hugged Weedy to her chest.

"I didn't know I could feel so much love," she whispered, sensing their two souls connate from a previous time. Yet beneath the joy there lingered still a thin sheath of fear. He would always be stolen goods. Something could easily shatter her newfound joy.

She stepped back inside. When he first came home with her, she had tucked him into a nest on one end of the sofa, and fixed a worn fleece blanket around him. She'd sat beside him stroking until he made a sigh and she saw he was resting. Even then she didn't want to leave his side. She'd sit beside him, whispering words of comfort while lightly brushing her fingers over him when he made the little raspy sounds in his dreams, and sometimes his legs twitched and ran. Finally, she'd stand up quietly, slipping off to brush her teeth and get into her own bed. At first he stayed the night in his nest, but after a few days, she'd wake to find him standing beside her bed, making the strange sounds.

"I'm right here, Weedy." And she'd get out of bed and take him back to the sofa. But one evening, she simply lifted him and put him atop the covers beside her and from that night onward he slept beside her in the bed and never made the raspy crying sounds again.

CHAPTER THIRTY-ONE

On her first day back to DVX after being out for over a week, Sylvie worried so much about Weedy, she turned around and drove back to her apartment, knowing she'd be late. She ran through the door and found Weedy right where she left him, curled on the sofa.

"What a good boy." She ran to the kitchen and grabbed the treat bag. Weedy jumped off and followed her and she held out a dog cookie. "What a good, good boy you are. Breathe," she said to herself. "Just breathe." She walked back toward the front door. "Come, Weedy," she called and he followed her as though he had lived with her his whole life. She bent and lifted him onto the sofa and dropped another cookie beside him. "I'll be back tonight. You rest and be good."

She hurried to her car, but she'd only driven a few blocks when she pulled over to the side of the road and called Carol. No answer. Carol always told her to text instead, but Sylvie didn't like texting. Too many people walked around in a perpetual bent-necked daze. Still she texted Carol, who was going to Sylvie's at lunch to check on Weedy.

Please, can you go over sooner? I don't know what he'll do all day.

The thought of leaving Weedy and her cozy home to work all day without windows in the sickly air of DVX almost made her turn back a second time.

Carol texted back immediately.

Plz don't worry. I'll go ovr.

Sylvie parked behind DVX, stepping out in bracing fall air. In the distance, someone was burning leaves.

When she entered the lab, she knew at once something was different. When she walked through the small reception area, the first thing she heard was a dog howling. The sound was so foreign to the lab, it stopped her for a moment and she listened as the sound filled the halls.

The howling stopped and she pushed through the swinging doors. She saw the dark-haired doctor walking toward her. Fear crept up her body as possessive as poison ivy proclaiming a fence post. In that one instance she was certain everyone working at the lab knew what she'd done, and they were awaiting her return to arrest her. So rapidly were these thoughts racing through her mind, simultaneously with the thought that she must and would tell them anything to get away and get back to Weedy, that she stumbled, tripping over the thick hose. She ducked into the mop closet to collect herself. She was bent over the buckets, when she felt a hand on her back. She whirled around only to find herself looking into the eyes of the young doctor.

"You startled me."

"I didn't mean to. You must startle easily."

She stared dumbly.

"Look, I need to ask you something."

The walls were closing in. She knew if she spoke her lips would tremble.

"Do you go out with that cop?"

"What?" She asked caught off guard.

With a smile, he said, "I asked, do you go out with that cop?"

"*No,*" she breathed out, relief sluicing like a river through parched earth. "What cop?

"Come on."

Her eyes flickered beyond his head to the hall, where she sought her escape. But she was cornered in a closet. She looked at the floor. "It's complicated."

"Ah, yes. Isn't it always?" He smiled looking at her, perhaps willing her to meet his eyes and smile back. He was attractive behind the thick glasses. Perhaps a bit too suave. "I want you to take a dog."

"*What*?" She asked sharply.

"Hey, are you okay?" He touched her again.

At the touch, she flinched.

"It's okay," he said in a gentle, soothing tone. "My name is Kenneth.I just thought . . ." He didn't finish, because just then there was the clanging sound of a bucket or something crashing onto the floor. "But you better hurry," he said stepping aside to let her out. "They'll be pissed off. Number 13."

She walked by number 11 to get to 13 and when she did, she felt a spasm in her body—a feeling of holding onto a thread that attached to the lifeboat carrying the ones you loved in the midst of a hungry ocean. Weedy was not in there; there was relief for that. But there another beagle stood.

When she was leaving the treatment room, she heard the slapping of Sharon's shoes. Could Sharon not keep her soles together? She pictured her stout frame, a force in itself, barreling forward, ready to chew her out for her absence. She straightened her shoulders. Sharon would stand in her 'vitally' clean lab coat, in all her righteousness, and state: "Rule number one, don't get sick."

But Sharon was not wearing her lab coat today. Sylvie noticed the same T-shirt she'd seen the day she applied for the job. But the shirt was ripped and dirty. Her pants too were stained. A bruise was darkening and swelling the side of her face, and there was blood congealed on her lip.

"That dog," Sharon panted, trembling. "I need your help."

"Of course. What happened?"

"It went psycho on me. I was just trying to get it to the treatment room." Sylvie realized Sharon must have been doing her job.

"Come with me," Sylvie said and led a docile Sharon to the bathroom, where she sat her down on the toilet and, with paper towels and soap, began cleaning her face.

"You need to get some ice on that bruise."

"Maybe I pulled too hard on the leash. But then it was all over me, crushing my face against the wall. I hate this job. I hate the prick doctors. I could tell them what happened, but would they care? *Bring me number such and such. We have an important trial to finish.*"

"Here, turn your head just a little. There. Can you go home, and get some rest? I can do what you need."

"You think I want to be doing this job? I only do it because it's the only job I could get after applying for a makeup artist at Belk and Penny's and about twenty other places. I hate it here. I do it because my mother lives with me and she has diabetes, and who else is going take care of her? If I had my life over I'd not be stuck here with a bunch of animals."

Sylvie let Sharon talk. After a while she stopped and looked up at Sylvie.

"Thank you, Jane. You're good with the specimens. This wouldn't have happened to you." She groaned as she shifted off the toilet. "I think I will go home. To hell with the doctors. If they ask for me, tell them you don't know." As she shuffled out the bathroom door, she turned and said again, "Thank you."

By the end of the day Sylvie's legs and feet ached. There was an early darkness when she stepped outside. Shards of light slipped between buildings, leaving shadows. Thinking only of seeing Weedy, she was walking quickly to her car, when she heard someone calling to someone else.

"Jane! Jane!" She heard the man calling, and realized that Jane was her name. She turned around and saw Kenneth walking toward her.

"Are you leaving?"

"Yes," she answered.

"Let me buy you dinner."

"Thank you, but I can't."

"Please. I insist."

"Maybe another time."

He reached out a hand as if to get her attention. "I need to talk to you. I don't think it can wait."

Beneath her shirt the sweat pooled on her skin, cold and damp.

"Okay," she said as nonchalantly as she could. "Go ahead then. Talk."

"Get in my car."

"I'd rather you tell me right here."

"Not private enough. Get in my car."

"No."

"I think we both know that we need to talk. Maybe you have something urgent you need to get back to, but I'm telling you, nothing—absolutely nothing right now—is as urgent as this." At the words, Sylvie's blood went cold. "I'm taking you to dinner. No room for arguing. And you might actually have a good time," he added, a smile altering his face to something softer.

Anxiety combined with overwhelm and most of all impotence. It must be how the ordinary people feel who live in countries run by dictators and corruption. Would you turn to the police for help only to find that they, too, were corrupt?

The sun slipped below the houses behind the lab and Sylvie felt a chill run over her clammy body.

"I need to make one call." But no, he would hear her. She turned her back to him and texted Carol.

You need to keep Weedy with you. Please. I'm onto someone who knows something.

When she received an immediate text back, she was grateful to texting in a way she'd never been before.

Grt that yr on to somthng

Ok to WD

Find out all u can

"Okay." She turned to Kenneth and walked beside him to his car saying nothing. Dread and exhaustion, her constant companions, walked with her. Her body would just give out. A body couldn't sustain this level of stress and adrenaline forever.

She settled back in Kenneth's car, nearly closing her eyes and letting the movement lull her. But there was no lulling to be had. He knew what she'd done. Why else this insistence on talking. What she wanted was to be home with Weedy. What she wanted was for Matt and Weedy to be well. What she wanted was to be able to forget about what went on in the lab. To stop working there. To stop laboratory testing on animals. For all humans and all animals to live in peace.

"What are you thinking about?" Kenneth turned to her.

"World peace," she answered.

He laughed. "Of course. Me too."

He pulled into a parking lot before a cedar-sided restaurant she'd never seen.

"I thought you might like it here." When she didn't answer, he added, "Indian, mostly vegetarian." Still she didn't answer him.

She followed him in, passing fake potted plants and diners with bent heads against mustard yellow walls. They were seated in a booth opposite each other. She found that meeting his intense dark eyes every time she looked up was unnerving.

"I'm not looking for a relationship," she bluffed, as if she assumed it was the reason he'd asked her out. The waiter approached and when Kenneth asked her, "You'll have some wine, won't you?" she nodded, yes. The waiter left. She heard tinkling water and turned her head to see a fountain, its blue lit water falling upon smooth stones.

"I'm not looking to go out with anyone either. But sometimes the experiments we do on the animals takes it out of me. I just needed some sympathetic company. Or non-sympathetic company. Just company. You seemed a safe bet." He cleared his throat. "I'd like to ask you something."

She nodded, uncomfortable.

"Have you ever heard about the Diving Dog experiment?"

Sylvie felt her cheeks color. "The what?" She knew very well what the Diving Dog experiment was.

"Diving Dog. It was only one of the tests that the navy performed on dogs. It should have been called the drowning dog experiment." He stopped and looked across at her.

She didn't respond.

"And it wasn't just dogs. It was monkeys and cats and rats, too. They were all used to study the physiological effects of decompression. There were three common experiments. In the first, dogs were placed in stereotaxic devices, the skin and muscle over their nose and skull was peeled back, electrodes inserted into the skulls, then the dogs were subjected to simulation diving. After the experiment the animals were killed with a cardiac injection."

She felt his eyes studying her face. She took a sip of her water. The ice was cold and bothered her teeth. "The second method is when the animal was intubated and decompressed." He continued explaining what she already knew. "Dogs have been used since 1937," he was saying. "And as many as one hundred dogs could be used in one single experiment. That's a lot of dogs, all to test the psychological effects of decompression." When he paused, she realized she'd been holding her breath.

"A lot of taxpayer money," she answered, putting a hand to her mouth in a feigned yawn.

"But the thing about the Diving Dog experiment," he continued as if he hadn't heard her. "Is that, like many experiments on animals, it came with a caveat that many of the findings on dogs could not be extrapolated to man. And still they continued to do it. Why?"

"Money and profit, I suppose. That, and the fact that a lot of humans are stupid."

He stared across intently again, and she imagined herself in some kind of test as if her answer would prove her innocence.

But then, without warning, he said: "What's very interesting to me is that you didn't even flinch when I told you of the three methods of the Diving Dog experiment. To me that says that either you're a psychopathic personality type yourself, and you experiment with torture to animals. Or you're an animal activist and you're already familiar with the Diving Dog experiment." When she didn't answer him, he said, "So which one is it?"

"Those are two somewhat extreme options that you've limited me to."

"You didn't answer me."

"I'm tired." She picked at the cardboard drinks menu.

"You probably want me to change the subject, don't you?"

"I probably want to eat quickly and go home."

"So you're not really looking to have a relationship, so that's why you go out with that moronic cop? Because you're not looking to go out with someone?"

"I don't go out with him," she said.

"You don't know me, so why don't you give me a chance?"

"Why did you assume I liked vegetarian food?"

"Because you like the animals. In fact, you're working in the lab because you like them."

She was about to ask, "What do you mean?" when he leaned forward and grabbed her hand. "I do too. Don't you understand? I'm like you."

She had a floating feeling of falling away from her body. Sudden relief, but like sand that churns beneath the surf, dirtying the water, she felt it tinged with danger. She wished for Carol.

Be real, she said to herself. Neutral, but real. Don't overreact. "I guess I like them. I feel sorry for them. They deserve some kindness and respect before dying." The truth of her words hit her.

"Come on. Don't play dumb."

She didn't look at him. The waiter returned and let Kenneth smell and taste the wine, before filling their glasses.

"Who do you work for? PETA?"

"No, I don't work for PETA. I only just learned what PETA was from Sharon." She reached for her glass, almost spilling the red liquid onto her shirt, and took a large swallow.

"*Stop pretending. I'm onto you.*" She tensed. Perhaps he sensed it, for he said more gently, "Jane, don't treat me like I'm stupid." Then in a hushed, yet urgent voice: "Don't you get it? I'm undercover too."

For a moment she stared at the table. Then ever so softly: "Are you really?"

"Yes."

This time the relief was real. "Oh, thank god."

He smiled across at her. "Yeah, or you could thank me."

"Then who do *you* work for? How long have you been at DVX?"

"Two years and I've learned a lot."

"How'd you know I was?"

"Just a hunch. Maybe it takes one to know one. So many people miss the essence of life. I watch. I'm aware. I see things. I knew what you were doing with that dog. He was alive, wasn't he?"

"No," she said too quickly. "He was dead." Relief receded, and the little voice inside her head began shouting.

Kenneth gazed back into her eyes.

"Truly. That dog was very dead," she said.

"Oh, can you be only a little dead?" He smiled.

"I think half the people I see walking around are half dead," she answered, desperate to change the subject.

"Whereas that little dog was very dead," he said but he let it drop.

She glanced across the restaurant to an Indian or Pakistani family all sharing food and she felt the familiar pang. The faux stone fountain tinkled melodically in the background. A couple in the corner sat side by side on the same booth, feeding each other. She sipped her wine, letting it travel to her stomach, warming her, numbing her.

She caught the eye of a woman sitting by herself with a book, and wondered what people glimpsing her would think. Would they assume she was married to the nice-looking man and envy her? That she was a woman who had stolen a dog to help give it a better life, because she longed to give all animals a better life, was a fact known by only one person in the entire city. Even Carol didn't understand completely. It was an unimportant piece of knowledge, but what made it fascinating was that only she knew it, and she wondered how many other people seated and dining had secrets that only they and no one else knew.

"What are you thinking now? You go far away."

"I got caught up thinking about the other people in this place. I'm just incredibly tired. I probably shouldn't have come with you. You said you needed to talk to me."

"I just did. I wanted to find out about you. And I needed to tell you about me. You can trust me."

"Okay." And when her Navratan Korma arrived, she ate it with waning appetite, anticipating her exit, and wondering what tomorrow would bring when she saw Kenneth at the lab.

"Okay, you were right," Kenneth broke the silence. "There is more." She looked up at him. "Jane. You could be in danger. That's why I asked you here."

"What do you mean?"

"The labs are cracking down on undercover agents. And when they find them, they can make your life a living hell."

"Then please don't tell them."

"I think they might already know."

"How do you know?"

"Come home with me tonight. You can stay. You'll be safe. I'll sleep on the couch, and I'll drive you to work early tomorrow so nobody knows."

"I can't."

"Yes, you can. I live just around the corner."

She felt the conversation had taken a murky turn that she hadn't foreseen to an already surreal evening. She could not tell him about Weedy. "I'm sorry but no, and if you force me to stay here and call a cab, it will be somewhat awkward for us tomorrow. Remember we work together. Sort of."

"The truth of it is, you're not safe. I'm thinking of your safety."

"No, you're not. You're thinking of something altogether different than my safety." She held eye contact with him and didn't look away. She had only to think of Weedy to feel the adamantine column of flesh and bone that perched in the booth further harden in its resolve to resist any invitation he thrust her way.

He must have sensed her resolve, for he persisted in trying to convince her of an imminent and grave danger, but with less and less conviction. She sat opposite, hardened like ceramic glazing, until he finally agreed to drive her back to her car.

He was silent on the drive back to the lab, and that scared her. Not his anger, but by the amount he now knew about her, and how he could use it against her. But she couldn't rack up yet another guy she had to go out with because he helped her with this mission.

Standing alone in the DVX parking lot was eerie. A lopsided moon balanced on the tops of black tree branches. She shivered, and all at once it was as if she could smell fear in the same way she knew the animals could. She sensed fear skulking around her, and fear smelt dank and putrid. *Weedy.* She needed to get to Weedy.

As she drove through desolate streets, unease sat behind her in the backseat. But the feeling slipped away as soon as she walked into her small apartment and saw Carol sitting on the sofa with Weedy. A wave of emotion—something existing beyond joy, perhaps relief, mixed with exhaustion and grief—caught her off guard when she saw her friend sitting beside her dog, waiting for her to return home. As she came through the door, Weedy's tail flumped simultaneously with Carol saying, "Oh, my god, look at you. You look a total wreck."

"Thanks. That's what friends are for. Lift each other up. Lie a little when one looks like crap." She smiled and could not have imagined a half an hour ago that this much love and warmth was possible in her world. She thought the powerful emotion might well push from the inside out, bursting like a big red balloon.

"What on earth happened to you?"

Sylvie collapsed onto the sofa, stroking Weedy, his tail still flapping. "Little Weedy! I missed you, too," she said grasping his head between her hands and kissing it. She looked up to Carol. "Don't you need to get home to Matt?"

"I'm okay for another minute. What happened?"

Sylvie leaned over Weedy, sticking her nose into his coat. "He no longer stinks. I was a total wreck a minute ago, you're right. But now, I'm fine. I'm wonderful."

"We know you're wonderful."

"I love this little dog more than I have words to say."

"I know. Why do you think I took such good care of him? Mangy little mutt."

"You're my constellation. When I walked in and saw you with Weedy...."

"What?"

"Forget the containers...."

"The what?"

"Forget the physical containers, the bodies, him a dog, you a human. It's as if I saw only bright lights, the souls of each of you and it was like I was part of you, part of this small constellation of stars. A very, very small constellation."

"Three."

"That's right. But very bright."

"You're so crazy and so wonderful. I'm happy to be part of your very, very small constellation of containers or whatever. Unless one of us shoots or falls from the sky. So let's say that we will always, be together, okay?"

"Yes, let's say that. It would make me happy," Sylvie said. "This is the single best thing I've ever done in my life. For Weedy, yes. And for the world, to take a stand for what I believe is right. But also for myself. I love him."

"Sylvie, you're avoiding telling me what happened tonight."

"I needed to get away from what happened tonight." Sylvie massaged the insides of Weedy's ears and he made a small sigh then curled, settling into a ball beside her. "You're not going to believe it." And as she began speaking, Carol stared wide-eyed, then lay her head back closing her eyes.

"Sylvie," Carol said eyes still shut. "Are you sure you can trust this guy? I wish you hadn't been so quick to divulge yourself. I mean for your sake."

"I think I can trust him. I mean, how'd he know about me if he isn't the same? You don't notice what you don't know, right?"

"Maybe."

Sylvie started laughing.

"What?"

"I haven't had so many dates in months. Who would have thought that working as a handler in the lab would produce men in every parking lot? Does your life sometimes feel unreal to you?"

"Yes."

"I mean, when I was little, I always loved animals, but if anyone had presented me with a preview of my current life, I doubt I would have signed up for planet earth. I wouldn't have even considered. It's just not the way I thought things would work out."

"I know. It never is. Can I tell you something?"

"Yes."

"They're taking Matt back to the hospital."

"Oh, Carol, I'm sorry. I should have asked you about Matt first thing instead of going on about stuff that doesn't matter beside—"

"No," Carol waved her hand, her eyes closed. "It's exactly what I needed. And it all matters. My life just sucks particularly much right now. And anyway, that's not what I need to tell you."

"Okay."

"The doctors said there's a new drug, and there's a chance it could help Matt. At least help with his pain. Possibly prolong his life."

"That's fantastic."

"Wait. They'll begin clinical trials soon. He would be a guinea pig. The drug is not on the market yet. They're in a pre-clinical phase, testing it on mice and then they test on dogs and primates before clinical trials and then human use." Carol straightened and opened her eyes.

Sylvie turned but Carol didn't look at her. "Sil, I want them to hurry up with the tests, and I want them to *do* the tests. On mice, on monkeys, whatever it takes. I think if I were the one sick, I wouldn't want that, but if it could help Matt feel better . . ." She stopped, and they both sat looking ahead as the moments passed, one after another. "Okay, please say something, Sylvie."

"There's nothing for me to say."

"You're angry."

"Of course I'm angry. But not with you. Your husband is—"

"Say it. He's dying. He's young and he's dying and he's in pain, and that's why I want the tests. For his sake."

"But then what's the point? Why say we believe it's wrong if we bend the rules for our own loved ones?"

"You're not in my shoes. You never have been. You can't possibly understand. And I need you to be there for me, and understand, but you can't. So I'm alone with this."

Sylvie thought about the many times she'd felt alone, wanting to share with Carol something that happened at the lab.

"We're all alone," she said, aware of how empty her words sounded.

"I knew you were angry."

"I didn't—"

"If you were dying and testing on mice could save you, would you?"

"No," Sylvie said. "I've asked myself a hundred times. I've thought about it. And, *no.* How could I? Like Socrates in a reverse sort of way."

"Of course we never really know until presented in real life."

Sylvie shrugged.

Carol turned to face her squarely. "Okay, how about if I were dying and testing on mice could save me, would you?"

Sylvie swallowed and pushed her hair from her eyes.

Carol looked away from her, and said to the room in general, "I never felt it right to have animals suffer. Even the mice and rats that so many people don't give a damn about. Why should my life be worth more than theirs? But for Matt's sake. . . ."

"But so many times they test drugs on animals and get an okay, only to find out that they fail on humans," Sylvie answered her urgently. "Because humans are so very much different from animals. In all ways but one: animals and humans both suffer and feel pain."

"Sil, don't you think I know that better than anyone else? Don't judge me. That's not what I need right now."

"I'm not judging you," Sylvie said stubbornly.

Carol began to cry quietly. "I need to go."

Sylvie leaned over and put her arms around Carol's quivering shoulders. "I'm sorry," she said. But there was nothing else she could say. There was nothing she could do.

After Carol left, Sylvie curled herself into a fetal position encircling Weedy. Her body was overcome by a sorrow she could neither name nor assuage. She lay silent. But the night outside was not silent, and she lay listening to the sounds of sirens and alarms, to the wind as it moved through the tree branches. She lay listening to the sound of Weedy's breath. At length, she rose, locked her front door and undressed. She lifted Weedy gently then climbed into bed.

"Goodnight, Weedy. Stay with me a long time. I love you so much." She hugged him close to her breast as sleep ran through her with slender fingers and its potent caress, taking her away from the world and all its pain.

In the parking lot of DVX, Kenneth had watched her drive away. Once home he picked up his phone.

"I had dinner with her. Yeah, she's a snitch. How'd I find out? I simply told her I was too. Told you it would work. So now, how would you like me to proceed at the lab tomorrow?" There was the slightest pause. Then he'd replied. "Alright, if you're sure." But when he clicked off the phone, he felt conflicting emotions. The thing was, he really liked her.

CHAPTER THIRTY-TWO

Dawn raised the curtain on a vast universe and the stars paled. As the first light pushed through muted silver sky outside her window, Sylvie woke with Weedy down by her thigh. She placed a hand over her heart and felt it thumping. As she lay still, taking in the ordinary bedside table and lamp, the room's shape unfolded and the night's disturbing dream receded partially, less incubus seeking her demise, more sibilant unease, a cracked door seeping gas. She sat up in bed, murmured to Weedy, who stirred only slightly, then flopped back and closed her eyes, trying to find sleep again. The ghostly feeling of the dream would persist throughout the day, but distinct and tactile memories were already retreating from her tumbling thoughts to settle somewhere in her subconscious where they would visit her only with imperfect provocation. What she could remember easily were the events of the preceding day.

She rose, showered, dressed, and fed Weedy, who now pranced around for his food on her kitchen floor in a kind of shuffled tap dance, body wiggling, mouth yopping out a funny little sound of hope. She called Carol, got no answer, and texted her asking if she would please check in on Weedy. Then she added:

If you can't, it's ok.

She kissed Weedy goodbye and drove to work.

Once through the doors at DVX, she was immediately nervous that she would bump into Kenneth. Her mind was quickly distracted when two things happened that confused her. Big, burly Mike, who never spoke to her, stopped before her when she was on her way to lead out the dogs. She looked up at him briefly. He opened his mouth, as if he wanted to speak to her, but at the same time, one of the doctors called from down the hall:

"We've an especially full day today. Could you please be quick?"

She glanced to Mike, who was making a strange face. She smiled at him uncertain and walked on.

The second thing happened when she turned the corner and nearly ran into Sharon.

"Hi, Jane!" Sharon said, waving a stack of papers in Sylvie's face like she was fanning a fire. Sylvie said hi, noticing the bruise coloring Sharon's cheek. "Better hurry," Sharon added, but she flashed a smile of conspiracy.

Sylvie led the dogs to the research room, keeping her eyes downcast. She wanted to run back to her apartment, grab Weedy and drive away to a pristine lake in the mountains. If she couldn't do that she wanted to dive under her duvet and eat potato chips. As the afternoon wore on and she neared the end of her shift, she was thinking about returning home to Weedy, a little smile on her face, when she turned the corner and literally bumped into Kenneth.

"Hey," he said, reaching out a hand. "You okay?"

"I'm fine. Trying to finish up here."

"Look. I'm sorry. I mean about last night. I shouldn't have pushed you to come over. But, I *am* worried about you. I've heard some of the other doctors talking. They suspect you. You are, hmmm, how shall I say it?" He smiled. "Not the usual riff-raff that takes up a position here. You're too polished, despite your rather hopeless fake accent. And so, they suspect you. Please let me help you."

"I'm fine," she repeated.

"I don't think you are. I can help. You need to tell me what you're planning to do. Exposé on the lab, something like that?"

She stood in the hallway, breathing in the smell of bleach, and debating what to say to him. She did need an ally. That was true. All of a sudden she wished she hadn't told David. Kenneth, being undercover himself, was the much better ally.

"Okay," she said. "I'll tell you. Because I have a plan. But let's at least go outside to discuss it. I wouldn't think standing in here was the best place." She watched him smile and they agreed to meet in thirty minutes.

When they walked outside together, forty-five minutes later, dark clouds hovered in the west.

"Quick. Walk away from me," she said.

"Why?"

"Just do it," she said, glancing across the parking lot. Mike was ducking into his Toyota. But she'd seen him looking pointedly at them over roof of his car. "He was watching us," she said grabbing Kenneth's arm.

"He's a run cleaner. Just a big oaf. He can't hurt us."

"I'm becoming paranoid."

"Come on. I think we're about to be in a downpour. We can duck in over there if you're that paranoid." He placed his hand on the small of her back and steered her gently out of the parking lot and over a crumbled section of the cement wall. They passed the blackened brick and wood remains of a fire with once shiny, now fading, beer cans dazzling center stage. He opened the creaking door to the shell of an abandoned house. She stepped inside as startled birds flapped upward in different directions, unsettling dust to roost in rafters once, but now no more. Some of the birds flew out through a hole in the roof. Others darted back and forth. Sylvie's eyes followed them, taking in the water-stained remains of the roof and the cobwebbed, dust-devoured walls. She stepped carefully over broken shards of glass mingling with rusty cans and old newsprint.

"Do you come here often?" she asked.

"No. Only when I'm trying to seduce beautiful but very reluctant, women."

"If I'm to trust you, you're going to have to tell me a little about yourself. How'd you end up a doctor at DVX?"

"Okay. I'm Kenneth Watson. I graduated from Cornell, went to Rochester for my residency. Fell in with a group who were devoted to animal causes. Began studying up myself and realized we weren't helping humans by testing on animals. I also saw the extreme, and in many cases unnecessary, suffering we were causing to sentient animals. I decided I could do something about it."

Sylvie knew then that she could tell him about Weedy. She needed to tell someone to take the burden off Carol. "My mother divorced my father five years ago and moved here," Kenneth continued. "I came here two years ago and got the job at DVX. I've been here since. I'm kind of a nerd, but you have to admit, I'm kind of a handsome nerd." His smile stretched, reaching her. "That was the short version. If you want a longer, more fascinating version, you'll let me treat you to an expensive dinner. Candlelight, aged Bordeaux, very romantic, and with the promise of some dessert at my house afterward."

"You're not shy about stating your desires."

"Getting down to business. But I intend to show you how much fun business can be."

"But what good are you doing the animals at DVX? I don't see how you're helping them."

He didn't answer, but he gazed down into her eyes. "You're beautiful. Even more so when you're passionate. I don't want to find out if you're also beautiful when you're in grave danger. Come here."

He was attractive in a geeky way, and she felt a twinge of something in her abdomen. Carol said she had to go out more, have fun.

"You always wear pink under your coat."

"Not always."

Sylvie shrugged.

"Okay. My mother once told me it looked best with my dark hair, and I should wear it around the girls I liked."

She looked down, but smiled.

"So I have a lot of pink shirts. Real men can wear pink. I like pink."

And she knew then she liked him.

He stepped toward her, and was reaching his arms around her waist, when a streak of lightening illuminated the sky, followed immediately by a sharp crack of thunder. She jumped.

"It's okay. Come here."

She stood where she was. "Aren't thunderstorms supposed to be over in fall?"

"The weather's doing weird things. Global warming. We can expect a lot worse." He reached to take her hand, and pulled her to his chest, holding her against himself, stroking her back. "But don't be afraid. I'll take care of you."

"I'm fine," she mumbled into his chest. The rain began and beat down like gunshot on the old roof, splattering through the holes and onto floor in some spots. She stood letting his hands explore the curves of her back. "Sometimes I just want for someone to take care of me," she said, and pulled away as if afraid to have her desire granted. "I'll have dinner with you. Candles and all that. But I have to go out with David first, the cop. He transports dogs and I'm finding out as much as I can."

"Should I be jealous?"

"No. Also, I have a plan. And he's going to help me, because he likes me. Having the law help with an illegal action can only be a good thing, right?" She spoke loudly, leaning toward him to be heard over the rain.

He chuckled. "I like your style."

"And one last thing."

"Shoot," he said.

"I did take home that dog. You were right."

He stared at her for a moment as if not comprehending. Then quickly: "I knew that." Another crack of thunder startled them both and when the low rumblings followed, he again reached out to hold her. She turned from him.

"I need to get home."

"It's pouring with rain. You're not going anywhere."

He walked a few paces and sat down on one wooden step of an old stairway. He patted the space next to him and dust wafted up. "Come, sit down by me. Tell me all about your plan. Maybe I can help."

"Okay," she said, and she sat down in the dust.

Outside the abandoned building Mike stood soaking wet, straining to listen through the falling rain.

CHAPTER THIRTY-THREE

The rain had lessened by the time Sylvie explained her plan to Kenneth: how David would trick Nick into transporting the dogs to the lab himself, fibbing that his van was broken but he had dogs. There in plain sight would be the dogs taken from unsuspecting people. People who thought their animal companions were going to loving homes. Nick would be implicated, and so too would DVX. She told him it would have to be well after hours. She told him why she wanted to expose Nick, and wondered if a journalist could also be on hand.

"So you don't work for any organization?" Kenneth asked out of the blue.

"No, it's just me and—" She stopped short. Something was crawling up her neck. She brushed her hand at the back of her neck, but nothing was there. "Why do you ask?"

"Usually there is an animal rights group behind work like this. Not just one little lonesome person," he said reaching an arm behind her and stroking her back.

"Yeah, well. Just me." She couldn't disregard the alarm she felt that had not been with her moments before.

"Do you find it hard working there?"

He asked the question with such compassion in his voice, she wanted to let go and fall into his arms. "Yes," was all she said.

After a while he began, "You know love and compassion can trap you too." When she didn't answer, he explained, "You can care too much."

"Is that what you feel?"

"I'm trapped, but not in the way you think," he said turning away from her slightly.

"You're trying to help. We're all doing what we think we can to help." She spoke wanting to believe his words, her rational mind squelching her intuition.

He made a sound she couldn't interpret. Then: "So it's really just you? No one else? No organization?"

"Just me," she answered again.

He turned toward her on the step, his knees on either side of hers. "I like it that way." He leaned toward her, pushing her hair back and touched the hollow on the side of her neck where neck met collarbone. "Do you like that?"

She didn't answer him, and when the silence lengthened, he leaned in, hesitating slightly, and kissed the same spot. She pulled away.

"What's wrong?" he asked her.

"Nothing."

"Look, one thing I promise you, you can trust me."

She shivered in the damp air. Her intuition shouted for her to heed it: Surely, those who were most worthy of trust had no need to go forth pronouncing its presence. Trust made itself perceptible through deeds and time.

"I really have to go now," she said standing up. In a flash, he was up, reaching for her.

"Kenneth, not now."

"Oh, come on. I know you like me. I can feel it. And I really like you. I wish I didn't, but I do."

"Then let's have dinner and talk, and then . . ."

"I'm jealous of that cop. I don't want you going out with him." He backed her against a cobwebbed wall, then his mouth was over hers and he was kissing her.

"*Whack, whack, whack*!" The three knocks outside the building stopped them both. "Get out of there!" They both turned at the sound of the voice, somehow vaguely familiar.

"What was that?" Kenneth asked her sharply.

"I have no idea. But I'm not waiting around," she said, smoothing down her hair on each side. "I'll see you tomorrow."

"Jane, wait! Don't go. Please, let me talk to you."

But she was already stepping out of the old house, grateful for a breath under waves, crashing and relentless, that had become her life. She looked up and down the street but there was no one there. "You come in ten minutes," she called back to Kenneth. She hopped the wall and ran, zigzagging around tall weeds and trash, back to her car in the DVX parking just as the rain began again. Her mind mirrored the pelting rain, the sense that she was caught up in a dangerous whirlwind of events and she wanted one thing and one thing only: to be with Weedy again.

The rain was whipping at her face sideways. She jumped into her car, glancing back toward the old house. She didn't realize how hard her heart had been beating until that moment. She was searching for her keys when she glanced to the abandoned building and saw the door open a few inches then remain cracked. Heart pounding, she scrambled for her keys. Out of the corner of her eye she saw movement. She turned her head and saw the door of the abandoned house fly open. Kenneth was running toward her yelling something. He was beginning to scare her. Her keys fell from one damp hand onto the floor by the brake. She jerked a shaking hand and locked the doors then felt for her keys.

He was racing across the parking lot now.

Keys in the ignition. Engine started.

His hand hit the window. He was pounding on it.

"Jane, I'm sorry! It's not what you think! You're in horrible danger. You need to believe me. Jane!" He called through the window.

She couldn't slam on the gas; there were still a few cars in the parking lot. And in one horrible moment, she saw that Mike's Toyota was still there. Something was wrong. And now she had confided in Kenneth. She had gone and told him about Weedy.

"Jane, you've got to listen to me before it's too late!" Kenneth was yelling. "Just roll down the window!"

Maybe he was telling the truth. She equivocated. No. She'd talked to too many people.

She backed up slowly but he moved around to block her from going forward, and now stood before her, looking like an escaped lunatic, the set of his mouth contorted in a way that suggested struggle, and she wondered what he would do. Slowly, she inched along, ignoring his knocks against the glass, ignoring his pleas, focused on the route she'd take, definitely not directly home. Her only concern was getting to Weedy. Kenneth could not find out where she lived. Where Weedy lived.

She drove through the parking lot to the opposite side, as he yelled at her to stop, to listen, to trust him. She focused on the busier road just ahead where laid her escape into normalcy. She put on her right signal, her movements methodical to steady her mind, and pulled out into the traffic uncertain but determined. She turned right then she was driving with the other cars, freed from the craziness of a moment ago, and unaware that she'd been holding her breath until she let it out in one great rush.

The cars on either side purred past, helping her to feel a part of the quotidian activity of just another city evening, helping her to forget she'd just been in an abandoned building with an obviously desperate, and possibly dangerous man, contemplating conducting some kind of sexual congress with him. And not a soul had known she was there. She shuddered. What if something had happened to her and no one, apart from Carol, knew Weedy was home alone?

She could feel her love for the little dog mutating into attachment, and she realized then, trying to drive away her fears, that he depended on her. She and Weedy already shared a past.

She remembered the day he'd ridden with her to the distant veterinarian's office. Afterward, she drove to the CVS to pick up his antibiotics. She remembered how she'd shut the car door, walked a few paces, then turned and looked back. There, staring out, were a little pair of eyes. Just the eyes above the window and the brown top of his head. She couldn't see his nose, but she would always remember how she'd felt in that moment.

Walking up to the shopping center, the same CVS and Barnes & Noble and Burger King and Waffle House that could be found in every shopping center from east coast to west, she stopped a second time. She stood looking across the parking lot to a row of silver maples, yellow leaves fluttering in the evening air, the sky a misty patchwork morphing to sepia sunset before her eyes. In the beauty of the moment her pathos was transformed, and her desire to help Weedy lead a life of comfort and quality grew. The wind blew harder turning the leaves up and inside out, their undersides a lighter shade of gold.

When the girl behind the counter in the pharmacy told her his medication was not there, she'd stared, unable to find her voice. Aware of the impatient line of people, many elderly, waiting behind her for their own medications, she'd pleaded softly:

"But you don't understand. It's for my dog. He needs it now."

A ripple of murmurs behind her, moving from the back forwards, reached her.

"It's for her *dog*," the third woman in line behind her stepped forward, repeating to the pharmacist and Sylvie wondered later would the sympathy still have been roused had she said, "my mother" instead of, "my dog." *Love adheres to no rules but its own.*

"Okay, hold on."

Twenty minutes later and sixty-eight dollars poorer, Sylvie left the drugstore, the sky slate gray, with just a narrow strip of soft golden light lingering above a cloud. In her hand she clutched the long, thin paper CVS bag with Weedy's drugs. His face was no longer to the glass. Would that be how death would feel one day? His simply not being there. She approached her car, then stood a silent moment, as she peered in watching his sides move in and out, his body curled tight in a ball on her car seat, not on a cement floor, his mind lost to a world of dog dreams.

Letting the memory retreat from her mind, she turned into her street, parking on the side just beyond her building. She turned the key and the engine stopped. She settled the stick up to the middle neutral position, and listened to the rain ticking against the windshield. She didn't see Carol's car anywhere, but that didn't mean anything.

Tick, tick, tick.

The rain danced outside and she sat in the light from a distant streetlight, feeling drained.

"Weedy is safe inside," she said to herself. The inside light came on as she opened her door and got out. She leaned and reached in back for her phone and water bottle. Head and shoulders bent over into the car, her bottom half drummed upon by the rain.

And out of the rain-soaked city came the voice:

"Here, let me help you."

She heard it like a bad dream, recognized it immediately, and whirled around to face him.

Kenneth held up his hands. "Wait, don't say anything. You have to listen to me. You are in danger. But it's not what you think."

"How'd you get here and what are you doing?" There was both a numbness and hysteria in her voice.

"Jane, you have to listen to me. I lied to you. I'm not undercover. But I'm not lying to you now. I'm not lying when I say you're in danger. I work for the lab, and Dr. Donaldson suspected you. Please, Jane. They are on to you. They want you and your kind caught and punished."

She stood, soaked, listening to him, terrified, but not so much of the words as that he now knew where she and Weedy lived.

"I'll report you to the police if you don't leave at once." He was standing four or five paces away from her making no attempts to come closer.

"Jane, I know your plan. I also know you stole a dog. You are going to have to trust me. It's your choice."

There was no one in the sodden streets. The rain tapped down on her head, monotonous like water torture. She watched it mixing with oil and gushing in the gutters at her feet.

"My job is to find out everything about you and to turn you in. But I fell in love with you the first time I saw you standing there all upset in the treatment room. I'm not going to turn on you. But you better hurry up with your plan then quit. For good. Do you hear me?"

"I don't trust you."

"Well, you better." He sounded angry. "And you need to give me some information so I don't lose my job. Tell me who else knows. Tell me something, or give up that dog."

"I would like it if you would leave. I need to get home."

"Then I'll walk you."

"No. I live many blocks away," she lied. "It's just I saw the parking space here and decided, with the rain, to take what I could find. Go now please, and don't try to see me again," she said slowly, but defiantly. With her eyes on him, she locked her car and shoved the key into her pocket.

"I'm going home. You must leave." She made her voice nonchalant and fearless, hoping her emotions would follow the cue.

The thought of Weedy inside made her crazy and bold at once. She started walking down the sidewalk away from the house and her apartment. She wanted to walk backwards along the cracked walkway, keeping an eye on him, should he try to enter her home or do something crazy. She strained her ears instead, listening for any sudden footfall behind her. But the rain splattered and she couldn't hear. And then it came. Not a hand on her shoulder or racing feet, but a scream more chilling than either.

"*JANE*!"

She spun around. He hadn't moved from where he'd stood near her car, and he appeared larger than life, his dark brown hair plastered on his skull like a Neanderthal man.

"Jane, listen to me!"

She had to strain to hear through the rain. She stepped a few feet closer.

"I'm telling you, they *know*. You either tell me who you're working for, who put you up to this, or you give up that dog. Your choice."

She whirled around and began running crazed through the rain until she could find shelter and text Carol and find out where her dog was.

CHAPTER THIRTY-FOUR

Sylvie ran for two blocks panting and splashing through puddles on the street and sidewalks. Then she ducked into the convenience store that sold hotdogs and fish sandwiches. When she turned on her phone, there were two texts from Carol. She was on her way to Sylvie's.

Relief washed over her. But was Kenneth waiting behind a tree somewhere, watching for her? And did she believe what he'd said with such passion? She peered out to the street, watching, till she heard someone cough behind her. She turned around half expecting to see Kenneth. But there was no one save the old curly-white-haired man behind the deli case.

"Hey," she said, raising a hand and waving feebly. She looked for something to buy, saw nothing, and bought a bag of potato chips from him, thanking him. Then looking over her shoulder, she ran back to her car, drove around the block and out to the highway, gunned her small Peugeot, got off on the next exit, snaked her way back to her neighborhood, and parked three blocks from her apartment on a dead end street. She ran to her home the back way, looking left and right as she ran, and again when she stood on her front step and unlocked the door.

Within minutes, Carol walked through Sylvie's front door carrying Weedy in her arms.

Sylvie choked out a sound, and dropped to her knees, arms outstretched to Weedy as Carol put him down. Weedy ran to her. He braced his front feet on her chest, stern wagging back and forth. Carol stood watching. Sylvie clasped his wiggling body to her breast. She closed her eyes, "Oh Weedy, what have I done?"

"What is it, Sil? What happened to you?"

"One million thank yous. For keeping him safe. For being here." Sylvie stood then fell to the sofa. "Up, Weedy up!" She patted the sofa and Weedy sprang to her lap.

"Here, I bought this for the little one." Carol tossed a small hedgehog onto the sofa, and Weedy immediately snatched it up in his mouth, startling Sylvie as he *squeak-squeak- squeaked* the toy.

"Thank you. For thinking of that." She stared at him with the toy in his mouth.

"Don't you believe in umbrellas?" Carol turned and began making a fire in the woodstove.

"And thank you for keeping him safe," Sylvie said again.

"Anytime. You don't have to keep thanking me. It's what we do for each other. You'd do it for me. I'm starving. What do you have to eat?" Carol asked.

Sylvie tossed her the bag of chips.

"There's a lot of darkness out there."

"What?" Carol asked.

"I heard once that more than half the universe is dark matter, where it gives off no light. No light at all. But scientists don't know what it is."

Carol turned and patted Sylvie on the head like a child. "There's a lot of darkness, you're right. That's why we need bright sparks of light like you around here all the more. Have you taken your medication, Sil? You sound down."

"I'm okay." Shivery and shaken, Sylvie told Carol everything that had happened except the very end part. The part when Kenneth stood in the rain and told her she needed to tell him who else was involved or lose the one thing she loved most in the world.

"Why did he convince me he was undercover, only to tell me now he's not? Nothing makes sense. My world is churning, whirling, topsy turving. I don't know what to do." All at once she felt like a feather floating through life with no volition of its own, or perhaps an autumn leaf whose fate is always to fall.

"You're talking to someone who understands." Carol sat down. "But, Sil, you should do like he says and quit. You could be in danger. He could be just trying to get in your pants, but he also could be telling the truth. And if something happened to you, I'd never forgive myself."

"I can't lose Weedy. I live in fear now that someone will come take him from me. And now I've gone and told Kenneth. I'm a fool, a floundering, feebling fool."

"You're too trusting, that's all."

"I'm going to have to move. I can't risk losing Weedy."

"Maybe he really is telling the truth. Maybe he was supposed to rat you out but he became smitten. You sure seem to be picking winners."

"But I told him my plan," Sylvie said in an agonized voice.

"Which you haven't told me yet."

"That's right I haven't. And I'm not going to. I have to have dinner with David first and see if he'll really do it. He's the one transporting the dogs, and only he can get Nick to come. Kenneth is like us. Or so I thought. I thought he could help. Be a witness. He gets it. You'd like him."

"You just said he lied and turned psycho on you."

"He did. I don't know what to think anymore. He understands the animals. He said all the right things. But then—"

"Sylvie, be safe."

"I will. Carol," Sylvie began. "If something were to happen to me, you'd take Weedy and—"

"Nothing is going to happen to you."

"But if it did, will you promise me?"

"I promise I'll take Weedy and keep him safe. Now, tell me your plan."

"No. I don't want to implicate you, should I screw up."

"Sylvie, you have to tell me."

"No. I'm not going to tell you, so you can stop trying. I'll tell you when it's all over and you'll be so very happy. You'll see."

"Now you've got me scared."

"I'll be fine."

"Oh, Sil, please be careful. I don't know what I'd do if I lost you," and she started to say, "too," but stopped.

"I'll try not to get lost."

Carol kissed the top of Weedy's head, stood and hugged Sylvie goodbye. Tarnished light filtered in the front window, the storm past.

"I love you, Sil."

As Carol ducked into her car, waving with a few fingers, Sylvie waved and called, "Thank you!" She watched as Carol backed up and drove off. When she could see the car no longer, she turned to go inside but stopped, liquescent knees pulling her to all fours, and there on her front stoop she kneeled panting like a dog. A shunting spasm racked her spine. The love, the relief. But also the fear. Lurking, smirking fear. Somewhere in the distance, a horn honked.

Sylvie pushed up, straightening and went in to sit beside Weedy. But it had been at that moment—down on her hands and knees on the porch that she knew she would lie to Carol.

Realizing how badly she'd screwed up in telling both David and Kenneth about Weedy, Sylvie knew she could not involve Carol by telling her what she intended to do. That way, if her plan went wrong, Carol could say honestly she didn't know anything about it.

And it was then that Sylvie came up with the lie. She would tell Carol she'd abandoned the plan to stop Nick, all the while moving swiftly forward with it. She would tell Carol she was moving away. Far away. With Matt to tend to, Carol was unlikely to pursue Nick Drakas on her own. It was the only way to protect her friend.

The next evening, having slept on the idea, and thought about nothing else in her waking hours, Sylvie called Carol.

"Are you sitting down?"

"Sylvie, no! Not another dog."

"No, not another dog. I'm quitting."

"Well, good. I'm relieved. I never thought I'd say that, but I am."

"And I'm abandoning the plan. It's too risky."

"Really?"

"Yes. And, Carol?

"Yes?"

"I'm moving."

"What?"

"I have to move."

"What are you talking about?"

"I told both Kenneth and David about Weedy. I'm going crazy over it." At least that much was truth. "I'm moving to the West coast."

"You're kidding, right?"

"No, I've put Weedy in danger. You too, if you think about it. I love him. And I love you, so I'm leaving. It'll only be for a little while."

Carol laughed. "If you love me, you'll stay."

"I can't." When Sylvie tried to explain, albeit halfheartedly because she was a poor liar, Carol met her with: "You're hiding something. What's going on? Something's wrong, or you're not telling me something."

Back and forth they went until Sylvie was on the verge of tears and telling Carol the truth, and Carol, with no understanding and sensing her friend was in danger, was on the verge of hysteria.

"You can't just up and move. Where will you go?"

"I've family in California, remember? It'll be okay."

"Sylvie, why? Why *now*?"

"I have to. I'll call you when I'm settled. Weedy could be recognized here."

"Settled? No. You can't just leave. I need you more than I've ever needed anyone. Even with Matt sick, I was there for you. I came and sat with Weedy when my husband was dying! I did it because I see what Weedy means to you. How much you love him. Sylvie, you're my best friend. I need you. Can't you wait and see me through this?"

On the other end of the phone, Sylvie was silent. Her eyes were shiny and she swallowed twice. There was nothing she could think of to say.

"Sylvie?"

"I'm sorry." Her voice wavered. She inhaled willing herself to be strong. "I'm moving out west."

The phone clicked in Sylvie's ear. She stared at it like it was a murder weapon. Carol had hung up on her. In all the years they'd known each other neither had ever hung up on the other, no matter how upset. She sank down onto the sofa beside Weedy and only then did she let herself cry.

"Oh Weedy, I've messed up so badly," she said crying softly into his ruff. "And I don't know how to fix it."

CHAPTER THIRTY-FIVE

Wearing heavy black boots, David thumped down the hallway of Headquarters to Chief Thompson's office. Nick must have said something. Just what David couldn't imagine, but he didn't care. He was more than prepared to tell the truth, and just as prepared for Thompson to side with McMahon who sided with Nick. Screw them all. He thought of his father. *You lied to me, dad. You said Cilla would come back after a week. Some things hold you back, son. You gotta get ahead in life, son. Telling the truth ain't always the way to get ahead.*

Screw him too.

He knocked.

"Come in!"

A large man with a crew cut and blood-shot eyes lounged behind a desk of polished wood. A little gold titled plate stood on the right-hand side of the desk and read: *Robert L. Thompson, Chief of Police.*

"Sir." David stood in the doorway.

"Officer Sampson. Come in. Have yourself a seat."

David stepped forward and sat down, his large legs folded like a praying mantis before him.

"You've been doing good work for us, I hear."

David waited, wondering. Thompson must have expected him to speak, for when he did not, Thomas barked, "Are you daydreaming or hearing what I say?"

"No sir. Not daydreaming. Yes sir. I'm listening to you, sir. Thank you, sir."

"What I need to know is whether I can trust you or not."

Again David didn't answer, waiting for more. And again Thompson barked: "Son, did you hear me?"

"Yes sir. You can trust me." He felt it was obvious, the reason why he'd become a police officer in the first place. To do what was right.

"Then I need to know what you hear around here."

"I don't understand, sir."

Thompson brought his thick torso forward with a great show of effort and scooted his chair an inch closer, leaning in toward David. "Okay, let's just say what is spoken between you and I must—it absolutely must—remain con-fi-den-tial. Do you get that?"

"Yes sir, confidentiality."

"Let's just say, I need for you to tell me if there are any individuals harboring feelings of ill will toward any member of this here department. And let's just say that you will be adequately rewarded if you do well at your job. But if you do not, there will be consequences you won't like."

"But sir—"

"But sir, *what*?"

"Don't you imagine that there are always disgruntled officers? That it's human nature to complain even if men don't really mean half of what they say?"

"Are you asking me the questions?" The chief mocked.

"Honest questions, sir."

"Then are you saying," Thompson said in a quieter voice, "that there's some talk going on?"

"Just the usual stuff, sir."

"Then I think you'd better start talking to me right now."

When David left Thompson's office half an hour later he met Slice, who he'd always liked. Slice kept to himself, never appearing bothered by the talk from officers that Thompson had just urged David to rat on, and as a consequence, David had never come to befriend Slice or know him well. Now he envied him.

"What'cha doing, David?"

"Nothing much, going to the coffee machines. How are you?"

"Meeting with the boss man?" Slice smiled.

"Something like that."

"About anything in particular?"

"I think he's switching me," David said quickly. "Desk duty."

"Don't let it get you down. You'll do it for a while then you'll get back on the beat. None of them do it for any reason but the power of doing it. Anyhow, by the time you get used to it, they'll take you off. Don't let it get you down."

Something in Slice's unaffected manner moved David and he felt bad about evading the truth. David felt Slice watching him, and wanted to tell him all.

"Something eating at you?" Slice asked.

"Truth is, Thompson wants me for his spy."

"Figured as much."

"You did?"

"He asked me two and a half years ago."

"And you did?" David asked in a hushed whisper. They had both lowered their voices.

"Of course not. I didn't become a police officer to be their crooked spy."

For a moment David's childhood roiled then eddied. A swimming pool became the recoiling waves, sucking him under.

"Y'all right, David?"

"I got a lot on my mind."

"I'm sorry David. Sorry to hear you're troubled."

"I didn't say I was troubled," David quipped. But Slice's tone comforted him. There was no antagonism. Slice had no agenda, he thought to himself, and he wished he felt that way about Nick or Chief Thompson. Or anyone else for that matter.

"Can you keep a secret?" He asked Slice.

"Probably so."

"Well, I didn't become a police officer to become their crooked spy either. And what's more I didn't become a police to be Nick's gopher."

"Meaning what exactly?"

"Nick has me working some jobs for him."

Slice was looking directly into David's eyes. He seemed to be listening to the silence after David's words ended. Then he spoke. "You better watch out, David."

"Why?"

"If you're dealing drugs for Nick, you could get in real trouble fast. You could lose your job. You could go to prison." His tone was neutral.

"You know Nick's dealing?" David whispered back.

"Sure."

"I do too. I mean, I've seen him take the drugs. It's why he takes all the drug runs."

"Sure," Slice said again. "You don't buy a new Stingray on a cop's salary." Then he laughed, a boyish laugh. "I wish."

"I'm not dealing drugs. I wouldn't. I'm—" David stopped, aware of how absurd his words were going to sound. Slice stood waiting. "I'm selling dogs."

Slice nodded slightly. "Where do you get them?"

As David told him the whole story, Slice listened. "You can't say anything to anybody," David continued. "I just needed to tell someone. It isn't right, but I'm in a bind."

"I won't say anything. I give my word, but you got to turn him in. Simple."

"I can't."

"Well, if you won't, I will. I'll leave you out of it."

"But I'm implicated. I'll get charged too."

"I'll vouch for you," Slice promised.

"Nick will know I told you."

Slice shook his head. "We have to turn him in, David. We're the police."

And David knew he never would have risked his job, his security, his life, if it hadn't been for Sylvie. The night before, Sylvie had called him and told him she had another plan. Would he help her? His answer was an obvious, if anxious, yes. Therefore, he needed to keep transporting the dogs for Nick until her plan was executed.

"When's the next time he has you doing it?"

Before he could answer, David saw Slice look past him to something beyond. He turned and saw Nick walking their way. Slice stopped talking.

"How's my buddy?" Nick said, walking up to David without acknowledging Slice.

"Hey, Nick." Slice said. He laughed lightly and said, "The thief flees the crime and gets away." He shook his head at David.

"*What*?" Nick asked sharply, whipping around and looking from Slice to David.

"Come on, Nick."

"Shut up, Slice. Or I'll shut that mouth up on you one day."

Slice ignored Nick and turned to David. "They always do. Is there really any justice?"

"I like to think so," David replied.

"See you two later," Slice said and left them standing there.

When Slice had vanished down the hall, Nick made a derogatory gesture in his wake. "Fucking ass-wipe. You need to stop talking to that piece of slime."

"He's a good guy."

"You don't know shit about him. Stop talking to him. I'm telling you."

"Okay, I don't need to talk to him. But I don't like being ordered around."

"Just stay clear of him."

David turned away from Nick. He wasn't going to keep the conversation going.

"What are you up to right now?" Nick narrowed his eyes.

"Going to get coffee. What are you up to?"

"Wouldn't mind a word with you. Need your help with something."

"All right."

David poured coffee from the pot, breathing in the burned, nutty smell. Where once had stood the sturdy stanchions of his ideals, now rotting beams threatened, letting in filth. He sipped the coffee and it was strangely comforting.

"It's like this. I need to know what people are saying."

"What do you mean, what people are saying?" David questioned, the rotting walls collapsing. He had to get outside. He needed air.

"I think people are talking. Like they may be on to us. I just need you to listen to the wind, get the general current. People like you. They trust you. And . . ." Nick paused, and David watched thinking Nick acted nervous about something. But then Nick said, "I gotta go." He turned, and stopped. "David," he said urgently. "I'm going to need your help with something else."

Still clutching his warm salvation in its white Styrofoam cup, David left the building. He turned up his collar and for a moment stood listening to the day's symphony: the flutter of dried leaves in the trees planted along the sidewalk. The bump and whiz of cars and trucks, tires and exhaust along the city streets. The shriek and joyous shouts of children one block down. Old men muttering to one another, leaning forward on benches. To hell with Thompson. And to hell with Nick, too. Tomorrow he was seeing Sylvie.

CHAPTER THIRTY-SIX

David stood outside his building's door looking first one way up the street and then the other way. When he spied her walking toward him with a bottle of wine in one hand and the end of a leash in the other, he wasn't sure if he was thrilled, terrified, or simply amazed she'd shown up. He waved his hand back and forth.

As she approached he saw the dog had on a padded black harness that looked like a space suit.

"You found it," he said. "Come on up." He led her up three flights of wooden steps, worn to a lighter shade of brown and sunken in the middle. As he walked he tapped the smudged brass balustrade to quiet his racing thoughts so incongruent with the feeling of having nothing to say. A song, trapped in his mind, announced itself with each tap of the railing until both ended with a protuberant finial finale.

"Here we are." Forced confidence hovered behind a nervous smile. He pushed open his door.

He glanced at her, but she didn't appear disparaging, and his worries dissolved, replaced by quiet wonder. He wasn't embarrassed about his, at best, modest home furnishings, for he assumed every single man of his age would live in a similar style, whether rich or poor, until he made a family, when naturally the course of life, which included house and home furnishings and a wife to tend to such things, would improve.

She crouched on the floor with one hand on the dog, so he bent down beside her.

"Is he okay?" He asked dubiously.

"It's all brand new to him. I'm trying to get him used to things. Maybe I'm rushing him, but it's my neurosis too. I'm afraid to leave him for too long alone."

"Why? What would he do?"

"It's not that. It's—" She didn't finish.

She stood, setting the wine on the table next to a vase of yellow grocery store roses with baby's breath. Harsh light from a streetlamp pooled, painting blue-edged shadows.

"You didn't have to bring anything." Not a drinker, he was nevertheless pleased to see the wine, lending to it a liberating power, and he yanked the cork out listening to its satisfying pop.

"Do you like wine?" she asked.

To lie or not to lie, that is the question. Whether tis nobler in mind to tell a small lie, to prevent hurt feelings, (especially when you're trying to woo the girl of your dreams) or to take arms against a sea of future troubles, caused by one small lie, and tell the truth.

"I don't really drink it, but I'd love to learn." He gave her his best grin. "Since I'm such a novice, tell me about it," he said clutching the bottle, looking from label to her, then turning away from her in alarm, but at once relieved to find two dusty wine glasses—once his grandmother's—in the back of his cupboard.

"Abbaye de Valmagne. It's made and aged in a twelfth-century Benedictine monastery."

He watched her face and mouth as she talked, and felt unaccountably happy, knowing he'd just made the right decision to never ever for the rest of his life lie to this charming and innocent and very pretty girl. To always take care of her, knowing too that from now on things would be different, even if she as yet did not know it.

"The monks were behind everything," she said, settling herself into one of his four chairs at the metal kitchen table with its ancient yellow and black checked Formica top.

"Ah," he nodded.

"I like the French wines," she said, leaning forward slightly and stroking the dog who sat on the floor between her shins. "They carry more of the earth in them. Californians are more about fruit—"

"Hah!" he laughed.

"So easier to drink and appreciate I think, but I prefer the French."

"You know a lot," he said, embarrassed that he'd laughed at that which he'd perceived a joke.

"Not really. I just know what I like and I lived in Switzerland for a while. We drank wine every day at school for lunch."

"You don't say."

"I do."

"Switzerland?"

"Boarding school. My mother put me there while she was trying to figure out her own life. My father died when I was two. I never knew him. My mother was what I suppose one calls today absentee. There, now you have it. It all comes up sooner or later."

The ghost of a possible boyfriend was beginning to nag at him. He wanted to ask if she was seeing anyone, but decided to stay away from that topic for the moment. She wasn't overly talkative, and he longed to know what secrets she kept locked in her heart. What thoughts troubled her? What did she think about, dream about at night?

"Do you have brothers and sisters?"

"No," she answered. After a pause she said, "You?"

"I had a sister. A half-sister."

"Had?"

"Yeah. They came and took her away. Because of me, they took her away."

"They?"

"The people from the nut house. She had some problems. But not enough to be locked away. I did something and she got blamed." He had never admitted it to anyone in his life. The act of speaking about it dispassionately soothed him more than he ever could have explained to her, and he loved her all the more for it. Again, the longing to open his heart and tell her everything singed his soul with tantalizing proximity. He could almost imagine how good it would feel, and he knew he could trust her.

"I'm sorry," she offered.

"It's okay." He saw the chance slipping away and he knew he hadn't the guts to tell her everything.

He wiped his grandmother's glasses with a paper towel and carefully filled them with the wine.

He raised his glass. "Cheers. We're having omelets and salad. And wine. How does that sound to you? Oh, and dessert." He set the glass down, but knocked the vase of flowers as he did. "Whoa, sorry."

She'd said simple, but the meal now seemed exceedingly meager. Why had he not prepared more courses? She was cultured. She'd lived abroad. How could this possible satisfy her?

"It sounds lovely."

He relaxed feeling guilty relief at expending so much worry on such personal concerns.

"I thought it'd be safe. I forgot to ask if you were a vegetarian. I thought you might be, volunteering at the SPCA and all."

She smiled. "They never said being vegetarian was a requirement."

A warm rush of excitement filled him at her teasing. "I just thought—"

"And you're right, I am a vegetarian. I forgot to tell you. My mind was elsewhere. I'm grateful you made that choice."

"I'm grateful too," he said, feeling their bond strengthen. "My guess is too," he began and turned and let the oil heat in the old-fashioned black iron skillet, lifting it and tilting it, careful not to let it get too hot. "Is that you're a pacifist."

"I am. But that's kind of a funny thing for you to assume. Why?"

David dropped chopped garlic and onions into oil. "I don't know. Just a feeling I had." Just a feeling he had, no, more like a tremendous and unexplainable desire to talk to her about it, and to share his views about the police department, and have her admire him and find him right and Nick wrong. "I'm a pacifist too," he added. "Which may seem at odds with being a cop, but really it's not." He turned back to her and saw the dog sniffing the air. "Is he okay?"

"Yes, he's great. In fact he's doing amazingly well. He just had to get used to the new smells. His name is Weedy. I don't know if I ever told you."

"Yes," he said and watched as she reached down to Weedy, placing hands under his belly gently, and lifting him up and into her lap. He turned back to the stove.

"I love you, too," she said.

David whirled around. He saw her with the dog, kissing its face. He coughed, then broke six eggs into a bowl, and whisked them vigorously. He poured the mixture into the hot skillet with the onions and garlic and it spit back at him for a moment. He stood listening to the sound of hot oil cooking chopped bulbs and beaten eggs.

"Smells good," she offered. He glanced to her and saw the dog on her lap, his tail hanging down over her thigh. She ran her hand over his back, and he shifted his weight, rearranged his compact body and lay down on her knees bringing his head to rest between his front paws.

"Garlic and onions." David said feeling simultaneously calm contentment and fired elation, doing for a woman what he always dreamed he could and would do. Cooking and providing. He felt complete, his apartment no longer empty but filled with warmth and purpose and most of all love. He thought of the dog lying in trust and love across her legs, a picture of tranquility. And at that moment, he promised himself he would have her trust him and love him that much one day. He would be kind. Most of all he would be patient.

He imagined a video camera placed high in the corner of his kitchen, placed there by Nick and the department to monitor him and trap him for imagined violations. He imagined them watching him not lying like a lump on his sofa, but cooking for a girl who waited for him at the table with obvious devotion. He wanted to speak to her of compassion and pity. He wanted to ask her if she sometimes felt that love stemmed indirectly from pity.

"Okay, it's about ready," he said, and turned so she could watch as he placed a plate, a little larger than the skillet's circumference, against the shallow pan and flipped it. "Little trick I learned."

A perfectly formed omelet covered the plate he brought to the table. He set it in the center, handing her a plate with faded pink and blue flowers around the edges, also his grandmother's. He cut the omelet in half and served her a portion, certain his grandmother, if she were watching, would have been pleased to see her plates in use, but more pleased to see the "nice girl" at the supper table.

"Help yourself to salad. It's lightly dressed."

She scooted her chair forward as Weedy sat up, interested and alert now that the savory omelet had joined the previous assembly of dull-smelling inanimate objects and flowers.

David felt the moment as perfect as a slice of life could be. He felt happiness born of this one moment, with her across from him, an omelet between them, anticipatory happiness allowing for everything yet to come, suffused by an imagined future and the promise of hope that nothing could now breach.

"How do you feel about dogs on furniture?" David looked up surprised, and she continued. "If I put my coat down on your couch there, could he sit on it?"

"Sure, no problem."

She laid her coat on his sofa and David watched her lift the dog gently and arrange him into the blue parka like a mother bird laying one feathered wing over her young. "It's okay. You rest."

"He's not spoiled or anything is he?"

As Sylvie walked back to the table and sat down, neither Weedy nor David took his eyes from her. She wore brown jeans that fit well, but not too snugly, and a large cream-colored Aaron Isle sweater. "I'm trying to make up for the life he's endured."

David glanced once to Weedy who had risen and was now turning around and around in tight circles on her parka. Finally he curled up, the parker scrunched up in a little wad under his front legs while his rump graced David's couch.

When she sat back at the table, he was relieved the dog was not in her lap.

"I feel a little like I'm his father," he said glancing at Weedy who had cocked his head. He raised a hind leg and began scratching a spot behind his ear.

"What?"

"I did help with stealing him."

"The rescue, you mean."

"The rescue?"

"Let's not use the "S" word."

"You love him a lot." He ate a bite of omelet and decided it tasted pretty good.

"Yes."

"I've never had a pet. I never . . ." he trailed off, taking a sip of the wine, and waiting for her to offer the comment that she didn't. She picked up her own fork and cut sideways into the omelet.

There was a silence and he wanted to look across at her knowingly, but he was too shy to meet her eyes the way he'd done a hundred times in his fantasies.

"Why do you love dogs so much?" It was out before he could retract it. But instead of bothering her, the question seemed for a moment to remedy all that had been awkward, as she sat there pondering.

She hesitated as if giving consideration. "I guess I just do." It sounded like a quip.

"You just do."

"Yes. And it's all animals."

"What?"

"Not just dogs. All animals. But dogs and humans have had a particularly close bond for many thousands of years."

"Right."

"My closest friends have always cared about animals. They understand the power of the human canine bond, but many people don't. So with those people I remain silent, not pushing on them a love they might neither understand nor accept."

"You can tell me."

"I know the shrinks would say that lavishing so much love and energy on a dog to the exclusion of most people is an aberrancy, that I didn't receive proper love as a child, or that I'm afraid of being rejected in a love relationship."

"Sylvie," he began. He stopped without finishing, before saying that he would never, ever hurt her. He watched her eat. He had an image of the three of them, her, the little dog, and him, forming an eternity triad—at least until a baby was made, then their child would replace the dog.

She regarded him, but when he didn't finish she continued over a swallow of wine. "Perhaps there's some truth, but even that truth can't claim reason. It can't claim the full reason for my love of animals. I love them because I love them. Dogs are less complicated, true. Dogs are not judgmental, true again. Dogs offer unconditional love. In many ways they're innocent compared to humans who can inflict all sorts of awful things on them. But the reason I love Weedy is something no shrink would ever embrace. For really there is no reason. I just do."

"I think humans are capable of giving unconditional love, too."

"Reason implies a conditional love. In Switzerland we read all of Montaigne's essays but it's only now that I understand the deep emotion he felt toward his friend. Etienne de La Boétie. I can still remember his words."

"Tell me his words."

"Translated to English: 'If I were pressed to say why I love him, I feel that my only reply could be: Because it was he. Because it was I.' Beautiful isn't it?"

David nodded. "I guess I've always longed for a love that intense." Should he ask her now about past boyfriends or wait? Wait, he decided. "I keep hoping I'll find it with the right woman, someone gentle and kind."

"Oh, I'm sure you will. Don't your police buddies have sisters they could set you up with?"

"I'm not desperate," he laughed. "When the right one comes along, I'll know it." She's trying to see if I like her. She can't come right out and ask so she's asking about dates with the sisters. She may even be a little jealous. Good sign, good sign.

"I think with a love like that you really have no control. It just happens," she said and looked up and met his eyes.

He couldn't believe it. He stared back at her and waited.

"When you truly love, you forgive everything. You don't judge, you merely observe and accept. In real love, familiarity does not breed contempt but rather a deeper love and a bond so connected that," she glanced up to something beyond David. "You feel its devastation if ever broken."

Thank you, God. David raised his eyes to meet hers and they were very bright. She was reaching for the salad.

"Sylvie. I think we're alike."

"You do?" She served herself the greens and tomatoes. "We've barely said anything to one another. All you know about me is that I've said I like animals. You don't live with any animals. Not even a gerbil or a snake. Not even a hermit crab."

"I'll buy a hermit crab tomorrow."

She started to put a forkful of salad into her mouth, but she put the fork down. She looked across at him. "You want a family."

"How did you know?"

"It's pretty obvious," she said gently.

"Oh." He rearranged his lettuce leaves.

"That and the statement about humans and unconditional love."

"Okay," he said. "Well, I guess I do."

Sylvie looked down to her lap for a beat. "It's funny, perhaps ironic even, but you're right. We may really be alike in wanting the same thing."

David's mouth opened as if to speak, or perhaps it was in surprise, but Sylvie stopped him.

"No, no, not that," she said quickly. "I guess I should say I'm not really looking for a relationship. At least not—" she looked away.

"I won't hurt you, if that's what you're afraid of," he said in a rush. "I can go slow. You've been hurt, haven't you? I won't hurt you," he said again, speaking faster, his voice rising.

"It's pretty amusing to try to make up for a lack of family with one weaselly little dog, don't you think? Poor Weedy, he didn't know what he was signing up for."

"Weedy?" David said, watching her glance over at the dog. He turned too and saw at once that it was no longer watching them but was instead lying on its side inert. "It's dead," he blurted out. The dog's eyes were rolled back in its head and its tongue was sticking partially out.

She turned back to face him. "Why would you say he's dead?"

"Look at him."

But she didn't. Instead she spoke slowly. "He's sleeping. It's the most beautiful thing I've seen in a long time. Here I am in a strange man's apartment—"

"I'm not a strange man."

"And Weedy is calm, so calm and accepting of you that he's sleeping. I think actually our voices are soothing him. When I'm home alone, I don't talk much."

"He's knows a good person when he sees him." David countered.

"Maybe so."

"He hasn't moved. Are you sure he's sleeping?"

"You really don't know much about dogs do you?"

"But, I mean what would you do if he did die right there?"

"David. You're sounding somewhat morbid."

"Sorry, but I just began to wonder how you deal with a dead animal. I mean for people there are funeral parlors to take care of things. What do you do, dig a hole?"

She didn't answer and he was about to apologize and change the subject, when she said, "If Weedy died, I'd want him cremated. If anything were to happen to me, to him, remember that, okay?"

"Cremated? You've got to be kidding," he laughed.

"I'm not kidding."

"A dog?"

"Yes. You don't take him to the funeral parlor," she said, perhaps anticipating his question. "You just take him to the shelter."

"The shelter?"

"Yes, the shelter. The SPCA."

"Never thought about dog cremation."

After the dog cremation discussion, they spoke eagerly at times and awkwardly at other times, and after the meal he cleared their plates, and offered her chocolate tart and coffee.

"So David," she said, taking a bite of chocolate slowly into her mouth and raising her eyes to his. He knew his face had turned crimson.

"Yes?" The piece of cake on his own fork dropped off and he hastily retrieved it, breaking eye contact.

"You need to tell me about transporting dogs. That's why I'm here."

"Is that the only reason?"

"David."

"I hope that's not the only reason." When she only gazed back at him, he continued, his spirits taking a nosedive. "I only did it for the money. It was stupid of me, I know. I did feel for the dogs, taking them from their owners like that. If I could turn back time."

Sylvie raised an eyebrow. "You sound like Cher."

"But I mean it."

"So you answer ads and relieve people of older or unwanted dogs."

He couldn't look at her. "I really did feel bad, but I'd promised my friend."

"Your friend, Nick Drakas, he's the one behind all this, right?"

"Yes, but what are you going to do? Do you realize I'll get in trouble from both sides if you expose us? I'm trusting you, that's why I'm telling you everything."

"Well, then you're going to have help me with the plan. I won't expose you. I'm trusting you too, since now you know about Weedy. I'll give you my word if you'll give me yours."

"You have a deal," he said, liking the way they were bound up together.

When he had told her everything he knew, and she had explained her plan and practically scraped her dessert plate clean, she said she'd better get Weedy home.

In the doorway he stood, staring at her, the panicky feeling rising up in his throat. Then as if coming out of sleep, he began to step forward and when she didn't back up, he reached for her. She tilted her head slightly as he began to kiss her.

After a moment she pulled away. "Thank you for dinner."

"What are you doing on Sunday?"

"I hadn't thought about it."

"Spend it with me. I'll cook for you."

"You don't have to cook for me." But she smiled.

"Okay. I'll take you to the Steak House." Her smile disappeared. "I'm sorry, I mean, we could go anywhere. Just that I want to take you out."

"Yes, I get it."

"Here, let me walk you to your car," he said, quickly.

"No. I'm fine. Goodbye."

He started to protest, but she was talking to Weedy, and had begun walking down the stairs. He leaned over the rail watching her, listening to her footsteps getting farther and farther away. He leaped forward down four steps at once, then stopped himself. *You'll see her again. It's okay. Let her be. You'll see her again.*

CHAPTER THIRTY-SEVEN

Two days later, Sylvie sat on the sofa beside Weedy who curled himself under a fleece blanket. She sat watching the branches on the oak trees move as the leaves fluttered wildly, and the sky behind darkened. A plastic bag whirled by, rising and dipping, before finishing its wild dance in a puddle across the road. Sylvie ate a chocolate chip cookie and rubbed Weedy's side. She stared outside transfixed. Her fate felt like the plastic bag, whipped here then there. She was grateful to be cozy and warm inside before the storm began, but her heart ached. She wanted to call Carol and tell her all about dinner with David, and listen to Carol tease the ease back into her. She would replay the evening and they would laugh. Or not. But they would talk. Connect. She wanted to tell Carol how good Weedy had been. But every time she called Carol, there was no answer.

The splatter of rain began simultaneous to a streak of lightening illuminating the street for seconds, followed by the crack of thunder a few seconds afterward. She was staring outside at the pelting rain when she realized her phone was ringing.

She stood to answer it. "Hello?

"Sylvie."

"Carol!" Relief hit her. "Are you all right?"

"No."

Sylvie waited.

"Can you come to the hospital? Bring Weedy. You can leave him in the car."

"I'm on my way."

"I'm still mad at you. I'm more than mad. I'm in shock. I don't understand what you're doing or why you're doing it. But right now I need you. You're my person, and for the moment, lousy friend that you are, you're still here."

"I'm on my way," Sylvie repeated.

Sylvie grabbed a coat tripping over the toy hedgehog Carol had bought, and led Weedy down the steps, as the rain splashed on the cement. She lifted him, holding him for a moment in her arms before setting him into the car with the blanket he'd been nesting in. Last year, she hadn't known he existed. Neither had she imagined a love like this could exist—all-encompassing with its fierce yet fearful joy.

"Come on, little guy, we're going to help a friend. That's what we do in life, we help each other," she said, starting the engine and glancing back at him. As she drove, she steadied her gaze forward as headlights glared in her eyes. She thought about Carol loving Matt and having to watch him die. She thought about how much she loved Carol and didn't want Matt to die. She wondered how she would act if the one person she loved most were dying. She thought about telling Carol she lied to her and telling her why she had. Then decided, not now.

She looked to the constant, uninterrupted trail of red taillights ahead of her, her small car becoming part of the larger momentum. The rain hit her roof and windshield, and the perky wipers bounced back and forth. In the distance she heard a siren. The hypnotic *slap, slap, slap* of the wipers began to lull her, the same way that the small acts of brushing one's teeth or methodically doing the dishes countered the larger, metaphysical feelings of life and death, being and purpose, and she tried to force her mind to think of happy things.

Wet with rain, Sylvie slipped through the automatic doors and into the steamy foyer of the hospital. There was a strange stillness, silent like moss on damp stone. A woman bustled in after her, breaking the stillness, and Sylvie walked toward the information desk. She was standing before the desk when Carol came up to her from the side. She took her shoulders like she wanted to shake her, and turned her around so she was inches away from her face. Sylvie stood passively, aware that normally Carol would have hugged her or kissed her on the cheek.

"They've given Matt two weeks to live. His enzymes or something have risen," Carol spoke dully like an automaton.

Sylvie said nothing. There was nothing she could say.

"It's not what you think. It's that we have to get Matt outside. But I don't know how, and it's risky. That's why I called you here."

"What can I say?"

"Nothing. Just help me get him out."

"You know it's pouring with rain."

"It doesn't matter. I need to get him out of here."

When she entered Matt's room, Sylvie saw a white curtain, a bed with white sheets and a body in it. She smelled the stale smell of the room combined with something else—the decay of disease perhaps. The body in the bed turned and she startled. The Matt she knew had shiny dark hair and vivid blue eyes that twinkled when he smiled. The man who lay in the bed had hair that clung to his face, like damp thread, and sunken eyes with no sheen. Eyes that regarded her without seeing her. The Matt she knew was strong, virile and vibrant. This man was emaciated and yellow.

"Hey, Sylvie. Still beautiful," he said slowly, cranking his neck around, and sounding more like a stroke victim or maybe just someone on heavy medication.

"Matt . . ."

"S'okay, Sylvie," he said slowly. She could barely hear him over the beeping of some machine. "I'm used to people thinking I look dead. I do, don't I? Somewhat gray, Carol says. Or is it green?" He tried to smile at her.

"Enough of that talk, sweetie," Carol said. "Sylvie, help me with this." 'This' was a tube hooked up to the machine.

"Carol, you can't unhook him from that. It's doing something."

"I don't know what it's doing, but I know what I'm doing. It's what Matt wants."

"It's dangerous," Sylvie said and looked to Matt in appeal.

"I've seen the nurses unhook him from it a hundred times. It's just fluids or something. There. Done." She brandished the tube with a flourish.

"Done," Matt repeated.

"Sylvie, go find the nurse on duty and distract her or him," Carol said. "Keep talking and asking questions. Then come downstairs and meet us outside."

"Uh, what do I say?"

"You'll think of something."

"Right." Sylvie walked out of the room. There was no one in sight. She turned a corner and saw a woman behind a desk.

"Can you direct me to the nurse on duty for room, uh, for this floor?"

"What do you need?"

"Well, I was writing a paper for my graduate Sociology seminar and I wondered if I could ask you some questions."

The woman rolled her eyes.

Five minutes later, Sylvie thanked her and fled downstairs. She ran out the doors, looking up and down the street as the golden glow of lamplight reflected in puddles. She thought of Weedy alone in the car and hoped the sound of the rain hitting the roof did not frighten him. For a moment she stood watching approaching headlights, listening to the rain and the soaking street sounds. She saw two figures that looked like infirmed senior citizens. The man dressed in a hospital gown over trousers, leaning on the woman.

She ran toward them. "Carol, no!" She yelled. "He'll die of pneumonia!"

To Sylvie's amazement she saw that Matt was laughing—his head thrown back, the rain splattering his face.

"It's the most beautiful feeling!" She could hear him croak, as though trying to shout to the saturated heavens. And as she stood in the rain watching Carol and Matt, there came over her an incongruous, and perhaps inexplicable, joy, the kind of joy born of sorrow, or perhaps born in spite of sorrow. The way grace often juxtaposed itself with tragedy. She ran the rest of the way, catching up to them.

Carol was crying, holding onto him, and holding him up.

"Just this," Matt kept talking. "It's the last time I'll ever feel it. How beautiful it is. How wonderful it is."

Sylvie touched his arm on the other side.

"Carol told me you were moving," Matt said, turning to Sylvie and talking with labored breath between pauses. Before Sylvie could reply, he continued. "She loves you so much, and she's going to need you without me. If I could do anything to keep you from moving away, just say the word, Sil." He stumbled.

"Matt, watch out!" Carol cried.

"Really, just say the word, Sil."

"Hush, Matt. Stop worrying about me," Carol said up against his ear.

Sylvie looked to Carol. Matt continued talking. "Please, don't ever take the rain for granted. Or the sun. Or life."

Sylvie felt crushed beneath the weight of life. She loved these two rain-sodden people, and their pain became her own. But shimmering through was a realization that someplace deep within her she also knew a gentle quietude whose calm she'd not known for years. Maybe never known. It was a joy so quiet the outside sounds—the rain falling, the cars splashing on asphalt, the city sounds—almost drown it out. But not quite. It was a joy so different from the sharp and fleeting moments of happiness, and she knew this quiet joy could withstand the sorrow. She'd tell Carol everything after her plan was completed. And she'd be there to help with Matt just as Carol had helped her with Weedy.

Taking Matt's other arm, she said with conviction. "We won't, Matt. We won't take any of it for granted. Isn't that right, Carol?"

"Yes, that's right," Carol said through the rain and tears.

"I'm right here," Sylvie said to Matt and Carol. "I'm right here."

PART III

PRESENT
February 2015

Stone walls do not a prison make/
nor iron bars a cage.

—Richard Lovelace

Only the people who have attained salvation or liberation are the really free people. Others are in prison. When you are not free, you are imprisoned; that is the prison then. Is it within the walls, behind the electronic doors? No. It is with in you. Your ignorance of your true nature is, itself, a prison.

—Sri Swami Satchidananda

CHAPTER THIRTY-EIGHT

Two weeks passed in which Eleanor did not see Jane. While Jane had recovered in the infirmary from a concussion, Eleanor had not recovered from sleepless nights where her mind spun out the same obsessive vagaries unable to focus on anything except the silent girl. She had to see her, thank her, apologize to her, and, most of all, talk to her. Perhaps more than talk she sought to comfort Jane and in so doing also allay her own tumultuous mind. Never had anyone or anything held her as Jane was now. For the first time since working at the penitentiary, she argued with Helen—arguing about what had happened when the guard hit Jane over the head.

"Jane had *nothing* to do with it," Eleanor said speaking rapidly, feeling not only the impotence, but also the injustice of the very system supposed to grant justice. "Except perhaps the misfortune of having her session when Mimi Kramer chose to assault me, bringing yet another inmate onto the receiving end of Mimi's venom and vituperation."

Helen spoke slowly. "Eleanor, I understand your concern. But inmates are strictly forbidden to have contact with other inmates and what holds true for inmates with inmates holds doubly true for inmates with their therapists. Jane is a high risk inmate."

"Oh, balls to that! *Look* at her."

Startled, Helen regarded Eleanor, but Eleanor continued. "She poses no threat to anyone, except perhaps herself."

"Dr. Hartley," Helen's tone changed. "An institution crumbles without laws and regulations to uphold it, which, I might add, are needed nowhere more than in a prison. For heaven's sake, Eleanor," Helen implored. "There are exceptions, of course. But it's not your job to find or make them."

Eleanor squared her shoulders. Out the window behind Helen the sun lay shrouded against a cottony sky. Eleanor kept her eyes on the window and beyond, as the suffused light entered her being. It covered her and spoke to her of past and future lives. Its contradiction was that it was both muted and bright. All humans contained the capacity for good and for evil. Jane might have committed an evil deed in the eyes of the law, but Eleanor knew the quiet, fair-haired girl, and she *knew* she was good. People could change—they did, didn't they?

Rationality told her Helen was doing her job and could not act differently, yet a small but growing voice was nudging her to take action. Did Jane matter to anyone in the world except Eleanor? What became of a life that reduced time to the measured counts behind prison walls? She could not forsake Jane—and she knew she could also no longer tell Helen her thoughts.

"Helen, I'm sorry. I guess I have what I've always asked for—a challenging job. And I guess we get what we ask for but not always in the way in which we want."

"Oh, thank goodness, Eleanor. I know it doesn't always seem right, but . . . anyway, thank you." Helen paused. "I count on you more than you know."

When she left Helen's office, Eleanor's mind was made up. And when she knew the segregation inmates were outside sharing their one hour of Association, she walked to building eight, the Isolation, Segregation and Detention unit.

She spoke with the guard and unit manager on duty, then, with permission, entered, pulling forward the heavy door, listening to it snap shut behind her. She was uncertain what she was going to do. She only felt the growing need to act.

"Which one is Jane Doe's?" She asked.

"Fourth down on left."

Eleanor moved like a slow and silent phantom, the only witness to herself, carrying with her thoughts about things she had never allowed herself to think. She saw the present as though it were already her past, and cared little if she was caught somewhere she ought not be.

She did not glance in any of the other 12 by 12-foot cinder-block cells, but when she reached the fourth cell on the left, tiny and sparse, with just enough space for a cot-like bed and a small chest of drawers, she stood contemplating the bare room through the wire-meshed glass pane. She touched her right palm to it, the glass cool and smooth as she traced the small surface with an index finger. Her eyes moved first to the only avenue of light within the cell, a tall narrow rectangular window on the opposite wall, and suddenly she saw herself old and sick in a bed somewhere with the windows pulled down tightly avoiding the living air of outside day, a stuffy sick smell in the room, no light, no fresh air, and she wondered if these girls were unwittingly preparing for death. Would death really come like that? A beautiful day unfolding outside and oneself oblivious? The gradual attenuation of a once vibrant life into mildewed desuetude. No children to care for her when she became old and feeble. Who would touch her and give her that needed human connection?

Touching the inmates was forbidden at the penitentiary. How many times had she longed to pat an inmate's shoulder in compassion or reassurance? But while she knew others had breached this regulation, she had upheld it in attempt to remain committed to her work. If she began breaking rules with which she disagreed, or taking everything into her own hands, she was headed down an equivocal and slippery slope as Helen had just reminded her. She realized the rule was a safety precaution meant to curb harassment and violence, but she also knew that living every day without touch paved a slow road to dysfunction, illness and despair. How many experiments with hapless monkeys attested to the enormous significance and magnitude of touch, its necessity among people in order to create functioning, stable, happy human beings? How could they, herself included, talk about right and wrong in the face of this? It was wrong to torture monkeys. And if it was wrong to torture monkeys, what about inmates? She shivered. Imagine no hello handshake, no shoulder of a friend, no hug after a hard day.

Her eyes scanned the room searching for clues. Who was the silent girl she sat with three times a week? What did she do daily, confined to this box? She remembered Jane lifting her, holding her, protecting her from Mimi.

She felt her legs quiver and she began to breathe differently. What precision of mind and movement it must have taken for Jane to act in the way she had. She shook her head and stared back into the cell and was aware not so much of the absence of presence, as of the presence of absence, an almost seductive austerity, or purity, not unlike the Cistercian orders. Compared to the cells she'd seen in G.P., this one appeared unused. There was not, on the low and insignificant chest of drawers, an array of nail polish, shampoo or deodorant. There was no food in view, although that was understandable for inmates locked up food in their plastic containers, fearing theft, in a way they'd never lock up more valuable items like cosmetics or clothes. There were no markers, no colored pencils, no cards or address books. No tissues, no toiletries, no sense of being lived in. There was, however, one bound notebook on the bed and beside it a pen.

Within the mind of Eleanor Hartley, desire wrestled with will, waded near to the shallow depths of obsession, as a longing to read whatever might be written, scribbled or drawn upon the pages within that notebook overtook all sense, and for a moment she contemplated speaking to the guard, citing professional or medical injunctions. With difficulty, she overcame the temptation, storing the idea in a far cavity of her brain, and recognizing as she did that it had not been entirely erased.

She heard footsteps coming nearer, the quick sharp tap of stealth. Then they were running. She moved quickly away from the doorway of Jane's cell and looked up to see a C.O. hurrying by, lips pursed. The C.O. passed without a word but gave her a suspicious look. The loudspeaker droned on and off, its constant angry calls an assault to any sensitive human being. There was a casual cruelty that prevailed in prison, which was all the more cruel for the very assumption that it, and not decency or compassion, was the norm. It coerced prisoners into becoming the very creatures the system advertised them to be, often stealing their last trace of humanity.

Eleanor stepped back to Jane's room and stared at the little empty bed where Jane slept. How could conditions such as these not dehumanize? Or was it assumed that these women were no more human on arrival than monkeys? Again the picture of the laboratory monkey flashed before her eyes, and she wondered if their wrongful imprisonment wasn't the greater of crimes. She thought of Jane and the crime she had committed. Substitute the word "murderer" for "Jane" and watch the reaction. Did her feelings subtly shift? Did she feel brutal abhorrence replace the softer emotion? Where a *taker of precious human life* slept. Come on, damn it! Where a *killer* slept. But it was no use. She could not change how she felt.

Eleanor sat behind the desk, the small beds of the isolation unit a recent memory.

She heard the perfunctory knock outside and her heart stumbled against the walls of her chest. Leading Jane, the guard entered and nodded to Eleanor as he handed over the small key that meant Jane was again handcuffed. Eleanor did not look right away at Jane. Her heart was beating too fast beneath her blouse.

When the guard left, Eleanor willed herself to glance up. She saw a silent girl with downcast eyes and sorrow cast over her face. This girl had killed a man.

One doesn't necessarily kill because one hates. One may also kill because one loves.

But why? *Why*? As Jane sat down before her for the first time in two weeks, Eleanor felt suddenly she could breathe easier. Her heartbeat was settling down. Now she wanted to tell Jane that she'd stood before her lonely cell. She wanted to ask her what mystery churned inside the notebook. She wanted to understand, if not possess, the courage and compassion, despite the risk of physical harm, to say nothing of punishment, that Jane had displayed during their last session.

As she stared across at Jane she tried, in a series of studied glances, to see beyond the closed and quiet mouth, to discern what had prompted her to act. Uncertain how to begin the session, she sat without speaking. But as the girl across from her did not move and the clock on the wall ticked reminding her that minutes were wasting, minutes in which she was here to help Jane, the heavy stillness became too much. She broke it with her own words.

"I hope the last weeks have been kind to you. I don't know what to say."

She waited, knowing Jane would not speak, but more than hoping now she would. She was answered with an unsettling hush.

"I want to thank you for what you did. I'm grateful. More than grateful—" She glanced up and found Jane looking at her, patiently. "Oh," she began, startled, but quickly closed her lips and thought how infinitely more appropriate Jane's silence had been compared to her blundering sentences. After a beat, she cleared her throat. There was no choice but to continue:

"What you did took courage and . . ." She stopped again and looked away from Jane. "You should not have been punished for it." She heard herself talking on, for now she could not stop this alien desire to share. "I know for a fact that there are girls in this prison who are innocent, but I haven't a clue what to do about it. Of course it's not my job. That's what they'd say to me, the authorities, that is. The powers that be. *It's not your job,* they've said to me before. And they'd say it to me about you. Sometimes, it's funny, but sometimes I have this feeling you're innocent, but then I know you're not. I guess. I guess I know it . . . what I mean is, even though you've committed a crime, murder to be precise . . . decidedly not your average run-of-the-mill crime. Well, in most places it's not. But regardless of that, of that detail, the murder . . . regardless of that, I believe you are *good.* I really do. And you can, you really can, trust me enough to talk to me. I mean you can confide in me. Jane, or whoever you are, I don't know the circumstances around your particular case, but you seem a good and gentle soul to me. And again I want to—" Eleanor was about to utter the words "thank you," when she looked up from her lap and across to Jane—and abruptly stopped.

Eleanor knew that what she next said, or didn't say, was absolutely crucial. Crucial to her work and success as a psychologist, and crucial to Jane's future. She glanced back down at her hands. For what she had seen pass over Jane's face was a moment of trust.

"Why did you risk your life to help me? You must have known that you also risked punishment, however unjustly delivered." She spoke one level above a whisper. And across from her pale eyes regarded her. Eleanor waited, expecting. But within the four walls of the room there was only silence.

"Look, I can help you get out of here. I feel you *need* to get out of here." The feeling had passed over her then—that if she didn't do something soon, Jane would be in trouble. She had never spoken her thoughts aloud, always monitoring and thinking before she spoke, but she was breaking through every membrane that had ever been herself, like crossing a swift river whose current allowed no return.

"I *want* to help you." Another flicker across the passive face. But like the other, it vanished just as quickly, the outside gate falling shut. A microsecond later Jane merely raised her eyebrows to match the extended corners of her mouth. Eleanor read it as easily as she was meant to.

"Okay, no, not immediately, maybe not . . ." She couldn't finish, for to finish would mean the inevitable retraction of her previous words and an unmistakable retreat. She regretted her impetuousness, but she'd seen the trust, however fleeting, and she'd trusted her interpretation, and now she was trusting her intuition. But no, it was impossible. She could never take Jane out of prison. She'd blown it. Why hadn't she said something kind and soothing instead of the omnipotent, *I can take you out of here?* Like she was God's first lieutenant or something? Who was she kidding?

To add hurt to shame, she remembered she had even fantasized about Helen agreeing to let Jane leave for a day. She'd imagined taking Jane home and baking cookies. They would make cookies and drink tea and Eleanor would talk to her soothingly until Jane saw life was not going to devour her and, in return for Eleanor's kindness and dare-devil feat of breaking her out of prison, she would, with a mouth full of warm, fresh-from-the-oven Tollhouse cookies, speak her first words to Eleanor. But no, that was a fantasy and Eleanor knew she had breached her own code of ethics.

"What I meant was . . ." She cleared her throat. "I can take you out of your own self-imposed prison," she said, grappling for a meaning that would not spell cop-out to Jane. "The prison of your mind."

She was focused on Jane's eyes, and begging her mind to tell her what her next step ought to be, when something caught her periphery vision. She turned to behold a tiny spider shimmying down its magic thread. The spider absorbed her, distracting her for seconds. She glanced at Jane to see if she'd seen it, for it was remarkable really. Jane was eying her oddly. Eleanor waited till the spider had landed gently like a lofty parachuter onto the desk.

"I wonder where it came from," she stated aware of the inane way the words sounded. "I guess this isn't really a place to have spiders," she said watching the spider. She looked across at Jane. Jane's eyes had altered since her last look and Eleanor could not read them clearly, but she saw the uneasy emotion, and realized what it was. Jane was afraid of the spider.

"Don't worry," Eleanor said softly. "I'll take care of it."

She reached for her briefcase, and pulled forth a tissue. With uncertainty she raised her hand to wipe away the arachnid. And as she did, she heard the words across from her as clearly as if a bell had begun chiming in the room:

"Don't kill it."

Eleanor stopped.

Time stood still and the voice in her head was silenced. For a moment she sat frozen. Then regaining herself in seconds that seemed spun of hours, she sucked the words deep inside like a spring of cool water in the Sahara. Shock, relief, desire granted. The words were the stars she'd tried to touch and thought she never would. The voice was beautiful. It was ordinary. It was different from the imagined version that would soon recede from memory without recall. Beautiful, fantastic, incandescent. Sensations, thoughts, epiphanies, revelations all occurred to her within the space of an instant then dissipated.

Proceed slowly. Proceed wisely. Don't screw this up, Eleanor Christina Hartley. Don't make a big deal and, for God's sake, act normal.

She looked up.

"I didn't want to kill it. I just thought for some reason that you were frightened of it and I wanted to show you I'd kill it if that was what *you* wanted. If that would help you to trust me. But no, I didn't want to kill it, and no, of course you weren't frightened of a spider. I'm sorry. I made a mistake."

Jane regarded her calmly, then, this time, no mistaking it, moved her chin upwards in one movement.

Keeping eye contact with Jane and speaking deliberately, Eleanor placed both palms face down on the desk. "You, you cared enough about . . . a tiny spider to break your silence?"

Jane looked as she had always across from her, but there was a new light in her eyes—a face lit from within, and Eleanor knew that from now on their sessions would be different. Like the child who has won the spelling bee and is bursting apart inside, Eleanor sat across from Jane trying to remain calm.

The spider, oblivious to its close call, climbed back up its invisible thread.

"Why do you care about the spider?"

Silence as tenuous as the spider's web.

"That's okay," Eleanor said. She coughed. "You know, I've felt bad, or, that's perhaps not the right word, but uh silly perhaps, calling you Jane all this time. So, would you like to tell me your name?"

"You know I could become silent again."

Eleanor looked down briefly, but the top of her skirt taut across her crossed legs offered no answers. "Yes you could. If you wanted to. But I think this will be better for you. Much better."

Jane sat motionless.

"I won't push you, if that's what you're thinking."

Jane nodded.

"But, I would like . . ." She felt a thought pressing her. Where was the thought? "I would like to know your name. So I don't keep calling you Jane."

"Jane is fine."

Jane closed her eyes. She looked tired, but she did not look sick, disturbed, or mentally unsound. She just looked . . . what? *What*? What was it about this one face that Eleanor Hartley found so difficult?

"Jane is not your name then."

Silence.

"Do you want to talk to me?"

Jane blinked. "I don't know." She stopped and seemed to be watching Eleanor. "It'll be hard. And I'm not sure where you should start."

Now added to a gesture, a micro expression, an arm or leg movement, was the long desired gift of voice, words which Eleanor thought would make for much easier therapy sessions. But in fact, she understood a fraction of a second later, they only added that much more information, too much information, and she found her ears straining and stuck on the words—like pieces of chocolate of which she was once deprived, now being thrown out to her in bagfuls.

Compared to the silence and rare shifts in posture, the words seemed now awkward, attached unfamiliarly to the previously silent mouth to which Eleanor had grown accustomed. Like a blind man who has compensated for his loss of sight with an acute sense of sound or a sixth sense, Eleanor wondered whether she would now lose the ability to read Jane's gestures again. All her patients emanated an energy field that was most evident upon first meeting: primal impressions, nonverbal expressions in the moments before language became dominant, when she could better sense her patient's inner sense of mind. As soon as the inmate spoke, the voice, in trying to assume a position often other than what was truth, paradoxically diminished Eleanor's ability to perceive.

"Where *we* should start," she corrected Jane.

Jane nodded.

"Do you want to tell me your real name?"

"I'd rather talk about the spider," Jane said quietly.

"The spider? Okay," Eleanor said quickly. "What about the spider?"

Jane didn't answer.

"Most people have a . . . well, if not an aversion, then certainly," Eleanor laughed, "no great love for spiders. I've never particularly cared for them. But neither am I afraid. What I mean is that I don't mind them." She paused. She was talking too much. She made eye contact with Jane and waited. When Jane made no more attempt to speak, Eleanor said, "Why do you care? Or I suppose I should ask why did you stop me from killing it?"

Jane looked across at Eleanor and there was no belligerence to darken her face. She said softly, "Is there any difference between killing a spider and killing a man?"

Eleanor stared at her a moment before answering. Jane's quiet tone told Eleanor more than her words and Eleanor knew she was serious about her question, however absurd it sounded to outside ears. "You're asking me if—" And Jane nodded. "Well, in our society yes, there is, but . . . ."

"Yes, I know, but—" Jane stopped.

"Go on," Eleanor urged.

"I know if I say that I don't see the difference, you'll think I'm crazy, but since you already do and since I'm already locked up, I guess it really doesn't matter, does it?"

"I don't think you're crazy," Eleanor said quickly. "Perhaps you'd like to tell me what you felt when you saw I was about to kill the spider?"

"I can imagine what it would be like to be squished. And I know I wouldn't want that so neither do I want it for this spider, that's all."

Listening avidly and studying Jane's face, Eleanor nodded. She noted that Jane spoke carefully and well. She was definitely not uneducated as Eleanor had readily assumed this entire time. Eleanor also noted that her words, far from sounding angry or challenging, seemed to be doled out in a neutral fashion. If she detected anything, she would have said there was a shyness to the voice, and also, however faint, a warmth. And Eleanor felt one pressing question rising to the top above all the rest: *What had led this girl to kill?*

"Go on Jane. You may keep talking."

"I'm not sure if there really is a point."

"In talking? Why do you say there's no point?"

Jane did not answer.

"That's okay. I know it must be hard. But often—" Eleanor began then thought to herself, easy does it. "Often," she began again, "talking something out helps you." She smiled at Jane as she delivered the words.

Nothing moved on Jane except her eyebrows, which Eleanor again easily read.

"Talking helps because you can share with someone the things you think are too dark to reveal, like," she stopped short of bringing up shooting two men in the face and heart just yet. "Like many things. The things we all carry around with us from childhood. Shame and guilt for starters."

"And sorrow."

"Yes, *and sorrow,*" Eleanor said too emphatically, feeling excitement course through her body. The last words Jane spoke to her during the session were to ask if she would please release the spider outside the walls of the prison. And Eleanor took pride in promising she would use a tissue carefully and release the spider.

That evening the rush of emotion that had welled up in her and spilled out, first to Helen, then in the parking lot of the prison as a guard looked over on her burst of joy—the flinging of her briefcase up into the air and the missing of it so that it landed on the asphalt, simultaneous with her shout of, "*Thank you, spider!*" after she'd carefully released it without, miracle of all, squishing it—found its finale at home with Lewis as she recounted the exact details of how Jane had spoken her first words to her.

"I haven't been this elated in months."

Lewis shook his head and laughed silently.

"What?"

"Nothing."

"No really, what?"

"*Nothing.*"

Eleanor poured herself a glass of wine from the open bottle.

"She cared enough about a tiny spider to break her silence. I find that remarkable."

"Or completely insane."

"I'm just afraid that Friday I'll walk in and she won't speak to me at all. And it will all seem like a dream."

"Well, maybe so."

Wife shot husband a look that even a non-expert in face reading could decipher.

"So do what you always tell me to do when I play," Lewis amended. "Picture and believe. Just believe and imagine she's going to talk to you again. 'Yeah, I killed the sucker. Shot him in the balls.'"

"Lewis!"

"What?"

Eleanor began to laugh out loud, surprising herself and her husband. But the thought that had persisted in her mind from that unprecedented session with Jane until now would not release its grip.

"Lewis, she would not let me kill a spider and yet she could gun down two humans in cold blood."

"Actually, it would be in warm blood."

That night as Eleanor sat on the edge of the bed unbuttoning her blouse and feeling happier than she had in months, she felt her husband's eyes upon her and she turned toward him and smiled.

"Yes?"

"I didn't say anything." He turned away so that he spoke to the wall, not to her.

Crawling like a long-legged crab, albeit an elegant long-legged crab, backwards across the bed to him, she reached out and stroked his back.

Lewis pinched his nosed between his thumb and finger like it itched, and turned his head to her. "I'm beat."

Eleanor scooted off the bed, stood, and let fall from her frame the tidy wool skirt. She waited for Lewis to turn his head and see that she wore only her blouse. She would finish unbuttoning it slowly. But Lewis didn't turn, and she sat back down upon the bed, glancing at his back. As suspicion alchemized into fear, she moved over to him a second time, hoping her false eagerness wouldn't let her down.

"Told you, I played hard today." He nodded his head up and down like puppet.

"All the more reason you need some tension released." She kissed his neck, the fear so bold now it swam from her stomach up into her throat like a fish trapped in a small tank. She ran her fingers over his chest and collarbones, then reached around and massaged his hard rhomboids.

“Relax,” she instructed him.

He lay back and she ran her hands over his stomach and down to his groin.

“Elle.”

“Relax.” Maybe soothing words spoken to a reticent husband would calm her own queasy self.

As the light outside swapped shades of gray for black, Lewis groaned and lifted his body up and brought it down against the naked woman beside him.

Later when he rose to take his well-toned body to the bathroom, Eleanor sat up and watched him before he shut the door. She heard the toilet seat being raised. She heard the trickle of running water in the sink, and imagined him washing his hands. She moved her eyes to the bed sheets in their after-love state of disarray, and thought of the bunk beds in each of the cramped prison cells. She thought of the small single, narrow cot-like beds that stood against the wall of each isolation room. Jane’s bed. A bed with covers neat, not marked by the sudden fleeting passion of bodies who meet to crush their distance with kisses rabid upon their lips. What did Jane do to lessen the solitude of isolation? Where could she find human contact and warmth, let alone passion? How many others before Jane had lain down on the hard little bed quietly losing their dignity in the wake of despair?

CHAPTER THIRTY-NINE

The worst thing I ever did, in the eyes of humanity, was, in my own eyes, the very best thing. So how can that be? Am I really mad as they say? And if so—

"Come on, Miss."

She looked up, pen mid-sentence. It was the nice guard, the one she called "the little one." He was short and slight, with Tootsie Roll-colored skin, and he was always professional with her, never giving her knowing looks or running his hands over her body in the ostensible search for illegal items the way the two white guards did.

She rose, held out her wrists for the cuffs and walked ahead of the guard to the therapy wing, propelled toward the same sterile room she entered three times week, but feeling a change in the air, knowing now everything would be different.

She could turn back, retreating into her igloo of silence, but she'd stepped out as she'd known over the past days she would. The disturbance with Mimi had set in motion a chain of events that, while apparently triggered by external forces, wound their way into the hidden limits of her mind and she asked herself had the outcome always been there, perfectly mapped? Or had her will and changing emotions set it moving—like a successful landing after a difficult flight, the auspicious outcome seems obvious, yet does it only obtain such confidence in its role as past not present? And once passed, can we see the divine design, or might the results have been altered at any point along the course?

How unrecognizable her life now was to her. She took a deep breath as she saw the door ahead. She hesitated when she was opposite the door. The guard knocked.

"Keep moving, Miss," he said, and she stepped forward.

Once inside the room, she heard the lyrical voice say, "Thank you," to the guard. She glanced at her therapist. She looked nervous sitting there behind the desk—the desk she'd always perceived as a protective fortress, shielding normal therapists from psychopathic murderers.

She sat down and looked up to meet the therapist's eyes staring steadily into hers. The pounding in her chest began, and she looked away. She wanted to look into the green eyes across from her, the face she thought about alone in her cell, trying to picture it and never succeeding beyond a blurry image, while the feelings that thinking of the face produced came to her at times whether bidden or not. She wanted to look at her therapist's mouth and the small ears, and her hairline where her hair swept up, pulled away from her neck, but she knew the eyes staring fixedly across from her would see her do it.

"Hello, Jane."

She wanted to speak to this woman who had sat with her now some four or more dozen times. Who sat with her patiently, often in silence, where there flourished a world of unspoken sentiment.

She heard her speak again.

"I was pleased with our last session. And I want you to know I won't push you to say anything you are not comfortable saying." Therapist paused, probably waiting. The minutes ticked by. "How have you felt since we last met?"

She knew that the piercing grief and pain she felt when she sat in her cell hour after hour, and day after day, was, when she sat before Dr. Hartley, relieved. But, even sitting there with the therapist, the small crack was always present. The crack was her. And whenever she felt the crack threaten to open, she fled to an oasis of silence where nothing of the past had ever happened.

"Jane, will you look at me?"

The request was delivered so kindly, not to mention beseechingly, that she obediently looked up and met her therapist's eyes and steady gaze.

"Thank you."

"You're welcome," she answered carefully.

"I don't want to keep calling you Jane if it's not your name." Again spoken softly and kindly.

But she was not nearly as concerned with revealing her identity as was the therapist, for it certainly did seem an immense deal to her.

"It must be somewhat strange having me sit here and call you by a name other than your given name."

No stranger than having your life stop abruptly. No stranger than sitting in prison for the rest of your days. It was odd, she thought, what one gave importance to. She saw that nothing mattered anymore; nothing and perhaps everything. But would Dr. Hartley see that too? The rumble, jumble of thoughts gaining unwelcome momentum.

"It's not your name, is it?"

"It is now."

"Interesting. Why is that? Why do you say that it is your name now?"

"I've become used to it. I'm comfortable with it," she answered with difficulty, clouds passing through her mind. Only one thing had mattered to her. Everything else, by comparison, seemed a flutter of feathers upwards, or perhaps backwards, in time. She remembered once standing on the corner watching a truck laden with factory-fattened snow white turkeys careen around a corner. A few faces stared their penetrating dark turkey eyes directly at her, as if they knew their fate, or maybe knew she knew. The truck roared on, disappearing into the distance. All that was left were the white feathers floating through air like clouds.

"You're comfortable with it." The therapist's voice brought her back from the fluttering feather-filled highway to the room. "I see." There was one of those long pauses where she knew she was meant to speak. But she didn't. "Why do you think that is?"

But this was silly. What did a name matter next to life and death? Next to being and not being? What did anything matter now? If she could see him again—but perhaps everything was an illusion anyway—the past as uncertain as the future, for she certainly couldn't find much of her past now.

"Are you seeking to become someone else? Did you give up your identity so no one would find you or know you again? Or did you . . . perhaps dislike the person you were before?"

The person she was before. Was the therapist implying that she was not that person now? That she was now a new person? And if she was a new person, where did the other go? Back to the question of past. There were no absolutes and the truth was inherently un-retainable, like those little epiphanies she would receive when she was with him, brief moments like little sparks of light where, jolted by joy, she understood and loved all.

"Would you . . ." She heard the therapist say, and she realized she'd again gone to another world. But for how long she couldn't have said. "Would you like to tell me your name?"

The name again. She could see she was going to have to tell Dr. Hartley her name if they were to get anywhere. "Maybe," she answered, thinking. "But first you must tell me if there is really any need to talk."

Dr. Hartley looked startled. "Of course there is."

"Why?"

"Well, first of all, it's my job to help you."

"That will really encourage your patients to talk."

After a pause. "Okay. You're right, of course more than that."

She could hear the clock ticking.

"I want to help you. If you don't think I can help you then tell me why you think that."

"Do you have any idea what my days are like?"

"Some idea. But tell me from your side."

She shook her head back and forth.

"You go to the commissary?" A cheerful, hopeful voice. "Does that bring any amount of pleasure to . . . ." Therapist stopped as if searching for the right words to give meaning to something that could never have meaning. "To an uneventful day?"

"What possible reason would I have to enjoy a trip to the commissary?" Not annoyance, just genuine confusion. Fatigue.

"Well, it seems to be, for many of the inmates, the high point of the week."

"Consumerism. Stuff. What need, or desire, do I have for any of that?"

"I don't know. You go to the cafeteria now don't you?"

She laughed then.

"Why do you laugh?" The therapist looked befuddled.

"The cafeteria," she answered. "That's not what we call it."

"What do you call it?"

"Never mind." She thought back to her first lunch outside of isolation. It blurred with her last lunch, two days ago, and her longing to stay alone in her cell, however much her stomach announced an opposite desire. It was always the same: women pushing and shoving to get there first, then the long wait in line to get through the door.

Finally she got her tray. The women on the serving line were ill-humored by this time. The vegetables were steamed a grayish brown beyond recognition. She looked out across the lunchroom. Against a wall stood a handful of administrators. Wardens, guards, therapists, and she wondered how they were assigned the job, or if it could possibly be they volunteered willingly. She also wondered why her therapist was never there. She would have liked that. An ally of sorts. A familiar, or kind, face. But no wonder she never volunteered. What sane person would? She knew the policy was that the administrators be available to the inmates to listen to requests. Some carried notebooks into which she'd seen them write the prisoner's name, smile and say, "We'll look *into* it."

Leaving, on her first day, a kitchen guard strode over near her. It was a short woman with a pinched face. "*Just a minute, inmate. Bring her this way!*" She yelled to the man leading her. She froze, wondering if she had unwittingly committed a prison crime. "Come 'long," her guard said softly.

"*Spread your legs!*" Barked the female guard when she was opposite her. The patting down and feeling up was done ostensibly to prevent women from taking the flimsy plastic forks or maybe some bread from the dining room, but as the squat hands continued their groping romp across her body, asserting their right to paw all over her, she realized how far she would need to retreat into her mind, even her muddled, befuddled mind, in order to find freedom within the prison's walls.

"Jane . . ." she heard her therapist say.

"Yes, I know. You want me to talk." She wondered what Dr. Hartley would have to say if she knew of the extracurricular activities the guards practiced with her body. She considered for that moment telling her.

"*Yes,* I do."

"Any subject in particular?"

"Well, let's see. If nothing comes to you, then perhaps you might begin by talking to me about what you saw in that poster that upset you so much."

"Which poster? Who said it upset me?" She said quickly but did not turn to look at the happy family with the smiling beagle who now had a tear through his tongue.

"I saw that it did."

She shook her head again, feeling the slight hope she'd had walking through the door dissipate. "This is all so pointless."

"Now you seem angry with me." More a question than statement.

She shut her eyes for a moment.

"You don't feel that?" She knew her therapist was looking directly at her when she asked it.

"Feel what?" What she felt was that she'd made rather a bad choice in deciding to speak. Silence had been so much easier.

"Feel that you're angry."

"I hate this."

"By 'this' do you mean talking about feelings that bring up your past?"

She was shaking her head back and forth. "I can't do this."

"What did you feel just now when you said that?"

"*Merde.*"

"Okay, what did you feel when you looked at that family?"

She didn't answer and refused to look over at the poster.

"Jane, do you have family anywhere?"

"No, the stork brought me."

"But you never have visitors here."

"They come at night."

"What?"

"You know nothing about me."

"I know." Dr. Hartley was looking at her awaiting mutual understanding and when she offered nothing, therapist said again, "I know. But I want to know about you."

She looked up. She'd lost the rebellious spark, born of frustration, and now an emotion surpassing sorrow surfaced. "But you can't know me," she said softly.

Therapist stared at her. "Why do you say that?"

"You can't."

"Why do you say that?"

She knew the therapist was watching her intently.

"Why do you want to try to know me?" she asked.

"I'm concerned. Very concerned about you. Do you have family anywhere?"

"Why is that your concern? Can't I exist apart from my family?"

"Yes and no. Jane, where *is* your family?"

"I could become silent again."

"So you've said."

She closed her eyes for a moment. "If you're going to insist that I talk, and it's obvious that you want me to," she spoke in a low, slow voice without sarcasm. She was very keen on her words. "Then I suggest you try talking about things that at least somewhat interest me, and not things that repel me."

Dr. Hartley studied her. "Repel," she stated. "That's an interesting choice of word."

Silence.

"All right." Her therapist cleared her throat. "What would you like to talk about?"

"I'm not really sure. I don't know until you start on something. So you talk, and if I don't like where you're going, I'll tell you."

"Okay. Do you want to talk to me about why you stopped talking?"

"Not really."

"Do you know why you stopped talking?"

"Yes."

"But you don't want to share that with me?"

"No."

"Do you want to talk to me about what you did and why you're in prison?"

"No."

Dr. Hartley closed her mouth and sat, watching her.

"I said no."

"I'm not here to judge you. Are you sure you won't?"

For a moment no one spoke.

"Tick, tock."

"What?" The therapist asked.

"The clock."

"Yes, the clock. But it's not time yet."

"You've heard the saying, the path to hell is paved with good intentions?"

"I have, yes."

"Let's just say I thought I was doing something good. It felt so right. So . . . good."

Therapist nodded. "Go on."

"That's it. That's all I have to say. It doesn't matter now, anyway."

Therapist said nothing for a few moments, then asked: "Were you high, Jane? Is that why it felt so good and you thought you were doing the right thing?"

"Oh for . . . *no,* I wasn't high."

"Okay."

"That's not at all what I meant. Just forget it."

"Okay."

She exhaled. A sigh.

"Do you want to tell me what you do with your time?"

She sighed again, deeper and more pronounced. "Time? You talk of time? Time doesn't exist. You couldn't know that unless you'd . . ." She stopped.

After a few moments, Dr. Hartley said, "What were you going to say just then when you stopped?"

"Nothing."

"Unless I'd spent time in prison, like you?"

"No. Unless you'd . . ."

"What, Jane?"

"Nothing."

"Why does time not exist?"

"I don't know."

"But you do know, don't you? You were going to tell me something."

"I heard one of the girls say during Association, 'You don't want to think too hard about the future. It may not come.' In prison there is no present. Inmates either remember the past or dream about the future." She stared back at the therapist. All at once her face broke into a smile. "Be anxious not for the morrow, for it may not come."

She knew she'd pleased, or at least surprised, her therapist, for she smiled back, and seemed to be waiting for more. She looked away. The clock tick-tocked. Dr. Hartley spoke:

"In some ways, Jane, I think you all, most of you, live more, or perhaps are forced to live more, in the present than anyone else. Taken from you are all the material possessions that give most people identity and individuality, but in reality only clutter the shelves of recognition. Stripped bare of the material, I think sometimes the true essence of all of you shines more brightly. Who are we really? A pair of Gucci's? A gold Rolex? Are we personality, or emotion? Or is there maybe something else? I've been taught to believe these things constituted the being, and if not, surely we were our emotions, leaving no room for spirit or soul. Are we amalgamations of our likes, dislikes, opinions and quirks? Or are these but a cloaking of the soul? Maybe when you take away the material, you begin to glimpse the soul of a woman. What I've seen in prison isn't always pretty. But it's human."

Dr. Hartley stopped suddenly, and there was the quilted silence again.

"Thank you," she said softly to her therapist.

"For what?" Dr. Hartley asked her.

"For talking to me. Really talking. Sharing."

"You're welcome."

"I'm not sure I see it the way you do, though," she said carefully.

"You don't believe what I said about the present? You don't have to, but I can also share with you that I've worked with women who actually found peace in prison."

She thought what that would be like—finding peace as the hours became days and the days lengthened to weeks, morphing to months."

"As if there could be a paradoxical peace in prison where you each live and breathe the present moment, trying, as you say, to forget the past and not dare hope for a future," Dr. Hartley was saying.

"Maybe. But, my god, what a present," she whispered. She knew she was speaking to her therapist differently now. She knew something had opened up. Something had changed.

"What?" Dr. Hartley leaned forward. "I didn't hear you."

"There's too much time for reflection. I can never escape my thoughts. I see certain moments over and over in my mind," she said looking down.

"Which moments are those?"

"Never mind."

"We're all prisoners of our minds. But breaking free begins with awareness. Then sharing. Letting go of the shame."

"I no longer hope. I no longer daydream. It's as if that good and positive part of me has dried up. I'm no longer capable of doing good because I can no longer perceive it. Can you understand that?"

"I honestly don't know."

"I can only perceive of despair," she continued.

"Do you think you perceive of despair because you're in here, or is it despair over something else?" Dr. Hartley asked.

"I don't want to talk about it."

"Okay. Do you want to tell me how you like prison?"

"What?" Had the woman really just asked her how she *liked* prison?

"I'm sorry. It's just that I remember working with a patient who told me that her idea of what prison would be like was far worse than prison itself. She told me that on the inside of the prison she felt free, removed from the day to day pressures of the outside world like earning a living, keeping a home and family and that she quite enjoyed life in the penitentiary and intended to stay for as long as she could." Dr. Hartley laughed a funny laugh.

She didn't answer, and after a while she heard her therapist asking, "Do you want to talk about which thoughts you can't rid from your mind?"

They both turned to the sound of a knock on the door.

"It looks like time," her therapist said. "I'll see you day after next."

"Okay."

She rose and was ushered out by the guard.

Brows knitted in concentration, Eleanor watched as Jane stood and was then gone. A thought was pressing into her mind and, believing it was important, she tried to bring it into clearer focus—like remembering a dream upon waking that might perhaps make sense to some part of you.

Her eyes darted once around the bleak room and she shook her head. It was as though Jane had taken with her all life and color from the room, as if the walls and ceiling and sparse furniture had been a brightly colored quilt that Jane now snatched up and dragged out behind her, leaving the room empty, dull, bleak, and devoid of animation.

Eleanor remembered the sparse room. She'd thought about telling Jane she'd stood before her little cell. Mimi had been taken out of isolation and when she had, Eleanor argued again with Helen, insisting Jane be given more privileges. She wanted to tell this to Jane too—but to what point, as she had not been successful. She remembered Helen's reply: "*Mimi* is not a high risk inmate. *Jane* is." But Eleanor had succeeded in seeing that Jane had more free time than she had before, and she felt victory nudge at the thought that Jane could now enjoy lunch with the other inmates, protected by guards.

The thought was pressing her harder now, but still lay just beyond her grasp. Jane's expression retained a gentleness. It did not suggest violence within. The kind of violence needed to murder a man. The thought wrapped around her brain. It would not let go.

The thought was cool white marble.

Eleanor tried to bring back the feeling her unconscious had slipped her way. Cool, smooth and white. Eternal Idol. Rodin's *Eternal Idol.* All tenderness converged within her, and she longed to kneel before Jane and beg her to tell her everything.

The thought was of sitting in Art History class, a hundred years ago, listening to professor Crosby discuss Rodin. "*To understand these lines, so tenderly modeled, traced and caressed, one has to be lucky enough to be in love.*"

CHAPTER FORTY

"So, what is it, dahlin'?" Cory sat beside Eleanor on a green bench. She wore a fuchsia and purple paisley scarf wrapped partially around her chin. The temperature was about forty-five, but the sun extended tentative rays down on them. About thirty yards away, a group of young boys kicked a soccer ball back and forth.

"Nothing." Eleanor watched a boy in a red shirt who seemed the ring leader of them all.

"Oh."

"Not nothing. Everything."

"Tell, honey."

"I think Lewis is having an affair."

Coralee caught her breath. "*No*! Do you *really*? *Why*?"

"Because he's not a good liar. Maybe he deserves to."

"*Lie*?"

"No. Deserves to . . . ." Eleanor trailed off. "How's Jim?"

"Jim's fine as peach pie. Tell me, dahlin. Do you have any *i*-dea who it is?"

"Probably a nurse. I don't believe it's the first time it's happened."

Cory stared for a moment before gasping, "A *nurse*?"

"I work to solve everyone else's problems and I can't even keep my marriage together."

"But—"

"It's as though everything I've ever worked on in other people is coming back to haunt me. It's killing me. Well no, it's not killing me, but—" She kicked at a partial piece of Styrofoam beneath the bench.

"No, honey, I *know*."

"Thank you. Lewis always says I'm too literal."

"I know he does. I mean—"

"I am literal. It's not killing me. But it does hurt. I know it's just my ego speaking, because—" She stopped.

"Because what, dahlin'?"

"I think the problem may be that . . ." She looked up and into her friend's eyes, with no idea of how to convey the language of her shuddering heart. "Have you ever wanted to go home so badly, but not really known where home was?"

"Well, I know where my home is."

"Have you ever been in love with someone at the same time you loved Jim?" Cory blushed scarlet from her neck up to her hairline, answering the question for Elle. Eleanor patted Cory's knee and said with a weak smile, "It's okay. I guess it's normal."

Cory did not speak and Eleanor removed her hand and looked across the park. One of the soccer boys had kicked the ball into a jogger and now the jogger stood in tight black pants talking to them, perhaps lecturing about park etiquette, and the necessity of not kicking errant balls into unsuspecting joggers. "I don't know. It may be that, well, I guess I'm not in love with Lewis anymore."

Cory's mouth hung open. "Really?"

"I don't know. What's love? We've built up a life together, a history together. Of course, I love him, but there's—"

Coralee shut her mouth then blurted, "Elle. I haven't been in love with Jim for years, bless his heart. He tries but . . . ."

"Then that's a pity."

"A pity? But you just said . . . ."

"I know. Don't listen to me, Cory. I don't know who I am some days. Most days. I haven't been myself. I feel I'm falling apart. There's a girl in the prison—"

"Do you really think it's a *nurse*? Right now?"

"Oh, I don't know. I should probably just confront him. Talk to him face to face, calmly. Nothing accusatory."

"Maybe you'd better wait."

"Why do you say that?"

"Well, it might be best to, I don't know, give the poor boy a chance to . . . ."

Eleanor glanced over to Cory. Her head was bowed, her chin hidden in the colorful scarf, but her eyes, brow and mouth had a strained appearance. Eleanor had never seen her fun-loving friend appear so uneasy. And there it was, so quick, so obvious, Eleanor felt embarrassed. She looked away. Coralee fidgeted then cleared her throat. Eleanor felt the shock. Then only a hollowness, like a room after love. She took a deep breath and turned to face the woman she'd known for more than half her life.

"Cory, do you know anything about Lewis's indiscretions?" She asked quietly, probing the side of Cory's face as if she could penetrate it with her eyes.

"*Me*? Why . . . why, I mean, why-*eva* would I know anything?"

"No, of course not. I'm sorry, Cory. I'm just rambling."

"Elle."

"*Oh God,*" Eleanor whispered, shaking her head back and forth. She longed to let her head slide off her shoulders into her hands. It would roll down and over to where the boys played their soccer game. Would they kick it? Maybe she could bury it here in the park. But her brain would continue thinking. "Tick, tock," it mocked. Was her brain the problem or was it her heart beating beneath her blouse? "Poor Lewis," she said.

"Poor Lewis?"

A breeze changed the air temperature. A squirrel scampered by their feet and over to the base of a nearby walnut tree. Eleanor's eyes rested upon it, in a blissful moment defying laws of psychology. For a moment her thought held no content. She saw the gray, furry, scurrying animal without taking it in. Out of focus.

Then slowly it came into focus. A good marriage was a thing of slow growth, an arrangement in which both parties agreed to their partial and mutual imprisonment. Love eased the limitations and expectations imposed on one another. Lewis had married her and he had promised to be faithful, et cetera. But why should he be made to act in a way alien to his natural instincts if those instincts were harmless? Harmless to everyone save Eleanor. John Stuart Mill would argue for the greatest happiness for the greatest number of people, bolstering Lewis's and Cory's case, while leaving Eleanor behind in the dust for the buzzards to pick over.

The epiphany struck her then, sitting on the park bench beside Coralee, watching but not seeing the squirrel. She knew people's lives were built on anticipatory pleasures. It was not the having, the obtaining, that made them happy, because few people knew how to appreciate the present moment. Few people knew how to live in the present and simply be. So they filled up their lives with material objects, or chased after other women's husbands, for they knew not how to fill the void. Only that there was a void. Yet, it was so much easier to take the moments as they came, easier than reliving the past, which would always retain an abstract flavor. And easier than anticipating or planning for the future. A future that might not come.

She thought about the prison girls, forced to live out their days in the vibrant present, confronting their worst demons. They tried to forget the pasts that had delivered them behind bars and didn't dare think to the future. Within the prison walls they awakened, living lives completely present, and for an instance she envied them their freedom.

When she looked up, she saw the boys had packed up their ball and left. Around her the afternoon was quiet—all except for the emotions roaring within the deepest hollows of people strolling past. Were those outwardly tranquil couples walking past her now arguing, over and over again with their lovers in their fractious minds, fighting for the imaginary and unobtainable control that never came? Fighting to be right? Defending opinions and actions? Were those white-haired folks seated serenely on the benches beside her and Cory harboring murderous thoughts?

She shifted on the bench. She would try to speak of this to Cory. No, she could no longer share anything with Cory. Perhaps she would drive back over to . . . she struggled for her thought back, but the thought that had been there a second ago was gone.

"Elle?"

"Yes." Eleanor turned to face her best friend and wondered why people did the things they did.

"What?"

"I'm sorry, Cory. I shouldn't have brought it up now. I haven't the time to go into it." Someone had told her long ago that there were only two reasons for doing anything. One was fear. The other was love. She looked to Cory. "I must get home to Lewis." Cory turned her head away and made no reply so Eleanor stood, running her hands over her hips, smoothing out her skirt. The squirrel darted away and climbed up a tree.

At length Cory looked up at her and Eleanor thought she would speak and she had no idea how she would respond. "Honey, you don't look well."

With the banality came relief. "I'm okay. I really must go."

"Well, call me, okay?" Cory's voice trembled. "Call me if you need to."

Eleanor looked at her friend and turned away.

CHAPTER FORTY-ONE

When Lewis walked through the door that evening, Eleanor wanted only one thing. But the shock of her realization sitting beside Cory had dulled her perception, leaving a fresh wound that now, from years of habit, she analyzed, and hurt though she was, she found it hard to condemn her husband. Didn't she stress to her patients reason and forgiveness over rash anger and blame? Even though she had not herself broken any marriage vows, was there really more than scant difference between herself and Lewis? As she stumbled down from her victim's perch of superiority, she strove for a combination of reason and wisdom with a stiff leavening of human compassion, realizing how little her angry righteousness would serve any lasting notion she had of happiness. Over the years she had always sought, when the choice presented itself, to choose being happy over being right. She knew couples who had destroyed perfectly workable marriages to prove a point, and to show, "I was right."

What's wrong with humans? Why does it take losing something to value it? But it was only a whisper reverberating within the walls of her mind that only she could hear.

Lewis was whistling. The piccolo notes bounced into her ears like unwelcome gnats, and any words she'd rehearsed dissipated as quickly as ice in the oven, and in their place settled a black, bubbling sludge of fury, fueled not so much by misplaced jealousy as dark-water fear and unfulfilled desires. He walked from the hall towards the kitchen and saw her standing there before the large glass window. He stopped whistling and stood still. "Elle?" he asked tentatively.

Not yet composed enough to speak, she took a breath and gathered her strength, but the right words didn't come.

"What's wrong?" Lewis asked.

"I know about Cory." She saw him freeze. She didn't speak. She just stood staring at him, waiting.

"*What?*"

"I know you've been seeing Cory. I need for you to talk to me." *Please let him tell me the truth. Anything but a lie. I can forgive the truth.*

"What are you talking about? Who told you this crap?" He was talking fast. He walked over to kitchen counter and reached for a bottle of wine. He pulled the cork from the neck roughly, his dark brows in a concentrated frown. He looked up.

She saw the ballad being played out across his face. "Lewis, I need to hear it from you."

"Did Cory talk to you?"

"Yes. Well, no, not really." She guessed then he was sorry he'd spoken. "Lewis, I want to know how long you two have been lovers." She flinched at the sound of the last word. She wanted to pour herself a glass of wine too, but she didn't want to walk over to where her husband stood.

He looked back at her as though surprised at her failure to grasp something momentous. But when he didn't try to answer or speak, she said, "They say the French somehow manage to separate love and sex, thereby gaining access to both."

Lewis shifted his weight and with the movement he seemed to relax. "Dammit, Elle," he said quietly. "Don't you ever get upset over anything? Everything's got to be able to be explained away with some analytical answer. Your husband's screwing your best friend and you bring up French mating habits."

"Thank you, Lewis." However much she'd needed him to admit his wrongdoing, his outburst and critical analysis of her, not to mention his phraseology, hurt her almost as much as his infidelity.

He imitated her then, his quick, abrasive actions, becoming the smooth, polished and controlled movements of his wife. He mimicked, in the authoritative, quiet tone, Elle's tone, "Thank you, Lewis."

It was said under his breath, but she heard it anyway. Meeting his eyes she said, "Is that what you want, for me to get upset? Is that why you did it?"

"It's not why I did anything." He stopped. "Maybe I wanted to feel—" He stopped again, leaving unsaid words.

Eleanor was fighting fear and rage simultaneously. She tried hard to use her intellect the way she always could in the past, but emotion beat it backwards. She knew, as the one betrayed, she had the easier role, even if she'd not asked to be hurt, for Lewis must not only feel sorrow and guilt, and whatever lack of fulfillment led him to Cory in the first place, but worse, the claustrophobic nightmare of being trapped between two women that he—if he didn't love them both—still must have cared for in some way or he wouldn't be there. Eleanor felt pain in her chest. She latched onto the last time he had told her, 'I love you.' Had it all been a charade or a habit worn into his personality, performed perfunctorily with no emotion left behind the three empty words?

She spoke the next words with all the courage she could muster. "Do you love Cory?" What it cost her to ask the question was written on her face, and when Lewis said nothing, her stomach began to fall away and she felt her chest rushing to meet it.

Lewis replied, although perhaps too late. "No, I just like—" He didn't finish.

"It's all right." She said quietly, holding onto that small scrap. "It's not as if I haven't had attractions myself."

"What?"

"Of course."

"*What?*"

"Of course," she said again. "But I didn't act on them."

Whether he realized she'd given him the gift intentionally or not didn't matter. Whether it backfired and caused jealously and anger didn't matter either, for these, in their own way, would be gifts. None of it mattered, for in that moment Eleanor felt better. Into her anxious, fearful and angry thoughts slipped the pale face of a girl behind bars, and she felt emotions she knew she could label if pressed, but in labeling them she would circumscribe what never should be. In that moment she found it easier to forgive Lewis. How could one want such different things? For what reasons? It made no sense. Her intellect, on which she had always been able to count with steadfast security, was now grievously failing her.

"I've never wanted to have an affair, Lewis," she offered.

Lewis moved his mouth as if to speak, but in the next moment his face began to collapse and Eleanor moved towards him.

CHAPTER FORTY-TWO

If a few moments can represent the essence of a lifetime, for Eleanor it was one particular afternoon in early spring. The days stretched longer and with the lengthening light came winds giving voice to thoughts unspoken.

Eleanor walked across the courtyard feeling the cool, new air cut through her jacket and blouse. It was the kind of day from which people would later say they caught a cold, opting for skimpy clothing in anticipation of the sunny warmth to come. She paused for a moment breathing in spring's sharp sweetness.

"I'm afraid it's going to be difficult to get her to talk about certain things, the important things," she said, sitting in the swivel chair across from Helen.

"Look on the bright side, a month ago you would have been over the moon that she'd opened her mouth at all."

"Yes, I know. I've thought of that. But in an odd, paradoxical way this complicates the matter. She seems angry now, too. I never once, strange as it sounds, found her to be angry with me when she was silent."

"I never really thought you'd get her to talk. No offense to your abilities, which I think more than highly of, as you know. It was just her. She seemed so remote or removed, or . . . ."

"She was remote and removed."

"Was it transference, do you think?"

"What?"

Helen smiled. "Don't underestimate the inspirational force of love, or attraction rather. I suppose true love often arrives only after attraction has vanished."

Eleanor said nothing and Helen continued. "Don't pretend not to know that they all fall in love with you. And don't pretend not to know that your success rate with them is higher than anyone else's is."

"But how can you measure success with this?"

"Girls who walk out of here with new awareness. With new attitudes. Girls who turn their lives around."

"Yes, I suppose."

For a moment neither woman said anything. Then Helen tapped the desk with her pen. "How are you?"

"Fine," Eleanor answered. She thought for a moment she might confide in Helen. *My husband's having an affair with my best friend, and for some weird reason, I'm not angry at him or at her. Just a wee bit hurt, however.* But since she had never met with Helen socially, she decided that keeping their relationship professional was in her best interest. What surprised her was that no one, including Helen, whose perception and intuition she respected, detected even the slightest change in her.

"You look well," Helen said.

"I need to get her to trust me," Eleanor said after a moment.

"You will."

Eleanor sensed that Helen was busy with her own problems, problems the penitentiary provided daily. She rose, glancing out Helen's window to the brown grass giving way to green on the near side of the high fencing, said goodbye, and walked to the psych room.

When Jane walked in, Eleanor studied her, taking in as much as she could in the seconds that passed. She also studied her own reactions: increased heart rate, nervousness, excitement, anxiousness. Had she been observing the same reactions in another, she might have laughed knowingly. She waited a few moments after Jane had sat down.

"How are you today?" Eleanor's tone was flat and uncompassionate, instead of her normal lyrical voice: *So, how's life behind bars this week* that both Mimi and Shina found fault with for different reasons. Today it said, *Look, I know you're here in prison, and I know it sucks,* to use the girls' lingo, *but, given that, how are you doing? You can tell me the truth today. My life sucks, too.*

"How do you want me to answer that?" Jane responded and, shaking her head back and forth lightly, she adopted the same tone as Eleanor—devoid of hope, all passion renounced.

"Just tell me how you feel. Angry, sad, joyful, hopeful, scared, depressed, none of the above."

"I feel fine."

Okay, you're obviously angry, Eleanor thought, with not a small amount of irritation herself. "Very well then," she said back to Jane.

"How do *you* feel?" Jane asked her.

"I feel fine," Eleanor answered automatically before she realized what she was doing.

"No you don't. Now, see what I mean?"

"What?" Eleanor asked caught off guard.

"I mean, there you sit across from me, upset as you can be, just like me, although I suppose for different reasons, and when I ask you how you are, you say 'I feel fine,' even though it's obviously the farthest thing from the truth."

Eleanor stared at Jane.

"So you see how hard, or misleading, or whatever, that question is? Especially the more you have not to feel 'fine' about?"

Eleanor swallowed. Silky strands of Jane's hair hung down on her face and Eleanor longed to reach over and push them back.

"Yes. All right then, I'm sorry. Let's agree then that you don't feel so fine, but without me asking the question—"

"And that you don't feel so fine either."

"During these sessions we're not concerned with how I feel," Eleanor replied.

"But it obviously affects the work we do," Jane said softly and smiled for the first time. "How could it not?"

Again Eleanor stared across at Jane, uncertain who the girl was, uncertain how to proceed. "As I said, how I feel is not the concern, and in these sessions you are going to have to adhere to that, so," she continued, the effort it took to do so surprising her, as if she were running a race and the outcome was dependent on her moving forward, using blinders, not looking back. "You don't feel so fine, and I can certainly understand that you might not. So," she said again. "Why don't you just tell me, in your own way, at your own pace, what the past day has been like for you? For instance, what do you do? I'd really like to know. I'd like to be closer to your world."

"I really can't talk to you."

"You have been."

"I can't."

"Try," Eleanor said.

"What you really want for me to talk about is what's inside my head, right? Or maybe, actually, what I won't allow into my head. Then you can write up some fancy paper in some fancy psychological journal, right?"

"No." Eleanor said. "Just tell me what goes on in prison. How you cope. What you do. How you react to other inmates. I'm not writing any fancy papers."

"I don't interact."

"Okay. What do you do then? What are your days like?"

Jane closed her eyes for a moment. Eleanor watched.

"Jane," she said in what she thought was a quiet tone of voice, but she heard its urgency, hoping against hope that only she heard it. "You can talk to me. It's okay. I don't have to tell the authorities everything."

Jane opened her eyes. "Actually you do."

Eleanor looked into the blue-gray eyes. She saw a contradiction of gentleness and strength. "But if you don't want me to, I won't." She knew she was breaking every code she'd ever agreed to as a prison psychologist, but she also knew in the depths of her soul she was doing the right thing in offering those words, and, she would have to honor them. But would Jane believe her? How could she?

"I *could* talk to you," Jane replied softly, "but it wouldn't matter, you wouldn't understand." Then more forcefully she added, seeming to have changed her mind, "No, I can*not* talk to you."

"I'll tell you one more time, the murders are not my concern. They're in the past, now," Eleanor said, and meant it. She found that she cared little now that Jane had murdered. It was neither her job nor her desire to judge the women with whom she worked. Besides, Jane had already been found guilty and convicted of murder. Yet, suppose Jane told her not only about the two murders, but about other murders, multiple other murders about which nobody knew? Could Eleanor then keep her word and keep her mouth shut before the authorities? What about the rights of the victims' loved ones? She shook her head to clear such thoughts. She knew in her heart Jane had not killed more people, so it didn't matter.

"What would it take to get you to believe what I say to you? That if I make you a promise today, I will honor it."

"It's not that. I can't *talk* to you."

Something had changed. Eleanor furrowed her brow, staring back at Jane. The emphasis had shifted from "*cannot*" to "*talk*." She struggled to understand, but Jane's words halted all thoughts.

"You don't have a dog, do you?" It was a statement, not a question.

"What?"

"You have no children, do you?"

"No. How did you—?" Confusion and hurt flickered within her, as if Jane had accused her of not doing her civic or womanly duty.

But Jane said nothing more.

"No, I do not. Why do you ask me?" Eleanor knew she'd been thrown a line and missed it.

Jane looked at Eleanor a long time, but in her look there was nothing reproachful, nothing angry, certainly nothing accusing. Her expression seemed resigned. Eleanor had seen the look before, and then she recognized it. It was the same look of utter hopelessness she'd read, however faintly, on that face the first time she saw it. But today, five months later, there was, under the exterior scrim, something more in the features. If Jane's expression cried resignation, then coexisting with it, Eleanor saw timeless acceptance. And it was this peace that rattled her even more.

Eleanor stared, reading the familiar face, not realizing her own expression had contorted into a confused gape. Jane looked to the floor, and in that one gesture was Eleanor's complete dismissal. The impassive mask was back.

"Jane, don't do this to us!" Eleanor's hand flew to her mouth the second she'd said it, and she stared with disbelieving eyes at the girl across from her, mortified at what she'd done.

And the girl across from her looked up, perhaps deciding Eleanor momentarily more interesting than the floor, and much to Eleanor's surprise, there was again no smirk, no contempt in her look, merely confusion, perhaps curiosity.

Beyond relieved that she'd not frightened, or worse, disgusted her patient, Eleanor decided an apology was in order.

"I'm sorry."

"It's all right." Jane's expression was as gentle as a pink balloon floating up across the sky. Her head tilted to the left, and her eyebrows arched. "My best friend was always throwing forth blurtations like that. It's not a big deal, is it?"

"Only in psychology." Eleanor smiled and Jane smiled back. Thoughts were coming to Eleanor faster than she could address them. She was going against every textbook rule and she was succeeding. She hadn't succeeded any other way, so she would continue on this perilous course, a single rope bridge across the abyss. She could very well fall, but there was no back-tracking now.

She shook her head then let it rest in the cup of her hand.

"Oh me, I feel like crap." So liberating to her were the words that she forgot to look up at Jane. When she did, she found her patient staring at her. Then Jane burst into laughter.

"Well, guess what? Join the club!"

Eleanor let her shoulder muscles relax, laughing along with her.

"I'm not being very professional."

"And it obviously feels good. You should see your face."

Eleanor stopped laughing.

"What's wrong?"

"Nothing." She inhaled. "Yes, it feels good. I've been . . . I've . . . I'm sorry Jane, or whoever you are. I'm sorry."

Jane smiled gently. "You don't have to keep saying that. Why don't you take a deep breath?"

Eleanor hesitated. The first ounce of her faltering doubt began in that second. "Okay." Confused, she looked back at Jane. She needed to gain some control. She made her eyes as compassionate and sincere as she knew how and looked directly at Jane. No, balls to that, she'll see through that. She looked down at the table to show submission. No control here. Talking to the table, she said:

"If I asked you, would you tell me why you asked me about not having any children?"

"Are you asking me?" She heard the mockery in Jane's voice and looked up. But it wasn't mockery. Jane was smiling, her brows raised and her head once again cocked to the left side.

"Yes, I'm asking you."

Jane considered. "I asked you because I needed to know the answer. It mattered."

Eleanor didn't want to blow it, but she too needed to know the answer. It mattered. And a thought swept by, its proximity tantalizing her, its inaccessibility taunting her. She had no children. She had no dog.

"How? I mean why?" Damn it, she was blowing it again, pushing too hard. Jane was retreating.

And then it happened.

All at once she caught it. Just a light being flicked on in a room for less than a second then quickly out. As if Jane's entire emotional life had crossed her face in that amount of time, less than a second. Eleanor finally understood. It rammed up against her full force, and trying, but unable to harness her emotions she blurted out:

"A *dog*! It was a dog! This has to do with a *dog*!"

The *poster*. Her analogy of the dog wagging its *tail*. How had she ever missed it?

Jane looked away from Eleanor, but try as she did, she could not stop the tears, and the small crack became a chasm, opening against her control for Eleanor to see, one tear leading to a fountain. She cried silently—tears she'd been holding back—her head bent over the desk, her shackled arms clutching her stomach.

"Yes, it was a dog," she sobbed. "It was a dog. It was a dog."

At first, Eleanor was beyond movement. Then as her own victory was consumed by all-encompassing compassion, she moved like a phantom around to Jane, slipping the small key into the keyhole of the handcuffs, letting them fall open onto Jane's lap. In one movement, Jane reached her arms up and around Eleanor and she held her, her first real human touch in months, while her body still heaved in its awful and elegant grief, and the sound filled the small room.

"It's all right to cry. *Cry, cry, cry.* I'm right here. Just let it out," Eleanor said in soothing tones, stroking Jane's hair. She didn't know how Jane was going to be all right, but she had the feeling that she would. She wasn't so sure about herself.

CHAPTER FORTY-THREE

In the days that followed, Eleanor found herself withdrawing from the world she once knew outside of the prison, and delving into Jane's case with a passion that left her enervated by nightfall.

She was talking to the girl who hadn't talked in a way that she had never talked with any previous patient, and she looked forward to her sessions with Jane with terrifying, guilty pleasure. Many gaps and questions still remained to fill and answer, but she was bold in asking Jane what she wanted to know, if only because Jane was just as bold in telling her when she did not want to answer. Eleanor found out many details, such as the fact that Jane was not twenty-something years old, but actually thirty-two, and that the dog in question was a beagle. Yet many pieces of the puzzle were still missing. The question that had bedeviled Eleanor the most was answered one day as if Jane too wanted to get it done with, irritated by Eleanor's compulsive desire to know.

"I don't suppose you're ever going to tell me your real name," Eleanor had said in an offhand manner one day.

"Why is that so terribly important to you, if it isn't important to me?"

Eleanor had sat quietly.

"You know you can be pretty difficult." Still Eleanor did not respond. "*All right.* My real name, since it seems you're going to keep obsessing about it till the earth cools, is Sylvia Marie Marshall." Jane had fixed Eleanor with a challenging stare and continued flatly, "But that girl is dead. So call me Jane. Jane lives in a prison, and Jane will die in a prison."

"Sylvia," Eleanor said softly to herself. Then a little louder, "Sylvia."

"*No.* You weren't listening. Not Sylvia. *Jane.*"

"I'm sorry. Jane."

Eleanor repeated the name to Helen, but Helen was at first unable to come up with much information, causing Eleanor to wonder if Jane had perhaps offered a fictitious name, only to later feel guilty at her lack of trust.

Eleanor found herself acting in ways that neither she nor anyone else would have ever predicted. Like in Freddy's market, embarrassing not only herself, but those around her, as she overstepped invisible boundaries.

As she stood behind a young girl who might easily have skipped out of the women's penitentiary yesterday, she listened over her shoulder to the local gossip between Freddy Phillips, Little Eddie and a man she'd never seen.

"Heard about Jeffries, didn't you?" The man she didn't know said.

"With the Lord above now. About as old too." Freddy smiled softly as the other man looked uneasy. "An old codger he was, was old Mr. Jeffries," continued Freddy in a genial tone. "Can remember the kids called him the Old Beagler. We all did. And he was, too. He loved them dogs more 'an he loved his own kids. When he got to being old and infirmed and he couldn't no more walk, he used to sit out on the porch of the field house. All his hounds been dead and gone some thirty years or more. I used to go over there to keep the old man company. Some days he be real talkative, and then some days he just sits there lookin' out to where his beagles used to be. One day I'm sitting beside him, and this little grin come to his mouth."

"He don't turn to me," Freddy continued, "but he says, looking straight ahead, '*You could see the hounds run from here.*' And sure if I couldn't see them hounds in his eyes."

Eavesdropping on the story, Eleanor felt funny. There was a lump wedged in her throat. She wanted to whirl around and demand of Freddy that he tell her everything he knew about hounds and hunting.

Swallowing the lump away, she stepped sideways over to where the three men stood. She glanced at Freddy whom she liked and he turned at that moment meeting her look.

"Evening, Miz Hartley," he said kindly, dipping his head down the way he always did.

"Damn register. It ain't working right again. *Freddy,*" the girl behind the cash register yelled and Freddy nodded again and excused himself. Eleanor watched with disappointment as he walked away, and she turned reluctantly to Little Eddie. She cleared her throat.

"I overheard you talking about Mr. Jeffries and . . . ."

"Didn't know you knew him. God rest his soul."

"Yes. I mean, no, but, well, I was just wondering where one might get a beagle around here?"

The two men eyed her oddly. "What's that, Ma'am? A beagle?"

"Yes. I'm wondering where you find them."

"Running all over the roadside," the man who was Eddie's friend said, and Eleanor wasn't sure if he was teasing her or insulting her. In his tone there was a dark note, jocularity tinged with resentment.

"What you planning on using that there beagle for, Ma'am, if you don't mind me asking, rabbits or deer?"

"Well, neither actually." She turned gratefully to Eddie. "I know they're used to hunt rabbits with, but," she paused awkwardly, "I was just wondering about them."

"About beagles."

"Yes. Yes." She pushed her shoulders back, rubbed her fingers and smiled. "Yes, about beagles."

Little Eddie regarded her the way she'd seen him and Freddy look at the resort people who drove up to Freddy's market in their SUVs and ask for bottles of French wine, sun-dried tomatoes and mangoes.

"I just like them," she added. But I know very little about them.

The men nodded their heads at her.

"Well, I guess just about anyone round here can tell you about beagles," the words rolled out of Little Eddie's mouth in measured congeniality, but his expression read something altogether different: *Now why would you, a fancy psychologist, want to mess with beagles and our hunting ways. Something fishy here. You leave the hounds to us. You nice and all, especially when you spend your money in our store, but you don't know nuthin' about hunting and country ways. Go on home now, and stop poking into things you know nuthin' about.*

"Thank you Eddie." Eleanor had said before she turned and left.

It was as if she'd stepped so completely from the mold that had once been Eleanor Christina Hartley.

Phone held to her ear, she listened to it ring, somewhere far away, and ring and ring. She was about to click it off when the familiar voice answered, "Hel-*low*?" The word was drawn out slowly. The voice sounded confused, as though it had, perhaps, just woken.

"Hi Cory. It's Elle."

"*Elle.* Why, dahlin, how *are* you?" Too strained. The easy, casual note absent, and in its place, caution.

"I'm . . . Cory, look. . . I know about you and Lewis." Awkward, not the way she'd planned it.

"What?"

"I know you've been seeing Lewis." There. She'd said it.

"Elle, what*ever* do you mean?"

"I want you to stop. I'm not calling you to rant and rave. I just want you to stop seeing him."

There was a silence.

"Cory?"

Still the silence. "Cory, listen to me." She spoke softly but in a tone she tried to make firm, not at all certain she was succeeding. "He's not strong. He's not strong like you are. You must help him." She wanted to say, "Help *me*."

"I do help him! I give him *everything*!"

At the words, Eleanor flinched, but continued. "He wants to stop seeing you, but he hasn't the strength." She inhaled deeply. "Cory, help him."

"He does *not* want to stop seeing me." A hushed tone. "I make him happy. He said so."

Elle caught her breath.

"He told me so." Cory continued. "I do things to him that—"

"*Stop it, Cory.*" Any thought she'd had of begging, pleading, confiding in Cory: *Why Lewis, Cory? Have an affair if you want, I won't judge you. But, of all the men, why Lewis, my husband?* dissolved as she listened in horror to the woman she thought she knew. Life wasn't supposed to go like this. She could counsel wayward girls, but she had not the tools to deal with the two people who she'd believed cared about her, betraying her quite so blatantly. Instead she continued in the same quiet, yet steady voice as before.

"I think he wants to bring it to an end. He feels trapped." But her tone changed, and she heard herself, against her intention, pleading. "You *must* help him."

"I wasn't the one who started it," Cory said in a hushed voice.

That hurt.

"He *loves* me Elle." But there was perceptible uncertainty behind the emphasis.

"Lewis has done this before," Eleanor bluffed. "It's nothing. Boredom. You must stop it. I have reason to believe he's unhappy."

"Unhappy? *Unhappy?*" Shrill and on the verge of hysteria. "I make him feel *loved,* I make him feel *wanted.* You don't see to his needs! You haven't for years! *You haven't got the slightest i-dea!*"

Had Eleanor said what she'd wanted, but hadn't the courage, to say: "Cory I don't hate you. You're my best friend. You're my *only* friend," Cory might have realized that sleeping with Lewis wasn't worth destroying a friendship of twenty plus years, not to mention two marriages. But Eleanor didn't say it. Instead she said:

"*Cory,* you have a husband and family. Think about them if you won't think about me."

Eleanor had hung up shortly thereafter, feeling she'd accomplished nothing, wishing she hadn't called Cory, feeling the now near constant sensation of being out of control of her life.

Suddenly, she whirled around throwing the phone across the room so that the plastic broke into two pieces when it hit the far wall and the battery fell out.

"No!" She screamed, slamming a fist onto the table. The pain shot through her hand and she cried out to the room, "*Help me!*" She jerked her arms up and grasped at her waist. *No, no, no. Don't lose control.* She shot a glance out the large window as if someone might be watching her disintegrate. She hugged her body, shaking her head. *Stop it. Stop it. Get a hold of yourself.* But she was sinking down to the floor, heedless of her mind's frantic commands. Lying on the floor, the emptiness of the house seemed to observe her, judge her and in one careless motion, dismiss her. It terrified her. She would get in the car and leave. But go where? The only thought that soothed her was the women's prison and she began to laugh until the laughter turned into hysterical sobs.

When Cory hung up the phone her face was red, her fists clenched and her eyes wet. She glanced around her empty bedroom bug-eyed, and returned her swollen eyes to the telephone in her hand. She punched in Lewis's office number even though he'd told her never to call him at the practice. *Was Elle telling the truth? God, could she really be right? Perfect Elle, she always was.* The phone on the other end rang twice, then a voice: "Internal medicine?" Cory hung up. Tears ran from her eyes. The memory came to her then, a visitor from the past. She was sitting beside Eleanor in their dorm room, clutching a phone in one hand, and a letter in the other hand. Eleanor held a wet Kleenex and kept leaning her long frame over Cory dabbing at her eyes.

"The low-down bastard! The *coward! A letter!* The coward sent a letter! What kind of a slimy, no-count, low-down, conniving bastard sends a letter? He had better not ever, *ev-ha* try to see me again! Cowardly bastard!" She had cried and cried and bubbled and choked. For, in fact, she had hoped against hope that he would indeed try to see her again, because Jonathan Parker, for all his cowardice in breaking up with her in a letter had been Cory's first sexual experience and she was in love with him. But Elle had wiped at her eyes, and even mopped up the running nose, and said in the soothing legato voice that she was certain the slimy, no-count, low-down, conniving bastard would not try to see Cory again. "Don't worry Cory, you'll get through this. You will, you'll see. And we'll look back on it together one day and laugh."

Cory had turned her mottled face towards Elle, hugging her tightly like Elle would try to leave her, smearing her mascara-smudged eyes and snotty nose into Eleanor's shoulder. "Oh, Elle. Thank God you're here. I hope one day I can be there for you too."

CHAPTER FORTY-FOUR

"Can you talk about . . . him or her?"

"Him."

"Can you tell me?" Eleanor wore a light green cotton blouse and now she leaned across so close to Jane that Jane might have stretched out an index finger and touched the silky fabric if she'd acted on the impulse she'd felt before to stroke the expensive-looking clothes and body beneath.

Jane looked away from Eleanor.

"He's gone, right?"

"He's gone."

"Why didn't you tell me of him first?"

Jane didn't answer.

"Did it hurt too much?"

Jane only shifted in her chair. "Tell me, Jane. Tell me, and help me understand what your life was like. Let me in just a little."

"They were killing him. They killed him."

"Who was killing him?"

"That's why I . . . ."

"What?"

"All of them."

"All of who?"

"They were killing all of them."

"Who?"

"I killed him."

"*What?*"

"I killed him."

"Are you speaking of Grady Smith, Jane? Who are you speaking of? The officer?"

"No! I took him in, only to be killed."

"Okay. Go on, tell me about it."

"I can't do this. Not now." She could feel Eleanor's eyes even when looking away from her, green eyes that matched her shirt. She looked toward the tiny window behind Eleanor, but there hung the de Kooning, taunting her with its violent brush strokes. She willed her mind not to see the red smear of dog across the pavement.

"Okay, okay. It's all right. Take a deep breath. Are you hyperventilating? Breathe Jane. Breathe."

"Okay."

"You've got to keep going. Keep breathing."

"That's what the guards all say. 'Keep moving.'"

"In this instance they may be right."

"Why do I have to keep going?"

Eleanor hesitated. Then she spoke the words. "Because I need you."

Jane didn't move but she registered the words. "Okay."

After a moment, Eleanor said, "That's better, isn't it? Deep breaths."

"It's like you're my constellation now. Still very, very small."

"What?"

"I had a constellation once, a very small one. But it's gone now."

"A constellation?"

"A few bright lights. Poor Carol. She must hate me."

"Who's Carol?"

"Someone I loved." Eleanor leaned forward, watching Jane intently. "My friend. My only real friend."

Eleanor listened, without speaking. But when Jane said no more, she urged, "Go on, tell me more about Carol."

"Please, I can't. It hurts too much."

"Okay," Eleanor said softly, letting Jane breathe. "Just feel it. Feel your sorrow."

"Sorrow is a luxury. This is different."

"A luxury? What you mean?"

Jane shook her head.

After a moment, Eleanor said, "Give me your hand." Jane was still cuffed, but now in their sessions Eleanor used the small key to release Jane's wrists, if only for that short time. She sat forward and motioned for Jane to scoot her chair closer toward the desk. Jane obeyed and Eleanor took her left hand in both of her own hands. "It's okay."

"All right," Jane said but did not look up. There was a jolt of current as Eleanor's soft fingers touched her palm.

She couldn't look at the face, so close. She glanced to the capable hands holding hers. Beautiful, strong hands, webbed with a few prominent veins. Perfect nails. "You hurt your hand. What happened?"

"Nothing. I'm fine," Eleanor answered.

Only then did Jane glance from Eleanor's hands to her face.

"How about you talk to me about anything at all?"

"Okay," Jane answered, but was silent.

"Your first time in prison. Coming here must have been a shock for you."

"What?"

"Prison. Coming here to prison."

Jane paused. "Not really. I've been here before."

"What? You have?" Eleanor questioned.

"Just from the other side. And while I'm not overly thrilled about being locked up in here, sometimes it's easier than watching someone you love stay locked up day in, day out, and there's nothing you can do."

"What do you mean? Who was locked up in prison?" When Jane didn't answer, Eleanor said, "Please, Jane. I want to help you."

Jane watched Eleanor's face trying so hard to process all the meaningless words. It made her tired. She knew where the conversation would go and she wasn't ready to go there. Casting her eyes away from Eleanor she said. "I really don't want to talk about prison anymore."

Eleanor took a cautious breath in. "Sure, okay. We don't have to." She smiled but Jane had turned away. "Let's try something different," she began. "I want you to think about a moment from your past, if you can. If you want to. A happy moment. And tell me about it. Close your eyes and let your mind go. Just let your mind remember something happy." Eleanor had a *déjà vu*, remembering a bespeckled and bald-headed psychiatrist delivering these very same words to her: *Remember something from your past. Something happy.* She remembered also all too well what she had said. *No, I can't. What use is there in remembering? I'd really rather not.* But Jane would do better than she had, she was sure of that. She repeated, "A happy memory Jane, something from your past."

"Okay."

"Take your time," Eleanor said.

"Okay."

"Where are you?"

"In prison."

"No, no. I mean, yes, okay. But now let yourself remember something really good from your past, and then tell me about it."

"Oh."

Jane sat still, but her body had fallen away like a person sinking into wave upon wave of sleep. Eleanor thought she looked far away, and when she closed her eyes it was as if she had shut Eleanor out. Eleanor studied her face: clear, clean with just a hint of color to the cheeks. The absence of angst written with wrinkles or groves, did not dispel the sorrow, and yet there was also peace. What was Jane thinking now? What was she feeling? Eleanor wanted in.

"Where are you?"

"I'm walking through a field."

"Can you describe it?"

"Thistle and goldenrod and Jerusalem artichoke. They're all around us. The purple thistle smells like jellybeans. The bees must think so too, don't let your nose get stung. The grass is already brown in some patches. Crows caw and fly from fence post to tree limb. I hear the Bob White calling over and over. The air is brilliant. Pure. I feel it on my body." Jane spoke as if in a trance far from the room where they both sat. Eleanor clasped Jane's hand, her own breath held. Jane continued. "Weedy walks forever beside me and a little in front, nose against the earth, smelling scents I'll never smell. It's all so different from the place he was condemned to live. Condemned to die. I watch him and smile. It's a miracle. And I want nothing more than to walk beside him forever. To be able to watch him outside in the sunlight forever."

Eleanor squeezed Jane's hand. "That's good, Jane." She let go of Jane's hand. "Go ahead and open your eyes. That was really, really good." Yet Eleanor longed to understand why, if it was really, really good, did she feel so sick inside. Breathing in through her nostrils, she tried to collect her thoughts.

"You believe in miracles?" she asked Jane.

"No."

"You just said it was a miracle."

"Then I didn't mean to. I don't believe in miracles."

"I didn't used to, but I think I do now. You sitting here, talking to me, well, that's a small miracle. Don't you think?" She was watching Jane closely, probing with her eyes, when she saw darkness pass unmistakably across her face—a cloud overtaking the sunlight in Jane's crow-cawing field.

"What happened just then?"

"Your exercise brought him back to me. I wish you'd not asked me to do that."

Eleanor was about to respond when Jane continued.

"Why I brought him that night, I don't know. I mean, I do know. I was scared."

"What were you afraid of?"

"I was scared to leave him since I told Kenneth about him. I knew Kenneth was up to something. But who the hell was Kenneth anyway?" Jane said, asking herself. "Maybe he really did like me. But now I think I understand that, crazy as it sounds, Mike was the one who was undercover. Not Kenneth. It was Mike all along." She shook her head as if agreeing with herself. Then suddenly she stopped and looked directly at Eleanor. "I have been such a fool. Blabbing my mouth. I might as well have just shot Weedy myself. It'd be the same thing, you know?"

"Jane," Eleanor said carefully. "Will you tell me who Mike and Kenneth and Weedy are?"

"I take medication. No one here knows that."

"*What?* You're on medication and no one knows?"

"No. I'm not on it. Not since coming to prison."

Eleanor folded her hands in her lap. She arranged her face in a look she hoped conveyed both concern and solemnity. "If you were on medication before entering the penitentiary, it's very, very important that you remain on it."

"Maybe. Maybe not."

"What medication is it?"

"I don't want you stereotyping me."

"I won't." She paused, waiting. "Jane, don't you think you should continue taking it?"

"No. I'm okay."

"There's a pharmacy. You can get what you need, you know. But you'll need a doctor to—"

"I said I'm okay. What's it matter in here, anyway? Although if you could help me find some medication to dull the pain."

Eleanor looked to her folded hands. "Jane, I'm going to ask you something, because I trust you to tell me the truth." She paused somewhat dramatically. "Are you angling to get your hands on narcotics?"

"You can ask all you want. And now I'm going to pretend you didn't."

Eleanor hesitated. "I asked because I've seen it quite a lot. I've been approached by inmates for recommendations for painkillers, and you did say, 'dull the pain.'"

"Yes, dull the pain. That's what I said. I didn't say, 'Could you please write me a prescription for narcotics?'"

"No."

"I didn't used to be so scared."

"Scared. You're wanting to dull the pain of fear?"

"How can you not be scared when there's only suffering in the world?" She said it as much to herself as to Eleanor. "Who other than humans could devise something like L.D. 50?"

"L.D. 50?"

"Never mind. See, even now I'm blithering. And it does no good. It harms. I can listen if you want to talk, Dr. Hartley, but I'm done talking. About everything."

"I wouldn't exactly say you've been blithering. You've been silent. You've been silent for a long time. It's normal to have a reaction—whether it's silence or its opposite—after extreme trauma. It's normal to want to process it all in your mind. And this, this blithering as you call it, is good. You're processing, Jane. Allow yourself whatever you feel."

"I feel like I can't talk about it—ever. When I try, it doesn't begin to touch it."

"Touch what?"

"Nothing."

Eleanor sat, taking in Jane's words. Holding eye contact, she said, "I can't recommend painkillers for you. I'm sorry about the pain. The fear. But talking about it might help. Will you tell me who these people are? Will you tell me what this L.D. 50 is? Is it a drug you've taken?"

Jane rubbed the back of her hand against her mouth. In a monotone she said, "L.D. stands for "lethal dose." The lethal dose required to kill fifty percent of the animals in testing a product." A startled sound escaped Eleanor's lip.

"Millions of dollars are spent on testing and it rarely correlates to humans. I wouldn't be surprised if big pharmacy was in cahoots with the pesticide companies. We eat fake food put out by Montsanto, and the like, and then get cancer and big pharma makes out like a bandit. Do you know the acid reflux drug, Nexium, costs around $23 in the Netherlands and in the U.S. it costs something like $215?"

"No, I didn't know that."

"Who pockets that? The CEO of Turing hiked the price of a drug used to treat a life-threatening parasitic infection from $13.50 a pill to $750. There are cancer drugs that cost more than $10,000 a month. And you know what? All these drugs are first tested on animals. Pesticides too. As many as 13,000 animals are killed to approve one single pesticide and there are more than 10,000 pesticides on the market today. All your cosmetics and the stuff in your medicine cabinet, tested first on animals." She stopped abruptly like before.

As if coming out of the trance but with eyes open, Jane retreated from Eleanor, almost as if unaware she'd spoken.

"Go on, Jane. You have a lot of facts at hand. What you're saying is very interesting to me. Horrifying, but interesting."

"It doesn't matter now, anyway. One person can't do anything to help."

"Jane, you can trust me. You can—"

"I said never mind. I told you I didn't want to talk anymore."

"Okay, but if you—"

"I heard you."

For a moment they sat together in silence. Then Jane spoke again. "In prison I'm taken from the one thing that gave my life meaning."

"Your dog."

"Well yes, of course, him. But even greater than him. The outdoors. What he was a part of. Or should have been a part of: the trees, the grass, the air, the breeze on my skin, sunlight on my face. The sounds of birdcall, the sound of the spring peepers. Clouds. The pure light of morning. All the beauty of the natural world." She stopped and Eleanor said nothing. Jane finished: "I get one hour outdoors."

Eleanor nodded. "I'm sorry. I wish—"

"You have no idea what it's like, so you don't need to try to appease me."

"I'm not trying to appease, I'm just trying to—"

"You don't have to say anything," Jane said, cutting Eleanor off. "There's nothing you can do to help me. So you see, really, how it is. Now I know how they felt everyday of their lives."

No, Eleanor thought to herself, she didn't see at all how it was. She wanted to be able to help Jane. She didn't like Jane thinking she couldn't help her, either.

"Where was your home?" she asked.

"With Weedy."

Eleanor nodded, taking this in. "Weedy was your dog, right?"

"Yes."

"Right. Okay, but I mean, where did you live, where would you go home to . . . if released?"

Jane regarded her, and Eleanor realized her mistake.

"I have no home." She said it patiently, answering Eleanor's question. She said it without bitterness. "Wherever he was, was home."

"Talk to me about him." Eleanor reached out to take Jane's hand, but Jane pulled away.

"I can't."

"Why you'd name him Weedy?" She smiled at Jane.

After a moment, in which Eleanor treaded water, Jane began: "He was so skinny and sickly like a weed, not a beautiful flower. The name just came to me at lab, just somehow fit him and stuck."

"He was in a lab?"

"Yes, that's right."

"You said Weedy was a beagle, right?"

"Yes. A beagle, of sorts."

"Like the dog in the poster," Eleanor said with a sharp intake of breath and realization.

"Right."

"Will you describe him so I can see him as you see him? I want to feel him and share him with you."

"He'd been experimented on a lot and had a wound. After I got him home, he began to heal and his fear lessened. He had a beautiful face with a white stripe. He had a kind face and kind eyes. Once he started to heal and his hair grew back in, he stopped crying so much. But no sound came out when he cried, you see. His vocal chords had been cut."

This time Eleanor gasped audibly.

"That's right," Jane said again. "In the lab they cut the dogs' vocal chords so they can't cry out in pain or frustration." She paused, as if letting Eleanor take in this information. "Weedy's cry was this airy, rasping sound. I'd listen and I'd see his dark eyes long after I'd left him."

Eleanor kept her eyes fixed on Jane. The barren and bereft feeling of when Jane had described the field persisted and she longed for a glass of water. Her face felt fragile and her gut a roiling mess, yet she sat regarding the homeless, imprisoned girl across from her. She wanted, and yet she didn't, for Jane to tell her more.

Jane spoke for her. "If you're tired today, I can talk. I don't mind. I know I said I didn't want to, but it's okay. I will. For you. It's just hard sometimes. Everything's hard."

Don't cry. Above all, don't cry. She needs to feel you're there for her, strong and commanding some ounce of respect.

"I'd love for you to talk to me. About anything you want." The remainder of Eleanor's faltering doubt was vanquished in that moment.

"I can't talk to you about his death."

"I understand."

"I can talk to you about the love I felt. I mean, I think, without sounding mushy. Talking about him like this has made me feel him again. It's brought him back to life for me. Which is both incredibly difficult and also beautiful."

"Anything you want. I think you'll find that talking helps you more than you realize. But if you don't want to . . . ."

"I know." Jane looked down. "I loved him more than I thought it possible to love."

Eleanor nodded.

"You probably think I'm bonkers. I mean to outside eyes, he was just a raggy beagle."

Eleanor didn't think her bonkers at all. She did wonder why Jane never spoke of family, or a boyfriend, or problems from her past that might have placed her where she was now, but now wasn't the time to ask about all that.

"Go on. Tell me how you loved this raggy beagle."

Jane looked at Eleanor quickly, searching her face. "Okay," she said. "I'll try. I remember something Montaigne said . . . ."

Eleanor stared. "What?"

"Oh," Jane said. "Montaigne. We studied him."

Eleanor sat very still, looking at Jane.

A quick frown passed Jane's face.

"Go on," said Eleanor softly. She felt her powers of perception fleeing her.

Jane shifted in her chair, and Eleanor saw a change of expression, perhaps relief? "I always said that without love life is meaningless. Life is nothing. I always believed in living life, simply yet fully, and never fearing it—even when the worst happened. I always said life was, and I didn't care what had befallen you, a gift. I tried to hold onto that and didn't fret about the things that didn't really matter, because I think things work themselves out in the end. Life proves this time and again." She paused. "At least it used to."

Eleanor closed her eyes.

"Are you all right?"

"Yes."

"Sure?"

"Yes. I used to think the very same thing."

"Really? But not now?"

"Remember we're not in here to talk about my thoughts."

"Come on. Do you know how silly that is?"

"Well . . ."

Jane was now smiling gently. "It seems to me that you'd get further with me, since that seems to be your goal, if you just acted normal, shared your thoughts, and we had a . . . a dialogue, no?"

"Perhaps." Eleanor felt close to tears. She wanted to say to Jane: "I'm falling apart. I think only you can help me." Maybe, she thought and hoped, it was just her body becoming menopausal. "Tell me more about Weedy. If you want to."

"Montaigne also said . . ." Jane was looking at the desk and she paused, clearing her throat again. When she raised her eyes, she found Eleanor looking at her closely. She held Eleanor's gaze for a moment in silence then finished, "that love is an attempt to gain the friendship of someone whose beauty has attracted us."

Eleanor felt the fire burn up through her neck and into her face, and she turned away. She cleared her throat and said the first thing that came to mind, "Ah yes, good old Montaigne. I didn't know anybody still read him." As she said it she glanced back at Jane, and saw Jane's pale face was now pink, and she realized then that Jane had not only seen her flush, but she had understood it, and she blushed again. For a moment, she could find no words. Apart from the clock's tick, the room was silent. But there was a loud pounding in her chest that made it impossible to think. She cleared her throat again, searching for words. "Excuse me, Jane."

But Jane was silent.

Finally Eleanor said, "Do you want to talk to me more about Weedy?"

Jane's eyes darted once to Eleanor, as if in a wary, orchestrated manner, then away again. She hesitated, and Eleanor spoke at the same time as Jane.

"You look disappointed."

"He wasn't always happy."

"I'm sorry. What did you say?" Eleanor questioned.

"He wasn't always happy," Jane said quietly.

"That must have been hard."

"I learned to understand him and not project my own human emotions onto him."

Eleanor listened without taking her eyes from Jane. She breathed through her mouth, her lips slightly parted. Her body retained the stillness of a winter tree.

"Anyone can do it. You just have to focus your attention. I'd focus on him and what he was telling me and not on my own thoughts about what was going on. I doubt I could do it with all dogs." She stopped.

"Go on," Eleanor said in a strange voice.

"I'd give him special free-range chicken, after he'd gone through his throwing-up phase. He'd prance around. He'd make this little noise. An airy little "yop" sound, almost like a yawn. He'd do it when he was excited, just before I was going to feed him. Then I'd feed him the chicken he loved, and I'd sit down on the floor beside him and eat curled cookies."

"Curled cookies?" Eleanor asked, relief flooding her veins.

"Tollhouse cookies. I'm so impatient to get them off the cookie sheet and eat them, and of course they're still warm, so they curl and stay that way when they've cooled."

Eleanor remembered her own fantasy with Jane and Tollhouse cookies. She encouraged Jane to talk further of curled cookies or anything she could remember, aware of the immense importance the details could have. In many cultures, part of the ritual surrounding the grief of a death is that family and friends keep asking to be told all the details—exactly how and where it happened. They seek to know even the smallest of details for their own understanding, and relating the story over and over again forces the mourner to review the situation continually. There was wisdom in these customs. American society often shied away from directly asking the details, finding it ill-mannered and disrespectful. Therapy, on the other hand, often began where manners left off.

Eleanor and countless other therapists had found that more often than not a patient would in fact want to talk about their deceased loved one. The exceptions, she knew from experience, belonged to the more horrific and premature deaths. Exactly how, she wondered, had this dog died?

"If you can speak of his death, it might help you," she now said to Jane, remembering passages from psychology texts: *Humans are unique in that they have the ability to re-create events from the past, and if the griever was benumbed at the moment of the tragedy and incapable of experiencing the real feelings that usually engulf the survivors, a directed re-creation of the sequence of events will provide him or her with the opportunity to relive and retrieve the hidden feelings and experience what really happened.*

She knew firsthand that over time the pain in speaking about death was a pain one could bear, like the pain of a massage over sore muscles. Hurt, but also relief. She knew, too, that when given the choice, she had not always followed her own counsel.

"We don't have the right vocabulary or language for grief, do we?" Jane said.

"No, we don't. I suppose that's why we resort to clichés. Sometimes, they're all we have."

"I think tragedy occurs so that we can turn it around," Jane said, "as we inevitably do, to something good. Great change, needed change, often arises from great tragedy. Tragedy is random. And the human need to see and greet it as something other than random is tremendous. So whether it truly is random or preordained doesn't matter if the result is something better and good. But you see, I didn't have that chance. The chance to set up a fund in Weedy's name to help all the other dogs in there. His death does no good as long as I'm in here. And yet I can't imagine ever going back."

Eleanor sat listening to her own private thoughts revealed and spoken from the young convicted murderer.

"You think you'll never forget. And then you forget."

"Forget what?" Eleanor asked.

"How it was. You can't remember how it was." Jane stopped and looked over at Eleanor. "What were you thinking just now?"

"Me?"

"Yes."

"I was just listening to you," Eleanor said. When Jane made no reply, Eleanor cleared her throat. "Jane, I'm wondering if you'd be willing to tell me more. Would you be willing to tell me how it was for you? Life before prison. Maybe it was so awful—so awful you had to shoot those men. Would you think about it and consider that in our next session?"

"Maybe," Jane said. "If I'm still here."

"*What?*"

Alarm pushed away everything extraneous in Eleanor's mind, and she was about to question Jane, when there was a knock on the door. She looked across at Jane with a stricken expression on her face, a mix of confusion and fear, but Jane was not looking back at her.

That night Eleanor stood in her bathroom. Slowly, she opened the medicine cabinet door. She stared at the familiar brands, hearing Jane's soft voice. There was her one perfume and her face creams and body scrubs. The elegance of certain brands with their intended status became sickening to her. She reached, grabbing bottle after bottle and pitching them into the trash can, listening to how each landed with a portentous thud.

CHAPTER FORTY-FIVE

As the overcast sky turned the afternoon to muted gray, pushing the hope of spring to a corner, Eleanor tried to push Jane's mysterious, and chilling, remark from her mind, and walked toward the neatly landscaped brick house to ring the bell. Maybe Jane would tell her, and maybe she wouldn't. But Eleanor needed to know. The sensation of needing to understand was like harsh whiskey burning her stomach.

From inside the house emerged short woman, older than herself by ten or fifteen years, wearing a worn navy and gray cardigan, pleated kilt, knee-socks and old-time loafers.

Eleanor extended her hand. "Mrs. Cartwell?"

"Please, call me Alice." The parched voice matched the eccentric face. Her blue eyes protruded, instantly supplying the image of a busy-body, but in the next second that image gave way to an appearance equal parts kindness and pathos, as if the woman standing in the doorway was eager for any good cause, eager to supply information if it might soothe the downtrodden children. She had a low sagging, full bosom under the cardigan, which added to the image of a perpetual nursemaid, breast feeding the world. She had a large mole on the upper corner of her mouth, and her creased and lined lips smiled easily at Eleanor.

"I'm Eleanor Hartley," Eleanor said, extending a hand and stepping closer. As she did, she caught a sharp whiff of the woman's perfume.

"Yes, come in." Alice Cartwell led Eleanor down a hallway covered by an old, worn oriental runner, and into a pale yellow drawing room. She motioned to a sofa near the center of the room.

"Oh, you needn't have," Eleanor said spying a copious tea service set out on the low table before the sofa.

"Nonsense on stilts. I have it every afternoon at this time. Please sit."

Eleanor sat, feeling very much like she'd disrupted this woman's Sunday afternoon ritual, but feeling also that she liked the feisty, odd little person. She glanced quickly around Mrs. Cartwell's living room—a mahogany writing desk, a tall cupboard in one corner, dust collecting on the shelves, tarnished silver settling into the dust, yet juxtaposed with these were vases filled with fresh cut tulips.

"Thank you for taking the time to see me. As I explained on the phone I work with the women in the state penitentiary. I thought it might help me to . . . ." Eleanor looked down to her hands folded on her lap.

"Yes, quite. About time one of you came to me. I tried to volunteer some years back, but they wouldn't have me." Mrs. Cartwell's right cheek and shoulder met each other in one giant nervous twitch like a mutual kiss. She continued as though oblivious. "My age I suspect."

"No, no. I'm sure you would have been wonderful. We . . . they must be very careful and strict with volunteers. There's a lengthy application process. They probably had enough."

"Don't worry about hurting my feelings," she chuckled. "I'm a tough old badger."

Eleanor looked at Alice Cartwell. She certainly was not the kind of woman Eleanor expected to be mixed up in a drug bust. She was, however, the type of woman who might wear Chanel No. 5, and Eleanor identified the scent as soon as Alice had taken her seat beside her.

"I suppose what would be of greatest help to me would be if you could simply tell me what happened and what you told the court."

"I told the court very little, for they didn't seem to want to hear my opinion on the matter. Any more than you did over at the penitentiary. Just the bare facts. I suspect they had already made up their minds. Perhaps if your superiors at the penitentiary would like more information, I could arrange a visit."

Eleanor cleared her throat. "I don't think that will be necessary," she said, adding, "I'm ever so grateful you agreed to see me, though."

"I'd agree to see the devil himself if I thought I could help out. You see, I have my own theories about why our youth are turning to crime and dereliction at earlier and earlier ages. If I could urge you to please speak with your superiors, I might be able to offer formative information."

"All right," Eleanor conceded.

"I understand their needs, those locked away behind bars. You see for many of them, the volunteers may be the only visits they get beyond the razor wire behind which they live. I believe their faith is strengthened by such people who see the pain, suffering, and brokenness—the humanity that exists in the prisons. I challenge the churches to take up Jesus's instruction to visit the imprisoned. One might be surprised what one would find there. You see, I realize that many a prospective volunteer may be intimidated by crossing the threshold of a prison, but once they have crossed that line many will recognize, just as I have, that what they see before them are but the children of God, simply abandoned or forgotten by friends or family, but not by God."

"Yes, I see," Eleanor said and cleared her throat again.

"You, too, are dubious about my abilities, I can see. Or perhaps, you are not a believer. Very well. You came for information about that particular night. I am happy to oblige you."

"I'm very grateful to you, Mrs. Cartwell. Alice."

"I don't remember the girl's name. She had no close relatives, you know. One or both parents deceased. No siblings."

"Her name is Sylvia Marshall. But we call her Jane."

"Very well. I would not want to question your logic."

"She prefers Jane, so I call her Jane," Eleanor added feeling not a little defensive and embarrassed that she'd said it. "But you may use either name."

"Very well," Mrs. Cartwell's shoulder jerked up to her cheek again, as if remembering some detail it had to tell. "You are probably wondering about me. When the prisons and what not won't have me, I volunteer with families in need. Many of them take me to the less desirable parts of the city, sometimes late at night. Such was the case on that night. I can't help but think I was beckoned out that night for a reason. I have always been aware of the possibility of danger when I make my rounds, although I have never feared it. Even when the shooting began, I still could not say I found any reason to have fear. I was a block or so away when I heard the shots, and I went like an arrow to its source." She paused and picked up the teapot. "Tea?"

Eleanor reached for her cup and brought it towards the pot as Alice poured.

"I was leaving a meeting with a family. I happened to look down the alley behind the apartments. The projects, we say here in America. Council Housing in Great Britain. H.L.M. in France. But they are all one in the same idea." She smiled. "My mind, you see, is full of trivia that will go to grave with me unused."

"You were telling me about what you remembered."

"Yes, I will get back to that. But I can't help thinking, we of this modern age rush through life without listening to others, without any real connection."

"I couldn't agree with you more, but unfortunately—"

"I understand. You, too, are rushed, needing to get on with your life," Alice Cartwell said knowingly and shut her eyes for an instant. "I can't recall if I actually heard a skirmish prior to the shooting, or if my intuition took me to the scene. I have, for as long as I can remember, had a keen sense for trouble. A very keen sense for trouble." She opened her large bulging eyes, and they stared from their sockets into Eleanor's own eyes.

Eleanor poured milk into her tea and raised the cup to her lips. As she did so she listened to the strident, yet oddly calming voice of Alice Cartwell, losing herself in a darkened alley, and forgetting the comfortable surroundings.

"I remember thinking something irretrievably bad was about to happen. One must learn to follow one's intuition. Would you agree?"

Caught off guard, Eleanor cleared her throat and replied, "Intuition combined with intellect can be a powerful tool, yes."

"We're such a literal-minded society. I'm so glad you dropped in on me, today. I do so enjoy a lively chat with another intelligent soul."

Eleanor nodded and smiled. "Yes. Unfortunately, my time today is somewhat limited."

"Of course. As you so plainly stated earlier. My mind often wanders and thus, I find my words following along with the nomadic thoughts." She closed her eyes a second time, as if summoning the evening in question. "I remember thinking quite clearly, and yet it all happened swiftly. Or perhaps very slowly, the quality a dream takes on. It doesn't matter, for it was quite nutty and incongruous. To this day, I can smell the fetid air of that neighborhood." She opened her eyes, took a sip of tea, then closed her eyes again. Eleanor wondered if she were going into some kind of trance, or maybe just smelling within her mind the fetid air. She realized she could be there for hours at this rate.

"I believe the man had been backed into a corner, and shot trying to scale the barrier. The police cornered him. Three of them. A plainclothes one too. Or perhaps a civilian."

"Three? Did you speak to any of the police officers?"

"Indeed, I did."

"Were you aware that an Officer Bread was shot and killed?"

"Oh, yes."

"You saw him shot?"

"As I said, it was all quite nutty and incongruous. Their faces . . ." At this point, something in Alice Cartwell's demeanor changed and she turned from Eleanor with a slight hiccupping noise. "It was a gruesome sight, I cannot deny that, and I am not inclined to revisit that aspect, even with you. Do forgive me."

"Of course," Eleanor replied. "I'm aware of the nature of the murders."

"So much messiness. Such commotion. Not at all like the movies." She laughed merrily. "I suppose a younger soul with less life experience than my old self might have been frightened out of his or her wits. Whereas I simply observed."

As Alice Cartwell continued speaking, all at once Eleanor was aware that the pitch of her voice had altered. It seemed to Eleanor that she now spoke with the importance of what she had to tell, and not, as she had before, with the compassion for the needy families with whom Eleanor already associated her. She watched the odd face as the woman spoke, trying to discern if its expressions offered a truth incompatible with its words.

"I do believe it was a standoff," Alice stated. "That is, I understand it was, until that odd little misshapen dog trotted into the alley. The one officer told me everything, you see. It was after that that everything turned to utter chaos. The man on the fence spun right around. Perhaps seeing the shadow of the dog. One of them shot and killed that poor little dog, why I do not know. Perhaps it was reflex. Perhaps he had meant to hit the police officer. She shot back, of course. Multiple times."

"You saw her kill officer Bread and Grady Smith?"

"Yes. I saw the gun in her hand. Then she was knocked unconscious."

"What?" Eleanor asked.

"She lay unconscious there beside her dog. I thought at first that she had been shot. But fortunately that was not the case."

"So she fired at Grady Smith because he shot her dog?"

"Correct."

"What about Officer Branston Bread? Why did she shoot him?"

"I do not know. That part is indeed peculiar."

"All right," Eleanor said, but there was uncertainty in her voice. "And she was not buying drugs from Mr. Smith."

"I couldn't answer that."

"But she fired at Mr. Smith because he shot her dog."

This time Alice Cartwell said, "To the best of my knowledge, that is correct."

"Might it have been in self-defense?"

"Oh yes, most likely. But unfortunately this is not what she said on the witness stand. She told the court he shot her dog so she shot him back."

Eleanor frowned. "But she shot him in the face and through the heart," she said softly, almost to herself. "That's a level of marksmanship not found in a woman just trying to defend herself." Then more loudly, addressing Alice Cartwell, she said, "I was never told anything about a dog on the scene."

"No. Dogs are not often seen in our criminal courts."

"And why was she carrying a gun?"

"Young people possess handguns today. You should not be surprised by that. However, you may be absolutely certain that I have never voted for any politician in favor of handguns, but then there is our second amendment and—"

"You said there were three officers," Eleanor said, cutting her off. "I only ever heard there were two."

"Oh no, there were three. Distinctly. And the young gentleman in pink. Civilian or police, I do not know."

"Wait a minute. Can you go back to the police officers? You said three. There was Officer Bread, Officer Sampson, and—"

"Yes, Sampson. He was some relation to her. At least he knew her. He kept calling her."

"What?"

"He kept calling to her."

"What? Officer Sampson did?"

"Yes, that's correct."

"Sylvia? Did he call her Sylvia? Did he call her by name?"

"Yes, I believe that is the name he used. Sylvie. I believe it was."

"What did he say?"

Alice closed her eyes again. "He shouted, *No, Sylvie, stop. No, Sylvie, stop.* I was just around the corner when I heard the words. That's when I knew I had to get help. Later he said, *It's okay. I'm here.* Something of that nature."

Eleanor nodded, her breath rapid.

"The girl was hopelessly, I emphasize hopelessly, distraught when she awoke in the hospital. She was only semi-conscious when they brought her in, and to awaken in a hospital, how dreadful." She shook her head remembering.

"You went with her to the hospital?"

"I did, indeed." The earlier tone of voice was back, signifying genuine compassion. Eleanor listened, aware of an odd sensation of jealousy. "The police were arguing," Alice Cartwell continued. "I remember that. But Officer Sampson told me to go. He'd follow, but he had something he had to do. But he never arrived. At least not during my stay."

"But Mrs. Cartwell, Alice, tell me, then do you believe, do you truly believe, she could have shot Mr. Smith in self-defense?"

"I would agree that it is quite possible."

"And in her fear, and the confusion, she may have shot Officer Bread, too?"

"Again, in my opinion, it is quite possible."

"Dear God," Eleanor said aloud. It was an accident. Jane had just gotten in the wrong place at the wrong time. There was no intent. It was only an accident. She had *nothing* to do with this. Except she shot two men dead in cold blood. But if Eleanor could prove it was self-defense. Or even that she had no reasonable means of retreat.

"I was there with her when she regained her consciousness," Alice continued. "She awoke, calling, '*Where's my dog? Help me find my dog. I want my dog.*" The poor thing. Completely beside herself. Distraught beyond all measure. I have never seen anything like it. There she was all bruised and cut and all she could think about was finding her dog. She started yelling to the nurse, 'I need to get out of here. You don't understand. I need to find my dog! *Let me out of here!*' They had to bind her arms and legs and tie her down. It was a terrible sight."

Eleanor sat in Alice Cartwell's sitting room feeling like a guilty voyeur, a vicarious guest of Jane's past.

"The nurses had to sedate her. By that time it was quite late and I had to leave her. When I returned the next day, I was not admitted to see her. No one would answer my questions. I was not a relative. The police had come for her. The murders. Of course she had to be tried."

"Oh God. Poor Jane." Eleanor's mind was whirling. She accepted "a drop more tea" from Alice Cartwell, all the while desperate to get back and pose questions to Helen. Or Jane.

She excused herself shortly thereafter, thanking Mrs. Cartwell and insuring the privilege to call upon her again should the need arise in the future. The last question she had pressed upon the older lady was: "Tell me about her dog. What happened to it?"

"Oh well. The poor, helpless thing. I—" Alice shook her head. I believe the officer who knew her took care of it." A tear, a first tear, had formed in Alice Cartwell's eye.

Eleanor saw. "That's okay."

That night Eleanor sank down into her reliable friend, the armchair in the den, feeling nothing like the person she had been two months ago. She wished for the hundredth time that she'd hear the front door open and close. Hear Lewis removing his shoes, and come padding down the Turkish runner to find her, to tell her what he was planning for dinner. But he didn't come. Her thoughts were spiraling in her head like a plane out of control. In the vast blue sky that falls off to infinity there should be such little room for error and yet a plane goes down anyway. Thoughts were rushed and uncomfortable like commuters pushing onto the approaching train or squeezing and hurrying to exit. They were a jumble of unwelcome images and words she could no longer control: a failed marriage, the loss of her best friend, a double betrayal, the girls at the prison, a girl named Jane, and then one last thought, the one that would not leave her.

Death. The death of her parents and her own death one day. She closed her eyes thinking and, without resisting this time, relaxed into the thought: Death comes to us little by little, not simply as the inevitable dilapidation of physical bodies, but by ceasing to be who we once were. So painless and benign, this change over the years that the end when we will cease altogether should not be feared. Just as she, Eleanor Hartley, was no longer the person she had been at age five or sixteen—how vaguely and imperfectly she remembered herself then—so too will this present age and self one day no longer be. Inevitable and painless. Evolution of self to the eternal. The seed of the forty-eight year old who now sat collapsed in an armchair was contained in that five-year old, who is no longer. Then it followed that the seed of that future spirit was contained in this woman who is now. All part of Eternal life.

She shut her eyes not wishing to remember that girl of sixteen, yet marveling at the past's beguiling capacity to surface in the present. In a paradox fit only for scientists or neurologists, childhood grew nearer as she grew older, real for her in memory but, like a mirage on a highway, nonexistent, even if real to her every, living, remembering cell.

She remembered the house at Christmas, decorated and shimmering with all the light of childhood hope and innocence. She remembered returning home in the evening from the golf course where she'd been skiing, the sky behind the hill orange with the sunset and the shadows on the deep snow a sparkling blue. The evening star would climb over the tops of the pines into a darkening sky. The brook was frozen with black water flowing under the ice, showing only in the broken spots. There were ski tracks crisscrossing, made from her own skis and the other kids who'd been out during the day. She knew that once home there would be cocoa and marshmallows waiting for her and her sister in front hall, and she'd sip the hot liquid by the fire before supper, and she'd hang her mittens and socks on the grate in the hall. Her mother would greet her with her apron still on and say to her, "And what wild and wooly thing did you do today?" And Eleanor, even at age sixteen, would throw her arms around her mother and hug her tightly. Then she would hop over to where her father sat in his armchair reading the paper and smoking his pipe and she would ask to eat one of his Nonpareil candies. He'd answer the same answer he did every night. "Okay, but just one, and don't tell your mother." Anticipating this comfort, sliding over the snow in the gelid air, she was happy. It would be the last time she would ever feel that kind of indelible happiness.

She knew something was wrong even before she heard her sister's screams. Sliding up to the house, her face expectant, believing that if she willed everything to be all right then surely it would, but feeling her heart thumping beneath her rib cage harder than it ever did whizzing headlong down a dangerous ski slope, she felt her first fear. She popped off her skis, and with calm, systematic precision lay them against the house in the same spot underneath the window where she always did.

"Lizzie?" she called out to her younger sister. "Lizzie, what is it?"

The screams did not abate and Eleanor opened the door of her house and entered. Her parents lay one atop the other, her mother's apron speckled with dark red. Lizzie, with her hands over her eyes, was barely recognizable squatting and pressed tight into a corner, the ragged wails still surging from her mouth. Eleanor was trembling, but otherwise remained calm. Like a visitor observing herself, she saw herself walk over to her younger sister, stepping over her beloved but now dead parents and, in her state of shock, state plainly:

"Tell me exactly what happened here, Lizzie. *Lizzie hush.* We will have to call the police. They will want to know."

Her detachment didn't puzzle her until years later after she'd been in therapy with four different psychiatrists. She would wonder had her riven heart, at such a young age, hardened and annealed so that the capacity to accept love, or even to feel it, became as remote as an island in a distant sea. Because of her apparent callous and non-feeling reaction to her parents' murder, her sister, Elizabeth, had remained estranged from her for nearly a decade.

The two men were eventually caught. They had been in prison before, had been released on parole and, on that day, had sought to steal whatever they could in the affluent neighborhood. They hadn't expected Dr. and Mrs. Hartley to both arrive home. The lawyers and Aunt Clarice went to great extremes to keep Elle and Lizzie away from the sensational case. Reporters flocked to the small New England town and shot pictures of the beautiful hundred-year-old house from the outside where the senseless murders had occurred.

The girls went to live with Aunt Clarice in Iowa beside the train tracks. And for a long time at night Eleanor would lie in bed and listen for the sound of the trains going by across the fields. She'd hear the engine coming a long way off and as it got nearer and nearer, somewhere along the way, the train whistle would blow, and she'd hear Lizzie's screams all over again.

When she and Lewis were engaged, she told him more about her past. Later, after they had moved to Virginia, he had asked her if she was quite certain she wanted to work with the women in the penitentiary.

"What's past is past. The only way to make anything come right from my past is use my personal experience to help others. I've worked through my past. I've come to terms with it, that's why I can do what I do. That's why I think I can be a good psychologist."

"Sure you're not repressing your feelings?"

She'd laughed. Repressing her feelings. "No. Sometimes it just hurts to remember. I loved them so much, it hurts. I'd rather not remember."

"But then you lose something that's part of you. You lose your past."

"There's nothing to lose. The past is already gone. Yours too if you're honest with yourself."

"Mine's alive in memory."

"No. It's not there; it doesn't exist. There is nothing real. What's the point of dwelling on something that's unreal?"

"I didn't say dwell. I just meant remember from time to time. You don't have to live in your past, but let it be alive and real by way of memory. Let them, your parents, live through your memory."

"Lewis, what I'm trying to say is that it's *pointless* to do that," she'd answered disliking the irritation she heard behind her words. "Not to mention that you waste the present moment in always going back to revisit the past."

"And what I'm trying to say, Elle, is that those memories make us who we are, make you who *you* are, like it or not. You shouldn't be allowed to forget. Memory makes our pasts eternal, so in a way we become eternal."

"Allowed?"

"Yes, *allowed*," he'd answered back stubbornly. Then, with a gentler tone born perhaps of embarrassment, added: "I don't mean remember and relive the . . . accident, but remember the good times, have some good memories. I think in time even the pain becomes a precious, if perhaps bittersweet, memory. The pain ensures that you will never forget. You only feel pain, Elle, because you once loved." He looked into her eyes then, and she knew he loved her, but she couldn't let him in. He continued, "The pain, the memory, will one day bring you comfort, and you'll be glad you didn't forget completely. Your love makes the pain endurable."

"You don't know what is endurable to me!"

"Okay, fine."

In her memory, he'd been angry. She wondered now if, instead of anger, he'd really been hurt.

"I'm sorry, Lewis," she'd said ashamed, the shame she always felt when she lost her composure.

"I was just trying to make sure you're doing the right thing with this prison thing." He said abruptly, turning away from her.

Regaining control and adding a certain aloofness, she had stated, "If my parents were alive, I believe they would want me to do this. They'd want me to do what interested me."

"And the looneys and half-wits interest you," he threw back.

"Yes. Why people do the things they do and what motivates them interests me. I'm a good psychologist. Maybe because of my history. Maybe in spite of it. I don't see that it matters."

She realized now what some part of her had known then too: Of course our histories mattered. We could step beyond them, but it took work. She knew the work she had to do. She needed to get to Jane. Before it was too late.

CHAPTER FORTY-SIX

"Jane." Eleanor let her eyes look at Jane for a moment without speaking before she said, "Was it the murder that made you stop talking?"

Jane rolled her neck around on her shoulders. "No."

"Was it because of losing Weedy?"

For a measured beat, Jane said nothing. When she spoke, she drew out the word slowly, "Partially." Then in a rush: "And because I got sick of people dismissing what I said because it wasn't their particular experience."

"What do you mean?"

"I mean people are so close-minded. So I loved a dog. I had boyfriends. I had girlfriends." She glanced at Eleanor. "I know what people think and what they say when you love an animal: 'Oh, but you really want a child, or at least a boyfriend.' But those weren't the reasons."

"What were the reasons, Jane?"

"And I just wanted to enter the animals' world. It seemed such a better place to be."

"Their silent world."

Jane made no comment. When she responded, her voice was quiet. "You think you have me all figured out, and it's that easy. You're mistaken."

Eleanor waited for Jane to go on, but when she didn't, Eleanor replied equally quietly, "I don't think I've figured you out, and I certainly don't think it's easy. I just wondered if your becoming silent had something to do with the animals who don't speak.

Jane made no response. "What made you talk to me?" Eleanor asked her after a moment.

Jane looked away. Eleanor turned to follow Jane's eyes and saw only the cracks in the floor tiles, a light coating of dust. Jane spoke without looking back. "I trusted you."

Eleanor waited for Jane to look back at her. When she did, Eleanor kept her gaze and asked, "Do you trust me enough to tell me what happened?"

"Maybe."

Eleanor waited.

"I shot a man. There. Big deal."

"You shot two men, and actually it is a big deal. But, I'm not judging you for it," Eleanor added quickly. "I want to understand why." She had decided not to tell Jane just yet about her conversation with Alice Cartwell. She would see if Jane remembered her. She knew some part of Jane did, conscious or unconscious, for she remembered now with a pang of remorse Jane's reaction on the day of her silliness with the Chanel No. 5. How the macabre and unbearable memory must have been brought sharply into focus by that one sense, the oldest and most primal of all the senses. Smell was more potent in evoking memory than any of the other senses because it went straight to the amygdala, the small almond-shaped gland which was the seat of memory, the center of emotion, intuition and, some might say, the soul.

"I'm a pacifist, I always have been," Jane said sounding defensive.

"You're a pacifist, but you pulled the trigger of a gun and shot two men dead. I know what that man did. I *know* he killed Weedy, but that doesn't make it all right to kill him. And why did you shoot the police officer?"

"You weren't there. You also have never been in that position. It all happened so fast. I don't remember what happened. They didn't believe me in court that I could shoot someone and not remember, but they haven't been in that situation, have they? My dog was shot. He was lying there bleeding. A man had a gun and was pointing it at me. All I was thinking was that I had to protect myself so I could take Weedy to the vets as fast as possible. And then," Jane had been talking emphatically with anger, or perhaps it was frustration, and now Eleanor saw she was close to tears. "He was hurt. I . . . you have no idea. . . I saw I was losing him and then I guess I lost all thought and I don't know what happened."

"But do you or do you not remember shooting Grady Smith and Officer Branston Bread?"

"Yes. No. I don't know. It all happened so fast and I don't remember accurately. You try it."

"What?"

"Just try to remember a recent event, however banal, in your life. Try being grilled in court and remembering *exactly* how it happened. You're at the grocery store parking your car. Where did you park? Can you remember? It was just yesterday. What color was the car to your left where you got out? How about the car in front of you? Did you see people? How many? What did they look like? What were you wearing? What did you do with your keys as you entered the store?"

"Okay."

"What did the checkout person look like? What did you buy?"

"All right."

"Were there trees near where you parked? Where did you go after the grocery store? Do you remember? Try it. Or try simply telling me what you did yesterday. Can you remember detail for detail? It's your *life*. But you notice hardly any of it. We just go whizzing through life. What a royal waste. We don't really see it."

"Maybe not."

"But you're not in a court of law so you don't need to. Then try losing the one thing in the world you love most. Try watching him die before your eyes and then remembering the exact sequence of events."

Eleanor sat quietly this time, and made no attempt to comment.

"You know it's weird," Jane kept talking. "Everyone you meet in your life thinks they know you. Thinks their perception of you is right, when in fact none of them is—including your own perception of yourself. We're composites. You may know one side of yourself well. I always thought I knew myself well. Those observing you from the outside see a side you can't. You see one side of me. Your perception of me is different from my own perception of me."

Eleanor listened, keenly aware that Jane had veered off the original subject. She wondered if Jane was equally aware.

"Jane."

"Hmm?"

"Can you or can you not recall shooting Grady Smith twice in the chest and in the face?"

Jane had been leaning forward in her chair. She now sat back, and looked at Eleanor and Eleanor saw at once a decision forming.

"What are you thinking?" she asked quickly.

But Jane did not answer. If she had reached a decision, she was not going to share it with Eleanor, and she looked away. It was only after a moment that she spoke but without the emotion of before. "I remember reaching for the gun. No, what I really remember is . . ." She stopped.

"Go on, Jane," Eleanor urged.

"Most of all I remember reaching for his body."

"Mr. Smith's?"

"*No*! Trying to carry him. And I just wanted to gather him all together. I've never felt such love and pain and, Dr. Hartley, even as a psychologist, you cannot imagine how that feels if you've never gone through it. I've never felt such love. Why did I bring him with me that night?"

"Do you know why you did?"

"If I could just have those few hours over again. I've never felt such *fear* as when I was trying to pick up his body."

Eleanor let Jane sit and breathe. "And then the police officers grabbed you?" Eleanor coaxed, remembering Alice Cartwell's words.

"I guess. I fought. I could have killed that policeman then and there, I can tell you."

"You did, Jane. You did kill him."

"No, not that one. The other one. I could've killed him."

"Well yes, so you told the court."

"To hell with the court. I could kill them too for sticking me in here."

"But you wouldn't really. You're a pacifist."

"To hell with you, too."

"I meant it sincerely, Jane."

"I fought him and he hit me and knocked me out and I'll never know what happened to Weedy's body. And if you think for a second that's something easy that you just bear . . . . If you think I don't live with that one thought day in and day out."

Eleanor heard Alice Cartwell's voice repeating Jane's words: *I want my dog. I want my dog.* How often over the past week had the words and their desperation come to her as she brushed her teeth, or sat and looked out the window, thinking of Jane miles away in the penitentiary? But the plaintiveness of the four words in Eleanor's silent mind was agonizing not because she could imagine the scene from which their tortured despair was derived, but for another, more unsettling reason, which left her feeling empty and void, doubting that she had ever in her adult life known a true moment of love, let alone deep joy.

"I live with the fact that I took him out of jail only to have him killed before my eyes. And I can't even have a gravesite or his ashes to mark his life by. To mark that period in my own life by."

Eleanor sat still, listening, gently encouraging Jane to continue talking if she stopped for long. When finally, Jane seemed finished, Eleanor said, "You knew one of the officers, didn't you?"

"What?"

"Did you know one of the officers?"

"No, well, maybe a little. He was semi-psycho. I didn't know him very well."

Eleanor eyed Jane oddly.

"He tricked me. He texted me to come, and I did, and Weedy got loose. And—" Jane stopped.

"Go on," Eleanor said, aware that Jane had stopped just short of telling her something important. Eleanor could feel the emotion in the room, a charged atmosphere with perhaps a coating of sorrow. Or was it regret?

"They took everything I had when I came here."

"I thought all your identification was stolen during the incident. That's why no one here knew your name or age. I mean, until they found your I.D. But even that was the fake, right? It also read Jane, right?" Eleanor asked, feeling increasingly confused.

"But I had a picture of Weedy still. They took my photo of him." Jane's voice was trembling. "All I remember now is the end. Why didn't I record more of the small moments? It's the small moments that make up our lives. I'm already forgetting how it was—forgetting the one being I thought I could never forget."

When the guard came, Jane's look begged Eleanor to help her, to take her away, to make her situation right again. Eleanor thanked her for being brave enough to talk about what she'd done. But when Jane and the guard's movement could be heard no more, Eleanor let her body fall back against the chair exhausted. She sat still, and she could hear her breath next to the granular ticking of the clock like muffled, aching heartbeats.

She stared at the dull, dust-coated pattern of the linoleum floor tiles, and the tiles became the months that had passed. She stared straining to see an answer in the pattern. If she stared long enough, without blinking, the pattern changed before her eyes. She thought of the men who had killed her parents. She had long ago sought to practice forgiveness, and now she could summon no lingering feelings of revenge. Love for her parents, sorrow and grief, but not the passion to kill. She tried to imagine loving a person enough to kill. She imagined Lewis being gunned down before her eyes. An anguished threnody of emotions filled her, precipitated not entirely by the thought of losing her husband. She visually placed her sister in Iowa before the gunman's barrel. Profound sorrow and more grief, the same results as with Lewis and her parents, but also the same budding realization and immobilizing anguish that accompanied it. She crossed herself quickly—an antique relic and automatic gesture left over from years of Sunday school—as if to remove all images of loved ones' death.

Perhaps only if she had given birth to a child would she enter the realm of what Jane in that one dark and unthinkable moment had felt. She felt the hair on her arms prickle. Very gently Eleanor shut her eyes. She visualized Jane being shot down before her. As her imagination gained on her, growing more and more vivid, she felt her hand reach for the gun and raise it. It was only with great restraint, and against her deepest desire, that she did not pull the trigger. She took a deep breath and opened her eyes, this time relaxing into the chair, her anguish vanished.

CHAPTER FORTY-SEVEN

"So you got Mute talking. Hmm-hmm-hmm."

"What?"

"Wake up, Hartley. You looks like you half in the grave. What's up? Trouble at home?"

"I'll remind you again, Shina, we are here to talk about you, not me."

"Now don't go getting uppity, Hartley. I didn't mean you look half dead. You always fine looking, you know it." Shina smiled an irresistible, contagious smile.

"Thank you, Shina. You're redeeming yourself." Eleanor smiled back unable to resist the girl's good mood. But then something happened that shook Eleanor's reserve.

Shina sat across from her showing pearly teeth and grinning. "I know. I know all about redemption. Now, you want to talk business, Hartley? Put it behind us so we can chit-chat?"

"Business?"

"Yeah, business. You need to listen to Shina, and listen to her good."

"I'm listening," Eleanor said.

"Hartley, that Mute, she didn't kill no one. They got the wrong girl."

"What are you talking about, Shina?"

"I'm talking about the fact that I know what each these women did. I have my ways."

Eleanor didn't respond.

"Truth is, I talked with her some. And that Mute, she didn't kill a soul."

Eleanor felt budding irritation.

"I ain't playing with you. I just am aware, is all. I *observe.* Like, for instance, I seen something interesting the other day. I like Mute, but you know she don't say much. She gotta like you, like she do me. But I saw her perk all up. You listening, Hartley?"

"I'm listening, Shina."

"I saw her perk all up and stare in a way that she don't usually when they asks a new inmate why she's in prison."

"I thought you weren't supposed to ask each other what crimes you committed."

"Shoot, Hartley. You not, but come on. Everyone wants to know what everyone else is done. So you want to guess what that new woman, Shelia, say that perked up our quiet friend so much?"

Eleanor shook her head. "No, Shina. I don't think it—"

"Well, tough titties, because I'm gonna tell you, anyway. She says, and I quote her exact words: 'I rescue baby bunnies. You got a problem with that?' That's exactly what she says." And Shina started laughing. "Funny, ain't it? Put someone in the pen for rescuing baby bunnies. Yeah, I figured she was lying, too, the way they all do. To listen to us, we all—every single one of us—we all innocent!" She laughed even more gleefully. "But then I read up about these animal-have-rights kind of people and yo! They really do put them in jail for rescuing baby bunnies. Now, ain't that some bullshit? Of course, them animals-have-rights people thinking a giraffe oughta vote is some crazy bullshit, too. Can you see a giraffe in a voting booth?" Shina laughed again heartily, imagining her giraffe voting.

Eleanor cleared her throat.

"So, as I was sayin' that Mute she didn't kill no one. Now, on the other hand," Shina wagged a long finger in the air as if testing the room's wind currents, "I wouldn't put it past the teasel-head to kill someone."

Eleanor hesitated, weighing the pros against the cons, and asked, "Who is the teasel-head?"

"Hartley honey, I'm sure you can guess."

Eleanor was sure she could too, but she didn't want to. Before she could open her mouth, Shina spoke for her.

"Teasel, you know, one those spiky-headed plants."

Eleanor nodded her head.

"Now guess."

Eleanor suspected the teasel-head was Mimi Kramer, but she had scant desire to be proven right.

"Shina, last week we discussed the people you missed most since coming to prison. And you enjoyed it. I thought a fun exercise might be to move on to the things you miss most."

"I miss my phone." Shina said without pausing to think. "You want me to enlarge upon that?"

Eleanor smiled. "Sure."

"Connection."

"Yes, of course."

"And information. Information is power."

"But now you have a dictionary for your power. Somehow, I like that better."

"No, Hartley, that dictionary is my way out."

Eleanor regarded Shina.

"My escape."

Eleanor nodded her head, and Shina grinned. "I played your game, now we going to finish our other little game, Hartley. Guess who the teasel-head is."

"*Shina*, I want you to forget the teasel-head. I want you to think about yourself and your life. Not to the point of selfishness. No one is advocating self-interest to the exclusion of helping out others. What I mean is, find your path, your truth." Eleanor heard her voice speaking words to Shina, but she knew that her mind was elsewhere. "Don't compare yourself to others, you're you. And don't worry what people say about you, because people will always say things. That's part of it. But find where you feel home. Find it in yourself. Okay Shina?"

"You boring me today, Hartley. But yeah, sure, okay. Whatever you say, baby."

Eleanor sat before Helen's desk, like her patients sat before her.

"I can't let it go. They tell me harebrained things all the time and I recognize it for such."

"Eleanor, you can't begin believing what every prisoner tells you. *Shina Jones* doesn't know. If you'll remember, she also told you she thought she was an anchovy."

"Yes, I thought that rather descriptive, not to mention creative and, given the nature of a prison, somewhat apt."

"Shina is not an anchovy, and she doesn't have the inside story on other inmates. No matter how intelligent she is on paper. Come on, where is the Eleanor I've come to count on?"

"I'm less inclined to believe them when the assertions are obviously spurious, when the assertions are wholly negative, invented for the purpose of putting down an inmate in attempt to try to raise themselves in my esteem. But you see, Shina wasn't putting Jane down."

Helen studied Eleanor. She shifted in her chair and glanced at the stack of papers on her desk. When she looked back at Eleanor, her face was tense. "Maybe you'd better focus a little less on Jane."

Eleanor jumped as a loud knock sounded outside Helen's door.

"Warden Huffington!"

As Helen rose to answer the door, Eleanor turned in her chair.

A C.O. stood in the hall. "We need a lockdown! We need a lockdown, right now!"

"What's happened?" Helen asked calmly.

"We've a woman hurt. *Assault.* She's in the infirmary. I got to her in the nick of time." After the C.O. had delivered the words to the warden, and they were no longer her sole possession, she seemed to shrink a little, stepping aside.

"I'm coming," said Helen, barely acknowledging the guard, then turning to Eleanor. "Come with me. I might need your help."

As the call for lockdown blared over the loudspeaker, girls scurried back to their pods, whispering to each other, guessing, assuming and wondering what had occurred. Helen and Eleanor walked quickly down the hall and across the courtyard, followed by many inquiring eyes.

Eleanor felt her heart pounding in her chest and wished for a glass of water, but she would not stop, for the nauseous fear was only kept in check by her movement. Helen opened the door to the infirmary and behind her Eleanor breathed in consciously, as her eyes traveled to the end of the room. She saw the large body of Cilla Hankins lying supine on the nurses' table. She let out her breath.

Cilla resembled a giant tortoise, flipped over on the sand. Something larger than pity began to take shape in Eleanor. Anger, injustice, an overpowering desire to help in ways she never had. But just as quickly as it had surfaced, the desire was replaced by a rush of futility, hopelessness and the feeling she had felt upon first seeing Cilla, an emotion that she would analyze in a profoundly disappointing and guilty revelation: relief.

Two nurses hovered over Cilla, while a third one washed her hands in the sink behind. Helen approached the third nurse and asked in a low voice, "What happened?"

"They try to strangle her," the nurse said turning to Helen. "Terrible thing," she continued then turned her eyes back to Cilla, regarding her the way a person might look at a fish that had washed ashore and, while flicking its tail and puffing its gills in a discomforting effort to live, was obviously destined to die. Eleanor walked over to Cilla, as Helen nodded to the nurse, but the nurse's next words stopped her. "They try to strangle her because she set fire to the room."

"Fire?" Helen repeated.

"Yes, fire. She got hold of some matches and tried to burn those girls up alive."

Helen put her hand to her head and turned to speak to Eleanor. But Eleanor was staring down at Cilla.

Cilla's face was a blotchy mixture of pale and red skin that had the effect of further distorting her features. Eleanor saw marks at her neck, and the area around her eyes looked gray. Even though it was against regulations, she laid a hand on Cilla's arm.

"Hi, Cilla," she said quietly.

Cilla turned her neck awkwardly on the table to regard this voice of kindness, and when her eyes saw Eleanor they filled with tears. Eleanor quickly saw it was a mistake as Cilla began to cough and choke, her chest heaving up and down.

"There, there now. Don't go getting yourself upset," the nurse scolded her. She motioned for Eleanor to back away.

"What is it, Cilla?" Eleanor whispered.

"They told me to do it."

"Who, Cilla? Who told you?"

"The voices," she gasped. "They told me."

"It's okay, Cilla," Eleanor said uncertainly, taking a step back, but Cilla was imploring Eleanor with her eyes.

"Lelia. I need to see Lelia."

"Who?" Eleanor leaned closer aware that the nurse was turning around.

"Tell Lelia I'm sorry. I can't reach her. I'm so sorry. Please tell her."

The nurse was returning. "Step away from her, please."

Eleanor patted Cilla's arm again and in the most reassuring voice she could find said, "I'll tell Lelia." She paused. "You're going to be okay, Cilla. You're going to be *fine*." She looked once more to the vitreous eyes and something cried out in impotent silence as though from fathoms below the sea's surface, and not from a body upon a table.

Eleanor spun around with a passionate force. "Helen, I need to—"

"Not now, Eleanor."

"I think it's important.

Helen turned to her.

"I need to get a message to a girl named Lelia."

Helen squinted at her. "Lelia?"

"Yes, Lelia. I don't know her last name but it's not that common a name."

"Eleanor, there's no Lelia here. Look, I need your help."

Eleanor stared back, immobilized. "Of course." It was a nickname then. Or worse, someone on the outside. How would she ever find her? She glanced over her shoulder to where Cilla lay, but the nurse was blocking her view. She looked back at Helen. "What happened?"

Under her breath, Helen said, "Mimi Kramer. I don't know the details. We'll have to hold a hearing. They found Mimi sitting on Cilla, holding her down, choking her. The fire was put out. It didn't amount to anything at all. I can't imagine what Mimi was thinking. Apparently Mimi saw it her place to strangle her for trying to set her room on fire. She's in isolation again."

"Isolation?" Eleanor repeated as cold fear enveloped her. She took a step backwards.

The voices started shouting at her louder and louder, and then they stopped. Cilla lay flat on her back looking up into a bright shining light. Her brain was going quiet but as it did, something else was coming alive. The birds were chirping and singing to her. She could even hear the bees buzzing, as one zipped over her head. She flapped one arm at it, and there was the hard ground beneath her, but it was covered with beautiful grass that she had never noticed before. The sky was blue and light clouds drifted across it. And the bright light shown down on her.

CHAPTER FORTY-EIGHT

Jane was in a house crowded by many people. At once she began to perceive that Weedy was nearby, but she could neither see him nor get to him. Ghostly lanterns hung from ropes, plunging back and forth and casting errant shadows of the bodies all around, growing denser. She had to get to Weedy. He was sick, or hurt, he needed her.

"Have you seen a little dog?" she asked a tall man with a strange mustache and a top hat, but he stared at her without comprehension. Pushing past human bodies in a frantic search to find Weedy, she saw a shaft of outside light coming from a far room, and she squeezed through a dark and narrow tunnel toward the light. She fell outside, landing on grass so alive and green she could have eaten it. She looked up and there was Weedy.

He trotted up to her, tail wagging, ears back in joy, and jumped into her lap.

"*Weedy. Oh, Weedy.*" She kissed his face and eyes. Love and joy so pure she could renounce the world for it alone filled her as she sat on the soft spring grass and held Weedy in her lap.

The call for morning count woke her from the dream, and she lay in the narrow bed overwhelmed by the feeling of love the dream had sent to her, yet feeling its embrace retreat as her surroundings became more real than the reverie.

Pushing herself out of bed, she stood as the guard passed her cell. How was it possible to feel such joy, and feel it that vividly in a *dream*?

She heard the door to her unit slam shut. The emotion from the dream persisted throughout the day, but as the hours passed, instead of reliving the tangible joy, she now felt the stark contrast of her present life to the life she'd once known. A spasm of grief snuck up on her, and she resisted for as long as she could until she could no more, giving in to it, and crying face down on her cot, all the while understanding her grief's provenance was not due to loss of freedom, or prison, or even the vileness of small cruelties that occurred within the walls. There was something worse. Absence. Carol, Weedy, the mother and father she never really knew. At length she wiped her face.

She sat in her cell staring at the wall. What are your days like? Dr. Hartley asked her.

Ever since speaking aloud of Weedy, she'd been aware of unease lurking as if she'd betrayed a secret she'd promised not to reveal. At first he'd been right there in the room with her and Dr. Hartley. She'd felt okay, but now alone in her cell, she was a dark tangle of limbs, strangled and scared. Talking about him had brought it all back, making it real again. She shut her eyes to the blank wall before her, trying to ward off another wave of grief in the same way she used to try not to feel the cold, afraid of giving in to the shivering. All was darkness. Like a curtain dropped. But the horror was not that she lay dead behind it. The horror was that life went on despite all. The horror was that she lay alive. But with no way out.

When she was silent somehow she could believe that she would wake from the nightmare. Now the reality was that there was not, after all, going to be a future in which both she and the dog she loved would be held together in tomorrow's promise throughout the long lazy summer afternoons.

She closed her eyes and she could still feel the fur on his ears and back. She could still see his sweet face looking up at her. She saw all their faces, and she saw all the fear. Saving Weedy had become symbolic of saving them all. But now all she saw was his face the last time, as he lay there uncertain what was happening, speaking softly to her with his eyes. And in failing him at the end, she had failed them all.

The door down her hall opened again and someone was walking towards her. For a moment, the open door brought sounds to her silence. She heard inmate voices coming from the courtyard. Someone beyond her hall was hollering that the TV was broke and who was the mother-fucker who messed it up? She shifted on the bed and it squeaked beneath her. She wondered over the fate of the television abuser.

Nearly a year into prison, the reliable, dependable, if monotonous routine of her new life had taken over, while memories of what she once had been grew dimmer. She retained certain stubborn images and she wondered why some moments got caught in the mind, when others disappeared completely, receding to oblivion like a name written in the sand by the edge of the waves.

She wondered at times if it was only the contrast—that humans needed the ultimate limit to squeeze out understanding, the same way it often took death to value life. She knew of people unable to love their parents until those parents were gone and it was too late to love them. Only then would the living love, loving fiercely, internalizing the love they could never feel, or at least show, face to face with that parent in the present moment of being. Only later, protecting that person in death in a way they never had in life.

Alone in her cell, with ample time to think, she began not only to hear the voice and words of her therapist and see a vague blurred image of her when she shut her eyes, but to feel the gentle hope that seemed to promise something akin to salvation. In her small cell, her small human self became less significant. Outside clocks ticked and the world moved forward, and inside this tiny cell sorrow welled, sometimes overtaking her, but beside her sorrow there was something else, more persistent. A voice of compassion, reminding her not to forget a dog she loved, for if she forgot, her love would have no meaning. And so it was, that in this cell chipping away the wall of her grief and spading down fresh mortar over pain, a world was born anew, soft and strange and full of wonder she almost dared not feel.

The guard stood before her door.

"Come on, Miss."

Jane stood. The guard no longer clipped the metal cuffs around her wrists, although he would remain by her side, a ubiquitous escort.

Now as the last cool days receded, she walked the perimeter of the courtyard twice, the polite shadow walking in step beside her yet never attempting to speak. She was called, 'Road Dog' like the others who walked during Association. When she was finished with the walk, she drifted back towards her building. The guard would let her do what she wanted for twenty minutes, and she knelt down on the dried grass and inhaled its scent and, with it, memory. A splotch of color caught her eye. A purple clover. There, as if transfixed, she remained on her knees, as the memory passed over her, almost crushing her.

"*Weedy,*" she whispered. "Weedy, I love you. I'll always love you. And I'll always be sorry." When the breeze touched her face, she came to and looked around, the shouts, laughter and voices now coming back to a world that had been silence. And there, not far from the clover, were the first daffodils of the season. She knelt beside the clover and the daffodils, understanding that this was it. The small moments. Wherever they occurred.

From her knees beside the flowers, she tilted her head. The clouds moved across the sky, and she remembered a tapestry of clouds above a landfill. "Onion-skied," she said quietly, allowing the ghost of that other life to crouch in the courtyard beside her, brushing lightly against her soul. "*Oh Carol,*" she whispered. "*I'm sorry, I let you down.*" She kept her face toward the sun and there was the faintest breeze across her forehead.

Only then—only for a few seconds, as she yielded to those few ticks of time's hand outside in the breeze—did her mind stop thinking of him, and still. She stood back up, eyes focused still on the sky above her head. Clouds moving and changing even as she watched.

She was staring at the patchwork of clouds, lost in their slow transition of shape when she heard the alarm. It was the fire alarm, probably one more false alarm set off by someone smoking. No, maybe it was to be a unit shakedown in which case she, unlike others, would be happy, more than happy, to be exiled to the courtyard for hours.

She heard a guard banging on doors and yelling, "Clear the unit! Clear the unit!" Another one shouted, "Everyone outdoors! Now!" Women were filing out doors opened only in emergencies and many were still in their nightclothes. They were the ones who had contrived to sleep their days away. They started to line up near her, faces she'd never seen before. New faces. The alarm continued to blare raking her eardrums. The smokers lit up and she moved farther away from the crowd to avoid the press of bodies. She turned and realized she could not see her guard through the rush of inmates. C.O.s walked purposefully through the crowd into the building. A minute passed.

A C.O. walked out the door screaming, "*You must stand behind the yellow line*!" The yellow line was a spray-painted yellow line across a third of the grass. She spotted her guard on the other side of the courtyard, and watched him running frantically scanning the mass of women for her. She started to walk toward him when she saw two Latino girls who didn't understand English or who hadn't been locked up long enough to know, and who now remained standing where they were, as resentment hovered dangerously above them. It was there all around them, and welling within the inmates, many irritated at the power play between guards and prisoners, irritated at the ignorant two who didn't know enough to move, forcing the rest to stand out in the chilly spring air. Some inmates rebelled intentionally, a last attempt to retain some modicum of their own autonomy. Jane watched the guards strutting in and out of the building, ostensibly ignoring the inmates yet often brushing past them roughly to provoke a fight.

"Get the fuck behind the fuckin' line!" An inmate yelled at the two girls.

"*Shut up*!" A guard hollered back in a threatening voice.

Jane pushed past some girls, crossed the line and gently steered the two girls to where they should stand. She was turning to retreat back behind the line and seek her guard when she felt something hard hit the side of her face. And everything went dark.

CHAPTER FORTY-NINE

"How's Cilla?" Eleanor sat before Helen.

"She's going to be fine. Physically. It was touch and go. She lost consciousness. The doctors told me she almost died, or did die for a moment. But they were able to bring her back."

Eleanor said nothing for a moment, then: "I wonder if she wanted to be brought back."

"She'll be hated more than ever now. Eleanor, did she ever give you any indication that she would try to, that she would . . ."

"Set fire to the room?"

"Yes."

"No. But her mental stability. . . . She should never have been placed in the state penitentiary."

"But she can't go around lighting fires."

"Yes, but we don't know what may have provoked her to do it."

"I understand. Are you thinking Mimi provoked her some way and then attacked her?"

"I wouldn't put anything past Mimi."

"Mimi will need her sessions with you doubled, if not tripled."

"Helen, I was wondering . . ."

"Yes?"

"I . . ." Eleanor began again as Helen waited. "Nothing."

"Anything else to report?" Helen said somewhat tersely.

"No. Nothing new." Eleanor had told Helen about going to see Alice Cartwell, and Helen had been as upset as Eleanor imagined she would. Helen told her the case was closed. Proving it was self-defense was the attorney's job, *not* the psychologist's or the warden's. Eleanor knew Helen doubted that Jane had killed in self-defense. But she also knew that Helen didn't know Jane like she did. She didn't spend time sitting with her, listening to her, witnessing her warmth and compassion and intelligence.

"All right."

"Helen?"

"Yes?"

"Perhaps if you and I and Jane could have a session together, you might see some of what I'm seeing now." She remembered observing the two indentations in the middle of each of Jane's cheeks, being mesmerized by seeing the dimples, realizing Jane was grinning at her.

Helen leaned back in her chair and regarded Eleanor with a strange look Eleanor had never seen before. "Eleanor, I know you care about her and want to help her. But you can't go getting attached to every vulnerable-looking girl who shows up here. Don't make me place Jane with another therapist."

"What? You can't put Jane with anyone else," Eleanor said in a rush, then caught herself and Helen raised her eyebrows watching.

Still regarding Eleanor, Helen said, "I must do what's right for each girl." She paused for a moment then resumed. "And what I'm telling you is that I'll leave Jane under your care for her therapy sessions—you were, after all, the one who got her to talk—but I'm asking you to focus a little less on her. She's not your only patient."

"Of course she's not," Eleanor answered.

Helen leaned forward. "Eleanor," She began, and instead of answering, "Yes?" Eleanor sat quietly, acutely aware that the room's tenor had changed. "Jane is in the infirmary."

"*What?*"

"She was assaulted," Helen said, and Eleanor knew she was being scrutinized. She was afraid her voice would quaver if she spoke so she waited a moment, breathing consciously, unable to meet Helen's eyes.

"Assaulted?" she said finally in a quiet voice.

"Yes. By a guard."

"By . . . a . . . guard?"

"A mistake, Eleanor."

"Again? *No.* No, that is not a mistake. That's either total incompetence or vicious retaliation. It's *absurd.* What happened? Was it as unmerited as the last time? I'm sure she did nothing to warrant—"

"Eleanor, get a hold of yourself. Jane is okay. She's going to be fine. I'm still getting the facts, but as I understand it she broke strict rules. I'm sorry, but I have to believe the guards over an inmate."

"The guards? Those ignorant, power-hungry sadists? You'd believe their word over a peace-loving girl like Jane?"

For a moment, Helen just stared at Eleanor, and said nothing. When finally she spoke, her voice was low. "Eleanor, Jane murdered two men. Are you forgetting the girl is here in prison for second degree murder? Peace-loving is not a term I would use to describe her." Helen looked at Eleanor over the tops of her glasses.

Eleanor tried to compose herself again, but there was a feeling that sifted to the farthest corners of her heart like damp sand, and it chilled her to the bone. Out of the two people she could trust at the penitentiary one was now turning from her and the other was in the infirmary.

"Helen, I'm sorry. Maybe I have let myself get too attached to her," she said casually. "I'm sorry."

Helen took off her glasses, and rubbed her eyes. "It's human nature. I'm amazed it's never happened to you before now. Look on the bright side, in all the years you've been with us, this is the first time. I'd consider that an accomplishment. I'm glad to see you're not entirely made of stone."

Eleanor nodded, but she gripped the seat to steady her shaking hands. What had happened to Jane? Helen misunderstood her silence and continued. "But you don't need me to tell you, you just can't afford to get attached to any of the girls here. That's why you're so valuable to us, Eleanor."

Eleanor nodded. "Thank you."

She bid Helen goodbye and walked toward her office. When she turned the corner, she stopped, her knees buckling. She put a hand up leaning against the wall. But she knew there was something else, invisible, that was holding her up. She remained that way, leaning against the wall, until she heard voices approaching. When the guards had passed, she straightened, and not caring who might hear her said, "Oh, to hell with it!" She began walking in the opposite direction from her office. She was going to the infirmary.

For the first time it hit her how Jane must feel having the one she loved taken from her. At first she hadn't taken the intensity of loving a dog, or anything other than a human being, seriously. Was it only last week—it now seemed another lifetime ago—that she had sat sipping morning tea by herself, and the brown dog, the one that had angered Lewis by performing its bodily functions in their yard, had trotted by her window, its gait easy, its tail up yet relaxed, its nose gently lowered to the earth. She knew she had never paid any attention to that dog. Its defecations hadn't bothered her the way they had her husband, and she knew all the years it may have lived beside her, its presence had barely registered in her brain.

But last week, she had seen the dog with fresh eyes and she had frowned, for the thought that entered her mind, like the quick flip of a switch, had left her tense with unease. Jane had lied to her. She had to be lying. One didn't love the brown dog as one loved one's own kind. But now as she walked, wanting to run, towards the infirmary, towards the girl she trusted more than anybody else, who she knew would never lie to her, she knew that the woman who'd sat in that morning's first light had stepped from her shell leaving the hard casing behind at the empty table in the frozen moment. Yes, it was a lifetime ago. People could change she thought to herself. It was time to stop using her parents' murder as an excuse. It was time to step past the dead, into the land of the living.

"Where are you going?" A female guard at the infirmary door asked her.

"The infirmary," she answered.

"Name?"

"I'm Dr. Eleanor Hartley. I'm a prison psychologist, and I'm here to see—" She stopped. The absurdity of not one person in the entire penitentiary knowing Jane's name, and the further absurdity of once knowing, calling her by another name, struck her as about as comical as murder. "I'm here to see Jane," she finished.

"*Miss,* do you have *permission*?"

"Yes," Eleanor hesitated a moment regarding the guard before her who stood erect and tight-lipped, eying her with obvious dislike. Would she run back and tell the warden? Was she required to report every admittance into the infirmary? Eleanor had no idea. She was taller than the guard. She squared her shoulders, reached into her briefcase to flash her I.D. and said, "Warden Huffington has given me permission."

"All right then," the guard said. "You can go in."

Eleanor pushed open the door to the infirmary. The first thing she saw was Jane. She was sitting up on a gurney. Eleanor felt a rush of blood to her face. *Oh, then she's okay!* The newness of seeing Jane somewhere other than in the psych room had the quick delirious effect of an orchestra starting up, syncopated heartbeats banging like drums, and chords of adrenaline that turned to nervousness and, when she saw the nurse take a hold of and raise Jane's arm, jealousy. She stood transfixed. Never had she seen Jane in anything but the white scrubs that gave the name to "icicle" and now she observed a white paper gown like the disposable ones used in doctors' offices. As the nurse moved to take Jane's temperature, the gown pushed to the side exposing white skin. Eleanor was about to turn and flee from the room when the nurse felt her presence and spun around.

"Hello," Eleanor began. "I was . . . I just wanted to say hi to Jane."

Jane turned her head toward the doorway at the sound of Eleanor's voice, and Eleanor saw a huge purple bruise. She gasped. Then Jane was looking at her, but Eleanor did not observe any excitement in Jane's features, certainly not such as she herself had felt upon seeing the girl.

"She's gonna be just fine. Her temp is normal. She'll be free to go." The nurse bustled over to the sink and pulled off rubber gloves. "Come on. Come on in, we don't bite," she called to Eleanor, and Eleanor advanced slowly until she stood face to face with Jane.

"Hi," she said to Jane as a wave of shyness overtook her. "How are you?"

Jane glanced at Eleanor and raised her eyebrows.

"You look tired today," Eleanor said, purposely avoiding mentioning the enormous bruise that covered the side of Jane's face.

Jane said nothing.

"I have something for you."

Jane's eyebrows rose again. Eleanor fished around in her briefcase, and pulled out a white piece of paper on which she'd written three lines and handed it tentatively to Jane.

"Okay, you're done. Hop down now," the nurse interrupted. "You two can sit together over here. I'll be back." The nurse motioned for Jane and Eleanor to sit in the corner by the sink on two cushioned chairs. Jane shifted one hip and slipped off the examination table until she was standing on the cold floor.

Eleanor tried not to stare at her, but she felt drawn to observe every detail, so much seemed new. She watched Jane walk carefully and sit down holding the little paper she'd given her and for some reason this pleased Eleanor. The white scrubs still covered her lower half, but she wore the flimsy paper top above. Eleanor knew the same excitement only, if it be possible, intensified that she'd felt upon entering the infirmary. When the nurse left there was a bubble of untainted joy as Eleanor thought of sitting the few moments, talking to Jane. She lowered herself quietly into the other chair.

"As I was saying, well, that's for you. I read it once on the back of a box of cereal. A long time ago."

Jane turned to her, eyes hooded.

"I always remembered it," Eleanor said.

Jane bent her face to the piece of paper and Eleanor watched her read it. Even though she now needed to depend much less on the muscles in Jane's face, she watched them tighten and she saw the face change shape. She was not surprised. It had been her intent, for she knew what was written on the white scrap by heart:

There is a land of the living
And a land of the dead,
And the bridge is love.

It was shortly after her parents were murdered that she read the lines one morning on the back of a Raisin Bran box. She was eating breakfast with her sister and aunt, the morning light streaming into the large dining room with just the three of them around the table. She kept an eye on the box, making sure her aunt didn't throw it out with the morning's garbage. She had asked for seconds on cereal—to Aunt Clarice's delight, for Eleanor until that day had shown little desire for food—then thirds so the box would empty faster. She knew what she was going to do. And for twenty-six years Eleanor had carried the cut-out piece of cardboard in her handbag, deriving strength from it when she came across it. Nostalgia combined with recognition, in the same way that discovering a toy or object from childhood produced certain long-ago feelings, or stumbling upon the Christmas decorations in the midst of summer could evoke the magic of the winter holiday.

Over the years, love had freed her from her own self-imposed prison. Love, not of other, but for her work. But in the early days, love was symbolized by that four-inch scrap of cardboard which, as the years passed, lost its totemic childhood power and took on instead a spiritual nature representing her parents. Incomplete or faulty memory allowed her to remember that time with fondness, even if the truth of the past would betray nostalgia for even the most reminiscent.

She never knew where she lost the piece of cardboard, but by the time she had, it didn't matter, the words were etched well into her heart. And last night she had brought them forth from her heart's hiding place, writing them out to share with Jane. How good it had felt.

Jane remained looking at the paper longer than it should take to read the simple lines, and Eleanor suddenly wondered how well she read. Perhaps her tense expression had been borne of embarrassment, but Eleanor's thoughts were quickly allayed when she saw Jane's eyes blink back tears. She hesitated only a moment before acting, aware that it was still not too late to stop, for to touch Jane in such a manner would be yet another breach in prison code for which she could well find herself relieved of her job. But she found she little cared for repercussions and perhaps freedom for Jane would spell her own freedom. In an instant she had pushed back her chair and wrapped her arms around Jane speaking gently.

"Oh, Jane. I'm sorry. I'm so sorry." And then what she did next would, in the quiet reflective atmosphere of her own home, astound her. With her arms around Jane's shoulders, murmuring, "I'm sorry, I'm sorry," she placed her lips to Jane's hair and kissed her.

After a moment, Jane's crying subsided and she shook her head.

"It's okay. I'm okay."

Eleanor moved, crouching on the floor inches from Jane and put her arms around Jane's waist. She moved one hand on Jane's back and the other on her arm until Jane looked up, wiped at her wet face, and let her eyes look gently into Eleanor's.

Eleanor answered Jane with her own expression, offering herself like a life vest. As she remained looking into Jane's eyes she saw the disparity of emotions: there was anguish; there was sorrow, but there was also something else.

Eleanor sat back down next to her and said nothing.

Jane cleared her throat. "What kind of cereal was it?"

"Ummm, let's see, probably Raisin Bran. I believe that's the one I liked best when I was young." Eleanor smiled. She reached over and touched Jane's arm. "I'm sorry," she whispered. "I didn't want to make you sad."

At a loss for what to say next, they both looked down.

Jane spoke first. "When I was little, I thought I could catch the moon."

"What did the moon symbolize for you that you wanted to catch it?" Eleanor asked, grateful and joyful in a way that she was only beginning to understand.

Jane didn't answer the question, but instead tilted her head back and let it rest against the wall. "God, this isn't how I thought my life would turn out."

"I know. It rarely is."

"Sometimes everything is all dark."

"I know," Eleanor said softly, stroking Jane's arm. "I know. It's at times like those that you stop and just try to breathe in the light. Let it in through the cracks."

"The cracks," Jane repeated with a strange little laugh.

"That's right, the cracks. We're all cracked. But sometimes you can try with all your will not to let the pain harden you. Let it soften you instead."

After a few seconds, Jane said, "When I was outside, I saw the purple flower of a clover. It made me remember something, and I wanted to die." Eleanor tensed. "But, a few seconds later, something happened. I saw another flower. A yellow flower. A daffodil. I hadn't done anything different. I was still me, but I *saw* it. And then I was watching the clouds. I often do. They're the same in prison as they are outside of prison. And then I felt the breeze, and I realized that even in prison I could still feel. I thought with or without a God, this was life. My life now. Single moments where I understand everything, and nothing. Where beauty nearly overwhelms, but in the end is . . . ." She didn't finish. "It was the first time I felt that even without," Jane's voice faltered. "Even without Weedy, or a family, or anybody, really, I could see the miracle of the purple flower, and the yellow flower.

"You're amazing," Eleanor said, but she said it so lightly and to herself that she wasn't sure if Jane heard.

"On the night that he died, I felt an intense love for him. I always did, but on that night it was stronger, almost as if some part of me knew. I'd had that feeling once before. The first time I bathed him, I felt this incredible tenderness. But on the last night, there was also something shallow and murky. It was like this really low-pitched sound, the rumbles and grumbles of fear, like a low warning bell that only I could hear. Do you know?"

Eleanor nodded. "A premonition."

"Yes. I had this feeling that Weedy was in danger. Kenneth might know where I lived, and he definitely knew I wouldn't be home. But Carol couldn't come stay with Weedy that night. And I wouldn't have wanted her to anyway. I couldn't tell her about the plan."

Jane was breathing hard, and when she stopped talking, Eleanor took a deep breath, as if breathing for both of them.

"I debated whether to take him with me or not. I had no idea things would turn out the way they did." She made a noise Eleanor couldn't interpret. "David knew I had him. Nick wouldn't know him. So I decided I shouldn't be superstitious and I made the decision to take him." She looked over at Eleanor. "My life would have turned out so very different, if I'd just made that one decision in another way."

"That's hard to think about, isn't it?"

Jane didn't answer.

"You can't beat yourself up for it. You know that."

Still Jane said nothing. Then ever so softly: "If we could just sit here together."

"What?" Eleanor asked, not sure she had heard right.

"Never mind," Jane said, and Eleanor was about to protest when Jane said, "This old man once told me something I've always remembered. That the only things worth saying are those that are un-sayable. It's like the more you know, the less you say. And most people talk a lot but say so little. More and more I find I can say most when I'm silent. In stillness I understand."

"Understand what?"

"I just *know,* and it's all okay. Well, sometimes it is."

Eleanor listened but she most certainly did not understand.

"Sometimes you have to know, too, that you don't know. And the uncertainty's a part of the mystery."

Indeed, Eleanor thought to herself, wishing for a little less mystery.

"It really is okay," Jane said, as if trying to convince herself. "Even the sorrow. Sorrow's a luxury."

"You said that once before, but you wouldn't explain."

"It's a luxury you can indulge, in the absence of stress."

"I see," Eleanor said, nodding. She wanted to reach out and touch Jane once more and say again, "You're amazing," but she didn't, and Jane continued without Eleanor's prompting.

"I don't know if I've always believed this, but I do now. That real joy is somehow tied to the sorrow. It encompasses sorrow, because loss is a part of all that's worth having. Just as birth and death are inseparable, and light and dark, so too are joy and sorrow. I had such joy with Weedy, even if it was short-lived. But I had no idea how closely it was tied to this, what I feel now."

And this time Eleanor did lay her hand onto Jane's arm. For there was nothing she could say.

"So why isn't that enough? It should be."

"Why isn't what enough?" Eleanor asked.

"The love that's left over after a death. If it's still there, then why . . ."

Eleanor nodded, finally understanding. She understood Jane needed an answer, needed for her to give her an answer to heal her wound, and if she could do that one thing, she might hold the girl, at least for these moments, in her heart. She reached back into her brain for something. The pages of her college psych book flipped before her. Yes. No. Not psychology. Find an answer that would satisfy *you*, not a textbook reply. Think about somebody *you* love then imagine a life without him or her. She glanced at Jane waiting for her response then blinked. She imagined a jury sentencing Jane to die for her crimes. She imagined the psych room empty of Jane, without the prospect of her ever walking through the door again, never again sitting near her as she was now. Sylvia Marie Marshall. Don't take her away.

Silently Eleanor prayed to a god she no longer believed in and in so doing she prayed for an answer. The answer came, but what exactly was it the saint had said? She disagreed with much of his teaching, but had remembered that one thing. She could see it written down and doodled over several times at the top right-hand edge of her open notebook, Cory sitting beside her, Professor Sedgwick lecturing in front. She closed her eyes for only an instant and thought of her parents.

Then she looked again at Jane, this time with confidence. "Saint Augustine had a simple but wise answer. He said, 'To love me is to want me to be.' To love something is to want it to be. Your love is still there, but you want him to be alive, that's all. It's natural. I'd guess you loved Weedy better than most people love each other—if love can be measured in such terms."

Jane nodded and Eleanor saw she was trying not to cry again.

"It's okay. As long as you love him, he'll live on. Death doesn't separate you from someone you've loved. It's other things that do."

Jane turned her head to look at Eleanor with an expression of gratitude, apparently this time unconcerned with the tears.

"He died knowing you loved him, Jane. Love may well be the most powerful force that exists. I haven't always seen this but," she paused. "Someone helped me to see it." She smiled. "You might have been denied love as a child, but you aren't scared. Anyone capable of loving as deeply as you did will be okay. Okay?"

Jane nodded through her tears. "If only I could go home once more, and see my little apartment, and see him lying on the sofa. In my dreams, I'm always there, filling his food bowl, giving him his medication. He's always there walking beside me." The words came out funny. It was the most Jane had ever revealed of herself. "No, death doesn't separate us, does it? He's still with me, isn't he?" And her voice begged Eleanor to agree with her. "Can you just . . ."

"Just what, Jane?"

"Just sit there, next to me. It feels comforting, and somehow . . ." She stopped.

"Yes?"

"Secure. "

"Okay."

Eleanor sat, thinking, *I'll stay all night if you want me to. Don't worry, I'll stay.* She listened to Jane's small coughing sounds. Jane leaned her head back against the wall again and Eleanor turned to regard her. She wanted to absorb the face beside her that she now knew so well—a sundial pointing to the joys and sorrows of a life. No more did Jane look blank to Eleanor. Now, the expressions marched readily across her face. There was new animation in the eyes that not even sorrow could shade. As Jane relaxed, Eleanor studied her. Across Jane's face she saw something more than serenity or contentment. She saw peace.

At length she reached a hand and touched the purple bruise. "Does it hurt?"

"It's okay."

Eleanor nodded and they were silent, sitting in the room together, side by side.

"Was he ever really here?" Jane asked.

Now curled into the edges of the face, Eleanor saw something darker than fear. "Of course he was," Eleanor answered Jane automatically, hoping to alleviate her doubt, with no way of knowing whether the animal she had loved with such devotion had been real or not. No way of knowing really if her parents had ever really been. Sure there were pictures somewhere, but where were they, the flesh and blood?

"But how do I know?"

Indeed, Eleanor thought to herself.

"He's not here," Jane continued. "I have no pictures of him. Nothing in here even remotely reminds me of him, except the dog in that awful poster." She tried to smile at Eleanor, but it fell short. "Although I do dream at night. And sometimes I wake wondering, how is it possible to feel *that* and feel it in a *dream*?"

Feel what?" Eleanor asked quickly.

"Never mind," Jane said and Eleanor felt her heart quicken in that now familiar and panicked way. "If I stop remembering him, then who will know he existed, and—" She stopped and Eleanor watched her.

"And what Jane?"

"Thanks for coming here. It means a lot. And for sitting. I look hideous don't I?"

"No. Not at all. You couldn't look— uh, go on, tell me what you were about to tell me."

"Nothing makes sense. Nothing's real anymore the way it used to be. That's one reason I stopped talking. Animals are better off."

"There is one real thing, Jane. This. This here." She touched Jane's thigh, uncertain for whom she was doing it, knowing that the nurse might come back at any moment, but knowing too that this was more important than anything else she had to do right now. "The moment. You here with me. You talking, sharing your world with me. It's okay. You can be scared. You can be upset. You can be confused. No one has the answers any more than you do."

"I thought I had it figured out the other day outside in the courtyard."

"Yes?"

"Not the day of the flowers, but on a different day."

"Your epiphanies happen outdoors, don't they? Epiphanies, or whatever you want to call them. You're always in nature."

"I guess. I'd saved a kind of beetle and set it down outside. First, I watched for hours as he made this determined march across my cell floor. I had to hide him from the guard. When I set him down outside, I felt the breeze on me. It really wasn't until I'd released the bug in the courtyard, and was watching him wave his feelers around madly in the outside air and set off on a new course—he didn't seem to know where he was going and didn't seem to care. It was only then that I felt this weird kind of knowledge take hold of me. Perhaps it was the breeze when it touched my face. I wanted to lie down and lose myself to the air. The bug was walking off into the unknown. I thought of Weedy, not existing, yet just as I felt the breeze persist, always existing. I'm sure I've lost you."

"No. Go on."

"I just had this feeling that he was with me."

"Because of the breeze. That's important to you, isn't it? You speak about it a lot." Eleanor watched her. "The breeze?"

"I don't know." She paused. "I think if I could just hear the music of some wind chimes somewhere, I would know he was here."

"Wind chimes?" Eleanor said, trying to follow.

"Wind chimes. Music always ends in silence. Did you ever think of that? They ring and then the silence. You need the silence to hear the notes. They ring and remind you where you are. There aren't any chimes in prison. At home if I heard chimes or church bells, I'd stop and feel the moment. Weedy lived like that continually. When I'd do that, I'd feel eternity. I wish I could always be that sure, as I was at that moment."

"Of what?"

"That he's here."

"It's said that all those who are loved live on." Eleanor said unconvincingly.

"I hope so." Jane's smile seemed forced. "We shared the same heart. Do you know what I mean?"

Eleanor looked down.

"No, you don't understand, do you? You never loved like that."

Eleanor regarded Jane, but didn't answer. The door was opening and the nurse was walking towards them. Eleanor heard the words as if from somewhere else, spoken softly. They sounded far away but she knew they were Jane's: "It's okay. Don't worry. It's going to be okay."

CHAPTER FIFTY

The phone call that he expected would one day come snuck into his life just as the first signs of late-thirties age did—a lone gray hair, a more sluggish reflex—quietly and insignificantly, yet carrying unmistakable magnitude. He was stepping from the shower, a baby blue towel wrapped around his waist, water droplets still clinging to his wide shoulders when he heard the telephone.

"*What?*" He said to himself and marched towards the insistent ring.

"Hello?" He said into it dully.

"Officer Sampson?"

"Yes?"

"My name is Eleanor Hartley. I work as a psychologist at the women's penitentiary. I suppose you know it?"

"Yes." The word was drawn out, spoken suspiciously.

"You were the arresting officer for a girl I am currently treating. Sylvia Marie Marshall."

Silence.

"Hello?"

David squeezed the phone tight in his hand. "What do you want?"

"I'd like to talk to you."

He held the phone so tight he thought he could crack it if he wanted to. He shut his eyes. "Yeah?"

"Could you meet with me?"

He stared out the window with its white paint smudge on the glass to the street beyond where he saw a girl and a boy walking together. She was laughing and swishing her hair as she pushed her body sideways, playfully, into his. The boy grinned but kept his gaze about four feet ahead, fixed on something or nothing. The girl kept laughing and speaking, her lips moving, her head turning to gaze up at him. The boy hunched his shoulders and took out a cigarette from his shirt pocket and glanced once at the tracery of the tree limbs as he cupped his hands and lit up. The girl took her hand suddenly and swept it up through his short, spiky hair, but still he did not regard her. Still he kept his gaze straight ahead. And as David stared out the window, he closed his eyes to the sight of them.

"Yeah, okay," he said into the receiver.

CHAPTER FIFTY-ONE

When Eleanor walked through the Sally Port her spirits were high. Her home life might be in shambles, but she was still one good psychologist. Two days before Jane had been upbeat and talkative.

"You know the Raisin Bran quote you gave me?"

"Yes." Eleanor smiled back.

"It's Thornton Wilder. *The Bridge of San Luis Rey*."

"That's right. How did you discover that so quickly?"

"Shina told me."

"Shina?"

"I figured she'd know, so I asked her during Association."

"And she knew, did she?" Eleanor wondered what else Shina told Jane.

"She did. She also introduced me to Cilla."

Eleanor gave an uncertain smile.

"I'm going to teach her to connect with her loved ones on the outside through telepathy. In particular Lelia."

"*Lelia*? You met Lelia?"

"No, I didn't meet her because Lelia is dead. Lelia was her baby, but after she died she came back as Cilla's Christmas tree and Cilla misses her. I understand that kind of missing because of Weedy. But as far as I know Weedy's not come back as a tree yet." Jane smiled.

Eleanor had stared, wondering if Jane were testing her in some way. "Her Christmas tree," she said slowly.

"Yes."

"Are you all right?"

"I know it sounds weird, but is it really any weirder than so-called reality?"

Eleanor had shrugged, smiled and agreed, finding anything Jane now said hard to dispute. Even Christmas trees. She thought back to her session with Shina that same day, and the smile on her face stretched in satisfaction.

"Guess what, Hartley? I mighta found out where I'm home. I got library for three hours yesterday. I love the library because excepting for here with you, when you ain't talking all your bullshit and asking bullshit questions, the library's the only place that's quiet. No crazy inmates talking stuff that don't matter. I sat down with that big dictionary, not my pea-sized one, and I start turning the pages, beginning with the A's, and before I know it, time's up."

Eleanor waited. She couldn't see Shina Jones working the rest of her life as a librarian, but then stranger things had occurred.

"Not a librarian," Shina said shaking her head. "A speech therapist. I'm gonna teach kids how to speak properly, how to use dic-tion," she enunciated deliberately, "and I'm starting with myself. I've already signed up for a grammar class."

"Oh, Shina!" Eleanor couldn't control her hands and they clapped together once, triumphant cymbals in the finale. "That's a beautiful idea."

"'Course Linda thinks I'm crazy, but she'll get over it."

"Indeed she will."

With the smile still lingering on her face, Eleanor passed the secretary's office, glanced in and called, "Hi, Asa! Beautiful day today, isn't it?"

"Oh. Hi, hon."

Eleanor stopped.

"Everything all right, Asa?" From where she stood, Eleanor could smell Asa's sweet baby powdered perfume, cavorting with the stale smell of the hall.

Asa stared at Eleanor then slowly shook her head back and forth. Eleanor opened her mouth, but Asa stopped her. "You best go speak to Helen." She was still shaking her head, but had returned her focus back to the paperwork on her desk when she said, "My husband told me not to take this job. He *told* me."

Eleanor felt paralyzed but she backed out of the doorway. "Have a good day, Asa."

"Same, hon."

Before Helen's office, Eleanor took a deep breath. She had no idea what to expect. All she could think of was Jane. She shivered, and knocked.

"Come in."

Eleanor opened the door and stepped forward.

"Eleanor, hi. Thank you. Close the door."

"Asa said to see you." She sat down before Helen.

"Oh. Good for her. I had a note on your desk, but I guess Asa beat me to it." Helen's normally thick straight hair stuck out on the side and dark circles beneath her eyes gave her face a coon-like mask. "I was told you went to the infirmary. People talk around here, Eleanor. Perhaps here more than anywhere else." She eyed Eleanor with a stern expression.

Eleanor returned her look, her eyes direct and unwavering, as she answered, "I did."

"Eleanor."

"And I'd do it again tomorrow given—"

"You went after I said you should show that girl less attention not *more.*"

Eleanor opened her mouth to speak, but Helen stopped her. It was not so much her words as it was the look on her face. It was a look of entreaty, but there was also another emotion coexisting. Something was scaring Helen. Eleanor saw it as plainly as if Helen were holding a placard announcing anxiety.

And as she looked across at Helen, Eleanor felt her own fear growing.

"I understand, Eleanor. I do. You think I don't feel for the girl, too? I'm not upset with what you did, just that we, of all people, must not break prison rules." Eleanor began to speak, but Helen cut her off again. "I'm willing to forget it this time. But this is a warning, it mustn't happen again. Can you forget about it?"

"I can forget about it."

"Good, because that's not why I called you here."

Eleanor ran her hands over her thighs smoothing her skirt.

"We've another matter at hand." Helen paused. "Do you want the short version or long?"

"Short, I suppose."

"Okay. Mimi Kramer is, well, she's dead. She was in critical care last night. Rushed to M.C.V. But she didn't make it. Her family is coming today . . . or what there is of her family, relatives . . ." She trailed off then finished. "I'll need you to speak to them. There will be an investigation. Obviously it's bad publicity for the facility. I imagine there will also be a lawsuit. As you can guess I'm not—"

Eleanor had been staring at Helen, listening to her words, but now unable to stop the hideous thought that was festering inside her, she interrupted and said, "What . . . what happened? Who—?" But she couldn't finish the question.

Helen looked at Eleanor for a beat, and spoke. "Shina Jones. Apparently, it was Shina Jones."

Eleanor opened her mouth, but no words came out.

"The girls are all a flutter. I'll need your help in—"

"Excuse me, Helen." Eleanor stood and walked out of the warden's office, and back down the hall to the Sally Port. She felt the nausea rising from deep in her stomach.

Eleanor sat down on the park bench where she had sat with Cory. An ordinary afternoon on an ordinary day, except she had left the penitentiary when she had patients to see. She saw people walking on the park's asphalt trails under the trees. She realized she was clenching her jaw and she tried to relax, but she couldn't. What if she were to cry out to one of those ordinary people strolling the park? "*Help me*!" Perhaps they wished to cry out the same thing to her, thinking her quite ordinary, sitting there poised on her bench.

What they didn't realize was that she, Dr. Eleanor Hartley, head psychologist at the women's state penitentiary, found it not in the least odd that an inmate's dead baby was now her Christmas tree and that another inmate was teaching her to talk to that tree. Now, who was crazy? Who would they lock up?

What was odd was that she, the respected psychologist, had failed so blatantly at her own life. She wondered how many of the women walking past her had simultaneously failed at being wives and failed in their careers. Usually the wife failure was forgiven if the woman in question was a successful career-woman, a C.E.O., or opera diva, maybe a prima ballerina, that sort of thing. And the woman whose career was less than illustrious could take pleasure in knowing that she had a happy home life: contented and fulfilled husband, beautiful, eager and capable children. Maybe even the continuity of grandchildren. But to fail at both took quite an unusual talent indeed. Perhaps she could go back to the shrinks. Perhaps they might kindly explain to her just how she might have succeeded in arriving at this particular point in her life.

She sat watching the people hurry along, returning to offices, couples entwined, seeking the first uncertain days of warmth. She sat quietly breathing in and out, trying not to lose herself but she felt she was losing control. All at once she hated the way she sat so erect and proper, one leg crossed over the other, in her smart suit. The longer she sat still, the more she felt an aversion to the woman who had thought she had control over everything, including her own life. The sham of it all.

She remembered having the epiphany sitting beside Cory, but now it dwelled just beyond immediate recall, something fragile like the thread the spider spun. In the past she'd found that by sitting still the answers to life's questions would surface like a sunset illuminating her mind with moments of beauty and clarity then fade back to gray, but now when she tried there was a gaping void.

She knew her behavior was different from ever before, and could quite possibly be considered destructive. People could change she thought. Yes, they could change for the worst. *Stop it. Just stop it.* She could not go back to the woman she'd been. She uncrossed her leg, slipped off her shoe and felt the crunchy blades of dried grass beneath her stockinged foot. Starchy brown blades with thin new shoots pushing through. She wanted to put her face against the earth and smell it. The woman she'd been before would have asked Helen every conceivable question and found out every precise detail, then sought to right the situation.

She thought again of the poet who'd spoken of the soul's eternal yearning, and in that instant she knew that if she yearned for anything in this life, it was peace. The quiet joy of watching one season become the next. She longed for what she called moments of the mind, and realized she sought these moments of mind more than fortune or fame, more than achievement or good sex. They were passing moments of memory, or maybe memories yet to come, passing moments of contentment, or stillness, what she thought the Buddhists or Hindus might call small Nirvanas. Moments, in between life's activities, of just being.

An older woman in corduroy trousers and tennis shoes stood with a small tan dog. She glanced over to Eleanor. The dog dug with pointed determination at the wooden slats surrounding a water fountain, perhaps in search of moles. His tail wagged back and forth as he dug, happy in his quest, not understanding he would never dig through the solid boards.

Scratch, scratch, scratch . . . dig, dig, dig. He stopped every few moments to regard his progress. How, Eleanor wondered, could he not realize the uselessness of his action and try to stick his nose up underneath the slats instead? She sat watching the frenzied, yet futile, dig take place.

Suddenly the dog stopped, almost as if he had sensed Eleanor's regard, and trotted over to her, mouth smiling, tongue hanging down, glistening, tail waving behind.

"Well, hi there." Eleanor stretched out a hand to touch the tan head.

"Fagin, come here."

Eleanor smiled at the woman, and motioned that the dog was not bothering her.

"*Fagin.* Leave her!"

The dog turned and sashayed back to the woman.

Eleanor knew she couldn't return to the penitentiary; she was in no shape to conduct sessions. She decided to drive home. When she pulled into her driveway, she saw Lewis's car. She shut her eyes and opened them, disbelieving, but the car was still there. She touched her hand to her hair, looking in the rearview mirror. She tried to smile at her reflection but the face looking back would not obey. She stepped out of the car and shut the door softly. Walking up the walkway she noticed that the grass was growing long on either side and she wondered if that bothered Lewis.

She stood a few seconds before opening the door to the house that she and Lewis had bought together. He was standing in the hallway, an old black suitcase beside him.

"Lewis."

"Hello, Elle. I thought you'd be at work."

She stepped around him and walked back to the kitchen to pour herself a glass of water from the sink. The water felt cool and steady and she wanted to follow it into the drain. To disappear. But she could not. She was an adult woman who had to face her problems head on and not dream of slipping down drain pipes. She walked back out to where her husband stood.

"You shaved your beard."

"I'm sorry. I thought if . . . maybe if I . . . Elle, I'm sorry."

It was the expression on his face that roused her compassion and made her want to touch the pale cheek, now exposed, in such vulnerable and milken contrast to his tan nose and brow. She looked at how his dark hair, salted with gray, lay in rumpled semi-circles on his head. How pity moved her to depths of feeling lust could never touch. She wanted to run her hands through the unkempt undulations of curls and have all—that carefree, childlike laughter they must have once shared—as it was before. Her eyes ran over his fit but nervous body, observing the way he stood defenseless and confused. She wanted to tell him it was all okay.

She remained standing in the hallway.

He watched, perhaps awaiting a response and when she didn't speak, she saw irritation replace hurt. "I wanted for you to just once show some feeling for something other than those girls in prison," he finally said.

She stepped forward, but stopped a couple feet from him. She looked into the dark eyes that were level with her own and saw what she hadn't seen before. His face was a wintery mix of emotions, and the momentary wave of pity was almost too much for her to bear. But she stepped closer and touched his arm. "Oh, Lewis. Lewis. You didn't lose, Lewis." She watched his brows raise slightly and his mouth open. She let her fingers tighten around his arm.

His face seemed to be crumbling like a forgotten sandcastle. "In sports if you break the rules, you lose."

She was shaking her head back and forth. "You didn't break the rules, Lewis. We both did."

He swallowed, staring at the floor, and she too looked down, noting the different colors and grains of the wood beneath their feet. She gripped his arm harder. He glanced up and met her eyes, and she noticed fine lines around his eyes and mouth she hadn't noticed before. All at once, Lewis shrugged, the shrug of one so completely at a loss there remains no other gesture appropriate.

"I know you didn't mean to hurt me," she said, still holding onto his arm. "I think I always thought I had to be the brave one, put on a stoical face. It probably came from trying to take care of Lizzie and coping with my parents' murder." There, she'd said it. "I did hurt. I did feel for you. Tremendously. I'm sorry I didn't show it better."

He stood listening to his wife, and the expression in his eyes told her she had, in uttering the words, given him the one thing he'd always needed. She wondered if she was too late.

"Thank you," he murmured, casting eyes down again. He shifted his weight, his free hand reaching down for the single suitcase. "Maybe we can go out to dinner or something."

She looked at him, willing him not to walk away. "Lewis, you can come back."

"I need some time."

"Lewis, can't we at least talk?"

He looked as though he might crack if touched too hard.

"You know where to find me," Eleanor said gently.

"Yes. At the penitentiary," he answered.

She opened her mouth.

"It was joke."

"Lewis."

"I need some time to think things through. I still love you, Elle."

He turned, walked out the door and down the steps, still a youthful, athletic man in the prime of life.

"Thank you, Lewis," she said quietly, once he had gone. "I love you, too."

CHAPTER FIFTY-TWO

"I think this will be among the hardest things I've ever done behind these walls."

"I know," Helen answered Eleanor. "I know you like her. Everyone here likes Shina."

"What hope does she have now? Why have her go over it and torture herself?" Eleanor shook her head. She'd listened to the details of Mimi's death: how Mimi had pounced on Cilla in fit of rage, probably acting out her own deep-seated unhappiness. Shina had rushed at Mimi knocking her down against the cement floor—then standing back in disbelief with the other girls in the pod as Mimi lay still, the dark pool around her head spreading and changing shape like a malignant cell, her mouth frozen open like her eyes in an unnerving rictal grimace, one last silent protest.

"If there's one lesson I've learned it's that nothing can be retrieved from the past. It's past," Eleanor said.

"Nothing except lessons. And wisdom," Helen answered her.

Eleanor inhaled. The relief in not hearing the word *memories.* "Maybe you should take my job," she said to Helen. "Helen I—"

"You've said that to me before. No, Eleanor, you're the best there is. I don't give a hoot if you disregard me and visit a girl in need in the infirmary. You're the best we've ever had. I know you're not feeling it right now. I know you think it's all your fault. That's flattering yourself a bit too much, don't you think?"

"Yes, thank you," Eleanor said, smiling just a bit.

"No, no, thank *you* for being so strong and not . . . ."

"Helen, I—"

"This is going to be hard for all of us. I need your strength and good judgment more than ever right now."

"Yes. Of course." She could have risen to leave then and not added a ruined career to her ruined marriage and the catalogue of failures of this one glorious year. She could have said, "See you," and smiled to Helen, her colleague and boss, and continued working with the inmates as Helen desired. But she didn't. She remained sitting and Helen asked quizzically:

"What is it?"

Eleanor took a deep breath. "I don't like saying what I have to say to you, but I'd be letting myself down as a psychologist if I did not."

"What it is, Eleanor?"

Eleanor wavered a moment, wondering if she shouldn't just shake her head as she'd done before and say, "Oh, never mind, it's nothing. Sorry." It would be so much easier for both her and Helen.

"Helen, I need to resign."

"Eleanor!"

"Not right away, of course. I'll give ample notice. I suppose that's what I'm doing now."

"Mimi's death was not your fault." Helen stopped then drew in her breath. "This is a prison, Eleanor. Things happen."

"I know. But maybe I never should have decided to work in a penitentiary. In the early years it nearly cost me my marriage. There has been a strain between Lewis and me ever since I—" She laughed softly. "Well, none of that matters now." Helen watched her avidly. "But that's not what this is about."

"Eleanor."

Eleanor pulled back her shoulders and took a deep breath. Her heart was pounding as she looked Helen in the eye. "I'm falling in love with an inmate."

Helen opened her mouth but did not speak.

"I can no longer pretend that I'm not. And I'm afraid I have been pretending, hoping, but—"

"Jane," Helen said reflexively.

And when Eleanor answered her there was resolution in her voice, "Yes, Jane."

Helen's face changed and she let out a little laugh. "Oh Eleanor, if that's all. I mean, I'm a little surprised but, but you're not really *in love* with her. It's transference. You of all people know that." Helen was speaking rapidly. "You've worked so intensely with her. I know she's been your pet project, so to speak. I know you don't have children." Helen trailed off and glanced away. "Look, Eleanor. You don't need to quit. Thank you. I mean really, thank you for such honesty, but this will pass and . . . we need to let it, because we need you here."

Eleanor was silent while Helen spoke. She sat still, digesting her words.

When Eleanor did not respond, Helen continued talking, "It's all right, Eleanor. It happens. I'm just surprised it's never happened to you before. That's why it came as a bit of a shock. That's all. How long have you been here with us? Goodness, longer than anyone else. It'll pass. It will. Just let it pass. You don't need to quit, but again, thank you for your honesty. That couldn't have been easy."

"Thank you, Helen. Let me think on it. I need to think." She rose and the last thing she saw was Helen's stricken face.

Eleanor was seated behind the desk when the guard led Shina Jones into the room. Her wrists were in cuffs. Eleanor tried not to gasp for Shina looked nothing like the girl she had worked with a week ago. The skin of her face hung dull and gray over sharp, prominent bones and her eyes had a hollow lifeless appearance like a woman years older, broken in spirit and physique by physical labor and mental decay.

Shina sat down and the guard left and shut the door. Eleanor could not for a moment take her eyes from the closed door. When finally she looked from the door to Shina, Shina was not looking at her, but staring to the desk with an expression that Eleanor had only seen once—on the face of a woman during a visit to the psych ward of the hospital.

"Hello, Shina."

Shina glanced up once briefly then back to the desk again.

Eleanor took a breath, pausing, and said cautiously, "I've heard what's happened."

Shina didn't move.

"I thought maybe you could tell me from your side. Talk about it from your point of view. If it's any consolation, I . . ." But she didn't finish.

Shina shifted, her arms and shoulders jerking.

"Shina?"

"*Don't fuckin' Shina me.*" It was so low it was nearly a whisper.

"What?"

"Ain't no justice in this world."

"There is. You just can't take it into your own hands."

"*Just shut up, Dr. Hartley. Just- - shut - - up.*"

"Shina—"

"*Don't you or nobody care what happens to me.*" Again a whisper.

Eleanor leaned over to Shina. "What?"

"They ain't no use talking to me anymore. Don't you get it?" Shina's voice was a tire leaking air. Both her expression and her posture lacked emotion. No buoyancy. No effervescence.

"No, Shina, I don't."

"Go on away, Dr. Hartley. Leave me be. You don't care shit."

"Shina, I—"

"I *said* go on with you. Ain't nothing nobody can do now and you know it." Shina looked at Eleanor then hissed, "*So just leave me be.*"

Eleanor sat up taller.

"*Shina.* Now you listen to me. I know you didn't mean to kill her. And I know that—" Eleanor stopped. Shina had looked up carefully, and Eleanor saw in that one protracted gaze all the individual hopelessness when life veered off its expected course. "You got tired of Mimi picking on Cilla, didn't you?"

Shina's expression changed.

"Yes, of *course* I know that, Shina." Eleanor said shaking her head back and forth with wide, imploring eyes. "You were trying to protect Cilla, weren't you?"

As Shina stared across at Eleanor, her eyes glistened, and she let her lids and lashes fall over them, blinking back the tears. Eleanor reached across the desk to pat Shina's arm, but Shina pulled away from her.

"I *know,* Shina. I *know.*"

"Yeah, but it ain't no use now. I killed her."

"Yes it is, Shina. *Yes,* there is use."

"Then you tell me why. You tell me *how.* I got about as much chance of parole as a sundae on a hot July sidewalk."

Eleanor nearly smiled for she felt a whiff of the old Shina back in the room for that quick moment and she saw that prison life would never completely crush the girl's spirit. But a feeling of hopelessness also filled her. How? Why? Shina was asking her. What use was there in talking about what had happened? What could Shina now hope for? Eleanor wanted to shout and scream and jump up and down to force the beautiful girl, with the wonderful words and high IQ back into the empty shell who sat across from her.

How? Why? But Eleanor did not know.

CHAPTER FIFTY-THREE

Handbag pressed before her, Eleanor pushed open the heavy glass door of the diner with her free hand and glanced around as the assembled heads looked up blankly to greet her momentary intrusion and incongruity. David Sampson had described himself as 6'1" with short, light brown hair, and wearing his police uniform. In an instant, her eyes landed on him, sitting hunched over the counter on a stool.

She walked toward him.

"Officer Sampson?"

She watched with interest as the initial suspicion layering his face retreated and boyish innocence took over. Something was wrong. The shift was forced. "Hello," he said looking at her shyly.

She glanced once at the cracked orange padding of the stool next to him, then sat down upon it, sliding her skirt toward her knees with her palms.

"We don't have to stay here." He sounded embarrassed, and she felt confused by him.

"Here is fine. You've a full cup of coffee. I don't mind."

"I'll finish and we can go somewhere more . . ."

"Here is just fine. I'd just like to ask you some questions."

She began by speaking about Sylvia Marie Marshall, aware of feeling defensive. He responded in an overly polite and almost ingratiating manner, Mr. Helpful himself. Again, she felt that something was wrong.

As she asked him innocuous questions and he answered them, she felt her mind flip-flopping back and forth. At times she liked his genuine nature. At times he frightened her for reasons she could not identify. There was about him a childlike quality, perhaps reinforced by the neotenic characteristic of a large head.

"I know she thought I was crazy," he stated after Eleanor had come to a hiatus in her questions.

"She mentioned something about being concerned about you," Eleanor replied, remembering Jane's true comment, "One of those strong, silent, psychotic types."

"She talked about me?"

Eleanor hesitated. "Yes." She saw in his eyes the desperate need for validation and wondered if she, herself, was no different from this police officer concerning the girl who occupied their thoughts.

"What did she say?"

"I'm sorry, I'm not at liberty to share that with you."

"Can't you just tell me a little?"

"I've already said too much. Now," She cleared her throat. "Officer Sampson, did you see Sylvia shoot Officer Branston Bread and Mr. Grady Smith?"

David hesitated. He was looking into his coffee cup, his large hands holding each side as though it were the Holy Grail. In his profile, she saw a frown of concentration. No, a frown of conscience. Then he spoke.

"She didn't shoot them."

Eleanor swallowed. She tried to find the right words to answer, but could not. So she repeated the officer's words. "She didn't shoot . . . *either* of them?"

"No, she would never kill. She—"

"Officer Sampson," Eleanor interrupted, aware her voice was trembling. "Are you telling me that Sylvia Marshall did not shoot Officer Bread or Mr. Smith?"

"Yes, that's what I just said."

"Then who did?"

"A police officer shot them."

"What?"

"A police officer."

"Both of them? Are you quite certain?"

"Yes."

Caught off guard, Eleanor gasped, and began to weep silently. The waitress behind the counter glanced at her, then shot David a contemptuous look. She nudged the napkins nearer to Eleanor.

David sat still, then reached out his arm and placed it around Eleanor's shoulders with awkward empathy. As the relief and emotion wore off, and Eleanor recovered herself, she raised her head to the handsome police officer, ignoring the fact that her eyes were smudged with tears.

"But do you know she's in prison for murder?" She said it in a hushed tone.

"I know." David answered regarding the depths of his coffee cup again.

"And what's worse, to me, is that she believes she did it. You let her believe she killed those men. What kind of person could do a thing like that?"

"A person who fell in love with her."

Eleanor stared, uncomprehending.

"If I talk to you, I'll lose my job."

Eleanor could find no words to utter.

"Come on." David set five dollars on the counter, touched Eleanor's back gently and motioned for her to follow him.

He took her to a darkly lit chain restaurant where he ordered another coffee and she, against her better judgment at 11:40 a.m., ordered a glass of Pinot Noir. She searched her handbag for an Advil, but found none. There in the dark restaurant with the red faux-leather chairs and imitation Tiffany lamps, David told her about the corruption in his department, a fact relatively well-known, perhaps even expected, by the scandal-hungry, crime-show-watching public. He spoke of his loyalty not only to the academy, but to his fellow officers, even though there remained no one now he felt he could trust. He admitted his actions on many accounts had been cowardly, but asked her what he would gain in standing up to a corrupt department. What could one man do, except tell the truth and lose his job? This course of action would not change a thing. And finally he told her how he had grown to love a quiet girl with a great sense of compassion, who couldn't bear to watch anything suffer.

"She stole a dog," he said to her.

"Okay, that was wrong to do. But you don't spend a lifetime in prison for stealing one dog from a laboratory. I'm sorry, but—"

"She was in danger. She was beginning to know too much. I was in danger."

"In danger? She's behind bars. She's in *prison*," Eleanor stated, her breathing short and shallow. The words sounded like a line from a bad *film noir.*

"But she's alive. I didn't want her life taken from her."

"What do you mean?"

"I mean someone would've found her and killed her. You don't know everything."

"What don't I know?"

"Just trust me. And if they didn't kill her, Nick would have. I didn't know it would happen. I didn't think Nick was capable . . . but once it had, I didn't try to fight it. Besides she was safe."

"Safe? Officer Sampson, if you'll forgive me for raising my voice, there is an innocent girl in there who is wasting her life behind bars for something one of *your* officers did. You killed her. Do you hear me? She might as well be dead."

David looked around the restaurant to the few people who'd looked over in their direction.

"They aren't *my* officers. And you know, I'll probably have to resign from my job, the only job I've ever wanted. But do you, sitting there across from me in your rich suit, understand any of that? I bet you have a husband who provides for you, and nice, adult children—like, about everything I lack. You can afford to sit there and question and accuse me. Look at you. You have no idea who Sylvie is. No, it isn't fair she's locked up, but at least now . . . never mind."

"What were you going to say?"

"Nothing."

"No, go on, tell me."

"No. But I'll tell you something else: 'Stone walls do not a prison make, nor iron bars a cage.'"

"What?" Asked Eleanor.

"It's a poem I had to memorize in high school."

"How very nice."

"True liberty comes from freedom of the soul. And it can't be threatened by chains or bars. She's freer than any of us. She always was. She's freer than I am, freer than Nick, freer than you. Freer than any of the people I know."

"Who's Nick?"

"My head hurts."

Eleanor leaned back against the fake leather. She rubbed her own temples. For a moment she couldn't speak, then composing herself, she stated very slowly:

"Would you feel free locked up in prison?"

"I don't know. Probably not."

"Then how very nice to be able to quote poetry and expound upon others' freedom when you're not behind bars. It's dangerous in a prison. We just had a girl *killed* in there. Jane, I mean Sylvia, could *die* in there."

He shook his head. "No, she's free. She won't die. Don't you see?"

"See what?" Eleanor demanded.

"She's better off."

Eleanor stared at him for a moment, in which neither of them spoke a word. Then:

"Officer Sampson," Eleanor began, her voice low. "Tell me, how well did you know Sylvia?"

"Very well."

Again she studied the young officer but said not a word.

"What's wrong?" he asked her.

"Were the two of you . . . intimate?"

"What do you think? Of course we were."

Eleanor watched the young officer and at once saw the lie flicker behind his eyes.

"Officer Sampson, might it possibly be true that, essentially, you put that young woman behind prison bars because you saw that you were not going to have her in the way in which you wanted her?" She paused, realizing precisely why she had understood the emotion.

"What?"

It was a hunch, but she persisted. "She barely knew you existed. She never thought about you."

"*No*! You don't know anything about it. About us!"

She knew she'd hit on something, and continued. "You became obsessed with her and realized you could never actualize your fantasy, and that's why–"

"*No! Shut up! Shut up!*"

David leapt to his feet, arms waving wildly. As he stood, he knocked against the table spilling coffee and wine across it, sending Eleanor's wine glass crashing to the floor. People turned to stare.

He stood towering over her. "You've made a bad mistake." He closed his eyes tightly. He opened his eyes but she was still there.

Eleanor saw the look in his eyes in enough time and leaped up.

"Stop! You're all right. You're all right. Don't make it worse for yourself." She reached for his arm. For once, she didn't care about the people around her, looking their way. She knew what she was here to do.

"*Leave me alone*!"

"No. I'm going to help you. I want to."

"Get off," he said shaking her away, but there was less venom in his voice.

She stood, still holding onto this arm, speaking softly, "It's going to be okay. I'm sorry. I didn't mean to upset you. Now, sit down." It was like taming a tiger. He sat down, and she sat, keeping her eyes on him should he erupt again. "It's okay. It's all okay." His face was tense, pouting like a child who's been told he cannot do what he wants. He was shifting back and forth in the chair not regarding her, and Eleanor saw then that he was damaged. Life had not always been kind to him. But then to whom had it been consistently kind? Watching him fidget uneasily across from her she understood at once what Jane had figured out that he had not.

Eleanor thought of her own life and how much she had tried to control it. She looked to the officer across from her, suffering when his desires went against his principles, creating his own living hell. Now she needed his help, and she would placate him in any way to get what she wanted. She knew that this was part of human nature, too. No different from him, she wanted her way. And she was human: happy when things went her way. Less so when they did not. But she'd become a psychologist for a reason. It's the things we do when things don't go our way, the things we do to get our own way, that cause the problems. She wondered what he had done.

She reached for the napkins and began wiping the table. He turned his empty coffee cup right side up and looked at it forlornly.

"David." She used his first name.

But he didn't look at her. She read his features.

"She's suffering. She needs your help."

"Yeah, I bet."

"You can help her."

"Help *you*, you mean."

"You can help her, David."

He didn't look up.

"David."

"*What?*"

"Just tell me what happened. Tell me all of it. Tell me the truth."

"I want another cup of coffee."

She flagged down a waitress who came hustling over, poured the coffee, made an attempt to wipe the unkempt table. Then she spied the wine glass.

"Oopsy." She reached down to pick up the broken glass. "Can I get you another glass of wine?"

"No, thank you," Eleanor answered while studying David's face. He was silent, but it was a silence from which omissions jumped forth readily. When the waitress left, Eleanor said, "I need for you to tell me what happened that night."

David looked away. He leaned back in the chair bringing his coffee to his mouth and took a large sip. Then, as a couple sat down at the adjacent table and Eleanor leaned forward on her elbows, exhausted and wide awake simultaneously, David began talking.

"It all started several years ago. Nick . . . it was Nick . . . he kept getting expensive cars and buying things and we don't make that much as cops. Once when I asked him, he said he'd share his secret with me, but if I ever told he'd kill me." David slurped his coffee and Eleanor sat silently watching him. He looked up at her.

"Go on."

"I'd forgotten I'd ever asked him. Then about a year later he comes up to me and presents me with a proposition. I see now it was all a cover, because he was taking the drugs from drug busts and selling them. And I think he wanted me to think the dogs were where he was getting his money, not the drugs."

"The dogs?"

"He phrased it like a Good Samaritan thing, and talked to me about his aunt who he loved dearly, and how she died of cancer." He took another sip of coffee.

"Okay. But I need to know what happened that night, the night of—"

"I'm getting to it. If I tell you, I need for you to understand why I did what I did. I really thought that . . ."

"What?" Eleanor asked.

But David didn't finish. "Anyhow, his aunt died and Nick wanted to help other cancer victims like her. Or that's what he said."

"Okay."

"It's big business. The government condones it. We save lives."

"What is? What are you talking about?"

"Selling the animals, dogs and cats and . . . to the laboratories. They test on animals to save lives, so we go to the shelters or go get the ones that no one wants." He stopped abruptly, and Eleanor thought that perhaps for the first time he heard the feverish swamp of his words when verbalized.

"You go to the shelters and adopt dogs and cats to sell to laboratories."

"Look, I don't steal and deal drugs and kill people. So I lied about some animals?"

"You're a police officer."

"Yeah, I am. Who are you? Those dogs were going to die anyway. This gave them the chance to be useful for something. But . . ." David stopped and Eleanor felt the omission.

"Go on," she said more gently.

"I did it some. I figured if they could save a human life, well, then their lives would have some purpose. But . . ." Again, he stopped. And Eleanor watched him for signs of mendacity. This time she said nothing.

"But Nick, he went too far. He got caught up in the cash. He got into drugs. Many of the guys who were stealing the dogs—"

"Stealing? I thought you said the dogs were from shelters and about to be euthanized."

"Those were just some of them. I found out there are whole rings of people who steal dogs from people's yards. Or they answer ads for animals free to a good home. It's big business. Nick, he can pay $5 for a dog and then sell it to the lab for $500. They call it the dog mafia. They sell puppies to use as bait for dog fights." Eleanor closed her eyes. "Look, I didn't do that. You said you wanted to know so I'm telling you."

"You're right. Continue."

"Most go to the universities, the big labs. That's where the most money is."

"What happened on that night?"

David made a big sigh.

"I need to know. Please."

Then, as David recited from his perspective what had happened on that night nearly two years ago, Eleanor found herself once again back in a tainted alley, the stark, gray streets of the city closing in on her, the scene of an egregious crime.

He passed the old red brick building that had once been a mill. Why it had always made him uncomfortable he didn't know. He tapped it to ensure its status as a mere building, and not some bloody red incarnate of the devil. The sides of the building smelled of urine. His phone read 9:58 p.m. He felt the earlier warmth of the day vanish into the darkness. He stepped back into his squad car.

Im 5 mins away. R U ready?

David had told Nick he had the dogs, but his van broke down. Could Nick collect the dogs and meet David at the lab late that night. David would say that a girl who worked there would let them in after hours. She had no key, of course, but Nick didn't know that.

David would meet Nick in the designated spot, then contact Sylvie and she'd be a witness. But not the only witness. What David hadn't told Sylvie was that he'd also asked Slice to come. When David had first heard Sylvie's plan, he was horrified.

"I can't double-cross him like that."

"But he's doing horrible things."

"Sylvie, I can't."

"Why not? What has he ever done for you except use you for his own ends?"

"I just can't."

"Okay, Nick or me. You choose."

And, in his anguish, he had chosen. He chose her, but he'd also asked Slice to be there. It would be Slice who turned Nick in, not David. Slice would be there as the arresting officer. Once committed to the plan, which was committing to Sylvie, he was desperate for it to work out. They'd gone over it so many times he was exhausted. Both would park near, but not in, the lab parking lot. She would wait in her own car, until he texted for her to come.

There were rows of shot-gun houses. Where they ended, an alley ran perpendicular behind the last few. A cement wall with graffiti flanked one side. David read in blue paint, *I saw Jesus yesterday*. He saw black stencils and the words: *You come to me, you die with me,* written underneath and he shivered, pushing away the sense of foreboding. Overgrown weeds from behind the wall crept over like conspiring assassins. He saw a lone car in DVX's vacant parking lot. He circled in the parking lot, allowing the swoosh in his stomach. He looked to his right and he saw the wagon Nick was using.

He parked on a side street, searching for Sylvie's Peugeot, and got out. A feculent stench leached into his nostrils. He began walking slowly, scanning the grounds, turning his head first one way then the other way.

He moved his large body with surprising speed, hopping a fence and landing with a *thud* on the other side. He radioed Slice to make certain he was in the unmarked car at the right spot. He was behind DVX now and he glanced to the windowless building. As he did, he saw something. Beside the lab, a man in a pink shirt was standing motionless. David squinted. The man was looking down at his phone. A disturbing thought ran through David's mind. But he didn't have time to pursue it, because from the opposite side of the man, David heard voices.

He heard the voices before he got there, and he stopped running, the crunch of the gravel beneath his heavy boots distracting and too loud. He listened in the silent hole of stillness and heard a foreign voice:

"I fill your body with holes if you try to stop me. Now just back off, and don't no one's gonna get hurt. That's right, stay right there."

"Drop the piece!" It was Nick's voice this time, but who was he talking to?

David lurched forward, gun before him. He turned the corner, to the abandoned lot just on the other side of the DVX parking lot. There he saw a slim man in a navy blue mechanic's suit with his back up against another graffitied wall. The man was crouching with bent knees, looking agile or nervous, and in his hand he held an automatic. Nick faced him, his shoulders squared, his feet braced, his blonde crew cut like a halo, and as David stepped closer to give Nick back-up, he realized he had to stop Sylvie. Without understanding what was happening, he backed up, madly texting Sylvie not to come, even while he knew he should run to cover Nick. Only later, when he reviewed the horrific unfolding over and over again in his mind, and in his texts, would he see what he'd done. In that crazed state of mind, texting Sylvie *not* to come, he had made two errors his phone auto-corrected. And without realizing, he sent the "corrected" text, and in so doing had instead told her to come to the scene.

He shoved the phone back into his pocket and leaped forward toward Nick. Nothing was going as planned. Minutes ticked by that felt like hours. Then out of the corner of his eye, he saw the pink shirt again. The man stepped forward and David saw his face. It was the guy from the lab!

Some twenty feet behind Nick, David lunged forward in a febrile rush, confused and distraught. Sylvie was double-crossing him. He stopped. What would he say to the man? His mind was spinning, figuring out what he should do when to his horror he saw Slice walking toward them too soon. David turned, his .38 out before him at stomach level. He motioned frantically to Slice to turn around at the same time he saw the little dog trot up from the opposite direction behind the second row of houses.

His senses blurred. It was all wrong! It wasn't supposed to go like this! The thought that Sylvie had betrayed him filled him with an explosive rage. First the pink shirt, now Weedy. Why was Weedy there?

"*Weedy*!" He heard her call, and for a moment he let the sound of her voice lathe his ears. "He's *loose*, David! He jumped from the car to follow me. Get him!"

In the next ten seconds he was swimming under water, fighting to save someone who'd slipped overboard. Everything happened so fast, yet when he recalled it, it was slow motion, like thick, dark molasses where he couldn't move his legs forward to act. Nick turned and David watched as his face registered Slice with confusion, then growing understanding.

Slice raised a gun as the man in the mechanic's suit, a Mr. Grady Smith, began to throw something over the cement wall. But Slice was not pointing it at Grady.

Gunshot broke the silence.

"*David!*" Slice yelled.

David jumped aside, aware he was leaving Nick wide open to the drug dealer. But he was still focused on executing Sylvie's plan, and it was also at that moment he'd seen his sordid chance. In the chaos, he leapt in front of Sylvie before Grady's bullets could find a home in her flesh, his thick boot kicking the dog forward with unusual force. And in the confusion, perhaps only Sylvie watched the face of her dog as the bullet found him.

But David heard him.

"*Aaaarrowff.*"

It was an odd sound, a sound more of sudden surprise than great pain. Weedy took a step then fell. There upon the dusty gravel the little dog lay on his side looking up over his shoulder to the girl who stared down at him in disbelief.

"*Weedy*!"

"Sylvie, get away!"

"*Wee-dee!*" She cried, pushing past David and collapsing beside the body, her hand reaching to touch the face that regarded her with a questioning look, but also with the serenity of complete trust. Then the head lay itself down and the small form was still.

Her cry did not come at once, perhaps she was too stunned, but David would hear it in the weeks afterwards reverberating throughout his tortured mind, and the smothering fog of guilt for actions he could never undo would seep into him like poison—the same feelings he had known all his life since the age of thirteen.

"*WEEEE-DEEEE!*"

It was a cry that halted his thoughts for seconds. A wail. It was the treble and tone that rent his soul like jagged glass and convinced him that she would never, ever live in this world again with anything close to normalcy. He had seen her face and heard her cry and there was no doubt in his mind that she would use any means on herself to follow the dog to wherever it had gone. And David knew he had to prevent that. At that instance he didn't know how, but his answer came to him a moment later.

As Sylvie flung herself on Weedy, trying to scoop him up, David ran to her. She swung her fists wildly at him, knocking him off balance, grabbing for his gun. He shoved her off.

"Sylvie, I'm here! It's okay."

"*No*! Help me! Forget the plan! Help Weedy!" David held out his hand and Sylvie ripped the gun from him. "Get away from me or I'll kill you!"

She was holding the gun out before her.

"Sylvie, no! Don't do it!"

"Get away from me or I swear I will pull the trigger!"

"Sylvie, please!" He leapt to the side, trying to fake her out, and lunged, swinging his fist hard at her left eye. Her head snapped back, the gun dropped from her hand and she fell to the ground next to Weedy. He grabbed his gun.

"Drop it," he heard Nick say. David's head was splitting.

He whirled around when he heard the three shots, followed in rapid succession by three more, and his mind ducked and darted making irrational leaps. There was the man from the lab, terror in his eyes. He turned and fled. David saw Nick, gun in hand, staring at Grady's inert body. Then David's reality ceased. He saw what couldn't possibly be. Slice lay on the ground some ten feet from Grady. David knew it was Slice, but few others would recognize the officer, aside from his uniform. In place of where the cranium had been there now bulged a purplish jell, dotted with gray mass.

Nick's arms dropped to his sides. He turned around to face David. "What the *fuck*? I mean what the *fucking hell* was that?

David couldn't speak. He staggered and his jaw trembled.

"What the fuck were you doing?"

"Nick," David began, lips still quivering. "Slice . . ." He was pointing his finger toward the body that lay still, apart from dark rivulets that pulsed from the torso.

"I'd say Slice got what was long overdue coming to him."

"Excuse me, is everything all right here?" Both David and Nick jumped at the sound of the female voice. "I've rung for an ambulance. One is presently on the way."

"Ma'am," Nick stammered. "Stand back."

The woman was short, in her late-sixties or seventies. A green, paisley head scarf covered her gray hair but a few strands slipped out around her face.

"I am quite adept in dramatic situations. Perhaps I can help."

"Thank you, Ma'am, but we have the situation under control." Nick's voice was taut.

"I note hostility in your tone, young man."

"What the—"

"I saw what happened. Perhaps I could be of help."

"Just hold on a minute, Ma'am."

Ignoring Nick, the woman shuffled over to the two slain men, first to Slice and then to Grady.

"*Ma'am!*"

She staggered and stopped, and when she turned back to face Nick, the look on her face spoke of the horror upon the ground in a way that words could not.

"Ma'am! Stand back! Please get away from them!"

The woman reeled, on the verge of vomiting, bent over and gulping out hiccupping sounds, but after several moments of deep breathing with her eyes shut, she seemed to collect herself. She spoke to Nick without looking toward the corpses again.

"You see, I am not afraid in times of crises. You might think an old woman like me would be. But I would prove you wrong.

Even in the face of something as atrocious and gruesome as what we witness before us. Nor am I afraid of scoundrels. But many are simply misunderstood," she said. "You must remember they were once somebody's child."

"*Misunderstood? What the fuck?!*"

"Your poor fellow officer," she spoke without looking to Slice. "Dying in the line of duty. What a brave sort he must have been. I suppose he had a wife and family. The grace in life is that they are not here to see what you and I must bear witness to."

"*Ma'am.* With all due respect. We've a somewhat urgent situation here. You need to leave this instant."

"But I can prove a most reliable witness."

"*Ma'am.*" A vein on Nick's forehead protruded. He lowered his voice, but there was a strained urgency. "Do you want to tell me what you think you saw?" He turned to David who listed to the side in shocked revulsion. David stumbled over to Sylvie and sat down on the ground like a child.

"David," Nick called.

David didn't look up. He checked Sylvie's pulse and breathing. "Sylvie?" he said, leaning over her. "Can you hear me?" He reached out a hand, allowing his fingers refuge in her hair. Her face was swelling where he'd hit her. Blood, perhaps the dog's, stained her shirt. The dog lay still beside her, and David glanced to him uncomfortably.

The woman followed Nick's gaze and saw the girl and the dog for the first time.

"Dear God. What happened? Was she shot as well? Is she also to be counted among the deceased?" She jostled over and knelt down next to the unconscious girl, and David felt a jealous and possessive urge sweep over him.

"She's all right. Just knocked out." He elbowed her away.

"Oh dear, oh dear. I must help. Here, let me—"

David saw two black boots stop in front of him and he looked up. Nick was towering above, but Nick was not looking at him. He was looking at the woman.

"Ma'am, perhaps you could be of help. Tell me, if you would, what you . . . saw." Had the woman seen the set of Nick's jaw, and had she seen his right hand fidgeting around his gun, she might have been afraid. But she seemed not to notice at all. She rose and looked into his cold, pale face.

"I saw everything."

"No. You saw shit. *Admit it!*"

"Excuse me?"

"You didn't see a damn thing, did you!?"

"Officer, I saw . . ."

"*What!? What did you see!?*" He was inches from her and he bellowed into her face. She stepped back uncertainly.

With what looked like supreme effort, she looked to the bodies of Grady and Slice, back and forth, before turning to Sylvie and Weedy. And finally to Nick, her eyes disbelieving. "Did the girl . . .?"

Nick squinted at her. "Did the girl w*hat?*" He spat.

"She . . ."

Nick stared down at her, his glare forcing her to take another step backward.

"Did she shoot him?" The woman was asking. David looked up and saw the incredulous expression on Nick's face, and for a moment no one spoke. David shivered as sweat made him cold in the night air. He heard Nick say, "You saw her shoot him? You actually *saw* it? You did, didn't you?"

"Yes, I saw it."

Nick was staring at her.

David stood, and Nick nodded his head up and down slowly.

David took a step forward, "No, she—"

"*Shut up, limp dick!*"

Nick turned back to the woman, smiling broadly.

"Yeah, she shot him, the sombitch. He was one hell of a notorious drug dealer. We've been trying to get him for months. It's done now."

"Yes, it's done now. He shot your fellow officer there, then she shot him. What a courageous girl. Oh my. But each individual life, no matter what mistakes were made, should have a chance." She bobbed her head from side to side. Emboldened, she began walking over to where the body of Slice lay. Nick followed close on her heels. "So young, such a long life ahead of him," she continued. "I believe he saved the lives of you two. You owe this poor gallant man your lives."

The woman bent bravely toward Slice and Nick said:

"*Step away from him!*"

A spasm jerked Slice's body, creating the sensation of life. The woman let out a anguished cry and fled.

"David!" Nick called, following her. "We'll have to write up a report. It won't look good that some young broad did away with Grady when you and I couldn't!" He made to laugh. "But truth is truth. Mrs . . ."

"Cartwell."

"Mrs. Cartwell here will be a reliable witness. And you and me, of course. We're much obliged to you, Mrs. Cartwell. Much obliged. Now, if I could quickly get a sworn statement from you."

"The poor, innocent thing." Alice Cartwell had shuffled away from Slice and stood hovering again over Weedy and Sylvie. Genuine compassion gave the empty words meaning.

A door slammed and lights had come on in several of the buildings.

"Hold on a minute," David began. "Nick, now you—"

"*David.* Come over here," Nick said tersely and motioned David out of earshot of Mrs. Cartwell. "You better listen to me good."

David glanced back at Alice Cartwell. He saw her look from Weedy to Sylvie and bend down. She untied her head scarf, placing it over the little dog's body and tied up the leg that bled. He watched as the green scarf took on a darker hue.

His mind was spinning out of control, and he closed his eyes to stop it. He was a boy again, trousers rolled mid-shin, letting the cold creek water wash him clean, his sister splashing her toes into the water, happy, his mother smiling at both, the defining events of childhood far away.

His mind continued to race. He would take Sylvie home to his apartment. He would be the first thing she saw when she woke up, and he'd explain gently the dog was gone, and he'd hold her in his arms and comfort her. But an uneasy feeling countered his thoughts, and told him she might not welcome that. And Sylvie might need medical attention. Only then did the idea bloom within his head. She'd loved the dog more than anything. He had to get out of there quickly. He would take the body to the SPCA and have it cremated for Sylvie like she'd said. Then she would see how sensitive he was. Then she would love him. Oh God, what had he done?

When David stopped talking, Eleanor said:

"She didn't kill either of them."

"No."

"But why did Mrs. Cartwell testify that Sylvie shot Officer Slice when she didn't know she did?"

"I don't know what Nick said to her later. I know he called her to go over the story. He went over the story with me, too. What could I do?"

"But you're certain Sylvie didn't shoot either of them."

"Yes."

"You'll testify in court won't you?"

"What do you mean?"

"We'll appeal her case. We'll prove it was an unfair trial."

"The woman already did."

A thought that had been nagging at Eleanor ever since her visit to Alice Cartwell was now answered.

"Mrs. Cartwell didn't see a thing. She came upon the scene afterwards, didn't she? She only repeated what you and your friend, Nick, told her to say and then she believed with complete conviction that she'd witnessed the entire drama. She must have been in shock after seeing the headless bodies at the time. That sort of trauma would wreak havoc with anyone's mind. You could have told her anything." Eleanor distinctly remembered hearing Mrs. Cartwell tell her, as they sipped tea together in her living room, that she had headed to the scene of the crime *because* she heard the shots fired. Therefore, she couldn't have witnessed the murders. She heard the gunshots, but that was all. She probably phoned for the ambulance before she saw any human figure, so great was her need to be of service.

"She saw what I told you she saw! What she told me and Nick she saw."

"Very well, but you will testify nevertheless, yes?"

He stared at the table.

"David?"

"Yes?"

Eleanor noted his jumping eyebrows, and their expression told her plainly he was hiding something, but she could have no way of guessing what. She continued:

"You believe in doing the right thing. You wouldn't have told me what had happened if you didn't."

He nodded, but wouldn't look her in the eye.

"Is there anything else you need to tell me?" She sensed he was withholding something more.

"I took her I.D. cards. Her real ones. I left the fake she used in the lab."

"I see."

"I was afraid she'd get in worse trouble."

Eleanor watched his face. "Were you also afraid you'd be caught for stealing dogs?"

"No! I'm telling you what I know. I was worried about her."

"You must continue to do the right thing. You'll testify, won't you? You'll tell the truth about what happened?"

"I already did."

"No. You testified for Nick, not Jane."

"What?"

"Sylvia, I mean."

"They'll think I was lying."

"That's all right, you were under duress. We'll work it out. David, you must."

An odd look was spreading over the handsome face.

"I don't know. Let me think on it." He shifted in his chair and Eleanor continued to stare watching the face change shape before her eyes.

Finally he looked into her eyes, and when he did he scowled. "*What*?"

Eleanor was often aware of the space that divided human expression from actual thought, how people frequently yearned to express a thought for which they had no words, how the uttered syllables fell short of the inspired thought. But now as she stared at David Sampson she found that thought and expression merged into one horrible word. She opened her mouth to speak:

"You."

"What?"

"You did it."

"What are you talking about?" A volatile brew of irritation and anger shadowed his brow.

"You shot—"

"No!" He yelled across at her. "It was Nick! Nick shot them both! That was his way. That was how he solved his problems."

Eleanor took in a breath and let it out, and when she spoke again, her voice was low and steady. "I wasn't talking about the murders." She watched David's face keenly. "I believe you. But," she began. "Grady Smith had no reason to shoot a dog."

She saw his eyes open wide. She saw the face contort as if he were about to explode a second time, then something altered. Perhaps it was that he felt great and final relief. Or perhaps he realized there was no way out.

"You set her up, and then you killed her dog."

"I had to. I mean, no! It was an accident! Really. I didn't set her up. The text auto-corrected. I swear! I *loved* her!" He was speaking fast.

"All right, all right."

"I did it because they could recognize that dog. She *stole* it, don't you see? They could kill her."

"She doesn't know it," Eleanor continued as if she hadn't even heard his words. "I don't know what she'd try to do if she found out the truth."

"I didn't mean to. Honest! I only meant to wound him. I wanted to rescue him and then she'd see I was good. I'd be a hero in her eyes."

"She *loved* her dog."

"I didn't mean to do it! I'm not a bad person. But I just wanted her to love me. She *did* love me! I know she did."

Eleanor was looking at him incredulously. She wondered if he'd ever been officially diagnosed, but she strongly suspected borderline personality disorder.

"She loved me, but her love for him was in the way. It was. I know that. I knew I could love her better than anyone else. I still know it."

Eleanor grimaced. "*Stop it. Just stop it.*"

"I'm not a bad person. I'm sorry. Really, you don't know how it was. I was jealous. I took her phone. I read her texts. She told that guy about our plan!"

Eleanor regarded him.

"I had to know! I was jealous of him."

"Who?"

"The guy from the lab. I read her texts. He's the reason she brought Weedy along. None of it would have happened."

"You took her phone and read her texts."

"But you can't tell her. You can't tell her I killed her dog. You *can't.*"

"I won't tell her. It will serve no purpose."

"It was an accident. I mean, I don't know why, I don't know how. . . Afterwards, I wanted to take it back, undo everything, make her dog live again. You can't know what I've suffered. And, and . . ."

Eleanor stared across at his contorted face, aware that he was struggling with something else.

"Please," he continued, the muscles in his face tense, the word strained. "That's not all. Listen. Listen to me. I have to talk to you. Please," he begged her.

"Go on," Eleanor said slightly nauseous.

"I'm not bad, really. But you see bad stuff, accidents, they follow me."

"What are you saying?" She asked him nervously.

"I'm saying that . . . I'm saying that I killed a boy. I killed a boy. I did. When I was thirteen."

Eleanor stared at him.

"Go on. Lock me up. I deserve it. I killed a boy and now a dog. But I've never killed anyone else. I'm a police officer and I've never used my gun."

"You're in your own prison. There's nothing I could do to lock you up further."

"It was an accident, see. He drowned. We were at his house, in his pool. He hit his head and drowned. But I pushed him in. But I didn't mean to. I never, ever . . . and all my life I've lived . . . . And then Sylvie's dog. And you don't know what

I've . . ." He was weeping. "I hate myself. I hate myself. But it wasn't my fault. But her dog was my fault. All my fault, but . . ."

Eleanor listened with a mixture of compassion and revulsion. She had no idea what to say. She thought about the inmates behind bars for committing rash acts. How many of them wished, seconds too late, for the moment back again and the chance to make a new decision, one whose outcome would not forever change lives? Or if it did, the change would lie in knowing they were women of restraint and wisdom, who did not succumb to impulse, opportunity or anger.

For the first time, Eleanor thought about Weedy in a different way. Only a few laws, nebulous at best, existed to protect his rights, and by extension the emotional well-being of the one who cared for him. Eleanor closed her eyes for just a second and she saw Jane's face filled with grief and sorrow. A rush of compassion, unlike any she'd ever known, filled her, illuminating what hours of questions posed to Jane could not uncover. The feeling was nudging a slumber that she had not wanted woken, but now as it persisted, she found part of herself awakening and with this new knowledge, she felt unbelievable joy. But the moment was short-lived, and she came back to the surrounding scene as though arriving in a traffic-clogged city from a hushed and sunlit meadow. David was talking, and she had not been listening to him. Not listening like his mother or father had most likely not listened to him. Was it ever that easy? Everything traced back to those carefree, torturous, idyllic, agonizing days of childhood?

"But that's not the worst. There's more," he was saying. "I blamed my sister. I blamed her and she couldn't defend herself. She had problems. She was retarded. At least that's what we called it back then. And I thought because of that she wouldn't get in trouble. But she did. They came and took her away. I loved her, my baby sister. And I couldn't see her. I found out later that she was raped in the mental house and she had a baby. All because of me. Because I blamed her."

As Eleanor sat still and watched David stumble and speak, she thought of Lewis holding Cory in his arms in attempt to lessen his loneliness. Perhaps, she thought then, having an affair was not the worst thing a man could do to the woman he loved.

"Haven't you ever done something you wish you could undo?" David asked, breaking her thoughts.

Eleanor looked across at the desperate face and into the officer's eyes. "Of course, I have," she answered quietly.

"Are you going to tell the police I killed that boy and blamed my sister?"

"You are the police. So I guess there's no need. Besides, it sounds to me like it was an accident. I'm sorry your sister was blamed, but you were a child. Children don't understand consequences like that." When he looked across at her, she saw something in him relax and change. "Where is she now?"

"Cilla? I don't know. I haven't seen her. If only I could find her, I'd care for her for the rest of her life, and I'd tell her I was sorry. Poor Cilla. Poor little Cilla."

The hair on Eleanor neck prickled. "Cilla?" She said, swallowing as if something toxic was lodged in her throat.

"It was short for Priscilla."

"Her name was Cilla? Cilla Sampson?" Eleanor asked calmly, all the while feeling a rampant beast set loose in her psyche.

"No. She was my half-sister. Cilla Hankins."

Eleanor became very still. It was as if the background hum of the restaurant stopped. Time froze. She opened her mouth to speak, and stopped herself. She couldn't talk about a patient, even to the police. Even to a half-sibling. But might he just be capable enough to care for her? Wouldn't a life with him be preferable to prison? They would have to do a home check, and he'd have to agree, but wouldn't it help them both? She could at least talk to Helen. Oh, Cilla!

"But Sylvie. You can't tell her about—" David said, unaware of the possibilities roaming through Eleanor's mind.

"I will not tell her." Eleanor said looking steadily into David's eyes. "But in return you will testify that it was your fellow officer who fired the shots that killed both Grady Smith and Officer Slice, I mean, Officer Bread. That girl is no murderer. She's suffered long enough."

He shut his eyes. "Okay," he said with his eyes still shut.

"Thank you, Officer Sampson. I must go." She stood. She was walking past him toward the door when she stopped.

"David. There is just one more thing." He had turned when he sensed her standing above him and now, his eyes open, he looked up at her with new fear. "What happened to the body? To Weedy?"

There was the slightest trace of peace across David's features when he replied, "I took him to the SPCA to be cremated. I thought one day maybe I could give her the ashes and she'd appreciate me." He stopped and Eleanor regarded him, waiting for him to continue.

"But you never went back," she said when he remained silent.

"No."

"Fine. Then I will then. You're not a bad person, David. I think you're a good person." She turned and walked to the door.

CHAPTER FIFTY-FOUR

A week had passed since Eleanor met with David, a week in which she had felt simultaneously like she was gasping for air in order to breathe, and also exhaling out great relief and tension. Time had stopped making sense. The words Jane had spoken came back to her: Time didn't exist.

But, now, as she sat across from Jane in the psych room she felt her senses heightened. Everything was intensified. The light and colors were sharper. It was the first time in the week that she'd felt like herself again. If also slightly panicked.

"Thank you."

"No. Thank you. You don't know it, but you've helped me," Eleanor replied.

Jane raised her eyebrows.

"Yes. Yes you have, but never mind that now. What will you do? What will be the first thing you do?"

"I don't know. I'm sort of dizzy thinking about it. I guess just walk. Outdoors. Feel," Jane's voice faltered, ". . . free. I just want to be able to see the sun when I want to. To go where I want to. Without handcuffs." She grinned.

Eleanor stared at the smiling face, to the dimples, then she turned slightly and followed Jane's gaze out the small window. New green leaves quivered on the trees. A gust of wind blew, bending a young tree, before it righted itself, its leaves fluttering up so that their pale undersides showed.

"To feel the air and the breeze. Watch a sunset. Walk my bare feet on the grass. Maybe go to the ocean."

Eleanor nodded, realizing no words she could utter could add anything to what Jane just expressed. Instead she said, "Here, take my card." She handed Jane a business card. "If you need a place to stay, you're more than welcome. If you don't need a place, come by anyway. We could make curled cookies together."

"Do you . . . do you—"

"I live alone, yes. My husband and I have separated."

"Are you okay?"

"Yes. Thank you."

"Sure?"

"Yes. Although . . ."

"Yes?"

"Although, I was thinking about, well, for some reason I was thinking about getting a cat."

"Oh, you should! You should go to the shelter. I can take you to the shelter. I'll introduce you. Let's go! We can go tomorrow! Well not tomorrow, but next week when I'm out. There are so many abandoned, yet wonderful—"

"Hold on a minute." Eleanor said, laughing. "I hadn't actually made a definitive decision."

"Definitive decision?"

"Whatever," Eleanor said, shaking her head and smiling.

"Get a cat. Just *do* it. Get a cat. You'll wonder how you ever lived without one."

"And you?"

"No."

"Even when there are so many dogs in need?"

Jane didn't answer and Eleanor knew better than to push her. She sat back in her chair. She would go to the S.P.C.A. that afternoon, but by herself, and not to get a cat. Neither one spoke for a moment.

"Jane," Eleanor began, "Sometimes inmates who have been locked up wrongly need time to adjust . . . time to get over anger or resentment. There are support groups that—"

"Thank you," Jane said. "But I think I'm okay. I won't need that."

"You think that now because of the relief you feel. But you don't know how you might feel in a week or so." Eleanor said, realizing that in a week or so she would not have Jane sitting before her. She wanted to be the one to take Jane to the support group. She was thinking this when Jane's words interrupted all thought:

"Dr. Hartley, I knew all along."

"Knew what?"

"I knew I didn't do it. I knew I didn't kill those men."

Eleanor stared, not understanding. Never had she seen a more serene face. "You told the court you shot them. You told *me* you shot them, or at least that you didn't know."

"I know. I'm sorry. I guess I really did have moments of confusion. Sometimes, especially afterwards, I wondered if maybe I'd shot them both. Sometimes I believed it. But it didn't really matter one way or the other, did it?"

"But why? Why didn't you say something to the contrary if there was even the slightest doubt? Why admit to it?"

The look was not so much confused as it was certain. "I knew I didn't do it," Jane said again evenly. "It didn't much matter, did it?" She said again.

"But you were blamed. The whole world condemned you for two heinous crimes you didn't do."

"But I knew. That's what matters, right?"

"I don't know, if it means you stay locked up in prison. What good could you do the animals locked up yourself?"

"I didn't care what anyone thought," Jane said, not answering Eleanor's question.

Eleanor studied Jane's face. "You didn't want to leave prison, did you?"

Jane was quiet.

"That was why, wasn't it? You believed the lie. You believed you deserved to be locked up."

Jane was silent.

"Jane?"

"I guess I thought I deserved it. I stole him. Of course that was wrong. Not by my code of ethics. But society would deem it wrong. But what was really wrong was that I killed him."

"You didn't kill him. You gave him the only love he ever knew."

"None of it matters now." Eleanor saw Jane try to smile, but there was bitterness behind the smile.

"I think love always matters, and I think you think that, too."

Jane didn't speak.

"Your being locked up in prison like them doesn't help them. You could empathize, but what good did it do?"

"Somehow it made it all right. All right that I had failed them all."

"You didn't fail them—"

"I couldn't—"

"What?"

"Weedy . . ."

"You couldn't go back to your life without him. That's why prison was okay."

Jane's gaze was steady, but Eleanor saw the tears threatening.

"Then what are you going to do now?"

Again Jane was silent.

"Do you have friends you can stay with?"

"*Carol,*" Jane whispered.

"Is there anyone?"

"I forsook my best friend when all this happened. I was afraid she'd be implicated. I couldn't risk that. And then . . ." She closed her eyes. "And then Weedy was dead. I just couldn't tell Carol how badly I'd fucked up. I wish I could talk to her, but I know she's given up on me. It's for the best. Who lies to her best friend and says she's moved away and is doing fine? Who just abandons her best friend when her husband is dying?" Jane paused. "Sorry. To answer your question, no, I don't really have anyone."

"Well, you can stay with me," Eleanor offered again. "If you want to. For as long as you need. I could be your family."

Jane didn't answer.

"If you need a place to stay."

"That's kind of you. Thank you. I think I'll be okay," Jane said.

"Are you sure? Where will you go?"

"You've helped me."

Eleanor looked down. "I'm glad I could help." She could feel Jane still looking at her. She looked up and met Jane's eyes.

"I will, you know."

"Be okay?" Eleanor asked.

"I'll get another. In time."

"Of course," Eleanor answered.

"We become what we seek."

"What were you seeking, Jane?"

"This. I loved him so much, I killed him. Shakespeare had something to say about that, I think. But I learned from it. I know now that I can love. All of them, just as much as I loved him. All of everything, everybody, all life."

"That's beautiful," Eleanor said unconvincingly. She broke eye contact. There was so much she wanted to say. Their time was almost up and she felt a rush of panic. She didn't want it to end. She remembered back to her first session with Jane, how stretched her nerves had been. How impatient she'd been to have the session over and finished. It seemed like lifetimes ago.

"Well." Eleanor cleared her throat.

Jane gave her an easy, gentle smile.

"Here, I have something for you. I mean other than a business card." Eleanor reached to the side and brought up her old brown briefcase. She pulled out a bulky object wrapped in tissue paper.

"Here."

Jane took the package from her.

"Soon you can hang them up in a tree somewhere and know that Weedy is near."

As Jane unwrapped the gift, Eleanor was not prepared for the joy that flooded her face. She held up the metal wind chimes, her arm extended, and as Eleanor listened to the gentle notes forming as each hollow bar touched against the other, she imagined the breeze. It seemed a pause unrelated to any time she'd ever known. And they sat for a moment without talking, the only sound that of the wind chimes as one note became the next.

"They're beautiful. Thank you."

"Will you think of him when you listen to them?"

"Yes," Jane's gray eyes looked back at Eleanor. "I'll think of him and I'll remember how it was. And I'll know he's with me."

Eleanor listened to chimes fade and she wondered if Jane would also remember how it was here in this room with her therapist. She knew that she would remember. She knew how hard it would be to sit in the room when Jane had gone, and she understood, as Jane had also realized during her stay behind bars, that perhaps remembering well was not the only homage one could offer. One could learn how to love again.

CHAPTER FIFTY-FIVE

Dressed in a pale blue suit that matched the sky above, Eleanor stepped out of her car and regarded the tattered building with apprehension that was at the same time giving way to curiosity about something she knew had once been a part of Jane. The same way a teen may take joy in finding a certain idolized movie star likes Dr. Pepper over Coke or Tupac over Snoop Dogg.

When she pulled open the door to the shelter a muted background noise of barking dogs and the pungent smell of animals greeted her. A wave of admiration ran through her for Jane. In front of her at the main desk a woman was pulling a furry white dog on a leash and Eleanor smiled at the lucky little dog getting a home. She waited patiently behind, wishing to be overheard by as few people as possible, aware that her question was going to sound unusual.

The woman in front of her was speaking to a girl behind the desk and Eleanor overheard pieces.

"Chews up everything when we leave, and peed all over the rug. I just can't keep a dog like that." Eleanor glanced to the dog again, this time stricken. She glanced to the woman then to the girl behind the desk for some reaction, but there was none, and she seemed to accept this information with indifference, leaning forward scribbling notes on a paper, while the woman with the dog continued listing the dog's many misdeeds.

"Carol!" The girl behind the desk called, speaking for the first time. Another volunteer, about Jane's age, walked out from behind a door, letting through a burst of loud barking as she did.

"A surrender. Can you take her back?"

"*Vivi*!" Carol exclaimed and ran to the white dog, smiling, but as she glanced to the woman, the smile lost its sheen. "Didn't work out?"

"No, I'd say not. She purposely peed all over everything she possibly could and ripped to shreds—"

"Did you leave her alone a lot?"

"Look, I'm not independently wealthy, I do have to work. She's just not a good dog."

"Come on Vivi," Carol said and walked back through the swinging door as the woman snapped her head back around toward the desk not watching her dog walk away.

When it was Eleanor's turn, she advanced hesitantly. She saw the girl behind the desk now plainly. She wore a harassed and tired expression, and glanced up at Eleanor but offered no greeting.

"What will happen to Vivi?" Eleanor asked timidly. All of a sudden she was filled with the rash idea of helping the poor dog, a thought struggling to become deed: she would adopt Vivi for Jane.

The girl flattened her lips into something like a duck's beak, and said, "She's cute, she'll get a home with someone who's got half a brain and can care for her." She shook her head. "I swear, *people*. What do they want? Are they forgetting you have to *care* for a dog? I mean—" She stopped abruptly, perhaps reconsidering speaking her thoughts aloud, and stared at Eleanor as if to say, "Okay, what do you want?"

Eleanor had been nodding in agreement as the girl spoke and now she felt the absurdity of her belated mission. "This is going to sound peculiar," she began, "But, what do you do with cremations that aren't picked up?"

The girl shot Eleanor a look that she could easily interpret. "Happens all the time. What do you think we do?"

"I—"

"When was it?"

"About two years ago, maybe a year and—"

"*Two years ago*?"

"Yes, I didn't hold much hope that—"

"Never had anyone come back two years later. May I ask why you want it now?"

"It's for someone else. It wasn't my dog. It would be to give to the person . . ."

"Yeah, yeah," the girl said and Eleanor knew she didn't believe her. "Well, I'm sorry."

"I understand. Thank you, just the same." Eleanor turned to leave then stopped. "Did you know Sylvia Marshall?"

The girl looked at her blankly.

"She worked here," Eleanor offered. "Or rather she volunteered sometimes, I think."

"How long ago?"

"Two—"

"Right, two years ago. Huge turnover here. It's hard. You know the work can be very depressing. I didn't know her." Just then Carol came back through the doors with an angry expression on her face.

"I can't believe she brought Vivi back. But *good,* I'm glad. Vivi shouldn't go to someone like that lowlife anyway. You know what? I may take her myself. Matt and I could use the company of a sweetie pie. Our little constellation of three could definitely stand to grow. Always good to take in more stars, right?"

"I have no idea what you're talking about ninety percent of the time," the girl behind the desk said shaking her head without looking up at Carol.

Eleanor felt a prickle along her spine. She was still standing regarding the two girls when they turned and looked at her at the same time. She was more than ready to get out of the depressing place and she'd only been there fifteen minutes. Yet something Carol had said lodged in her brain. She felt unable to turn around, and she stared at Carol instead. "Constellation," she said dumbly.

"Right. Don't mind me. I say bizarre things all the time. Honoring a friend of mine."

"Did you by chance know of a Sylvia Marshall?"

Carol stood very still without moving or speaking. Then something gurgled in her throat. Her eyes began to glisten. She stumbled as she took a step toward Eleanor, a twisted look painting her face with shades of disbelief. "How did you know?"

Eleanor did not understand. "Know what?"

"Sylvie. Why did you ask me that just then?"

"What?"

"*Sylvie.* Do you know her?"

Eleanor's mouth trembled as she stood looking at Carol.

"Who are you? Do you know her?" Carol asked again.

"I worked with her," Eleanor replied in a shaky voice.

"You worked with her?"

"Well, not like, I mean I—"

"Where is she? Where is Sylvie? What happened to her?" Carol demanded, speaking faster, like she was not in control of her words. "She just up and vanished. I mean truly vanished. She said she was going to go out west to see her mom and she'd call. But she never called, except to leave two very strange and brief messages, and that's not like Sylvie to say she'll do something and then not. Like, all of a sudden she just disappeared and we phoned and phoned but she never returned the calls. I needed her, in ways you cannot imagine."

Eleanor's chest heaved once and she let out a ragged sob.

"What's wrong? Are you all right?"

"Yes, yes. There has been a terrible mistake," Eleanor gasped, regaining her voice. "But she's okay. She's okay. But I must let her explain to you."

"Explain what? What happened to her? Where is she? Please tell me."

Eleanor was overwhelmed. She glanced around for a chair. It was like being in a foreign land where she didn't quite understand the language, but she was beginning to trust her instincts. Who else was out there who might have provided clues to Jane's innocence? What was wrong with the world?

"She was locked up in prison unjustly," she stated flatly to Carol. She felt the guilt of discussing what by right was Jane's alone to divulge, but then she thought that perhaps it would alleviate the astonishment and questions when Jane came back to her friends to explain, if she did come back.

"*Prison?*"

"I can't really discuss it now. I came because her dog. Weedy."

"She was put in prison for stealing Weedy? That's absurd. Oops," Carol looked around the shelter like the F.B.I. might be lurking. "I have not told another living soul about what she did. Even my husband doesn't know everything."

Eleanor nodded.

"She didn't want to involve me. Right? That's why she never called. That's just like her. Especially with Matt going through—" She stopped, bending over and taking a deep breath.

"You knew her dog, Weedy?" Eleanor began again.

"Of course, I knew Weedy."

"His body was dropped off here, and his ashes were to be collected and never were. So that's why I came, because I was wondering—"

"What are you talking about?"

"I know it sounds strange, but—"

"What are you talking about? Weedy's here. He's back there, right now."

"You knew Weedy?" Eleanor whispered, not yet able to grasp the meaning of Carol's words.

"You don't understand, of course I knew Weedy. Sylvie acquired him in a most unconventional manner. Well, I guess I just blurted it, although I promise that was the first time ever. He was a particularly pathetic case. If you'd have seen him at the beginning like I did, a real mess. But Sylvie worked miracles with that dog. And then at first I didn't know it was Weedy. This idiot banging on the door at 1 a.m. and won't stop, and thank God Donna was back there then. The idiot wants the body cremated and the dog isn't even dead. *That* was a first for us."

She was talking fast with the excitement of one who's found a friend who shares an interest and with the joy of retelling a dramatic, but happy memory. "But who would recognize anything, he was covered in blood. His front leg was nicked by a bullet and all messed up. Then when he came back from the vets, I was so happy to be able to tell Sylvie he was okay and would live. But Sylvie was gone. And I didn't see how Sylvie could part with him."

"How—" Eleanor began, but Carol continued talking.

"I worried something awful had happened. How'd he end up like that? Shot? Had Sylvie been shot too? Sylvie was always so strong, nothing bad ever happened to her. She was my strength, my crutch. For as long as I can remember, if Sylvie was there, I'd be all right. No matter what. She told me she was leaving, and we argued. I felt awful about it after, but—" Carol stopped. "Then, I picked up that strange voice message and I could tell something was wrong. She was trying not to cry. Sylvie didn't cry easily. Said she was excited about going, and taking Weedy, too. But I had Weedy, *so what was going on*? I started thinking something was seriously wrong. Either that or she'd lost her mind. How could she part with Weedy? She'd loved him more than I've ever seen anyone love an animal. Or love *anything*. But we couldn't reach her. Her phone disconnected. Nothing made sense. I went to her apartment and all her furniture and things were still there. I went to the cops, but then I was scared. Because she'd taken Weedy. So I let it drop."

"I was going crazy. Really, seriously crazy. Sylvie was never very big on technology. She didn't like to text, wasn't always great about calling. But then I got the message that said she'd made it to California. Weedy was fine. Something about her mother, who I knew she'd not been in contact with. I figured she'd explain to me when she was ready. That was her way. I missed her more than I can say, but my husband . . . it was a bad time in my life. I had to let it go for the moment. But I always thought . . ."

She paused for a breath. "The only part that didn't make sense was Weedy. How she could have left him. Why did she say he was with her? What had happened to him that he got hurt?" She stopped as if remembering the exact sequence of events. Then it was as if understanding illuminated Carol and, staring at Eleanor, she let out a strange, lone cry, "*Oh my God. Sylvie was in prison*? They should have put me in there. I was the one who told her to go undercover at DVX."

All the while Carol had been talking, repeating the same story in her confused memory of events, Eleanor was hearing snippets incompletely, because it was at that moment the slow seepage of understanding had begun. A thought, a flash of realization, one waiting for the other to catch up and connect and then faster, raging, unconceivable. It was like a sluggish daydream freed from centuries of repression, emerging now to both terrify her and elate her in its promise to at last become life. She began to sob in loud sloppy hiccups. She was speaking through her tears, but her words apart from, "Are you sure? Are you absolutely certain?" And, "*Weedy,*" were incomprehensible.

"It's okay, it's okay," Carol soothed, holding Eleanor's arm.

"I have to sit. I have to sit down," Eleanor sobbed.

"*Prison,*" Carol repeated again. "There was this guy, big and tough, with a crew cut like some Nazi. He came here one day, asking questions, and said something about Jane at the lab. I knew he was talking about Sylvie, so I kept quiet. He said he'd been undercover at DVX with her. That he knew she was undercover, but she didn't know he was. I thought he was trying to get me to talk, and I worried that he knew about Weedy. I didn't say anything."

"She thinks Weedy is dead," Eleanor said.

"No," Carol said in hushed disbelief. "Weedy dead? Oh, Sylvie! Oh *no,* poor Sylvie. He was all that mattered to her. Here, yes, sit. You don't look good."

"I'm fine," Eleanor said as Carol steered her around to a chair against the wall. "It's a miracle."

Carol looked at her funny. "That's what Sylvie always said. It's like you've brought her back to life for me. Sylvie always said miracles happen in threes. And this is it. Weedy was the first miracle. And then my husband was next, right around the same time. He was supposed to die. Misdiagnosed. He had a horrible and rare infection. I needed Sylvie desperately. And now you've brought her back to me. She's miracle number three. Sylvie, you were so right!" Carol shouted to the ceiling like Sylvie was up there hiding.

"Sylvie said that?" Eleanor said after a moment. "That miracles . . . ?"

"Yup, and she was always right whenever she pronounced something." Carol stopped and looked around the room. A cat leapt onto the desk. "I can't believe any of this is happening."

"But Weedy. You can't let him be adopted. Do not let Weedy be—"

"No, no, don't worry. He lives with my husband and me. My constellation of three. I bring him to work. He has a staff position. He's so even-tempered now, we use him to acclimatize really scared dogs. We'd never adopt him out."

"But he's Sylvie's!" Eleanor leapt up.

"Of course." Carol smiled and burst into song, startling Eleanor even more. "*Someone to watch over me.* Or Weedy, rather.

That's why I kept him. I always kept up the hope that Sylvie would call and come back and all would be like it was before. But Sylvie, she's my best friend, I need to see her. How can I see her?"

"I'll tell her. You'll see her. I'm sure she wants to see you, too. Now I . . . I would like to see Weedy."

"Okay, but he might look different from when you knew him."

"I never knew him. I just feel like I did."

"He's missing a leg. The bone in his front leg was shattered. He would have bled out, but someone tied up his leg. He was in shock or unconscious. I guess I can see how the idiot thought he might be dead. I *guess*." Carol kept talking and leading Eleanor by the arm, and although she was still sniffling, Eleanor knew she had never in her life been happier than at that moment entering a hallway filled with barking dogs and reeking of urine.

CHAPTER FIFTY-SIX

It was dark when Eleanor rose, slipped into her car and drove east to greet the rising sun. The sun set and the sun rose, all in balance and harmony, allowing human discord its ripple across the timeless surface and the illusion that it could alter any lasting course.

She drove past the turn off for the penitentiary, past the swarming subdivisions, and wound her way up the small hill that called itself a mountain on the green street sign, to the top where the grade was too steep to build. She turned her car towards the overlook, a favorite spot for teenage lovers to attempt their clumsy sex, and turned off the engine. From her seat she could look out to the vista of the countryside, dotted here with farmhouses and estates, there with growing shopping centers and suburbia. She waited. The sun was just beginning to emerge on the horizon, and she saw the valley below shadowed in the hush of dawn until the sun climbed higher, shortening shadows and burning out darkness. She rolled down her window.

The air that embraced her was cool and pure. How could the girls in the penitentiary live without feeling this? She breathed it in, closing her eyes.

She thought of the families, slowly waking to the new day, rising from bed and trudging into kitchens for freshly brewed coffee. Sitting down to kitchen tables pouring milk over Raisin Bran and spooning it into groggy mouths, or maybe cooking up pancakes, the comforting smell seeping into dreams. Flipping on the morning television or checking tablets to ensure nothing drastic had occurred during the night of slumber. The morning news blared into the psyche, eroding a nighttime of dreams and the slowly receding reality of the night and dream-life slipped away, and yet it had once been more real than the harsh reality of morning. Perhaps for some, then, dreams were the last, best refuge.

She wondered if Lewis thought about her as he rose each morning in his rented apartment. Was he still seeing Cory or had guilt bore its way into his conscience, forcing the cessation of carnal activity and, in so doing, denying the recipients their greatest assault against mortality? She opened her eyes and watched the glitter of the awakening suburbs, wondering how it would feel to not "be." She wouldn't feel. She would simply not be.

She heard a dog barking in the distance. *Arrwf, arrwf, arrwf,* three times, then stop. *Arrwf, arrwf, arrwf,* three more times. The birds were already telling the world a new day was dawning.

She thought about Officer Sampson and his notion of goodness. Again she thought to herself that it was not the desire for happiness that made people do the things they did. But perhaps she could help him. She had spoken with Helen and there was a chance, albeit slim, that Cilla could be released. She hadn't said a word yet to Cilla, and she thought about her and the traumas she'd endured throughout life. No help from anyone. No understanding. Only loss, upon loss. Brother, child, freedom, dignity. She would do everything she could to help right the wrongs perpetrated. She had to focus on the possibility not the improbability.

She thought about Shina Jones, brilliant and beautiful, so close to freedom, until the hand of fate tempted her to live up to her own notion of justice. Who are we kidding? We're no more in control than a baby is at birth. We think we have control then an event occurs that makes a mockery out of even the most planned-out life.

She thought about a girl who had loved a dog, and in that moment, Eleanor's anxious joy was tinged with fear, and nearly too great to contain. Jane would see Weedy this week. This one thing that Eleanor had done seemed to her now the only one good thing she had ever done—but at least it was that. Cars were moving on the roads below. The valley was coming to life. Already the light had changed. She felt the promise of spring touch her as a breeze came through the open window. She believed she, too, could love that dog because—it had taken her this long—she knew that she loved the girl. She turned the key in the ignition, started her car and backed up.

CHAPTER FIFTY-SEVEN

"How are you doing today, Shina?"

Shina sat across the desk from Eleanor without the handcuffs this time. Eleanor had seen to that.

"I don't need none of your Miss Mary Poppins bullshit this morning. I'm doing as well as can be expected, so just keep your mouth shut."

"Shina, I've arranged to get you out of the holding cell. I've spoken with Mrs. Hollit, the I.H.O. As you know, you have the right to a witness. You have the right to a staff advisor. And you have the right to question your accuser, which in this case . . . " Eleanor's tone changed and she didn't finish. "What you may not know," she began again more forcefully, "because I didn't know, is that you also have the right to use my notes and testimony to help you in your case, to get you a lesser offense, or to clear you completely. That is, if I'm agreeable to it. Which I am."

Shina stared at Eleanor without moving or blinking. "What can *you* say? Mimi's *dead.*"

"I know she is. But I can say what I know to be true. I'm not saying you didn't—" Eleanor found the words hard to say. "That you didn't kill Mimi. That's not what's in question. We're all in agreement there, aren't we?" She asked, thinking suddenly that all she needed was another girl falsely accused of doing something she hadn't done.

Shina nodded her head once, looking down at the desk.

"Yes, but what I can help you prove is that it was an accident, and also that your action against Mimi was provoked. Right?"

Shina watched Eleanor as she spoke.

"I can say that there was a history of animosity between you and Mimi and I don't believe that you were ever the instigator. *Ever*," she repeated. As Eleanor spoke the words, she felt disloyalty for the unhappy girl with whom she had worked in this same room. But Mimi was gone. She couldn't help her now. Shina was here, and she could help her. She knew without a doubt that Shina Jones was not dangerous. She believed too that Shina would be an asset to any company or work place or husband or future family on the outside world with whom she chose to apply herself.

"I will state that you did not intentionally try to hurt Mimi Kramer. It was a horrible, unfortunate accident, and she brought it on herself."

Shina sat still for a few moments. When she spoke, it was in a low, confident tone. "Dr. Hartley," she said then paused. "I tell you something and you listen good." She paused again. "You listening?" And with the words, Eleanor smiled.

"I am, Shina."

"I'm not sorry I did it. I mean, I'm sorry Mimi's dead. As many times I mighta wished her dead, I never wanted to see her dead, as in the flesh dead. But I ain't sorry I stood up for Cilla, and I'd do it again today knowing my consequences 'cause what's right is right. Otherwise, what's the point of all us girls being in here in prison in the name of justice? Some justice. Hmpf." She stopped, looked down to the floor but she continued, "And you could stand to take a page outta my book."

Eleanor swallowed and opened her mouth to reply, but Shina continued.

"You know what else?"

Eleanor waited.

"You a good soul, Dr. Hartley. A real good soul," Shina repeated, and Eleanor shifted, turning her head to look out the tiny window.

CHAPTER FIFTY-EIGHT

"Is it all right if I see Jane tomorrow, one last time?"

Helen had stared at her then spoken the few terrible words. "Jane has been released, Eleanor."

"What? She's already gone?"

"Yes. You knew that. The officer's statement is on record. We didn't need a retrial."

"No. *No.* She said you told her she had to get her housing sorted out," Eleanor had blurted in a rush. "She can't be *gone,* Helen. I need to see her, I have her *dog.* I mean, I'm going to have him."

"Eleanor . . ." Helen looked flummoxed shifting through paper on her desk.

"Where has she gone? Just tell me where she is. Please."

"Get yourself together. She's somewhere."

"I know, but where? I need to know."

"Oh, wait. Right, right, right. You're right." Helen laughed and looked almost as relieved as Eleanor. "You always are. She's still here. She had trouble getting housing. A convicted felon."

"But she's *not.*"

"I know but—"

"And neither am I."

"What?"

"Always right. I am most definitely not always right."

Helen looked at her in puzzlement.

"She can stay with me."

"I don't understand."

"It's no longer in conflict with my work. I'd like that. Of course, if she would, that is."

"Have you okayed that with Lewis?" Helen eyed Eleanor skeptically.

"Lewis has left me."

"*What?* Oh, *Eleanor.*"

"Hi," Jane said as she walked into the psych room in her street clothes, a worn pair of blue jeans and a loose white T-shirt.

"Hi," Eleanor answered, aware of a diffidence that had crept up between them now. But perhaps, she thought, only she felt it, and Jane was only thinking of being free. And maybe only she felt it because, now, she had no real purpose in Jane's life.

Jane smiled at the chair as if she and it shared a secret and sat down as she always had. Only this day was different. It was her last day.

"How do you feel?"

Jane nodded her head, "Good."

"You look good," Eleanor said, willing her face not to blush. "It's strange seeing you in something other than the dramatic white scrubs." When Jane didn't answer, Eleanor continued. "Which I thought somehow always suited you well."

Jane smiled and ran a hand through her hair, pushing it out of her face.

"I was wondering," Eleanor began. "Will you be Jane even once out of here? Or will you go back to Sylvia again?"

"I don't know. I guess I'll just have to wait and see. Maybe it's time to be me again. Sylvie. But take with me what I've learned from Jane."

"I see," Eleanor said, nodding. "I have something for you," she said, changing the subject.

"I can't wait to hang my wind chimes. They're so beautiful, but you didn't—" Jane stopped and Eleanor read in her unspoken words the slight embarrassment—no doubt born of the showering of gifts and, at one point in her life, Eleanor would have, in deciphering the emotion, felt the embarrassment extending to herself.

"Well, this is along those lines . . ." she began. "But I don't think you could possibly guess in a million years—" She felt her throat clench and she couldn't finish.

"A million years," Jane said, smiling again, and raising her eyebrows in amusement. "That's a long time. I won't try, then." But when Eleanor produced no package from her briefcase, Jane said, "I've decided not to go undercover again. It didn't help anything. But I want to work to end animal testing, for the sake of the animals and for humans. Did you know that ninety-five percent of drugs that test safe or effective in animal tests later fail in humans?"

"No, I didn't know that."

"I want to do whatever I can to help the new technology out there, like organs-on-chips. I don't know how, but I'll find a way."

Eleanor nodded.

"And I've also decided to go to the shelter. That's right, I'm going to ask them for their most ugly and unadoptable dog." She'd been looking at Eleanor and she paused and looked away. "Weedy would've wanted that."

Eleanor caught her breath. "That's just it. Maybe you'd better wait."

Jane glanced up and there was the quizzical look Eleanor had come to know. "Why's that?" Jane asked.

"Because—" Eleanor began, but she couldn't get out the words. She stopped, and in that moment Jane must have seen something was wrong.

"What is it?" she asked gently as Eleanor sat in front of her patient with tears wetting her eyes, unable to stop herself. "What's wrong?" Jane asked again. This time, it was she who stood and walked around to Eleanor. She squatted down next to the chair, stroking Eleanor's back and speaking in soothing tones. "It's okay. It's okay, whatever it is. I'll help you." But it was too much and Eleanor cried the tears she'd tried to hold in her whole life. The emotion too strong, she just had to let herself cry as she listened to Jane's gentle voice.

After promising that she'd continue working at the penitentiary, she had coaxed Helen into giving her permission to bring Weedy in, and he was waiting patiently down the hall with the guard. She wiped at her face.

"I'm so sorry." She looked at Jane for a moment and saw her concern. She realized at the same time how she must herself look. "I'm okay."

"You don't look it."

"I am. I have . . . never . . . ever . . . in my life been happier. And . . ." Now she was laughing, almost feverishly. "Those were tears of joy because I may never, ever be this happy again. I'm okay. Really. Go sit back down for just a minute. Just a minute, I promise. And I'll be right back." She looked into Jane's eyes, to the face that was questioning her, but that she knew now had always trusted her. She laughed again, more sanely. "Just believe me, you are going to have to be sitting down for this one. The very last thing I want is to give you a heart attack. And thank you. Thank you for trusting me."

Jane did as told. Eleanor stood, opened the door and left the psych room. She walked down the hall and turned the corner. And it was as if she was beginning a new life when she saw the little dog, standing balanced on his three legs beside the guard, watching her, almost as if he knew what was happening and had been waiting for her to walk into their lives for a very long time.

"Thank you, so much," she said to the guard when she approached. "Thank you." She bent down, and patted Weedy's head with the light touch of someone unused to animals. Yet someone familiar with emotion, and again tears stung her eyes. "I think this is going to make you just as happy as it's made me . . . and . . ." She couldn't finish, and she remained squatting before Weedy, staring through her tears into the quiet brown eyes.

Outside, something timeless, untouched by sorrow, was speaking in softer tones. Birds called back and forth and a breeze lifted leaves. She felt more than joy. She felt peace.

"Come with me now, Weedy." She stood and the guard handed over the nylon leash. And as Eleanor walked down the penitentiary hall leading Weedy toward the room, she spoke softly:

"Come on, Weedy. Let's go home."

ACKNOWLEDGMENTS

Despite the solitary nature of writing, many people help contribute to an author's work. Special thanks to Cecilia Soprano, artist extraordinaire, for drawing the spider's web and designing the cover with my own dog Sparkle's face. To Kathryn Ponn Muhler for helping proof for typos. To Audrey Brent for spurring me along. To Andrea Hurst and Sean Fletcher.

And gratitude as always to Ted, John, Amy, Sue, Margaret, Waverly and Kathryn for being there.

ABOUT THE AUTHOR

Author photo by Ted Pfaltz, www.Maxxis7.com

Kay Pfaltz works with numerous animal welfare organizations to help bring about more peace and compassion to our animal friends. To this end, she donates all profits from her books to animal advocacy groups. For more information, visit www.Kaypfaltz.com.

NOTE TO THE READER

The Things We Do was originally titled, *Stone Walls Do Not a Prison Make,* after Lovelace's poem, but I felt that title too cumbersome. This was a novel I worked on, visiting the Women's State Penitentiary for research, and then put aside for many years. When I decided to return to it, addressing more of the issue close to my heart, animal testing, much had changed in a short period. The digital age was well upon us. I adapted the manuscript slightly to fit the times, but my focus remained with animal testing.

Another difference with this text and the original manuscript (spoiler alert for those who haven't yet read the book) is that in the original, I ended with Chapter 54 when Eleanor meets with Jane and gives her the wind chimes, realizing that, "perhaps remembering well was not the only homage one could offer. One could learn how to love again." In other words, I did not bring Weedy back to life. I still think that made for a more realistic and literary novel. Yet, I find that as I age, I don't mind a happier ending. There is enough darkness in the world, why not let a little dog live? In a way, I felt I was actually saving one laboratory dog in letting Weedy live. I know I'm not alone in my sentiment because when my agent was shopping my first dog-story books, many a response was: "I don't want to read it if this dog dies." This seemed odd to me because, unless one has a parrot or an elephant, our animals do usually predecease us. But death needn't be a thing to be feared. In fact, it can be beautiful, if the life was well lived. It's a life of suffering one should fear, and that's what I try to address with the animal testing issue or any other issue of abuse, be it concerning humans or animals.

I realize for any animal lover this story is difficult, despite a happy ending for Weedy. I've written about some of the more difficult circumstances because turning a blind eye and pretending animal atrocities don't occur, be it factory farming or general abuse, doesn't make them go away. If we truly care for exploited animals, we will have the courage to see the truth and act, even in small ways, where we can with compassion and purpose.

I hope I have not come across too heavy-handed with my message and attempt to educate. It's never fun when an author's agenda is made obvious. If my message is too blatant or blunt, I ask your forgiveness. But there is a pressing need to speak out.

On February 3, 2017, the current administration shut down the Animal Welfare Database. On February 13, 2017, the Physicians Committee for Responsible Medicine and a coalition of other organizations took legal action to bring it back. A day later, 100 members of Congress sent a letter to the president. Four days later, the USDA restored a few documents, but most remain hidden from the public view.

As of publication of this novel, the database, which included inspection reports of research facilities, testing laboratories, and other institutions regulated under the federal

Animal Welfare Act and Horse Protection Act, remains essentially missing.

What you can do to help: visit PCRM.org/Database to tell Congress that the USDA must restore its animal welfare database. Donate to your local animal advocacy groups. Educate yourself about what goes into your food, or what goes on behind the walls of research laboratories, who lobbies for which pharmaceutical companies, and speak up with intelligence and compassion. There is much new and innovative technology, such as organs-on-chips, that is safer for and more relevant to humans and doesn't involve animals. Let's spread compassion, understanding and awareness to those willing to listen, and bring about a kinder world and greater joy to humans, animals and our planet.

Kay Pfaltz

Made in the USA
Lexington, KY
15 July 2017